MARRYING DR MAVERICK

BY
KAREN ROSE SMITH

MILLS &
BOON

First published in Great Britain 2013
by Mills & Boon, an imprint of Harlequin (UK) Limited,
Eton House, 18-24 Paradise Road, Richmond, Surrey TW9 1SR

© Harlequin Books S.A. 2013

Special thanks and acknowledgement to Karen Rose Smith for her contribution to the Montana Mavericks: Rust Creek Cowboys continuity.

ISBN: 978 0 263 90157 3

23-1113

Harlequin (UK) policy is to use papers that are natural, renewable and recyclable products and made from wood grown in sustainable forests. The logging and manufacturing processes conform to the legal environmental regulations of the country of origin.

Printed and bound in Spain
by Blackprint CPI, Barcelona

Award-winning and bestselling author **Karen Rose Smith**'s plots are all about emotion. She began writing in her early teens, when she listened to music and created stories to accompany the songs. An only child, she spent a lot of time in her imagination and with books—Nancy Drew, Zane Grey, *The Black Stallion* and *Anne of Green Gables*. She dreamed of brothers and sisters and a big family such as the ones her mother and father came from. This is the root of her plotlines, which include small communities and family relationships as part of everyday living. Residing in Pennsylvania with her husband and three cats, she welcomes interaction with readers on Facebook, Twitter @karen rosesmith and through her website, www.karenrose smith.com, where they can sign up for her newsletter.

To my family and friends who love animals as much as I do—my husband Steve, my son Ken, Suzanne, Sydney, Liz, Jane, Ryan, Heather, Abby, Sophie, Chris. Special thanks to my pet sitter, Barb, whose expertise allows me to leave home with a free heart.

Chapter One

Brooks Smith rapped firmly on the ranch-house door, scanning the all-too-familiar property in the dusk.

His dad didn't answer right away, and Brooks thought about going around back to the veterinary clinic, but then he heard footsteps and waited, bracing himself for this conversation.

After his father opened the door, he looked Brooks over, from the beard stubble that seemed to be ever present since the flood to his mud-covered boots. Tending to large animals required trekking through fields sometimes.

"You don't usually come calling on a Tuesday night. Run into a problem you need me for?"

Barrett Smith was a barrel-chested man with gray hair and ruddy cheeks. At six-two, Brooks topped him by a couple of inches. The elder Smith had put on another ten pounds over the past year, and Brooks realized he should have been concerned about that before today.

There was challenge in his dad's tone as there had been since they'd parted ways. But as a doctor with four years of practice under his belt, Brooks didn't ask for his dad's advice on animal care or frankly anything else these days.

"Can I come in?"

"Sure."

Brooks entered the living room where he'd played as a child. The Navajo rugs were worn now, the floor scuffed.

"I only have a few minutes," his father warned him. "I haven't fed the horses yet."

"I'll get straight to the point, then." Brooks swiped off his Stetson and ran his hand through his hair, knowing this conversation was going to get sticky. "I ran into Charlie Hartzell at the General Store."

His father avoided his gaze. "So?"

"He told me that when he stopped by over the weekend, you weren't doing too well."

"I don't know what he's talking about," his dad muttered, not meeting Brooks's eyes.

"He said you carried a pail of oats to the barn and you were looking winded and pale. You dropped the bucket and almost passed out."

"Anybody can have an accident. After I drank a little water, I was fine."

Not so true according to Charlie, Brooks thought. His dad's longtime friend had stayed another hour to make sure Barrett wasn't going to keel over.

"You're working too hard," Brooks insisted. "If you'd

let me take over the practice, you could retire, take care of the horses in the barn and help out as you want."

"Nothing has changed," Barrett said angrily. "You still show no sign of settling down."

This was an old argument, one that had started after Lynnette had broken their engagement right before Brooks had earned his degree in veterinary medicine from Colorado State. That long-ago night, his father had wanted to discuss it with him, but with Brooks's pride stinging, he'd asked his dad to drop it. Barrett hadn't. Frustrated, his father had blown his top, which wasn't unusual. What *was* unusual was his warning and threat—he'd never retire and turn his practice over to Brooks until his son found a woman who would stick by him and build a house on the land his grandmother had left him.

Sure enough…

"Your grandmama's land is still sitting there with no signs of a foundation," his dad went on. "She wanted you to have roots, too. That's why she left it to you. Until you get married and at least *think* about having kids, I can handle my own practice just fine. And you should butt out."

He could rise to the bait. He could argue with his father as he'd done before. But he didn't want his dad's blood pressure to go any higher so he stuck to being reasonable. "You can issue an ultimatum if you want, but this isn't about me. It's about you. You can't keep working the hours you've been working since the flood. You're probably not eating properly, grabbing donuts at Daisy's and potato chips at the General Store."

"Are you keeping track of what I buy where?"

"Of course not. I'm worried about you."

"Well, don't be. Worry about yourself. Worry about the life you don't have."

"I have a life, Dad. I'm living it *my* way."

"Yeah, well, twenty years from now you just tell me how that went. I'm going out back. You can see yourself out."

As his father turned to leave, Brooks knew this conversation had been useless. He knew he probably shouldn't even have come. He had to find a way to make his father wake up to the reality of his deteriorating health. He would...one way or another.

Jasmine Cates—"Jazzy" to her friends and family— stood outside the Ace in the Hole, Rust Creek Falls' lone bar, staring up at the wood-burned sign. She glanced around at the almost deserted street, hoping she'd catch sight of her friend Cecilia, who was tied up at a community meeting. They were supposed to meet here.

On the north side of town, the Ace in the Hole hadn't been touched by the devastating July flood, but Jazzy didn't know if she felt comfortable walking into the place alone. It was a rough and rowdy cowboy hangout, a place single guys gathered to relax. But when they relaxed, all hell could break loose. She'd heard about occasional rumbles and bar fights here.

Feeling as if she'd scrubbed herself raw from her shower at Strickland's Boarding House, attempting to wash off the mud from a disastrous date, she passed the old-fashioned hitching post out front and stared up at the oversize playing card—an ace of hearts—that blinked in red neon over the door. After she climbed two rough-hewn wooden steps, Jazzy opened the old screen door with its rusty hinges and let it slap behind her. A country tune poured from a jukebox. Booths lined the outer walls while wooden tables with ladder-back chairs were scattered across the plank flooring around a small dance floor. Jazzy glimpsed pool tables in the far back. Old West photos as well as those from local ranches hung on the walls. A wooden bar was situated on the right side of the establishment crowded with about a dozen bar stools, and a mirrored wall reflected the rows of glass bottles.

Cowboys and ranch hands filled the tables, and a few gave her glances that said they might be interested in talking…or more. Jazzy quickly glanced toward the bar. There was one bar stool open and it was next to—

Wasn't that Dr. Brooks Smith? She hadn't officially met him, but in her volunteer work, helping ranch owners clean up, paint and repair, she'd caught sight of him now and then as he tended to their animals. She'd liked the way he'd handled a horse that'd been injured. He'd been respectful of the animal and downright kind.

Decision made, she crossed to the bar and settled on the stool beside him. Brooks had that sexy, scruffy look tonight. He was tall and lean and broad-shouldered. Usually he wore a smile for anyone he came in contact with, but now his expression was granitelike, and his hands were balled into fists. It didn't even look like he'd touched his beer.

As if sensing her regard, and maybe her curiosity, he turned toward her. Their gazes met and there was intensity in his brown eyes that told her he'd been thinking about something very serious. His gaze swept over her blond hair, snap-button blouse and jeans, and that intensity shifted into male appreciation.

"You might need a bodyguard tonight," he drawled. "You're the only woman in the place."

He could be *her* bodyguard anytime. She quickly banished that thought. Hadn't she heard somewhere that he didn't date much? Love gone wrong in his romantic history?

"I'm meeting a friend." She stuck out her hand. "You're Brooks Smith. I'm Jazzy Cates. I've seen you around the ranches."

He studied her again. "You're one of the volunteers from Thunder Canyon."

"I am," she said with a smile, glad he'd recognized her.

When he took her hand to shake it, she felt tingles up her arm. That couldn't be, could it? She'd almost been engaged to a man and hadn't felt tingles like *that*. Brooks's grip was strong and firm, his hand warm, and when he took it away, she felt...odd.

"Everyone in town appreciates the help," he said.

"Rust Creek Falls is a tight-knit community. I heard stories about what happened after the flood. Everyone shared what was in their freezers so no one would go hungry."

Brooks nodded. "The community spirit was stoked by Collin Traub and the way he pulled everyone together."

"I heard about his proposal to Willa Christensen on Main Street but I didn't see it myself."

Brooks's eyes darkened at her mention of a proposal, and she wondered why.

"He and Willa seem happy" was all Brooks said.

So the man didn't gossip. She liked that. She liked a

lot about him. Compared to the cowboy she'd been out with earlier tonight—

A high-energy country tune played on the jukebox and snagged their attention for a moment. Jazzy asked, "Do you come here often?"

"Living and mostly working in Kalispell, I don't usually have the time. But I'll meet a friend here now and then."

Kalispell was about twenty miles away, the go-to town for everything anyone in Rust Creek Falls needed and couldn't find in their small town. "So you have a practice in Kalispell?"

"I work with a group practice there. We were called in to help here because my dad couldn't handle it all."

She'd heard Brooks's father had a practice in Rust Creek Falls and had assumed father and son worked together. Her curiosity was aroused. She certainly knew about family complications. "I guess you're not needed here as much now since the town's getting back on its feet."

"Not as much. But there are still animals recovering from injuries during the flood and afterward. How about you? Are you still cleaning out mud from homes that had water damage?"

"Yep, but I'm working at the elementary school, too."

"That's right, I remember now. You came with Dean Pritchett's group."

"Dean's been a friend of our family for years. He was one of the first to volunteer to help."

"How long can you be away from Thunder Canyon?"

"I'm not sure." Because Brooks *was* a stranger, she found herself saying what she couldn't to those closest to her. "My job was...static. I need a business degree to get a promotion and I've been saving for that. I came here to help, but I also came to escape my family. And...I needed a change."

"I can understand that," Brooks said with a nod. "But surely they miss you back home, and a woman like you—"

"A woman like me?"

"I'd think you'd have someone special back there."

She thought about Griff Wellington and the proposal he'd wanted to make and the proposal she'd avoided by breaking off their relationship. Her family had tried to convince her she should marry him, but something inside her had told her she'd known better. Griff had been hurt and she hated that. But she couldn't tie them both to a relationship she'd known wasn't right.

Maybe it was Brooks's easy way; maybe it was the interest in his eyes; maybe it was the way he listened, but she admitted, "No one special. In fact, I had a date tonight before I ended up here."

"Something about that doesn't sound right. If you had a date, why isn't he here with you?"

"He's a calf roper."

Brooks leaned a little closer to hear her above the music. His shoulder brushed hers and she felt heat other places besides there. "What does that have to do with your date?"

"That *was* the date."

Brooks pushed his Stetson higher on his head with his forefinger. *"What?"*

"Calf-roping. He thought it would be fun if he showed me how he did it. That would have been fine, but then he wanted *me* to do it. Yes, I ride. Yes, I love horses. But I'd never calf-roped before and so I tried it.

There was mud all over the place and I slipped and fell and I was covered with mud from head to toe."

Brooks was laughing by then, a deep, hearty laugh that seemed to echo through her. She liked the fact she could make him laugh. Genially, she bumped his arm. "It wasn't so funny when it was happening."

He gave her a crooked smile that said he was a little bit sorry he laughed, but not much. "Whatever gave him the impression you'd like to try that out?"

"I have no clue, except I did tell him I like horses. I did try to be interested in what he did, and I asked him questions about it."

"This was a first date?" Brooks guessed.

"It was the *last* date," Jazzy responded.

"Not the last date *ever*."

She sighed. "Probably not."

Was he thinking of asking her out? Or were they just flirting? With that twinkle in his eyes, she imagined he could flirt with the best of them if he really wanted to.

"So you came here to meet a friend and hash out everything that's happened," he concluded.

"My gosh, a guy who understands women!"

He laughed again. "No, not so well."

She wondered what *that* meant. "When I'm at home, sometimes I talk it all out with my sisters."

"How many do you have?"

"I have four sisters, a brother and parents who think they know what's best for me."

"You're lucky," Brooks said.

"Lucky?"

"Yep. I'm the only one. And I lost my mom a long time ago."

"I'm sorry."

He shrugged. "Water under the bridge."

But something in his tone said that it wasn't, so she asked, "Are you close to your dad?"

"He's the reason I stopped in here tonight."

"To meet him?"

"Nope." He hesitated, then added, "We had another argument."

"Another?"

Brooks paused again before saying, "My dad's not taking care of himself, and I can't give him what he wants most."

In her family, Jazzy usually said what she thought, and most of the time, no one heard her. But now she asked, "And what's that?"

"He wants me to marry, and I'll never do that."

Whoa! She wanted to ask that all-important question—why?—but they'd just officially met and she knew better than to probe too much. She hated when her family did that.

Her questions must have led Brooks to think he could ask some of his own because he leaned toward her again. This time his face was very close to hers as he inquired, "So what was the job you left?"

After a heavy sigh, she admitted, "I was a glorified secretary."

"A secretary," he murmured, studying her. "How long are you staying in Rust Creek Falls?"

"I've already been in town for a while, so I guess I'll have to go back soon. I work for Thunder Canyon Resort. I'm in the pool of assistants who handle everything to do about skiing. I had a lot of vacation time built up but that's gone now. I don't want to use all my savings because I want to earn my degree. Someday

I'm going to own a ranch and run a non-profit organization to rescue horses."

Brooks leaned away again and really assessed her as if he was trying to read every thought in her head, as if he was trying to decide if what she'd told him was really true. Of course it was true. A rescue ranch had been a burning goal for a while.

"How did you get involved in rescuing horses?"

"I help out a friend who does it."

Finally, Brooks took a few long swigs of his beer and then set down his glass. He looked at it and then grimaced. "I didn't even offer to buy you a drink. What would you like?"

"A beer would be fine."

Brooks waved down the bartender and soon Jazzy was rolling her finger around the foam on the rim of her glass. This felt like a date, though it wasn't. This felt...nice.

The music on the jukebox had stopped for the moment, and she listened to the chatter of voices, the clink of glasses and bang of a dish as a waitress set a burger in front of a cowboy.

Finally, as if Brooks had come to some conclusion, he swiveled on his stool and faced her. "If you had a job in Rust Creek Falls, would you stay longer?"

She had no idea where this was going since the town had few jobs to spare, but she told him the truth. "I might."

"How would you like to come work for me as my secretary and assistant?"

"I don't understand. You said you work for the vet practice in Kalispell."

"I made a decision tonight. There's only one way to

keep my father from running himself into the ground, and that's to take some business away from him. If I open an office here in Rust Creek Falls, I can take the load off my father and show him at the same time that he can feel confident handing down his practice to me, whether I marry or not."

She admired what Brooks wanted to do for his father. Would working for him move her life forward? She could learn a lot from him.

"Can I think about it, at least until tomorrow?"

"Sure. In fact, take a couple of days. Why don't you come along with me on my appointments to get a feel for my practice day after tomorrow? I'm going to have loose ends to tie up in Kalispell, but then you and I can spend the day together and you can see what my practice will involve."

When she looked into Brooks's dark eyes, she felt something deep in her being. In that moment, the world seemed to drop away.

They might have gazed into each other's eyes like that all night except—

Cecilia Clifton was suddenly standing beside Jazzy saying, "You should have come to the meeting. The town's making plans for the holidays." When her gaze fell on Brooks, she stopped and said a breathy "Hi."

Yes, Brooks could take a woman's breath away. Jazzy thought again about his offer. "I'd like to shadow you for a day and see what you do."

Brooks smiled and so did she. She had a feeling the day after tomorrow was going to be a day to remember.

Chapter Two

Two days later, Brooks pulled his truck to a stop in front of Strickland's Boarding House, a four-story ramshackle Victorian. Its once-purple paint had faded to a lavender-gray. Cowboys on the rodeo circuit had bunked here over the years, but right now, many of the folks from Thunder Canyon who had come to help were staying here. Melba and Old Gene Strickland cared about their guests in an old-fashioned family way.

He switched off his ignition, thinking he must have been crazy to ask Jazzy Cates to work for him. He really knew nothing about her except what she'd told him. He'd followed his gut instinct as he often did in his work. But that didn't mean he was right. After all, he'd been all wrong about Lynnette. He'd thought she was the type of woman who understood fidelity and loyalty and standing by her man. But he'd been so wrong.

He knew, however, he was right about opening the local practice and taking some of the workload from his father. After all, it was for the older man's best interests. Still…asking Jazzy to become involved in that undertaking—

She was so pretty with that blond hair and those blue eyes. When he'd looked into those eyes, he'd felt a stirring that had practically startled him. It had been a very long time since a woman caused *that* reaction. However, if he hired her on, he'd have to forget about her natural prettiness and any attraction zinging between them. He'd be her employer and he'd have to fix his mind on the fact that she was just a Girl Friday who was going to help him, maybe only temporarily. She might hightail it back to Thunder Canyon sooner than he expected. After all, Lynnette hadn't wanted to live in a small town like Rust Creek Falls. How many women did?

The wooden steps leading to the rambling porch creaked under his boots. He opened the front door with its glass panel and lace curtain and caught the scent of something sweet baking. Forgetting all about Melba's well-deserved reputation as a terrific baker, he'd picked up donuts and coffee at Daisy's Donuts, never thinking Jazzy might have had breakfast already.

Jazzy had told him the number of her room—2D, on the second floor. He climbed the steps to the second floor and strode down the hall to her room. He gave a double knock on her door and waited. Maybe she'd forgotten all about going with him today. Maybe she wasn't an early riser. Maybe she was down at breakfast. Maybe she'd decided going along with him today was tantamount to calf-roping!

She opened the door before he could push aside

the flap of his denim jacket and stuff one hand in his jeans' pocket. She was wearing an outfit similar to what she'd had on the other night, a snap-button, long-sleeve blouse and skinny blue jeans that molded to her legs. He quickly brought his gaze up to her face.

"I was running a little late," she said breathlessly, "but I'm ready."

She'd tied her wavy blond hair in a ponytail. Her bangs straggled over her brow. Forgetting she was pretty might be a little hard to do. "I brought donuts and coffee from Daisy's if you're interested."

"Oh, I'm interested."

They couldn't seem to look away from each other and her words seemed to have an underlying meaning. No. No underlying meaning. He just hadn't dated a woman in a very long time. He was reading too much into cornflower-blue eyes that could make a man lose his focus.

Brooks never lost his focus. Not since his mother had died. Not during his years at Colorado State. Not during his engagement. His focus was the reason his engagement had gone south.

"Let's get going, then. I have an appointment with Sam Findley at his ranch at seven-thirty to check on a couple of horses that almost drowned in the flood. One of them has PTSD and gets spooked real easy now."

"Were they hurt physically?" Jazzy closed and locked the door to her room, slipping the key into her hobo bag that hung from her shoulder.

"Sparky had a few deep cuts that have taken their good time healing. I want to make sure he hasn't opened them up again."

"Is most of your work with horses?"

"Lots of it is with horses and cattle because of all the ranches around here. But I do my stint in the clinic, too. Or at least I did."

At the end of Jazzy's hall, Brooks motioned for her to precede him down the steps. When she passed him, he caught a whiff of something flowery. Could be shampoo. Could be lotion. He didn't think she'd wear perfume for this little jaunt, but what did he know? Women mystified him most of the time.

Jazzy clambered down the steps in a way that told him she was high-energy. She went outside to the porch railing and stared up at the sky that was almost the same color as her eyes. She pointed up to the white clouds scuttling across the vista, hanging so low they looked as if a person could reach them.

"Isn't that beautiful? I never appreciated a day without rain as I do now."

She wasn't just pretty. She was gorgeous. Not in a highfalutin-model kind of way, but in a prettiest-gal-in-town way. He crossed the distance between them and stood at the railing with her.

"I know what you mean. I've never seen so much devastation. Half the town was affected. Thank God for our hills. The General Store, Daisy's and Strickland's were all on the higher side. The other side of Rust Creek is still recovering, and that's where we're headed." Standing beside her like this, his arm brushing hers, talking about the sky and the flood, seemed a little too intimate somehow. Weird. He had to get his head on straight and do it fast.

Jazzy gave him one of her quick smiles. He'd seen a few of those the other night at the Ace in the Hole.

Then she headed for the steps. She was a woman who knew how to move. A woman with purpose.

In his truck, he said, "You didn't wear a jacket. Even though we're having a bout of Indian summer, the morning's a little cool. Want the heat on?"

Glancing over at him, she motioned to the coffee in the holder. "If one of those is mine, that's all I need."

"Donut now or later?"

"One now wouldn't hurt."

He chuckled and reached for the bag in the back. "Cream and sugar are in there, too."

He watched as she poured two of the little cream containers into her coffee and then added the whole pack of sugar. She wasn't a straight caffeine kind of girl, which he supposed was all right.

"Dig around in the bag until you find the one you want."

She came up with a chocolate glazed, took a bite, and gave him a wink. "Perfect."

Brooks found his body getting tight, his blood running faster, and he quickly reached for his black coffee. After a few swallows that scalded his tongue and throat, he swiped a cream-filled donut from the bag and bit into it. Halfway through, he noticed Jazzy watching him.

"Daisy's Donuts are the best," she said a little breathlessly.

He was feeling a little breathless himself. Enough with the donuts and coffee. Time to get to work. Focus was everything.

Ten minutes later, Jazzy wondered if she'd said something wrong because Brooks had turned off the conversation spigot. He was acting as if the road was an enemy he was going to conquer. She supposed that was just as well. Eating donuts with him had gotten a little…sticky. She'd seen something in his eyes that had, well, excited her…excited her in a way that nothing Griff had ever done or said had. Downright silly. If she was going to be working for Brooks—

She hadn't decided yet.

Veering to the left, Brooks drove down a rutted lane that had been filled in with gravel. Yet, like on many of the Rust Creek Falls streets, there were still a lot of potholes. Paving crews had been doing their best, but there was only so much money and only so much manpower. Lodgepole pine grew on much of the property. Larch, aspen and live oak were color-laden in October with gold and rust. A couple of early snows had stripped some of the leaves and there were still a bunch fluttering across the ground as they climbed out of the truck and headed for the large, white barn.

"Does Mr. Findley run cattle?" Jazzy asked to soothe the awkwardness and start conversation between them once more.

Brooks responded without hesitation. "No. No cattle. Sam's livelihood didn't get affected like some. He's a wilderness guide. Hunters and tourists stay at the farmhouse, and he has two cabins out back. He stays out there if he has women guests who would rather be alone in the house."

"Sounds like a gentleman."

Brooks shrugged. "It's good business. A reputation goes a long way out here. But then you should know that. I imagine Thunder Canyon is the same."

"It is."

A tall, good-looking man with black hair and gray eyes came to meet them at the barn door. Brooks introduced Jazzy. "She's one of the volunteers from Thunder Canyon, but she's hanging with me today."

As Sam opened the barn door for Jazzy, he said, "Brooks has some kind of magic touch that I haven't had with Sparky ever since the flood." Sam shook his head. "I was the one who rescued him along with a couple of others, and maybe I hurt him without knowing it."

"Or maybe you just remind him of what happened," Brooks said easily. "Horses remember, just like cats and dogs. It's why a visit to the vet is so traumatic for some of them."

"He lets me feed him, but he won't take a carrot or sugar cube like he used to," Sam added regretfully. "And getting into his stall is a major undertaking. Are you used to being around horses?" Sam asked Jazzy, looking worried.

"Yes, I am. A friend rescues them and I help her out. I promise I won't go near Sparky if he doesn't want me near him."

"Do you want me to stay?" Sam asked Brooks.

"If you have things to do, and I'm sure you do, there's no need. We'll be fine."

Sam nodded, tipped his Stetson to Jazzy and headed back toward the house.

She watched him thoughtfully. "For a small town filled with gossip, I never heard anything about his tours while I've been here."

"Sam keeps a low profile, mostly advertises on the internet, attracts a lot of tourists from back East."

"Is he from here?"

"Nope, and nobody knows where he came from. He doesn't talk about himself much."

"Are you friends?"

Brooks thought about it. "We're something between acquaintances and friends."

"So that means you talk about sports and livestock."

Brooks chuckled. "I guess you could say that. You can add the goings-on in Rust Creek Falls, which is a topic of conversation for everyone. Come on, let's see Sparky. Sam has it rigged up so the stall doors open to the outside corral. He can come and go as he pleases."

"That's smart. Freedom's important to an animal that's been traumatized."

Brooks eyed her again as if trying to figure out who she was. *Good luck,* she thought. *She* was still trying to figure that out herself. Coming to Rust Creek Falls had changed her in some elemental way. Sure, in Thunder Canyon she had her family and her job. But she didn't want to live vicariously through her sisters and brother. She didn't want her family to be her world, and she certainly wanted her job to be more exciting than the one she had, or at least promise a better future. She couldn't get promoted without a degree, so she was going to get that degree.

"Let's take a look at Mirabelle first. Sparky will hear us and get used to us being around."

Jazzy had made a quick judgment about Brooks when she'd met him at the Ace in the Hole. The more she learned about him, the more she realized she'd been right. She'd been able to tell he cared about his dad. Now she could see he felt deeply about the animals he cared for. Just why did this man never intend to marry?

Mirabelle, a bay, was cavorting in the corral beside Sparky's. When she saw Brooks, she neighed.

Jazzy smiled. "She likes you."

"What's not to like?" He almost said it with a flirting tease, but then he sobered. "I've been treating her for a few years. One weekend, Sam had an emergency and couldn't reach my dad, so he rang up our practice. I was on call. Since then, I've been taking care of his horses. Gage Christensen's, too."

"The sheriff," Jazzy said, knowing Gage a little. They'd had a dinner date, but things never went any further.

"Yes."

"While I was at the elementary school working, I heard that he and Lissa Roarke are engaged." When she and Gage had dined at his office, his mind had definitely been elsewhere. Probably on Lissa, who'd flown in from the East to organize volunteers in Rust Creek Falls on behalf of an East Coast relief organization.

"So that's all around town, too?" Brooks asked.

"Lissa has been doing so much to get help for Rust Creek Falls that her name pops up often, especially with the volunteers."

"Gage went through a tough time after the flood, but he sure seems happy now."

"We had dinner," Jazzy said.

"Dinner? With Gage?"

"I stopped in at the sheriff's office to ask for directions. He and I started talking and one thing led to another. But his mind was elsewhere—I think it was on Lissa. That was soon after she arrived."

"You mean he asked you out because he didn't want to think about her?"

"Something like that, though I don't think he realized it at the time."

Brooks looked pensive as Mirabelle trotted toward him. He glanced at Jazzy. "Do you feel comfortable being out here with her?"

"Sure. Is there anything special you want me to do?"

"I'm just going to check her overall fitness, and make sure nothing insidious is going on. After a flood, all kinds of things can develop."

When Mirabelle came up to Brooks, Jazzy let the horse snuffle her fingers. That ritual completed, she petted her neck and threaded her fingers through the bay's mane. She talked to her while Brooks examined her. He checked one hoof after another, then pulled a treat from his back pocket and let her snatch it from his palm.

"She's the easy one," he remarked. "Now let's go check out Sparky."

Jazzy could easily see Sparky eyeing them warily, his tail swishing. "How do you want to do this?" she asked.

"We're going to sit on the fence and let him come to us."

"Do you think I should be sitting there with you, or should I go inside?"

"Let's give it a try. You can't force a horse to communicate with you. If I'm patient with Sparky, he usually comes around."

"He hasn't for Sam?"

"Sam was on a guiding tour when the rain started, but he got back in the nick of time. Sparky's tolerating Sam. But I think that has to do with the flood and the rescue, maybe a sense of abandonment. Animals have it, too."

Had Brooks felt abandoned when his mother died?

Had his father been there for him? Maybe that was at the root of their discord.

Brooks opened the gate at the rear of Mirabelle's corral, and they walked out.

"Sparky was watching us while we were tending to Mirabelle, so he knows we're here." Brooks went along the fence a little ways then climbed the first rung and held his hand out to Jazzy. She thought a man's hands told a lot about his character. Brooks's hand was large, his fingers long. Staring at it, she felt a little quiver in her stomach.

"Jazzy?" he asked, and she lifted her chin, meeting his gaze.

Zing.

Something happened when she looked into those deep, brown eyes. She took his hand and felt an even stronger buzz vibrate through her body. She could feel the calluses on his fingers that had come from hard work. She was curious about him and his life and she was afraid it showed.

They were both sitting on the top rung when Sparky froze midtrot and eyed them warily. He was a paint pony with dark brown swaths on his cream-colored coat.

"Now what?" she asked.

"We wait."

"Wait for what?"

"You'll see."

The horse did nothing for at least five minutes. He just stared at them. When Jazzy glanced at Brooks, she saw he wasn't the least bit impatient. Wasn't *that* a novelty. She shivered suddenly. The morning air *was* cool and she rubbed her arms.

"Are you cold?"

"The sun's warm."

"Not what I asked you." Brooks was wearing a denim jacket that fit his broad shoulders way too well. It was loose at his waist. She concentrated on the brass buttons on his jacket instead of contemplating other things about him.

He started to shrug out of the jacket and she clasped his arm, saying in a low voice, "No, really. I'm fine."

He chuckled. "You don't have to whisper around Sparky. He's not afraid of our voices, just of us getting too close when he doesn't want us to."

She felt herself blush, but she still held his arm because her hand seemed fascinated by the muscles underneath. Ignoring the fact that she said she was fine, he removed his jacket and hung it around her shoulders.

"You can give it back once the day warms up."

So he was protective, and...thought he knew best. What man didn't?

Although she protested, his jacket held his warmth and his scent. It felt good around her. She snuggled into it and watched Sparky eyeing them.

It happened slowly, Sparky's acceptance of them into his world. The horse tossed his head and blew out breaths. He lifted his tail and ran in the other direction, made a circle and then another that was a little closer to them. After about ten circles, he was only about five feet from them.

Brooks took a treat from his back pocket and held it out to the horse, palm up.

"Sam said he wouldn't take treats from him anymore."

"That's Sam. Sparky and I have an understanding. I

don't try to do anything he doesn't want me to do when he takes the treat."

"Rescue horses are often skittish like this," she said. "I mean, horses rescued from abuse, not floods."

"Trauma in whatever form has to be treated with kindness most of all, as well as a gentle hand and a firm determination to overcome whatever happened."

She'd seen that, working with the horses at Darlene's place.

It took Sparky a while but he finally came within a foot of Brooks's hand.

Jazzy didn't move or even take a breath.

Sparky snatched the piece of biscuit and danced away then looked back at Brooks to see if he had more.

With a smile, Brooks took another piece from his back pocket. "These get crushed by the end of the day, so you might as well eat them," he said in a conversational tone to the horse.

Sparky must have understood because he made another circle, but didn't dawdle this time. He snatched the biscuit and didn't dance away.

"How many times have you done this before?" Jazzy asked, completely aware of Brooks's tall, fit body beside her.

"Too many to count," he said, shifting on the fence but not moving away. "He and I go through this routine every time I come over. I'm hoping someday he'll see me and just trot right on up. I thought about buying him from Sam, but I don't think it's advisable to move him to another place right now.

"Can I look at you a little bit?" Brooks asked the horse.

Sparky blew out a few breaths but didn't move.

"I'll take that as a yes." Brooks slowly slid down off the fence, taking care not to jump too heavily onto the ground. The sleeves of his snap-button shirt blew in the wind, the chambray looking soft.

Jazzy was fascinated by man and horse.

Brooks found another crumb of the treat in his pocket and offered it to Sparky. The horse snuffled it up and Brooks patted his neck, running his hand under the horse's mane. He slowly separated the hair there and Jazzy could see a series of scratches and a five-inch long swatch that looked as if it had been stitched.

Although he pawed the ground, Sparky stayed in Brooks's vicinity.

"Come on down," Brooks said to Jazzy. "Slowly."

She eased herself off the fence.

"Stay there," Brooks warned her. "Let him catch more of your scent. Let him get used to you."

Rescued horses mostly needed to be cared for gently, then regularly watered and brushed when they'd let you do it. She'd never become involved with one quite this way before.

Brooks kept talking to Sparky and then gave her the okay to come closer. She did, feeling she was getting closer to Brooks, too.

Brooks gave her the last little bit of treat and she held it in her fingers. When she extended her palm, Sparky took it from her.

By then, Brooks was studying the horse's flanks. "He's looking good. Soon we can put him in the corral with Mirabelle and see how it goes."

"I think he'd like some company. Wouldn't you?" she crooned softly to the horse.

When she glanced at Brooks, he was watching her, listening to her, and her pulse raced.

At the end of the day, would he still believe he should hire her?

As Brooks drove to other ranches, Jazzy could see they were all recovering from the flood. In some fields, alfalfa had survived. Many ranchers had been soil-testing to find out what nutrients the flood had depleted. Some reseeded with fast-growing grasses, while others planted soybeans. All were trying their best to recover. Most were making headway.

She watched Brooks work with calves, with goats, with cattle. She helped however she could and realized she liked assisting him. They grabbed a quick lunch at the diner, talked about Rust Creek Falls and Thunder Canyon. Whenever their fingers brushed or their eyes met, Jazzy felt energized in a way she never had before.

At the end of the day when they were driving back to Strickland's, Brooks said, "I know I'm doing the right thing opening this practice. Dad's going to be angry about it, but in the end I think he'll thank me."

"You're doing something for his best interests, even if he doesn't see it that way. I guess roles reverse as parents age."

"And as children grow wiser."

She thought about that and all the advice her parents had given her. But she particularly remembered one thing her brother Brody had told her. He'd said, "You have to find the life you want to live, rather than settling for the life you've fallen into."

What life *did* she want to live?

Brooks drew up in front of the boarding house,

braked and switched off the ignition. Leaning toward her, he explained, "If you're my assistant, you wouldn't spend all your time in the field with me. Mostly what I need in the beginning is somebody to set up the office, make appointments, get the word out about the practice."

He paused for a moment, then honestly admitted, "At first I thought I'd been impulsive about asking you to work for me, but today I realized it really was good instinct that made me ask. You're great with the animals, Jazzy, and with the clients. You seem to be able to talk to almost anybody. That's a gift, and a great one in a receptionist. So if you take this job, you'll be a little bit of a lot of things—a receptionist, an assistant, a tech. What do you think? Do you want to work with me?"

Brooks was leaning toward her and she was leaning toward him. She felt a pull toward him and thought she saw an answering pull toward her in the darkening of his eyes. But if she accepted, they'd be boss and employee.

"Sure. I'd like that a lot."

Brooks extended his hand to seal the deal. When his hand gripped hers, she found herself leaning even closer to him. Whether he was aware of it or not, his thumb gently stroked the top of her hand, just for a moment.

Then he pulled away. "I'll wait until you get inside," he said gruffly. "Tomorrow I'd like to take you to the practice in Kalispell and let you talk to the office manager. Is that okay with you?"

"That's fine with me."

Looking into Brooks Smith's eyes, Jazzy realized their association was going to be more than fine. The thing was—he was a confirmed bachelor. So she'd better keep her head.

They'd *both* keep their heads because that's what bosses and employees should do.

Chapter Three

Jazzy had no sooner hopped into Brooks's truck Friday morning—he'd waited outside today—when she fastened her seat belt and turned to him. "I have a favor to ask."

Brooks cocked his head and his face said he was ready for almost anything. "I'd guess but I'll probably guess wrong."

"What makes you think you'd guess wrong?" she joked.

"Because I can*not* read a woman's mind. What's the favor?"

"I've been helping Dean at the elementary school when I'm not needed somewhere else, even though my carpentry skills are at a minimum. Still, I don't want to let him down. Can we stop over there on the way to Kalispell? I tried to call last night and kept getting his voice mail."

"He's engaged now, isn't he?" Brooks asked, obviously tuned in to the local chatter.

"He is. He bought a place with some land and he's just moved in with Shelby and her daughter Caitlin."

"Shelby works at the Ace in the Hole, right?"

"Yes, but for not much longer, she hopes. She's going to reapply for a job as an elementary school teacher once the school's up and running again."

"That could be a while."

"It might be, but that's what she wants to do. Anyway, he doesn't always answer his phone in the evenings. So I thought it might be just as well if we could stop at the school. I'll explain I'll be working with you, but I'll still help out around the school on weekends."

"You want his blessing?" Brooks didn't sound judgmental. He actually sounded as if he understood.

"Something like that."

"We can pick up donuts on the way and bribe him."

"Brooks!"

"I'm kidding. I often pick up donuts and drop off a couple of boxes for people who are volunteering. We all do what we can to say thank you."

After a stop at Daisy's, they drove to the elementary school property in a drizzling rain that had begun to fall. The low-hanging gray clouds predicted more of the same. Just what Rust Creek Falls didn't need.

At the school, the building crew had made progress, but it was slow going without money for materials, and work often had to stop while they waited for supplies. Today, however, Dean was there with a crew. They found him easily in the school library, building shelves. He looked up when he saw Jazzy and did a double-take as he spotted Brooks.

After Jazzy explained why they were there, Dean gave her an odd look. "You're not going back to Thunder Canyon?"

"I don't know when. For now working with Brooks will give me experience to open that horse rescue ranch I want to open someday."

"She's good with animals," Brooks assured Dean. To Jazzy he said, "If you're going to be a few minutes, I'll look around."

Perceptively Brooks probably sensed that she needed to convince Dean this was the best move for her. She nodded.

When Brooks left the library, Dean frowned. "What kind of relationship do you have with Brooks? I didn't even know you knew him."

"I didn't before the other night. But we hit it off."

"Hit it off as in—"

She knew she shouldn't get impatient with Dean. He cared as an older brother would. But his attitude was much like her family's when they second-guessed the decisions she made. "I know you think you have to look out for me while I'm here. But I'm thirty years old and old enough to know what I'm doing."

Assessing her with a penetrating glare, he asked bluntly, "Did you hook up with him?"

"No, I didn't hook up with him!" Her voice had risen and she lowered it. "He's going to be my *boss,* so don't get any ideas you shouldn't."

With a glance in the direction Brooks had taken, Dean offered, "Maybe *he'll* get some ideas he shouldn't."

Jazzy vehemently shook her head. "He's not like that."

Dean sighed. "I guess you'd know after a couple of days?"

"My radar's good, Dean. I know if I'm 'safe' around a man."

"Woman's intuition?" he asked with a cynical arched brow.

"Scoff if you want, but I believe in mine."

It was probably woman's intuition that had made her break off the relationship with Griff. Her instincts had told her he simply wasn't *the one*. There hadn't been enough passion, enough of those I-can't-live-without-you feelings. Something important had been missing.

"Okay," Dean conceded. "But be careful. I heard he's a confirmed bachelor with good reason. If you fall for him, you'll only get hurt."

She couldn't let this opportunity to find out information about Brooks pass her by. "Why is he a confirmed bachelor?"

After an assessing look that said he was telling her this for her own good, he kept his voice low. "He has a broken engagement in his history that cut him pretty deep. A wounded man is the worst kind to fall for. Watch your step, Jazzy, or you will get hurt. I don't want to see that happen. Not on my watch."

"I'm *not* your responsibility," she said, frustrated, and stalked out.

Ten minutes later with rain pouring down faster now, she and Brooks sat in his truck again, headed toward Kalispell. Dean's words still rang in her head. *A wounded man is the worst kind to fall for.* She wouldn't fall for Brooks. She couldn't. Besides, she didn't fall easily. Her relationship with Griff was proof of that.

Still, as she surreptitiously eyed his strong profile,

her stomach did a little somersault. To counteract the unsettling sensation, she remarked casually, "Progress is being made on the school, but it's going so slow."

"A ton of funds and a larger crew could fix that. But the way it is now, the elementary school teachers are going to be holding classes in their homes for a long while."

"The town has come a long way since I first arrived, though."

He nodded. "Yes, it has. The mayoral election next month should be interesting."

"Collin Traub against Nate Crawford."

"Yep. They butted heads trying to get the town back on its feet. Their families have a history of butting heads."

"A feud?"

"Some people say so. I don't know how it started. I don't know if anybody remembers. But because of it, the election is even more heated."

She wouldn't ask him who he was voting for. That was really none of her business. But other things were. "How did your clinic in Kalispell take the news you'd be leaving?"

He didn't answer right away, but when he did, he looked troubled. "I don't want to leave them in the lurch, and I won't. The other two vets in the practice understand why I have to do this. Family has to come first."

Her parents had always instilled that belief in their children, too.

Two hours later, Jazzy was still thinking about Brooks's broken engagement as well as everything she'd learned from the clinic's office manager about the computer programs they used, advertising and a multitude of other elements she'd have to coordinate to set up his practice. The rain had continued to pour as Brooks and the office manager had filled Jazzy in on what her job would entail.

Jazzy had worn a windbreaker this morning in deference to the weather and now flipped up the red hood as she and Brooks ran to his truck. He'd gone to her side with her to give her a hand up to climb in, but that meant he'd gotten even damper from the rain.

Inside his truck, he took off his Stetson and brushed the raindrops outside before he closed the door. Then he tossed it into the backseat.

"Where's your jacket today?" she asked.

"The same place yours was yesterday."

His crooked half smile and the curve of his lips had her thinking of other things than setting up his office. An unbidden thought popped into her head. What would it feel like to be kissed by Brooks Smith?

No! She was *not* going there.

Brooks looked away and she was glad because she was afraid he might read her thoughts. As he started up the truck, she said, "You need a name for the practice." It was the first thing that she could think of to say.

"I guess I can't call it Smith's Veterinary Practice, can I? That's what my father uses. Any suggestions?"

"Not off the top of my head. Once you pick a location, we might choose something geared to that."

"I like your ideas," he said simply, and she felt a blush coming on because there was admiration in his voice. When was the last time someone told her they liked her ideas? At work, she just did what was pushed in front of her. Sure, she offered suggestions now and then, but nothing that really mattered. Brooks seemed to make *everything* matter.

The rain poured down in front of them like sheets that they could hardly see through. Brooks didn't seem to be anxious about it, though. He drove as if he drove in this weather all the time, keeping a safe distance from whatever taillights blinked in front of them, making sure he didn't drive through puddles that were growing deep.

They were well out of Kalispell when he asked, "So you think you can handle setting up the office? The printing for flyers and business cards and that type of thing will have to be done in Kalispell, but we can accomplish a lot of it through email. I know this is a big job—"

Was he having second thoughts about her abilities? "I can handle it," she said with more assurance than she felt.

She must have sounded a little vehement because he cut her another glance. "I don't want you to be overwhelmed. There's a lot to think about. We can farm out the website design."

"I can do it. I know I can, Brooks. I've taken night courses that I thought might be useful at the resort, and I've never gotten a chance to use a lot of what I learned, including web design and graphics. I even took a course in setting up a small business in case I ever get the chance to start up my rescue ranch. I've put my life on hold for too long. By helping you, I finally feel as if I'm moving forward."

He was silent for a few moments, then asked, "Did you have other things on hold, other than your job?"

Was he fishing about her personal life? She could tell him about Griff—

And maybe she would have. But the water was moving fast along both shoulders of the road. As she thought about Brooks's broken engagement, how she'd told Griff she couldn't see a future for *them,* the truck suddenly dipped into a hole hidden under a puddle. The jarring jolt would have been bad enough, but a loud pop like a gun going off accompanied it.

Brooks swore and muttered, "I know that sound."

Their blow-out caused the truck to spin on the back tire until they faced the wrong direction. The vehicle hydroplaned on another puddle and they ended up near the guard rail on the opposite side of the road.

It had all happened so fast, Jazzy almost felt stunned, like she'd been on some amusement-park ride that had gone amuck. Her brain was scrambled for a few seconds until she got her bearings and realized they were half on and half off the highway.

Brooks unsnapped his seat belt and moved closer to her. "Are you okay?"

"I think so." Without conscious thought, she rubbed her shoulder. "We blew a tire?"

He nodded. "I'm going to have to change it."

"Oh, Brooks. In this rain? I can call Cecelia or Dean."

"There's no need for that. I've changed tires before. I've gotten wet before. It won't take long, Jazzy, once I get us set up right. Trust me."

Trust him. Could she? She didn't know if she could or not…yet. She'd be foolish if she trusted him on this short acquaintance. Yet she had seen enough to trust in his abilities, to trust that he'd do what he said he was going to do.

His gaze ran over her again. "Let me get us over to the shoulder on the right side of the road so I can take care of the tire."

"I can help."

"Jazzy—"

"We can argue about it or we can change the tire," she said adamantly, not accepting a macho attitude from him any more than she would from Dean, her brother or her dad.

"Are you going to tell me stubbornness is one of your virtues?" he asked warily.

"Possibly. Apparently we both have the same virtue."

He shook his head. "Let's get this done."

Jazzy was more shaken than she was letting on, and her shoulder *did* hurt. But she wouldn't be telling Brooks about it. Testing it, she realized she could move it, and she wasn't in excruciating pain. Those were both good signs. She could help Brooks and worry about her shoulder later.

Brooks managed to steer the truck around and with the thump-thump-thump of the blown tire, they made it to the right side of the highway over to the paved shoulder. Thank goodness the shoulder was wide enough that they wouldn't be in any danger as other vehicles passed.

Brooks touched her arm. "Stay here. I've got this."

But she, of course, wouldn't listen. She hopped out of the truck and met him at the rear of the vehicle.

He shook his head. "You're crazy. You're going to get soaked."

"So we'll be soaked together. I've helped my brother and dad change tires. I'm not inept at this."

He lowered the rear truck panel. "I didn't think you

were. Let me grab the spare and we'll get this done quick."

"Quick" was a relative term, too, when changing a tire in the rain. Jazzy had tied her hood tightly around her face and she felt bad for Brooks when his shirt became plastered to his skin. But he didn't complain and she didn't, either, though she was cold and shivery. That was so much the better for her shoulder because it was aching some. The cuffs of her jeans were protected by her boots, but from thighs to below her knees, she was getting soaked.

Twenty minutes later they were back in the truck with rain still sluicing down the front windshield.

Brooks reached in the back and took a duffel from the seat. "I carry a spare set of duds in case a calf or a horse drags me into a muddy field. It *has* happened. How are you under that jacket?"

Actually, the waterproof fabric had kept her fairly dry. "I'm good. Just my jeans are wet."

He switched on the ignition and the heater. "How's your shoulder?"

"Numb right now from the cold and damp."

He began unbuttoning his shirt.

At first she just stared at the tan skin and brown curly hair he revealed as he unfastened one button and then the next. For some insane reason, she suddenly had the urge to move closer...and touch him.

When his gaze met hers, her breath almost stopped. She quickly looked away.

She could hear the rustle of fabric...hear him reach into the duffel bag.

"Jazzy, take this."

Out of the corner of her eye, she could see he was offering her a hand towel.

"You need it more than I do," she managed to say, her eyes skittering over his bare chest.

"Wipe your face," he suggested. "Then I'll use it."

She took the towel and dabbed at her rain-splattered cheeks, the ends of her hair that had slipped out from under the hood. After she handed it back to him, her gaze went again to his completely bare chest, broad shoulders, muscled arms. Wow!

"Do you work out?" she asked inanely, knowing he'd noticed she'd noticed, and there was nothing she could do about that.

"No need to work out when I wrestle with calves, chop wood for my stove and repair fencing on my dad's property when he lets me."

"Do you have a house in Kalispell?"

"No. Because I fully intended to move back to Rust Creek Falls someday. I'm in one of those double condos on one floor. It's got everything I need."

She handed him the towel and watched as he dried his hair with it. It was sticking up all over. She wanted to run her fingers through it and brush it down, but he quickly did that and swiped the towel over his torso.

"Getting warmer?" he asked, with the heater running full blast.

"Yes. I'm fine. I can't believe *you're* not shivering."

"Hot-blooded," he said with a grin that urged her once again to touch him, test the texture of his skin, and see if there really was heat there.

Before she had the chance to act foolishly, he pulled a T-shirt from the duffel, slipped it over his head, maneuvered his arms inside and pulled it down over his chest. She could see denim protruding from the duffel.

"Is that another pair of jeans?"

"Yes, it is."

"You should change."

"I'm fine. Let's get you back to Strickland's and look at that shoulder."

"You're a veterinarian," she protested.

"I had some EMT training, too. Out here, you never know what you're going to run into. If you'd rather I take you back into Kalispell to the hospital—"

"No! I don't need a hospital or a doctor."

"Great. Then I'm perfect for the job."

After that, every time Jazzy glanced at Brooks, she envisioned his bare chest, his triceps and biceps and deltoids and whatever else she'd seen. He had tan lines from shirtsleeves on his upper arms. He had dark brown hair arrowing down to his belt buckle. He had a flat stomach and a slim waist and—

Okay, heating up her body wasn't helping her shoulder. In fact, it was starting to hurt a little more.

They didn't talk as he concentrated on driving and *she* tried not to concentrate on him. She thought about her sisters and brother and parents, and considered phoning them. She hadn't checked in for a while and they'd want to know what she was doing. However, should she tell them about her job with Brooks? She almost had to, because Dean probably would. Besides that, the news would soon get around to the other volunteers and some of them would be going back to Thunder Canyon. It was difficult to hide anything in a small town.

When Brooks pulled up in front of Strickland's, Jazzy said, "You don't have to see me in."

"I don't have to, but I'm going to. I told you, I want to check your shoulder."

"You're still wet. You'll catch cold."

He laughed. "Everyone knows you don't catch cold from the cold. I promise, this will be almost painless, Jazzy. I just want to make sure you're not really hurt."

Okay, so they were going to have to get this over with because he was persistent and stubborn. In a family as large as hers, she'd learned there was no point in arguing.

Once inside Strickland's, they climbed the stairs. Jazzy took out her key and opened her door. She'd already told Dean that Brooks was "safe," so why was she hesitating in letting him into her room?

Simple. He was half dry, half wet, and all imposing male.

Her room was small and the nice thing about it was it had a bathroom of its own. Standing by the single bed, Jazzy was very aware of it as Brooks came into the room and stood before her.

"I left the door open," he said. "I don't want you to think I have an ulterior motive."

He had left it open about six inches, and she realized how thoughtful it was of him to do that. She simply had to think about him as a doctor right now.

"Take your jacket off," he said gently.

At first her fingers fumbled with the zipper. Her nervousness was stupid. She had nothing to be nervous about. But unzipping her jacket, she felt as if she were letting him into her life in a different way. She shrugged out of it and hung it over the bed post. He took a step closer to her, and she suddenly felt as if she couldn't breathe. Her gaze locked to his for a few seconds, but then he directed his focus to her shoulder and reached out to touch it.

She thought she'd prepared herself. She thought this would be clinical.

The exam *was* clinical on his part as he kneaded around the joint and asked, "Does that hurt?"

"Some," she managed to say.

"Don't soft pedal it if it does."

"It's not that bad. Really."

As he felt along the back of her shoulder, she winced. His fingertips massaged the spot and she found that didn't hurt but felt good.

"You got bumped around and might have black-and-blue marks tomorrow. Put some ice on it for the first twenty-four hours, ten minutes on, half hour off."

"Yes, Doctor," she said with a slight smile.

His fingers stopped moving. His eyes found hers. The room seemed to spin.

No, not really. Couldn't be. But gazing into Brooks's eyes was like getting lost in forever. His hand was on her back now as he leaned a little closer. She felt herself swaying toward him.

But then he straightened. "Take it easy for the rest of the day."

Feeling reality hitting her straight in the face, she asked, "When do I officially start work for you?"

"Let's consider tomorrow the starting date. I've been talking to a real-estate agent and she'll have a list of places for me to look at. Would you like to go along to do that?"

"You bet."

"Unless you don't feel well."

"I'll be fine."

"Famous last words." He went to the door. "Ice the shoulder."

As he opened the door and went into the hall, she called after him, "Get out of those wet jeans."

She thought she heard a chuckle as he strode away from her room. She remembered his shirtless upper body. She remembered the feel of his fingers on her shoulder. She remembered the way his smile made her feel.

Working for Brooks Smith could be the biggest mistake she'd made...lately.

Chapter Four

The sun shone brightly in the brilliant turquoise sky as Brooks let himself into Strickland's Saturday morning, coffee and donuts in his hands. He'd found a property he wanted to show to Jazzy. She'd said yesterday she'd be ready anytime he was, but he hadn't wanted to waste her time, so he'd taken a look at three properties early this morning. He was confident one of them would work, but he wanted to see what she thought.

At the front desk, he greeted Melba who was shuffling papers into a file folder. She eyed the bag from Daisy's Donuts. "Jazzy didn't come down to breakfast," she told him. "Maybe she'll eat some of what you brought her."

He supposed Melba had seen him with Jazzy the past two days. The older woman watched over her guests with an eagle eye.

He climbed the stairs, glad he'd put lids on the coffee cups or he'd have sloshed it all over the box and donuts. He was just eager to show Jazzy the property, that was all.

But deep down, he knew the reason for his eagerness was more than that. When he brought Jazzy back here yesterday and examined her shoulder, he'd had to remind himself over and over again that it was a clinical examination. But he could vividly remember how she'd felt under his fingertips, the look in her eyes. They were attracted to each other and fighting it. Just how difficult was it going to be to work together?

Not too difficult, he hoped. They wouldn't have time for attraction, not if they were going to get a clinic up and running. So the sooner they looked at the property and got started, the better. It was silly, really, but he couldn't imagine doing this with anyone else. Jazzy was so positive and upbeat, so excited about new things. She understood the dedication it took to take care of animals, and she even admired it. Unlike Lynnette. She was so different from Lynnette. Jazzy wouldn't do anything half-measure. Dating Jazzy could be an unrivaled experience. More than dating her could be...

He thought about his dad's ultimatum. Marriage would be a solution. Yet after his experience with Lynnette, he couldn't even think about it.

It was a shame he couldn't erase the shadows of the past from his memory bank.

When he reached Jazzy's door, he shuffled the box into one arm and rapped. She didn't answer. Could she have gone out? Was that why she hadn't appeared at breakfast?

He rapped again. "Jazzy?" he called. "Are you in there?"

To his relief, he heard movement inside. Then Jazzy was opening the door, looking as if she'd just awakened from a deep sleep. Her blond hair was mussed around her face and she'd pushed her bangs to one side. She was wearing a raspberry-colored nightgown and robe over it, but she hadn't belted the robe and the lapels lay provocatively over her breasts.

He quickly raised his gaze to hers. "Are you okay?"

She seemed to come fully awake. Now she belted her robe, cinching it at her very slim waist. That wasn't a whole lot better, but she didn't know that. He'd just have to package his lusty thoughts away in mothballs. He was concerned about her and that concern must have shown.

"Tell me the truth, Jazzy." He didn't want some varnished description of how she was feeling.

"Can I tell you over donuts and coffee?" she asked. "That really smells good."

If she wanted coffee and was hungry, she had to be okay, right?

Without a second thought, he stepped inside the room. She moved over to the nightstand, clearing it of books and lotion. She set them on the small dresser.

After he settled the box on the nightstand, he pulled over the ladder-back chair while she curled up cross-legged on the bed. She was so natural...so unaffected... so pretty.

He opened the box of donuts, pulled out a chocolate-glazed one and handed it to her. "Tell me."

She wrinkled her nose at him. "As the day went on yesterday, I got more sore. Last night I couldn't get to sleep. It must have been about 4 a.m. when I finally did, and I guess I was in a deep sleep until you knocked. You should have called to warn me you were coming."

"You need a warning?"

She shrugged. "A girl doesn't like to be caught with her hair all messed up." She flipped a hank of it over her shoulder.

He laughed. "You look—"

She held her hand up to stop him. "Do *not* say fine. No woman wants to hear she looks fine."

"Then how about you look morning-fresh and pretty."

She'd been about to take a bite of the donut but she stopped and her eyes widened.

"What? You don't believe me?"

"I have sisters who look beautiful in the morning. They don't even get sheet wrinkles on their faces."

"You don't have any sheet wrinkles. Or *any* wrinkles at all."

Her skin was so creamy, he wanted to reach out and touch it. That was the problem. "You do have a few freckles, though. But I like those, too."

She blinked.

He could see he'd definitely surprised her, maybe even embarrassed her a little. He popped the lid off the coffee. "Sugar and cream, just like you like it." As he handed it to her, he asked, "So how sore are you this morning?"

"Just a little, really. I think some of it's from the seat belt."

That made sense.

"Do you feel like looking at a property I found? If you don't, we can do it another time."

"No, I want to go." She was about to lay down her donut, when he said, "Take your time. I told the real-estate agent I'd buzz her when we were on our way."

Jazzy suddenly got a determined look on her face,

and Brooks knew he was probably in for trouble. She pointed her donut at him. "Just because you're tall and strong and seem to know what you want in life, doesn't mean you can look at me as...fragile."

Now where had *that* come from? Honest to goodness, he just didn't understand women. "I don't."

She pointed her donut at him again. "You do. Maybe it's because you take care of animals, but you have some kind of protective streak. It's the same streak that argued with me about help with changing your tire, and being out in the rain and thinking I had to rest today. *You* were in the accident, too. *You're* not resting."

"I didn't bump my shoulder."

She lifted a finger and stroked the air. "Okay, point taken. Still, I'm not some damsel in distress. Got it?"

She was sitting there cross-legged on the bed—with mussed hair and a just-awakened look. Baser urges nudged him to move closer, to climb into bed with her...

As if he needed more proof she wasn't fragile, she said, "And I iced my shoulder yesterday like you told me to. I can take good care of myself."

Whether she could or couldn't remained to be seen, but he wasn't going to tell *her* that. After all, she'd left her home and her family and her job to come to Rust Creek Falls to help.

"You've been fighting having somebody look after you all your life, haven't you?" he asked perceptively.

She finished the rest of the donut and wiped her fingers on a napkin. "With a family as big as mine, it can't be helped. Everyone thinks they know best for everyone else. We do take care of each other, but sometimes it just gets very smothering." She licked one finger then picked up her coffee, took a couple of sips, then asked,

"Do I have time for a quick shower? I can be ready in ten minutes."

A woman who could be ready in ten minutes? This he had to see. "Go for it," he said and stood. "I'll go downstairs and wait. If Old Gene's down there, he'll want an update on how all the ranchers are doing. So if it goes a minute or two over ten, don't worry."

She hopped off the bed. "Ten minutes. Start timing."

He was still shaking his head, amused, as he went down the stairs. Jazzy was a bundle of…something. He wasn't sure what. She had energy and spirit and a smile that wouldn't quit. Maybe, just maybe, their partnership was going to work out.

Fifteen minutes later in Brooks's truck, Jazzy could feel his gaze on her and she knew she was just going to have to get used to that protective streak of his. It didn't feel so bad, really, coming from him—rather than from her brother or Dean or her dad. But she really was feeling better since the shower had loosened her up. Ice had definitely helped last night.

She was a bit surprised when he headed down Buckskin Road toward the creek. The properties in the lower-lying areas in the south part of the town had been the worst-hit by the floodwaters. Some of the properties directly north of the creek hadn't fared so well, either.

He pulled up in front of a refurbished one-story office. Another car was already parked there. When she and Brooks disembarked from his truck, an older woman in jeans, boots and a denim jacket nodded to them. Brooks introduced Jazzy to Rhonda Deatrick, who was a real-estate agent.

Rhonda handed Brooks a key. "Look around as long

as you want. You can drop the key back at the office when you're done. That way I won't interfere in your decision process."

He laughed. "In other words, you're not going to sway me one way or another."

She smiled. "You're just like your daddy. You know exactly what you want. So this will either work or it won't." She nodded to Jazzy. "Nice to meet you." She headed for her car.

"I guess she knows your dad?"

"Actually, she helped out my grandmother on some property issues. But Rhonda has a couple of horses my dad's taking care of, too."

"Everyone knows everybody here. But then Rust Creek Falls is even smaller than Thunder Canyon. Thunder Canyon used to be more like this, before money moved in with the resort and all."

They went up the short walkway that looked as if it had been recently power-washed. The building itself was sided in dark blue. Concrete steps led to the wooden porch with its steel-gray railing.

"Everything looks freshly painted and cleaned."

"From what I understand, there was a foot of mud in this place after the flood, so it was completely gutted and redone," Brooks explained.

"Was this a house?"

"No, it was a dentist's office. That's why it has a lot of good things going for it."

"The dentist didn't want to resume his practice?"

"Nope. He was near retirement age. He'd been renting the property for the past ten years. The owner was the one who decided to put it into tip-top shape again, and see if he could rent it to another doctor."

Brooks opened the door and stepped aside so Jazzy could precede him. She went up the steps, her arm brushing his chest. Even that swift contact affected her. The scent of his cologne affected her. Everything about him affected her.

Inside, everything was white. There was new dry wall in all the rooms, as well as new tile flooring.

"I think I'd leave the exam rooms in white for now," he said. "I can hang framed posters on the walls. But the reception area needs a coat of paint."

Jazzy examined the space. "An L-shaped desk would look good right there." She pointed to the wall across from them. "Or a counter. This would be pretty in a really pale blue, maybe with some stenciling around the ceiling."

"Stenciling?"

"Yes. You use a template and there are special paints. It's not difficult. I helped Mom do it in the kitchen. It could be on one of the walls or two of the walls, just around the doorways and windows. Whatever you decide. I'm sure there are plenty of animal stencils. It would look really cute. We can fill a basket with dog toys, another with cat toys."

"Everything in here has to be easy to clean," he reminded her.

She'd forgotten about that. "What's your dad's office like?"

"Practical."

"Animal owners are practical, but they want their pets to feel at home, too. Coming to the vet is often a traumatic experience. The more pleasant we make it for them, the more they'll be glad to come here."

"I like that philosophy. I'll try to have regular hours

here and make outside visits to ranches during speci-
fied times. I know there will be emergencies in both
instances. Once I take patients away from Dad and he
sees he doesn't have to work so hard, then maybe we
can combine our practices. I can take over the majority of the work, and he can help out when he wants. Or
else he can handle office visits and I can do the ranch
visits, which are harder on him. It would be ideal. I
think he just doesn't want to admit he can't do what
he used to do."

"Nobody wants to admit that."

"Maybe so, but life is about change, even for, or especially for, older folk."

Before she thought better of it, she clasped his arm.
"I think you're doing the right thing."

He covered her hand with his. "I surely hope so. Let
me show you the rest. You can see the creek from the
backyard."

Leading her into a hallway that led to the back of
the office, he opened the door that went outside. The
property had a huge backyard and beyond she *could*
see Rust Creek.

"This is nice."

"I can imagine kennels out here and runs, which Dad
doesn't have. Maybe eventually, if he doesn't give in to
a joint practice, I could buy this place. Because of the
flood, prices are down in this whole area."

"I imagine it could still be expensive."

After a long look at the creek, and then a glance
at her, he said, "I've saved most of what I've made
since I graduated. My rent's low, my scholarship paid
for schooling. I've invested a lot of it since I've been
working."

"How long have you been living in Kalispell?"

"Four years."

She saw something shadowy pass through his eyes and couldn't help asking, "But you really didn't intend to live there?"

"Life hasn't turned out as I expected."

She could keep silent, but that wasn't her way. Softly, she asked, "What did you expect?"

Again, he stared into the distance for so long a time she didn't think he was going to answer. But then his gaze came around to hers. "I expected to be married and practicing with Dad. But my fiancée broke our engagement and everything fell apart."

There was a lot of pain behind his words. From his broken engagement, or from his troubles with his father? If it was the broken engagement—

When she'd broken off her relationship with Griff, had it left this kind of pain with *him?* Brooks had confided in her and she realized that that confidence gave them an even more personal connection. If she reciprocated, their bond would grow. Unless he saw her in the same light as his fiancée. Right now, telling him about Griff just didn't seem to be the right thing to do, any which way.

They stood there in silence for a long time. Finally Brooks said, "I'm going to take it. This property seems perfect and I don't want to let it slip away. I can probably get all the paperwork done today. I'll start painting the reception area tomorrow morning."

"*You'll* start painting? I thought I was working for you now."

"Your shoulder's still sore and…"

The look she gave him must have stopped him. He

held up his hands in surrender. "Right. You don't want me to be protective. Do you want to paint, too?"

"Paint, and anything else that will help you get off the ground. If my shoulder's still sore tomorrow, then I'll decide what I can or can't do. Deal?"

A slow smile spread across his lips. "Deal."

But when they shook on it, Jazzy had the feeling she was agreeing to a lot more than a business arrangement.

The volunteers had carpooled for their initial drive to Rust Creek Falls, so Jazzy had left her car back in Thunder Canyon. She really didn't need it here because everything was within walking distance or she could catch a ride with someone. When Cecilia, who was also staying at Strickland's, dropped Jazzy off at Brooks's new clinic the following morning, she winked. "Have fun."

"We're going to work," Jazzy told her, for not the first time. She'd told Brooks yesterday, after they'd shaken hands on their deal, that she'd find her own way to the clinic.

"You can have fun and work, too," Cecilia reminded her.

But Jazzy was not looking at Brooks in any way other than as an employer. She simply was not. She was going to help him get his office ready. Period.

Glancing toward Brooks's truck, she wondered how long he'd been there. When she stepped inside his new office, she figured he'd probably arrived before dawn. There were tarps covering the floor, a flat of water bottles in one corner and a giant cup of coffee on the ladder.

"Did you have breakfast?" he asked. "I have donuts in the truck."

"I ate this morning. I knew I'd need some energy."

"How do you feel?"

"I feel like I should be here helping you paint. End of discussion, right?"

He gave her a slow smile. "Right. I only have one more wall. It would help me if you would do the trim around the windows."

"So I don't have to lift that heavy roller?"

"No. Because I think you'd be good at the detail work."

She laughed. "Very adept. Just point me to the brushes. What else is happening today?"

"Internet service will be hooked up tomorrow, same with phone. Equipment will also be delivered. I bought a secondhand desk at the used furniture shop and Norm said he'd actually deliver it today, even though it's Sunday."

"That's fast."

Brooks looked so tall and head-over-heels sexy this morning. He'd discarded his Stetson. His shirt might have seen a hundred washings because it was soft and a bit faded. He'd probably worn an old one in deference to the paint splatters he might get on it, she supposed. His jeans appeared worn, too, and fit him *so* well.

"I can't believe how fast this is happening."

"It has to happen fast for Dad's sake," Brooks said matter-of-factly.

"When are you going to tell him?"

"Once we're up and running. I don't want him to think it's something I won't go through with. I intend to present it to him as a done deal."

Brooks's cell phone buzzed. He took it from his belt and checked the caller ID. "I should take this. It's the Kalispell clinic."

Jazzy nodded and went to find the paint brush, but she couldn't help hearing Brooks say, "Clint can't handle it?"

He paused then added, "Yeah, I understand. Okay, it will take me about ten minutes." When he ended the call, he just stared at Jazzy. "I have to drive to a ranch outside of Kalispell, but I don't want to leave you here with this mess."

"No mess, just painting to be done."

"I don't like leaving you here without a vehicle."

"Strickland's is only a few blocks away. I can always call Cecilia or Dean if need be. Go, take care of whatever emergency has come up."

He came closer to her, so close she could see the rise and fall of his chest as he let out a long breath. He looked as if he wanted to…touch her and she wanted him to touch her.

His voice was husky as he said, "You're becoming indispensable."

Seriously she responded, "I don't think I've ever been indispensable."

He cocked his head. "That's hard to believe."

"In a large family, someone's always there, ready to step in. Sometimes when I get home after time away, it feels like no one's missed me. It's hard to explain."

Now he did reach out and touch her face, his thumb rough on her cheek. "I'd miss you if you weren't here."

"I shouldn't have said what I did." She could feel heat in her cheeks.

"You can say whatever you want to me, Jazzy. Sometimes it's easier to talk to strangers about the truth than to anyone else. Maybe that's why we hooked up at the Ace in the Hole."

Hooked up. But they really *hadn't* hooked up, not in that way. Still, she knew exactly what Brooks meant, and she couldn't help but say, "You're not a stranger anymore."

As soon as the words were out of her mouth, she wondered if she should have said them. Maybe he didn't feel the same way. But then his eyes darkened and he seemed as if he wanted to do more than touch her face, as if maybe he wanted to kiss her.

"No, we're not strangers anymore."

She tried to cover the excitement she was feeling, the heat and the speed of her racing pulse. "It's hard to believe we've only known each other less than a week. I feel as if I've known you longer."

"Much longer than a few days," he agreed, seemingly unable to look away. Then he appeared to remember he had something else to do, and someplace else he had to be. Whatever he'd been thinking and feeling got closed off. "I'd better get going. If there's any problem, call me," he reminded her.

There *was* a problem. She was much too attracted to Brooks Smith. *He's a confirmed bachelor,* she chastised herself. That was so hard to remember when he looked at her with his intense brown eyes.

Chapter Five

When Brooks stepped inside his Rust Creek Falls
clinic—and he was beginning to think of it that way—
he stopped short and just stared at Jazzy. She was sitting
at the desk that had obviously been delivered when he
was gone...in front of the wall that hadn't been finished
the last time he'd looked. She hadn't just painted the
trim, the baseboards, the door frames, she'd finished
that wall, too. He didn't know whether to shake her or...
Go ahead and think it. He wanted to take her to bed.

Not going to happen. He was her boss. They could
never have a decent working relationship if they were
involved, though that didn't keep him from imagining
what it would be like—bringing her into his condo, un-
dressing her slowly, leading them both into pleasure.
He'd wondered more than once about her romantic past,
and maybe it would come up because he had a question for her about it.

She stood when she saw him, all smiles. "I need to know if you're going to rely on word of mouth to get business, or if I should investigate some other advertisement opportunities." She had a pad and pen on the desk, jotting down ideas and the next items on a to-do list.

"Are we going to talk about what you did here this morning?"

"Not right now. There are more important things. I'll need to know your budget for advertising. Maybe you can tell me what's worked with the Kalispell clinic and what hasn't. What I think will serve you well now is to provide some kind of service that your father can't."

He'd been wrestling for the past few hours with recalcitrant cows. He'd washed off at an outside spigot but he still felt grimy, not at all as if he should be anywhere near Jazzy. Still, he approached her.

"You've given this a lot of thought."

"You want to succeed, don't you?"

"Sure, I want the practice to succeed, but more than that, I want Dad to see the success of this practice as a relief for him."

"So what service *doesn't* he provide?" she asked with that perky smile that made his whole body tense.

Keeping his mind on the question, he answered, "Dad doesn't do much work with small animals because he doesn't have time. He sets up office hours but then he gets called away. Ranchers can't bring horses and calves to him, so *he* goes to *them*. Traveling takes time. On top of that, Dad likes to gab. He spends a lot of time with his clients."

"Do you think that helps?"

"Sometimes it might, sometimes it might not. For instance, the first time I went to Sam's to help with his horses, we did spend a lot of time talking. I had to get a good feel for what was going on and what had happened to them. But since then, we talk very little, except if it's about the animals. Dad, on the other hand, would make a point of spending time with Sam with each visit."

"So what you're saying is that your dad's appointments aren't always on time."

"They're *rarely* on time. When he has office hours, his waiting room fills up and patients can be there an hour and a half to two hours before he gets to them."

"So that's a great place to start. His weakness can be our strength. We'll have to figure out a way to make sure you keep your office appointments, and I'll have to be certain I schedule them with the right amount of time."

"That envelope I gave you has a list of Kalispell services and the times that they schedule them. For instance, if you have a cat come in for an ear cleaning and a nail clip, that's a fifteen-minute appointment. A yearly check to discuss problems, get vaccinations, maybe flea treatments, would take a half an hour. Get my drift?"

"But I don't think it can be that cut and dried," she protested.

"You're right. After I get to know my patients, I can analyze their needs pretty accurately. I don't want to overcharge just because they take up my time, either. It's going to be a balance."

"I understand that."

He came around the side of the L-shaped desk unit. Jazzy was using a folding chair because the desk chair he'd bought wouldn't be delivered until tomorrow.

She ran her hand over the walnut finish on the desk.

"I like this. It's quality wood and sturdy. Your computer setup and printer should fit on here just fine."

"We'll see tomorrow. It shouldn't take too long to set up." He studied her. "But right now there's someplace I want to show you."

"Here in the office?"

"No. You've done enough work here today. I just want to show you something I like about Rust Creek Falls, and maybe you'll like it, too."

He was standing behind her as he looked over the desk and suddenly he couldn't keep from placing his hands on her shoulders.

She went perfectly still.

Jazzy felt warm under his hands. There was a comfort in holding her, but he felt a need to claim her somehow, too. Funny he should think of it that way.

He was grateful for her help, for her expertise in painting, for her caring about his practice and his dad. He cleared his throat. "Thank you for finishing this today, Jazzy. Tomorrow we can actually start setting up."

Releasing his grip on her, he stepped away.

She was silent for a moment but then her eyes sparkled in a way that invited him to get to know her better. "As soon as I wash up, I'm ready to go." Her voice was light.

They were going to keep everything between them *very* light.

As Brooks drove to the north of Rust Creek Falls, Jazzy recognized where they were headed—Falls Mountain. Tall evergreens were everywhere.

When the paved part of the road ended, Brooks

glanced at her. "This last stretch has been smoothed out some since the flood, but it could still be a little rough. Have you ever been to the falls?"

"I haven't. There just never seemed to be enough time to ride up here."

Brooks's truck bumped along the narrow road, which became a series of switchbacks under the never-ending groves of pines. One of the switchbacks led out onto a rocky point before doubling back. They could have parked there, she guessed, to get a view of Rust Creek Falls valley below, but they didn't. Brooks kept driving.

Suddenly they rounded a sharp turn and Jazzy could hear a tumbling, echoing roar. Mist wisped in front of them until finally as the sparkling sun reflected off shimmering water, she spotted the falls.

Brooks veered off the road to a safe spot and parked. "Would you like to get out? We can walk closer."

"Is it safe?"

"I promise I won't let you trip and fall over the edge." He grinned at her and she shook her head.

"I've done some hiking, I'll be—"

"Fine," he supplied for her and she had to grin back. There was something about Brooks Smith that made her want to dive into his arms. How could his fiancée have broken up with him?

After Jazzy climbed out of the truck, Brooks took her elbow as they walked toward the falls. They stood there a few moments in silence, listening to the fall of water, watching the mist puff up, admiring the late-day sunlight glinting off the cascade of ripples. They were standing close together. Brooks was still holding her elbow and it didn't feel protective as much as... close...intimate.

Because of that, because she wanted to know more about him, she asked, "Do you date much?" She knew what she'd heard from Dean, but she wanted to hear it from Brooks.

"I don't have time to date."

"If you did, would you?"

Instead of gazing at the falls now, he was gazing at her. "I don't know. Dating is meant to lead somewhere. I don't know if I want to go there for lots of reasons."

She knew she was prying but she asked, "Such as?"

The breeze and the mist wound about them, seeming to push them closer.

"Relationships require time, and I don't have it. Relationships require commitment, loyalty, fidelity and few people know how to give those."

She sorted that one out from all the rest. "You've put a lot of thought into it."

"Because I tried once and it didn't work."

Hmm, just what did that mean? Had Brooks's fiancée expected flowers, poems, rose petals and attention from morning to night? On the other hand, if Brooks really didn't know how to be a partner in a relationship...

She'd find out about the partner part.

"Did your mom and dad have a good marriage?"

"This is beginning to feel like the Inquisition," he grumbled.

"Sorry. I shouldn't have asked." She'd obviously pushed too far and she had a tendency to do that. She just hoped that she hadn't ruined their rapport.

But as if *he* needed answers, too, he asked, "What about *your* parents? Do they have a good marriage?"

She didn't mind talking about her parents. They were the epitome of what a married couple *should* be. "Oh, yes. They still hold hands. They enjoy being around each other. We can tell."

"You talk about it with your brother and sisters?"

She grinned. "Especially when we're trying to point out what we want for our futures. Three of my sisters are happily married. Incredibly lovesick." She sighed. "They sure have had more luck than I've had." Then, because she didn't want Brooks to think she was pathetic not being able to find anybody to love, she said, "But maybe that's because I don't like calf-roping. Maybe if I practiced, a cowboy would lift me out of the mud and he'd become my Prince Charming."

Brooks laughed. "That's a pipe dream if I ever heard one."

"Don't I know it. I limit my pipe dreams to achievable ones." And she could see, even if she'd begun to fall for Brooks Smith, that that road would lead nowhere. Whatever had happened to him had made him sure that a bachelor's life was the one he wanted.

What a shame.

The following morning, Jazzy was at the front desk, setting up the computer program. She glanced over at Brooks as he helped the delivery man move in more equipment and furniture. He was wearing jeans and a T-shirt today in deference to the work he was doing, and he looked good. All brawny, handsome cowboy.

They'd met here today and acted as if they hadn't shared those closer moments at the falls yesterday. But then she knew that was the way men acted sometimes. Her dad, especially, had trouble showing his feelings. And Brody, even though he was supposed to be a modern-day bachelor, didn't often put his into words, either.

In the reception area, Brooks pushed a few chairs into place and then asked Jazzy, "What do you think?"

"I think it's coming together. By tomorrow you should be ready to see patients. Later today, I'll see about putting the word out on local Kalispell sites. Getting the word out isn't always easy, but we'll do it."

Suddenly, a tall, thin woman with fire-red, frizzy hair burst into the office. "Brooks, what's going on here? I heard there was a bunch of commotion down here and came down to see myself."

With an expression of chagrin, Brooks turned to face the newcomer. "Hi, Irene. Have you met Jasmine Cates? Jazzy, this is Irene Murphy. She manages the feed department at Crawford's store."

"It's good to meet you, Mrs. Murphy." She wasn't touching this complication. She was going to let Brooks handle the woman and an explanation that might spread through the town like wildfire. Jazzy was an outsider, but Brooks wasn't, and the news would be better coming from him.

"I'm setting up a clinic here," he explained. "Buckskin Veterinary Clinic."

"You mean, you're like an annex to your dad's practice?" Irene inquired with a puzzled look on her face.

"No, I'm not an annex." Brooks didn't explain more.

Irene gave the place a good looking around, and her nose went a little higher into the air. "It looks like we'll have something to talk about at Crawford's today." Before Brooks could say another word, she'd swept out the door.

"Uh-oh," he muttered. "I'd better get hold of my father. She's the town crier. Nothing escapes her notice."

Brooks took out his phone and speed-dialed his dad's number. He frowned. "Voice mail. He must be out on a call. He leaves his phone in the car rather than carry it with him. That's a mistake for more than one reason. If he had it on him, at least he could dial 9-1-1 if something happened."

"Is there a reason he leaves it in his car?" Jazzy asked.

"He lost his phone once when he was tracking through a field and never found it again. When something happens once, Dad doesn't forget. He doesn't change easily, either."

When Brooks's face darkened, Jazzy suspected he was thinking about his broken engagement and his father's directive to get married or not join him in his practice. She didn't know how she'd feel if her parents gave her an ultimatum, like either get married or move out. But they'd never do that.

Nevertheless, she did often feel their concern that she hadn't met the right guy, that she wasn't settling down like her sisters, that she wouldn't have the grandchildren they were hoping for. That was a constant, steady pressure. She could only imagine the pressure Brooks was feeling with his dad's health being in danger. No wonder he wanted to do something about it.

A half hour later, Jazzy was proud of herself that she'd set up the computer program and it was ready to input patient data.

Brooks circled around the desk and leaned over her shoulder. "Great job, Jazzy."

Turning her head sideways, her face was very close to his.

"Thanks," she said, a little breathless. "Now I just have to round up some four-legged patients for you."

He didn't move away and she wondered if he liked the idea of being close as much as she did. His voice was husky when he said, "Once we get the sign up tomorrow, everyone will know we're here." He'd told her he had a friend who could paint a sign on short notice.

All of a sudden, the front door of the clinic banged opened and a tall, barrel-chested man, who was red-faced and almost looked as if he were breathing fire, came rushing in. "Just what in the hell are you doing?"

When Brooks straightened, he had a pained look on his face.

Jazzy asked, "Should I call the sheriff?"

"The sheriff?" the man bellowed. "*I* should be the one calling the sheriff. My own son is trying to put me out of business."

Now Jazzy saw the light. The irate man was Barrett Smith, Brooks's father. She couldn't believe he'd already gotten wind of what was happening here, but Irene Murphy must have put the word out.

Brooks rounded the desk so he was face-to-face with his dad, or rather boot to boot. "Calm down, Dad."

"Calm down? My own son is trying to humiliate me in front of the whole town!"

"I'm doing no such thing. I'm setting up a clinic to take some of your business away, so you're not working twenty hours a day."

"You've no right to interfere in my business."

"Just as you have no right to interfere in my life?" Brooks asked, a bit of resentment in his tone.

Uh-oh, Jazzy thought. This argument could really damage father-son relations. Yet she didn't feel she had the right to interfere.

"I'm older and wiser. I know best," Barrett blustered.

"You're older, but I don't know how much wiser. You won't see reason so I had to take matters into my own hands. We could see patients here today if we had to. We'll definitely be open soon, then you won't have to take all the night calls. If people in town start trusting me, we'll both have enough business."

"If they start trusting you? You're only four years out of vet school."

"Yes, and I know all the new techniques and new medications. Do you?"

"You think you know too much for your own good. If I put the word out that no one should come here, they won't. Then what are you going to do?"

"You don't have everybody under your thumb, Dad, including me. So just accept the inevitable and think about slowing down."

"The only time I'm going to slow down is when I'm in my grave." He pointed a finger at his son. "And you remember that. This isn't over, but I have someplace I've got to be." And with that, Barrett Smith left as brusquely as he'd come in.

"That went well, don't you think?" Brooks muttered as his father slammed the door behind him. Then he added, "Maybe marrying someone would be easier than all this!"

Jazzy felt bad for Brooks *and* for his dad. "You knew he'd be upset."

Brooks rubbed the back of his neck. "I should know

better than to get into a shouting match with him. It never does either of us any good."

"You weren't shouting," Jazzy reminded him.

"My father thought I was. I wanted to break it to him gently. Irene must have beamed it up to a satellite and disseminated it through the whole town."

Jazzy bit back a smile at Brooks's wry tone. "Did the two of you ever just sit down and *talk?*"

With a sad shake of his head, Brooks admitted, "No. We haven't had a decent conversation in the past four years."

She felt such a need to comfort him. "You know, our families just want the best for us."

"What they think is the best for them is the best for us, and that's not true. You asked if my parents had a good marriage. They seemed to. They didn't fight. I saw them kiss each morning before Dad left for work. He wasn't around that much because he was always working, but my mother never complained. She warmed up his suppers when he got home late. When he missed a school event because of an emergency, she was there for me and enjoyed it. She never wanted him to do anything else. When she was diagnosed with cancer, my grandmother lived with us to help out, but I hardly remember that time. In some ways, it seemed to last forever, and in others it was over in the blink of an eye. Three months after her diagnosis, she died."

Jazzy came from around the back of the desk and stood near Brooks. "I'm so sorry. I can't even imagine losing a mom. My mom...well, she's our glue."

"That's exactly right," Brooks said. "Mom was our glue, and when she was gone, it was as if Dad and I had nothing else to hold us together. I spent time with

Dad with the animals just to be around him because I felt so adrift. But it's not as if we talked about what we were feeling…how much we missed her. It's not as if we talked about much of anything except the cases he took care of. When I wasn't with Dad, I was spending time with the horses. We had three and we boarded a couple of others. I could ride and forget for a little while. I could ride and eventually start to feel happy again. But I felt guilty when I felt happy."

"I don't think that's so unusual. Did you get over the guilt?"

"Eventually, but my dad… After my mom died, he changed. He became more rigid…harder. Sometimes I thought he expected perfection and I just never lived up to that. Now I think, like you said, he just wanted the best for me."

"So when you were a teenager, did you rebel?"

"Nope. I didn't want to give him a hard time. I wanted to keep the waters smooth. I played sports, told myself I didn't care if he was at my games or not. I got scholarships and that seemed to make him happy. So we had a tentative peace until everything went south with Lynnette and I felt as if I had disappointed him all over again."

Jazzy was more curious than ever to find out what had happened with his broken engagement, but he didn't seem to want to talk about it. In fact, he turned the tables on her.

"So did you rebel when you were a teenager?"

"I put a few pink streaks in my hair, got a tattoo, but that was about it."

"A tattoo?"

"It's a butterfly," she said. "But it's not someplace

that usually shows." She wasn't being provocative, but she saw him glancing at her arms. Maybe she hadn't meant to be provocative, but his eyes got that dark look again.

"There's much more to you than meets the eye," he said as if that wasn't a good thing.

"You like simple women?" she asked.

"I like women who are honest."

That gave her food for thought. She was about to follow up and ask him if Lynnette had been *dis*honest, but her cell phone played, announcing a call. She'd laid it on the counter beside the computer. Now she reached for it and saw it was her sister.

"Family," she said. "I'd better take this."

"Go ahead. How about some lunch? I'll go get takeout at Buffalo Bart's Wings To Go."

"That would be great."

Brooks gave her one last look before he grabbed his denim jacket from a chair and left the office.

"Hey, Jordyn," she said as she answered her phone. "What's up?"

"Mom told us you took a real job in Rust Creek Falls with a veterinarian. What's he like?"

Leave it to Jordyn to hone in on that.

"He's a veterinarian," Jazzy said evenly, to stop her sister from wandering further.

"How old?"

"He's twenty-nine."

"Ooh, and you just turned thirty not so long ago. Same age. Now give me the real details. Is he tall, dark and handsome?"

"He's tall," Jazzy teased. "And he's cowboy handsome. He's really great with animals, and he's a…gentleman."

"Are you falling?"

"No, of course not. I'm working for him."

"Those two things *aren't* mutually exclusive," Jordyn concluded.

"He's a confirmed bachelor."

"Uh-huh."

"And his life is complicated right now. He and his dad are arguing and—"

Jordyn cut in, "I hear something in your voice I never heard when you talked about Griff."

Out of all her family, Jordyn had probably been the least enthusiastic about her relationship with Griff. Maybe she'd sensed Jazzy's uncertainty about it.

"I'm working for Brooks," she said again. "Let's leave it at that. How are Mom and Dad?"

"They're fine. So is everybody else. But we're concerned about you. Are you giving notice to Thunder Canyon Resort?"

Wasn't *that* a good question?

"I should know in another week or so. I like working with Brooks and the animals. It's great practice for that horse-rescue ranch I want to start."

"You've given up on the business degree?"

"No, but for now, I don't want to plan. I just want to go with the flow. I'm tired of trying to meet other people's expectations of what my life should be."

"You're mad at the family because they wanted you to marry Griff."

"I'm not mad. I just got exasperated and tired of being watched over. I want my own life. I don't want to make finding a guy a priority because my family wants it for me. Do you know what I mean?"

"I know exactly what you mean. You want Prince Charming to drop out of the sky and land right at your feet."

"Jordyn—" This sister *could* be just as exasperating as the others.

"I get it, Jazzy, believe me, I do. And whatever you want to do, you know you have my support. So take a picture of this veterinarian with your phone and send it to me. I'll decide if he's Prince Charming material or not."

Chapter Six

On Friday, Jazzy printed out Mrs. Boyer's bill as the woman stooped to her beagle, patted a chocolate patch on his head and cooed, "You're going to feel better soon. I'll take good care of you." She looked up at Jazzy as Jazzy told her the amount of the office visit and waited as the woman wrote out her check.

It had only been a few days and Buckskin Veterinary Clinic was already seeing clients. Brooks had put a sign in the window that they were taking walk-in patients, and that had helped business, too.

"You know, your clinic is going to be convenient for me," Mrs. Boyer said. "Barrett is hard to get a hold of in an emergency. And it will be nice to have a practice that focuses on the smaller pets, too."

"I'm glad you decided to give us a try," Jazzy said sincerely.

Brooks came into the reception area from the back, carrying a bag. He handed it to Mrs. Boyer, a brunette in her midforties, who seemed to love her beagle like a child. "If Hilda won't take the whole pill," Brooks explained, "you can open the capsule and sprinkle it on her food. Just mix it in. It's supposed to have a liver and beef taste."

Mrs. Boyer laughed. "Hilda will eat almost anything."

"If anything comes up between now and your follow-up appointment, just give us a call."

"I was just telling Jazzy it's such a relief to know I can get a hold of you on short notice."

Jazzy and Brooks had made a pact that they wouldn't bad-mouth his dad, or say anything derogative about his practice. This was about building up Brooks's practice, and providing service to their clients. If they did that well, they would be successful.

"I saw your father at the General Store," Mrs. Boyer went on, glancing at Brooks. "I didn't know if I should say anything, but he was looking a bit peaked. When he left, one of the men he'd been talking to said Barrett had been complaining because some of his clients were coming here."

"We're just trying to provide an alternative to Dad's practice," Brooks explained. "I think the area has room for both of us."

Hilda began to whine. She obviously wasn't getting the attention she thought she deserved.

"I'd better get Hilda home. I understand we could have bad weather later today, rain into sleet. I think I'd almost rather see snow than more rain."

"A lot of other folks here would say the same thing," Brooks agreed.

After Mrs. Boyer deposited her checkbook in her purse, she led Hilda out the door.

As soon as the woman left, Jazzy turned to Brooks. "Maybe you should have a talk with your father."

"You saw what talking with Dad is like. It just raises his blood pressure."

"But if he's not looking well—"

"Jazzy, he won't listen to me."

"Do you think your practice really is starting to affect his?"

"After just a few days, it's hard to believe. Maybe he's seeing something that isn't there. He's never had much time for small animals. Most people here call our practice in Kalispell for their dogs and cats and bunnies. But if he's heard people are coming in here to us, maybe it's a psychological thing. I don't know. I just know the two of us can't seem to have a conversation about anything that matters, not without his temper— or mine—flaring."

"I haven't said one bad word about his practice," Jazzy assured him.

Brooks put his hand on her shoulder. "I know you haven't. Thank you for that. I want to do this fair and square."

The fact that Brooks was a man of integrity drew Jazzy to him as much as everything else about him. His hand on her shoulder felt warm. In fact, she could feel the heat from it all through her. Every time they were together, they seemed to have a rapport that went beyond words. She understood him a little better now since he'd told her about his childhood and about his broken engagement, though she still wondered why he'd broken up with Lynnette, or why she'd broken up with him. However, looking into his eyes right now, she didn't care at all about his past, just about being with him.

"You did a great job getting the word out about the practice through Dean and the other volunteers at the elementary school," Brooks said with appreciation. "I think that's made a difference. Are you still volunteering there on Sunday?"

She'd told Dean she'd still help out when she could, so she didn't mind giving up her day off to keep her word. "Yes, I am. I don't know how much help I'll be, but Dean says they can use anybody who knows how to swing a hammer."

"You've had practice swinging a hammer?" Brooks's hand still rested on her shoulder.

"Sure. Abby, Laila, Annabel and Jordyn never wanted to get dirty so I'd help Dad with his at-home projects like the shed in the backyard, or even work on the stalls and in the barn. I really am a Girl Friday. I can do a little bit of everything."

"You're proving that," Brooks said, gazing into her eyes.

When Brooks looked at her like that, her tummy did flip-flops, her breath came faster, and sometimes she even felt a little dizzy. It happened at the oddest moments—after he treated a little patient, when they were sharing hot wings over lunch, when he dropped her off at Strickland's. She wondered if that zing in the air whenever they were together was evident to anyone but her. She wondered what he thought about it.

He's a confirmed bachelor, she warned herself again.

No sooner had she taken note of the warning, than

Brooks dropped his hand from her shoulder. "I'm thinking about helping out over there on Sunday, too."

"Really?"

"Don't sound so surprised. I told the Kalispell practice I'd be on call for them, but I know how far behind the elementary school is on their progress. It can't be easy for the teachers to be having classes in their homes. I think they're going to have more than the usual volunteers this weekend. I spoke to Dallas Traub from the Triple T as well as Gage Christensen last night. They're going to be at the school, too." He paused then went on, "You said you had dinner with Gage and it didn't go well. Is it awkward when you see him now?"

Was Brooks fishing to see if she might still be interested in Gage? If he was, he could put those thoughts to rest. "No, it's not awkward. We had dinner and that was that. He's a great guy. When anyone sees him with Lissa, it's obvious they're in love. I'm glad he's happy."

Just like her sisters were happy. Just like Willa and Shelby were happy. Sometimes Jazzy wanted what they had so badly that it hurt. Sometimes she could hear her biological clock ticking. Sometimes true love seemed to be a far-away dream that was never going to come true, at least not for her. She thought coming to someplace like Rust Creek Falls, she would stop the constant reminder. Maybe something was lacking in her that she couldn't find the *one,* that Mr. Right might simply not be out there for her.

The phone on the desk rang and she was glad for the interruption. However, before she picked it up, she studied Brooks. "I still think talking to your dad might be a good idea."

But Brooks shook his head. "I've never met a man

more stubborn than my father. He's solid rock once he's made a decision. But I will call his friend Charlie and ask him to keep an eye on Dad for me." He motioned to the phone. "Now see if we just picked up another client."

Brooks was a good man, she thought as he headed for the back of the clinic.

And a man who never intends to marry, she warned herself again as she picked up the phone.

It never should have happened.

Jazzy's dad had taught her to wear gloves when handling wood products. She usually did. But today, with Brooks working with her side by side, she didn't seem to have her head on straight. So when the two-by-four slipped and the splinter cut her, she knew it went deep.

Brooks was beside her in an instant. "What happened? Are you all right?"

"I'm fine," she said, unable to keep from grimacing in pain. "It's a splinter, that's all."

Brooks's steady gaze didn't waver from hers. He took her hand in his and saw the injury immediately. "I'm sure someone has a first-aid kit."

"Don't make a big deal of it."

"Jazzy, it needs to be looked after. Do you always try to fade into the woodwork and pretend everything's okay?"

Brooks's words shocked her somewhat until she realized they were sort of true. At home, she didn't want to cause anyone any trouble. It was simple as that. That's why she'd dated Griff as long as she had, even though she'd known there wasn't enough passion there. Her family had liked him. He'd come to dinner. He talked sports with her dad. Her parents had liked the fact that his sporting-goods store was doing so well and he was financially secure. She hadn't wanted to upset the family applecart. She'd wanted to be on the road they'd dreamed for her, and she'd dreamed for herself. But Griff hadn't been right. Pretending she was happy hadn't been right. Always standing in the background hadn't been right.

"That's what I do, I guess," she admitted.

"Let me see if I can get it out without a tweezers," he suggested. Taking a close look at it, he manipulated it a little, then pulled it out. "I think I got it all, but you really should ask Dean if he has a first-aid kit and put some antiseptic on it."

Brooks was close enough to kiss. He was close enough for her to see the tiny scar above his eyebrow. His caring and his attention were like a balm that she'd needed for a couple of years and hadn't even known it.

She heard the titter of laughter across the room and glanced at two volunteers who were eyeing her and Brooks. Uh-oh. She didn't want any gossip starting about the two of them.

Spotting a couple of other volunteers glancing their way, too, she sighed. Did Brooks notice how they were becoming the center of attention? Before he could, before any of it could get out of hand, she backed away from him and said quickly, "I'll find Dean and get this taken care of."

Her sudden agreement seemed to surprise Brooks.

She hurried to the hall. Dean was there and when he saw her, he scowled! What was that about?

Approaching him, she asked, "Where do you keep the first-aid kit? I have a splinter I'd like to bandage up."

"You can't leave it in."

"Brooks took it out. I just want to put antiseptic on it."

Taking her by the elbow, Dean guided her up the hall to a bathroom. "We've got running water in there now. Wash it with soap. I'll bring the kit in."

"To the girls' bathroom?" she asked with a laugh.

"It's the only one working. We do what we have to do."

With another smile, she went into the bathroom and did as Dean suggested. A few minutes later he was there with a plastic box. He removed a bottle of antiseptic and a tube of cream.

"I hope you know what you're doing," he said.

"I'm making sure my hand doesn't get infected."

"Don't play dumb with me, Jazzy. You don't do it very well."

She supposed that was a backhanded compliment. "What's the problem, Dean? Every time you look at me today, you're frowning."

"That's because there's been little ripples around you and Brooks today."

"Speak English, okay? What kind of ripples?"

"Whispers, under-breath comments like, 'Doesn't she work with him now? Maybe they're more than boss and employee.'"

"And you listen to gossip?"

"Of course not. That's why I'm asking you. Are you just Brooks's assistant or are you more than that?"

"I'm his assistant," she snapped. Then seeing that this was Dean, and remembering all the times she'd spent with Brooks over the past two weeks—the conversations, the lunches, the concern for his little patients, as well as his big patients, she added, "And his friend. You know how it is, Dean. You work with someone all those hours and you talk about family, friends. You become closer than just two colleagues who push papers around."

"You're sure this hasn't gone beyond friends?"

"It has *not*."

"I spoke with Brody. He said they all know you're working with Brooks, though they don't know much about him."

"Jordyn does. She and I had a conversation about it. I don't want my family thinking up stories about the two of us any more than I want anyone here doing it. I wish everyone would just stop worrying about my life and concentrate on their own. You're going to be married and have a beautiful family, a wife who's going to be a teacher here, a little girl to love. Isn't that everything you've always dreamed of?"

"Yes, it is, actually. I want the same thing for you."

"When you want it for me, it feels like angst. It feels like something I have to live up to. I want to fall into it, not live up to it. I want to follow my bliss and let it lead to my happiness."

Dean started to smile.

"Please don't laugh. Over the past couple of years, I've found that the more I tried to control my life, the less control I had. So now, here, I'm taking what comes day by day. I'm going with the flow. I'm adopting an attitude of seeing a glass more full than more empty. And good things are happening. I lucked into this job with Brooks."

"Does it pay as much as Thunder Canyon?"

"Almost. So please stop being concerned for me, and please stop passing your concerns onto my family.

I'll talk to each one of them individually over the next few weeks. I'll make them understand that being here is right for me."

"You do have a new softness about you, a new mellowness. Does Brooks do that for you?"

"I don't know. I haven't thought about it. Does Shelby do that for you?"

"Yeah, she can, when I've had a bad day. Instead of being all grumpy or silent, she gets me talking and I get back on an even keel. You're still staying at Strickland's, right?"

"Right. Melba is giving the volunteers a good deal on rent, so I'm still saving most of what I'm earning. I'm fine, Dean."

Brooks knocked on the bathroom door and called, "Jazzy?"

"We're in here. It'll soon be a crowd."

Brooks laughed as he opened the door and saw Dean. "What do you think? Do we need to rush her to the emergency room in Kalispell?"

"Nah, I think she'll live."

"You two better think up a new routine," Jazzy muttered. "Something that will make me laugh instead of cry."

At that, they all laughed.

"Okay, I'll take my kit and go." Dean headed for the door.

As soon as the swinging door slapped behind him, Brooks moved closer to the sink where Jazzy stood. "All fixed up?"

"Ointment and a bandage. I'm good to go."

"Are you? Or is the gossip a problem for you?"

"I just don't want the wrong thing getting back to my family. I don't want to cause them stress and worry."

"I understand that. But you have to shut off the gossip. In a small town, it could ruin your life." He took her hand. "We have nothing to hide, Jazzy."

No, they didn't. Not yet. The business relationship was front and center. But she wondered about the other part of their relationship—the heat, the quivering excitement, the pull neither of them could deny. Yet Brooks was trying to deny it. Again she wondered if that was for her sake...or for his.

"Are you still going to be able to work okay, or do you want me to take you back to Strickland's?"

"I can work just fine."

Brooks's cell phone buzzed and they both glanced at the holster on his belt. "I have to get this," he said. "It could be the clinic."

"If you need to make a quick exit, I can get a ride home with Dean, no problem."

"Let's find out." Brooks checked caller ID and frowned. "It's Charlie Hartzell." Brooks answered quickly. "What's going on, Charlie?"

Jazzy watched the color drain from Brooks's face, watched his back straighten, his shoulders square. "When did this happen?" There was a pause.

"Thank God you were there," Brooks breathed. "I'll head to the hospital now. I'll meet you there."

After Brooks clicked off his phone, he said to Jazzy, "Dad collapsed. Charlie thinks it was a heart attack. He's on the way to the Kalispell hospital. I've got to get going."

He'd already started moving and Jazzy walked after

him, catching his arm. "Do you want me to go with you?"

His voice was gruff. "You don't have to do that."

"I want to, Brooks. You should have someone there... for *you*."

His eyes got that deeply dark intensity that she was beginning to understand meant he was experiencing deep feelings he didn't share. All he said was, "I'd appreciate that."

Fifteen minutes later—Brooks's foot had been very heavy on the accelerator—they walked into the hospital, not knowing what they'd find inside.

Much later that day, Brooks and Jazzy sat in the waiting room. Charlie had left and Jazzy was glad she'd come along with Brooks so he'd have somebody with him. The lines on his face cut deep, his expression was grim and tension filled his body. She could tell when she sat next to him. She could feel it when his arm brushed hers.

Brooks suddenly muttered, "I never should have had those arguments with him. I should have stayed detached and calm."

"He's your father, Brooks. How can you stay detached?"

"I've pretty much done it the past few years, and I regret that, too. I feel so guilty about all of it. If anything happens to him—" He shook his head. "Before they took him in for the procedure, I didn't even say what I should have."

That he loved his dad? Those words were sometimes hard to get out, especially in an emergency situation when time was limited and medical personnel were buzzing around.

Jazzy had been part of this push to get Brooks's new practice up and running quickly, and she felt partly responsible for everything that had happened. Maybe if they had handled it all differently, Brooks's dad wouldn't be in the hospital. She laid her hand on Brooks's arm, knowing nothing she said would ease what he was feeling.

A nurse came into the room and said to Brooks, "Your father has been taken to his room. Dr. Esposito would like to see you there. Just follow me."

Although Jazzy had stayed in the background until now, she knew it was hard to absorb everything a doctor said in this type of situation. She asked Brooks, "Do you want me to come with you?"

He didn't hesitate. "I'd appreciate that."

When they stepped into Barrett Smith's room, Jazzy thought Brooks's dad looked ten years older than he had when she'd seen him last. He was hooked up to an IV and he was scowling.

Dr. Esposito, with his wavy black hair and flashing brown eyes, glanced at Barrett's chart and then up at the two of them. "You're Barrett's son?" he asked Brooks.

Brooks nodded and shook the man's hand. The doctor glanced at Jazzy. "And she is?"

"She's a friend of mine," Brooks said.

The doctor eyed Barrett. "It's up to you whether I should discuss this in front of her."

Barrett waved his hand. "After a man goes to the hospital, nothing's private. What's it matter?"

"Is that permission to let her stay?" the doctor asked Barrett.

"Hell, yes," the older man said. "Just get on with it. I want to go home."

The doctor's arched brows and patience said he'd seen this reaction before. "Your father experienced a myocardial infarction. Fortunately, not a severe one. We inserted a stent in a blocked artery."

"Is that going to take care of the problem?" Brooks asked.

"It will take care of the problem for right now. We're of course monitoring him and he'll have to get checkups. I'll set up a follow-up appointment when he's released. But as I was telling your father, I believe his attack was brought on by several factors—exhaustion, overexertion and a lifestyle not conducive to heart health."

Silence reigned in the room.

"What does he have to do to stay healthy?" Brooks asked.

"He has to change his habits if he wants to live a long life."

"I'm here," Barrett said. "Don't talk to them as if I'm not. I have a veterinary practice. I eat when I can. I work because the work's there."

"Yes, well, that doesn't mean you can't make adjustments," the doctor said. "I'll also be putting you on medication—one is a blood thinner and the other is to help lower your cholesterol."

"I hate taking medicine," Barrett grumbled.

"Dad, you'll do what the doctor says."

Barrett crossed his arms over his chest and looked very much like a rebellious teenager.

Dr. Esposito remained passive. "I'll be talking to your father again before he's released, probably tomorrow. I want to monitor him overnight. I also want to set him up with a consultation with one of our nutritionists about diet."

"I already know," Barrett said. "It's all over the TV and news. But I'm *not* going to turn into a vegetarian."

"You don't have to turn into a vegetarian," the doctor protested. "But you *do* have to practice moderation. I'll leave you to talk to your son." He said to Brooks, "If you have any questions, I'll be on this floor about another half hour or so."

After the doctor left, Brooks said to his dad, "You have to take care of yourself. You have to let me take over the practice."

Barrett looked up at Brooks, mutiny in his eyes. "No, I don't. This is just a little setback. I'm not giving up my practice until you're settled down."

A nurse bustled into the room to check Barrett's IV and they all went quiet. But as she began to take Barrett's blood pressure, Barrett waved his son away. "Go! Go home. I need to rest. I'm going to be just fine."

Brooks looked as if he wanted to go to his father, sit beside him, convince him to do what was best. But Jazzy knew Barrett was in no mood for that now. She gently touched Brooks's elbow. "Let's let him rest for now. We can come back."

She could see the torn look on Brooks's face. But when he looked at his dad and Barrett stared back defiantly, Brooks gave a resigned sigh. "All right, we'll leave for now. But I'll be back."

"Famous last words," Barrett muttered. "Go take care of your own life and let me take care of mine."

Outside the room, Brooks stopped in the hall. He

suddenly erupted, "He makes me want to put my fist through the wall."

"You don't need a broken hand on top of everything else," Jazzy reminded him.

Brooks studied her, went silent, studied her again. "He's going to die if he keeps up what he's doing."

"Brooks, all you can do is encourage him to do what's healthy. You can't do it for him."

Brooks stared down the hall, at the nurses' desk, at the tile floor and the clinical surroundings. Then he looked Jazzy straight in the eye. "Will you marry me?"

Chapter Seven

Jazzy gazed at Brooks in stunned silence. Her heart was tripping so fast she could hardly breathe. Had he asked her to do what she thought he asked her to do? *Marry* him?

"Can you repeat that?" she asked haltingly.

He ran his hand down over his face, then looked at her as if maybe he should have kept his mouth shut. "I asked you to marry me. I know you think I'm absolutely crazy."

"No…" she started and didn't know quite how to finish or where to go from there. All she knew was, the idea of being married to Brooks Smith made her feel as if she was on top of a Ferris wheel, toppling over the highest point. "I just wanted you to repeat it so I know I wasn't hearing you wrong. You want to marry me?"

He took her hand in his and looked deep into her

eyes. "This isn't a joke, Jazzy. I'm not out of my mind. Really. But I need to solve this problem with my father. The only way he's going to let me in on the practice, the only way he's going to rest and stop wearing himself down, is if I'm really settled. I thought he was bluffing up to this point. I truly did. But he's not. Something is making him want this for me. A rival practice seems to have made the problem worse. So I can only see one solution. I have to give him what he wants."

"I don't understand," she said very quietly, his assessment not making her feel so tipsy anymore.

"He wants me to be married. Settled. So I need a wife. The way we've worked together the past week, I just know you'd be perfect."

"So you really *do* want me to marry you?"

"It wouldn't be a *real* marriage."

When he said those words, she found herself amazingly disappointed. How stupid was that?

He squeezed her hand and went on. "We would stay together for a year. In exchange, I'll deed over the land my grandmother left me. You can have the ranch you've always wanted, rescue horses, maybe even earn that business degree."

Suddenly Jazzy realized *she* was the one who must be crazy. She didn't want a ranch as much as she wanted a life with Brooks. She was falling for him, and she was falling *hard*. Working beside him for a year, living with him for a year, she'd be altogether gone. On the other hand, if they actually fell in love, maybe he'd change his mind about not wanting to stay married. On the other hand, if their relationship didn't work out, she'd have an out.

Living with Brooks, eating breakfast with him,

working in the office with him, spending evenings with him... What was she thinking?

"What would your grandmother think?"

"She would understand. She loved animals, too. And she'd be proud to watch you use it for good. She'd also understand I want Dad around as long as I can have him. Think about it, Jazzy. I'll show you the land. It's a great place for what you want to do. Imagine how long it would take you to save up to buy your own property."

"I don't even know if I could do it in ten years," she murmured.

"Exactly. We'd both be getting just what we need out of this deal."

The longer Jazzy looked into Brooks's eyes, the longer he told her all the reasons this would work, the more she believed him. She thought about his dad in that hospital bed and how this fake marriage could possibly set his mind at ease. Really, they'd be saving his life.

"Maybe you should think about this a little while," she said.

"I don't need to think about it. I'm not usually an impulsive person, but when I see the solution to a problem, then I take it. You're my solution, Jazzy. We can make this work. We like each other. We respect each other. We'd look at this as a partnership."

Yes, they would. It would be a bargain...a good deal. They'd each be getting something they needed. She'd definitely be moving her life forward.

"But didn't your dad say he wanted you to build a house on that land?"

"We'll have to take this piece by piece. I think he'll just be so overjoyed I'm getting married, that the house won't matter."

"But what happens at the end of the year? With your dad, I mean?"

"By then his health will be stabilized. He'll be on the road to healthier living. I'll be taking care of most of the work at the practice, maybe even bringing in a partner. We'll just tell him it didn't work out. We jumped in too soon. But that's not to think about now. Now, we just need to convince him we fell in love and this is exactly what we want."

"Will you keep the new office?"

"Yes, I think I would. Dad would feel as if he still had a say over what was going on at his place. Little by little, I'd handle the whole load."

"You'd be giving up a year of your life for your father. Is that what you really want to do?"

"Didn't we both say family is what matters most? A year of my life is nothing. I don't know how much longer I'll have him. I have to do this, Jazzy. Will you help me? Will you make it work?"

She thought about a wedding, a bridal gown, vows. She thought about the ranch and the horses that needed to be rescued and a life in Rust Creek Falls. She thought about being far enough away from her own family to have a life of her own without their meddling. This really could work.

And her and Brooks? Well, she'd just have to keep her growing feelings under wraps and pretend this was business all the way. But in the meantime, she'd enjoy every minute she was with him. How much of a hardship could that be?

"There *is* another big advantage in this for me," she confessed with a smile.

"What's that?"

"My family will be getting what they want. They want to see me married and settled down, too. Maybe they'll stop worrying about me, at least long enough that I can put my own life in the direction *I* plan without their interference."

He was still holding her hand and now he squeezed it gently. "So you'll do this? You'll marry me?"

Her heart felt fuller than it ever had before. "Yes, I'll marry you. What do we do first?"

Brooks stood beside Jazzy as they looked up at the pine-filled mountains, snow-capped peaks, the quiet serenity of the property his grandmother had left him. Was he absolutely crazy?

After his father's adamant refusal to do what was best for him, Brooks had known he had to do something drastic, really drastic. He'd asked himself what would settle his dad's mind most; what would provide the opportunity for him to change his health in the right direction? Brooks had realized only one thing would do that—his own marriage.

Of course he wouldn't ask just any woman to marry him. That would be truly stupid. But he knew Jazzy's background. He knew what she thought about her family. He knew she worked hard. He knew she had a goal, but wasn't sure how to get there. A marriage on paper for a year would suit both their purposes.

"What do you think?" he asked her.

They stood by his truck pulled helter-skelter over a rutted lane. This property, like his dad's clinic and ranch, was located on the higher end of town. There had been some erosion from the waters, but overall, it had survived quite nicely.

"How big is it?" Jazzy asked in a small voice, and he wondered if she was anxious or nervous about his proposal and her acceptance. Of course she was. They were stepping into untested waters.

"Ten acres."

"The property looks like it's never been touched by a man's hand."

"It hasn't. My grandmother's ranch, next door so to speak, was sold when she died. She'd subdivided this parcel for me, and I never knew that."

"Are you sure about this, Brooks? You really want to let this property go?"

"It's a pretty piece of land, Jazzy, and, yes, it was my grandmother's. But it's not as if I'd be selling it for a housing development. You want to do something worthwhile with it, and you deserve compensation for giving me a year of your life."

She gazed out over the hills and pine forests, rather than at him. "When do you want to get married?"

Was that a little tremble he heard in her voice? Was she as terrifically unsure about this idea as he was? Maybe so, but Brooks only knew how to do one thing— forge ahead.

"As soon as possible. In fact, the sooner, the better. As soon as we put Dad's mind to rest, the quicker he'll take it easy. I'm hoping we can get this planned and accomplished in a week to ten days."

"That's fast."

"Having third and fourth thoughts? You can back out."

Now she did turn toward him. What he saw in her big, blue eyes made his chest tighten and his throat practically close. She was vulnerable, maybe more vulnerable than he was. Maybe planning this wedding put an impediment in her road instead of clearing it. From what he'd heard, little girls had dreams of Prince Charming and happily-ever-after. He certainly wasn't offering her that. The good thing was, however, she'd be free and clear of him in a year. Then she could resume her search for Mr. Right and think about having babies.

The idea of Jazzy and babies didn't help that tight feeling in his chest. "This wouldn't be a real marriage, Jazzy. You'd have nothing to fear from me. We'll be... housemates."

That caused a crease in her brow. "Housemates," she repeated. Then after a huge breath, she asked, "Where would we get married?"

"Dad won't believe this is the real thing unless we get married in a church."

"I'll have to shop for a wedding dress."

"And we'll have to order a cake. I'm hoping we can use the church's social hall for a small reception."

"You've already planned all this out in your mind."

"Yes, I have, but all the details can be up to you. After all, it's your wedding."

"And yours," she said softly. "There is something I'd like to know before we move on with our plans."

"What?"

"Can you tell me why your fiancée broke her engagement to you?"

The wind sifted in the branches of the pine boughs and Brooks felt snow in the air. Not a big one yet. Maybe flurries tonight. He knew he was distracting himself with the idea of the weather because Jazzy's question turned the knife that sometimes still seemed to be stuck in his heart.

"Brooks?" Jazzy asked, looking up at him, expecting the truth and nothing but. Jazzy wasn't anything like Lynnette. Nothing at all. That was a terrifically good thing.

"There were several reasons. You want me to run down the list?"

"Brooks—"

He shook his head. "Even after all this time, it's still hard for me to talk about."

"Do you ever talk about it with anyone?"

His answer was quick and succinct. "No."

Instead of prompting, poking, or encouraging, Jazzy just stood there and waited, looking at him with those big blue eyes, her blond hair blowing in the breeze.

"We were at Colorado State together and engaged for a year. She was three years younger than I was and I didn't see that as a problem at first."

"At first?"

"She still liked to go out with her friends. Since I was buried in studies or practical vet experience most of the time, she went. I really didn't think anything of it. My parents had had a good marriage and I just expected the same thing to happen to me."

Jazzy's expression asked the question, *Why didn't it?* She didn't have to say the words. A nip in the air made his cheeks burn, or maybe it was just thinking about the whole thing all over again.

"She'd come home with me on holidays and vacations. When we were home, I helped Dad and she knew I expected to join his practice after I graduated."

"So you thought everything was on the table?"

"Yes, I did." He realized Jazzy was getting an inkling of what was coming next. "A few months before my

graduation, Lynnette started asking questions like—
Did I really want to practice in Rust Creek Falls? Did I
really want to live there all my life? I told her that was
my plan. I'd never been anything but honest about it. I
think the real turning point was a job offer I had from a
practice in Billings, and one in Denver. When I turned
them both down, she began acting differently. Or maybe
that had started even before that. I don't know."

He saw Jazzy take a little breath as if she guessed
what he was going to say.

"A month before I was scheduled to graduate, she
told me she'd fallen in love with someone else, someone else who wanted the same kind of life she did. She
didn't want to be married to someone who might work
eighteen-hour days, whose phone could beep anytime
with an emergency, whose small-town life was just too
limited for what she had planned."

"Oh, Brooks."

This was why he didn't talk about what happened.
This was expressly why he hadn't told Jazzy. He didn't
want her pity. He turned away from her to look in another direction, to escape the awkwardness, to bandage
up his pride all over again. He was looking up into the
sky for that snow when he felt a small hand on his arm.
It was more than a tap, almost like a gentle clasp. Her
touch was thawing icy walls that surrounded his heart,
had surrounded it for a long time.

"Brooks?" There was compassion in her voice and
he had to face it. That was the right thing to do. He
turned back to her.

"Thank you," she said simply. "For telling me. I understand a little better why—" She shook her head.
"Never mind. It helps me understand you."

"So you think you have to understand me to marry me?" he joked, trying to shake off the ghost of the past, trying to look forward.

"That would help, especially in front of your dad. If we're going to pretend we're madly in love and this was a whirlwind courtship, understanding each other goes a long way, don't you think?"

Madly in love...whirlwind courtship...pretending.

Just what were they getting themselves into?

"You're what?" Barrett asked, looking stupefied an hour later.

"We're getting married," Brooks said, with more determination than enthusiasm, Jazzy thought.

"Of course we'll wait until you're feeling better," Jazzy explained.

Barrett looked from one of them to the other, his eyes narrowing. "And just when did this romance start?"

"Jazzy's been here since July," Brooks answered offhandedly. Then he took her hand, moved his thumb over the top, and smiled at his dad, though Jazzy thought the smile was a little forced. She was aware of his big hand engulfing hers, of how close they were standing, of how her life was going to be connected to his.

Studying them again, their joined hands, the way they were leaning toward each other, she wondered exactly what he saw. After all, she and Brooks had developed a bond. They wanted the best for his father. They had their own goals. They believed this was a good way to achieve them. Besides all that, they genuinely liked each other. If she could just keep that liking under wraps, if she could just pretend Brooks was a good friend, not a man she was extremely attracted to, everything would be fine.

The flabbergasted expression left Barrett's face, but he still seemed wary. "You two have been spending a lot of time together, haven't you?"

"For more than a week, we've been together most hours in the day," Brooks supplied easily.

"Yes, I know. Setting up a *rival* practice."

"Dad, it doesn't have to be a rival practice."

Barrett took another look at their clasped hands. "We'll talk about that after this marriage takes place. Why is it you don't want a long engagement?"

"You and Mom didn't have a long engagement, did you?" Brooks countered.

Barrett looked surprised that Brooks remembered that.

"Mom used to tell me stories about when the two of you met." Brooks added, "Come to think of it, you had a whirlwind courtship yourself, didn't you?"

"So your mother told you about those days?"

"She did. She was visiting friends in Rust Creek Falls and went to a barn dance. You were there. She told me as soon as you do-si-doed with her, she knew you were the one."

A shadow seemed to cross Barrett's face and Jazzy wondered if he was in pain. But the monitors were all steady. He was silent for a few moments and then said, "Those years were the happiest of my life. She was right. We both knew that night. So maybe...so maybe this sudden engagement of yours is in the genes. Maybe waiting is stupid when life is short."

"But you're going to have a long life, as soon as you change some of your ways," Brooks suggested.

"No one knows how long they have," Barrett said thoughtfully. "I'm going home tomorrow if some blasted machine doesn't beep the wrong thing."

"Are you sure you're ready to go home?" Jazzy asked.

"You know hospitals and insurance these days. I'm sure the doc wouldn't let me go home if he didn't think I could."

"You're not going home alone. I'll stay with you," Brooks concluded.

"There's no need for that."

"Dad, I insist. Even if it's just for a few days…to make sure you're back on your feet. Our practice isn't that busy yet and I can help out with yours. You've got to start taking care of yourself, and this is one best way of doing it."

Barrett assessed the two of them for a long time, then finally he addressed Jazzy. "I heard some of the volunteers are staying at Strickland's. Is that where you are?"

"Yes, sir, it is."

"Then let me propose a bargain. I'll let Brooks come and stay with me if you come and stay, too. I want to get to know my daughter-in-law-to-be."

Jazzy fought going into a panic. Staying with Barrett wasn't all that far-fetched. The problem was, she and Brooks would be under his eagle eye. They'd have to watch themselves every minute they were together. They'd have to watch every word they said, and really, truly act like a couple who'd fallen in love. She wouldn't look at Brooks because that could be a dead giveaway that there was a problem.

Instead, she focused on his dad. "That is an option, Mr. Smith. I'd like to get to know you better, too. But

I do think Brooks and I should discuss it before we decide."

Barrett didn't look at all upset with her suggestion. In fact, he waved his hand at the two of them to go outside the door. "So discuss! Then come back in here and tell me what you decided." He studied Brooks. "I think you chose a gal with a practical head on her shoulders. Go on now. Talk this out."

In the hall, Brooks pushed his hair back over his forehead and his eyebrows rose. "I can't expect you to stay at Dad's with me."

She was quiet a moment but then she decided, "Maybe it's for the best. We have a wedding to plan, and your dad needs somebody to keep on eye on him while you're at work. I can do that."

"Are you sure you don't want to back out of this whole venture? Dealing with two Smiths in close quarters might be too much to ask."

She thought about the horse-rescue ranch she wanted to manage. She thought about Brooks's dad and his health. She thought about staying at his dad's ranch with Brooks. Did she really want to do this?

Her answer came easily and freely. "We'll plan a small, quiet wedding, and we'll take care of your dad. It will be a piece of cake."

A piece of cake, Brooks thought wryly the next day as he handed his father his remote and made sure he was settled in his recliner. "Is there anything you need? A glass of water? Something to eat? Jazzy and I went shopping last night in Kalispell and the refrigerator is stocked with good stuff."

"Rabbit food, probably," Barrett grumbled. "You know I don't like rabbit food."

"I have a copy of the diet the doctor recommended."

"Fine. I'll eat what you want when you're here. But as soon as you two leave—"

Brooks stepped in front of his father's chair and stared him down. "I lost Mom. I don't want to lose you. So try to cooperate a little, all right?"

Barrett was about to answer when Jazzy came into the room with a tray. On it, Brooks saw a turkey sandwich, a salad and a dish of fruit. He didn't know what his dad was going to say about that.

Jazzy glanced around the living room. "This is nice. Homey. This is where you raised Brooks?"

If his father had been about to argue with Brooks, he seemed to have changed his mind. "Yeah, it is. He was born here, in the downstairs bedroom, in the four-poster bed." Barrett waved his hand toward the hall in the back of the house.

"Really? A home birth? Was that planned or an accident?"

"It was in the middle of a snowstorm is what it was," Barrett elaborated. "My mom happened to be here so I didn't have to handle it myself. He came out squalling."

Jazzy set the tray on the table next to his father. "I hope you like this. The turkey is supposed to be the deli's oven-baked kind. The salad is something I cooked up. It's my own dressing. And the fruit—I hope you like apples and strawberries."

To Brooks's surprise, his father looked up at Jazzy and smiled. "It looks great and I think my stomach just growled. Good timing."

Brooks felt like shaking his head and rolling his eyes but he knew better.

"I'm going to make soup tonight if you're okay with that. My mom's vegetable soup can make anybody feel better about anything."

"So you know how to cook?" Barrett asked with a wink, taking a big bite of his sandwich.

"I'm not a wonderful cook, but I can make anything basic. And I can always call my mother to find out what I don't know."

"Did you tell your family about the wedding yet?"

Jazzy's face was serious for a moment then lightened. "Not yet. That's on my list of things to do today."

"I have a couple of Dad's outside calls to make, but then I'll be at the clinic for a few appointments this afternoon," Brooks informed them both.

Barrett scowled. "You think you'll be able to handle that on your own with Jazzy here? I'm really fine alone."

"You're not going to be alone, Dad, not for the next few days. So just get used to that idea. Jazzy, if you need me, or he becomes too bullheaded, call me. I put your suitcase in the upstairs bedroom, the one with the yellow rose-print wallpaper." To his father, Brooks said, "I want to talk to Jazzy about some wedding details. Will you be okay for a few minutes?"

"I'll be fine." His father pressed a button on the remote. "Don't worry about me."

Brooks crooked his finger at Jazzy and they went into the kitchen. She wore khakis today with a red blouse and looked like a million bucks. He'd been trying not to notice but that was hard with her blond hair swishing over her shoulder as she moved, her blue eyes flashing up at him, her smile curling like an old, forgotten song around him. There was something about Jazzy that was starting to make him ache. That was the dumbest thought he'd ever had.

"You want to talk about the wedding?" she asked.

"I called the courthouse this morning and all we have to do is go in and get the license and we're good. I also checked with the church and we can have the service next Wednesday. Is that all right with you?"

"If you think your dad will be okay by then."

"Not okay, but I have the feeling we'll have to tie him down long before then. He listens to you much better than he listens to me. So anything we want him to do is better coming from you. Do you think you can handle that?"

"I'm used to dealing with a younger brother. I can handle it."

Brooks chuckled, and then he looked at her and he wanted to kiss her. No way, but yes, that was definitely what was on his mind.

To change gears and to drive in a different direction away from that train of thought, he asked, "So you're going to call your family later?"

"I suppose I'll have to now. Your dad's bound to ask me about it."

"Do you want to wait until I'm around to do it?"

"No. I'll call Mom and she'll spread the word. Everyone else will probably call me. I might have to turn off my phone for the next few days. What bothers me most is that I can't be completely honest with them, at least not yet."

"It's not too late to back out."

She looked as if she wanted to say something about that, but she bit her lip and didn't.

With that gesture that was both innocent and sexy, he couldn't keep himself from reaching out and pushing her silky blond hair behind her ear. "We're in this together and it will work out."

She turned her cheek into his palm and they stood there that way...in silence. Finally she was the one who straightened and leaned away from his hand. "You'd better get to work. Covering two practices yourself isn't going to be easy."

"At least mine's just getting started. I'll manage. I forgot to tell you with bringing Dad home and all, the Kalispell practice found another vet who's relocating from Bozeman. So now I can focus here."

"That's wonderful news." Jazzy threw her arms around his neck and gave him a hug. "I'm so glad. I was worried about you spreading yourself too thin."

All of his senses registered her sweet smell, her soft skin, her genuine hug. On top of that, he realized he couldn't remember when a woman had last worried about him. That aching took up residence in his chest again. He pushed it away as he leaned away from her.

Taking his jacket from the back of the kitchen chair, he shrugged into it. He felt her watching him as he walked to the door.

"I'm just a phone call away," he reminded her, meaning it.

As Jazzy gave him an unsure smile, he wished he was staying right there in that kitchen with her. That thought drove him out of his childhood home. It drove him to concentrate on where he was going and the animals he'd be treating. It drove him to think about *anything* but Jazzy.

Chapter Eight

"Mom, take it easy, I know what I'm doing."

Jazzy glanced in the living room and down the hall to the first-floor bedroom. Brooks was in there with his dad setting up a baby monitor he'd bought so he'd be able to hear his father if he needed anything. She really didn't want either of them to overhear this conversation.

"How can I take it easy when you broke up with someone recently, and now you're getting married?" her mother asked.

"Griff and I were never right. You and Dad, Abby and Laila and Annabel liked him. Jordyn and Brody liked him, too, but they understood better how I felt."

"And how did you feel?"

"Like all of you were rooting for a relationship I didn't want. When Laila told me she knew Griff was going to propose, I had to break it off."

Her mother sighed. "Griff was such a good catch."

"Mom—"

"How can you be getting married when you haven't known this man very long? What's his name again?"

"It's Brooks Smith. I told you. He's a veterinarian."

"That's about *all* you've told me. You didn't even tell us you were dating him. Dean didn't even mention it."

"Dean doesn't know everything," Jazzy said, holding on to her temper.

"So is this going to be a long engagement?"

Jazzy swallowed. This was the hard part. "No, we're getting married in a week to ten days. I don't have the details yet. As soon as I do, I'll let you know. But Mom, I know this is quick, so it's really not necessary for all of you to come. Really. But if you do, I can reserve rooms at a Kalispell motel."

"A week to ten days! Jazzy. Why the rush? You're not—"

"No, I'm not pregnant. This is just…right. Brooks and I know it." Jazzy was realizing more and more that this marriage *would* be right for her. How Brooks might feel at the end of the year was another matter.

"I wish your father was here." Her mom had mentioned that her father had gone to visit a friend.

"Dad won't change my mind."

"Then maybe your sisters can."

Jazzy knew she was going to have to say what she didn't want to say. However, maybe it was time. "Mom, do you know why I left Thunder Canyon?"

"Yes. You went to Rust Creek Falls to help the flood victims."

"That's true. But I also needed to get away from all of you. I needed to find out who I am on my own without four sisters' opinions, and Brody telling me what he thinks is best, too. I needed to make up my own mind about everything from work to getting a degree to dating."

Her mother was silent for a few moments and Jazzy was afraid she'd hurt her. But then she said, "You never told us any of this."

"I don't think I fully understood what was happening until I was here. I mean, I knew I wanted to get away from something, but I wasn't exactly sure what it was. After I was here, I realized there's so much noise in our family, and its growing in leaps and bounds with Laila, Abby and Annabel finding their dream husbands. I felt lost sometimes. I felt invisible sometimes."

"Oh, Jazzy." Her mother's voice was filled with the compassion she felt for her.

"I don't feel that way here," she murmured. "I don't feel that way anymore. I feel like Brooks needs me— with work, and personal things, too. I feel like an equal…a partner."

Again, her mother went quiet. Finally she asked, "Jazzy, is this truly what you want?"

"It *is*. And as soon as I know more about what's happening, I'll let you know. I promise."

"Your sisters are going to call you."

"I know."

"Brody might, too."

"I know."

"And you won't get upset with them because they care."

"I won't. But you might as well tell them my mind is made up. I'm getting married to Brooks Smith."

After the conversation was over and Jazzy had ended

the call, she felt worn out. This afternoon, she'd made soup and generally checked on Barrett, yet she'd also had to dodge *his* questions about her relationship with Brooks. She'd sidetracked him with anecdotes about her brother and sisters and her family. She'd done pretty well, but she didn't know how long she could keep it up.

At least Barrett was turning in now, and she and Brooks wouldn't have to deal with his scrutiny as they had during dinner and a few games of gin rummy.

She went down the hall to Barrett's room and found Brooks plugging the small monitor into a receptacle.

"So you're going to hear me snore all night?" Barrett was asking his son.

"I'm sure you don't snore all night. I'll sleep a lot better hearing you snore than I would worrying about the fact that you could need something."

Barrett gave a harrumph and turned to Jazzy. "So you called your parents?"

"I spoke with Mom. Dad wasn't there."

"And—"

Jazzy felt her cheeks getting a little hot. "They're concerned, of course, because it's short notice. But my mom just wants me to be happy." She went over to Brooks, took his hand and looked up at him adoringly, though it really wasn't much of an act to do that.

This is what they'd been doing all evening, and he played along with her, too. Leaning toward her, he wrapped his arm around her shoulders. "They'll come around. I can't wait to meet them."

Something in his eyes told her that he was being honest about that. Did he want to meet them to learn more about her? Or because he'd be dealing with them, maybe, for the next year? This was all getting a bit confusing. Boundaries were blurring. Were they colleagues or were they friends?

Taking his arm from around her, Brooks said, "You're all set up, Dad. You don't have to do a thing. Just leave it on, and if you need anything, yell."

"If I yell, you'll hear me without the monitor."

Jazzy had to smile at that.

"So you two are turning in, too?" Barrett asked with a quirked brow, as if he wondered if they'd be sleeping in separate rooms.

"I have a few journal articles to catch up on," Brooks said.

"I'll turn in early because I want to get up and make both of you breakfast," Jazzy added.

"We're both early risers," Barrett warned her.

"No problem there. I am, too. We'll see you in the morning."

But before she and Brooks exited the room, Barrett called after her, "That was a fine right soup. I'm glad there's leftovers for tomorrow."

Jazzy laughed as she and Brooks entered the living room and headed for the staircase. They climbed it in silence.

After Brooks walked her to the guest-room door, he frowned. "I didn't think being around him was going to be so tough."

"That's because we're pretending."

They stared at each other, each weighing the other's motives, needs and ultimate goals. After what Brooks had told her, she understood now why he was a confirmed bachelor. He'd been hurt badly. As far as she knew, he'd never trust another woman. Yet there was something in the way he looked at her that told her he wasn't immune to her as a woman, and she knew there was something in the way she looked at him that told him he was a very attractive man.

"We're going to have to do a lot of pretending with my family, too," Jazzy warned him. "They're probably all going to call me. I told Mom I don't expect them to all make it to the wedding. After all, Annabel's husband is a doctor."

"So from what you've said, there's Abby and Cade, Laila and Jackson, Annabel and Thomas. Brody and Jordyn are still single."

"That's right. I told Mom I could reserve rooms at a Kalispell motel if they want to come up and stay overnight."

"That's probably a good idea."

"How many guests do you think we'll have?"

"Maybe about fifty."

With Brooks's eyes on hers, with him close and the memory of his arm around her still fresh, she said, "So we're really going to do this."

"We really are." He changed the subject before either of them thought too much about it. "Dad wants to help with chores tomorrow morning, but I told him that's out of the question."

"I can help."

"You're making breakfast."

"Breakfast takes about five minutes. I help with chores at home, you know."

He grinned at her. "You do, do you?"

"I'm not a city girl. I'm used to small-town Montana." Maybe she'd said it because she wanted to make the distinction between herself and Lynnette.

Brooks's eyes narrowed. "Are you trying to tell me something?"

"I'm trying to tell you, you can trust me to keep my word. You can trust me to be a partner in this. Helping you look after your dad means taking a load off your shoulders. I'll do that with you, Brooks. After all, it's our agreement."

Even without the agreement she would do it for him if he asked.

Brooks was close, but now he moved a little closer. The nerve in his jaw jumped and his eyes darkened. She thought she knew what that darkening meant. It was his desire. He was fighting it for all he was worth, and she had been fighting hers, too. But now, she didn't know what was more prudent. She wished he'd act on that desire.

As he leaned closer to her, she thought he might.

But he didn't even touch her this time. His lips, that had been so sensual moments before, thinned and drew into a tight line. His shoulders squared and his spine became even straighter.

Then he let out a breath and he shook his head. "I confided in you about Lynnette, but that's not something I do very often. And even though I did, trusting is tough for me."

Although he hadn't touched her, she had to touch him. She clasped his arm. "Brooks, I will help you with your dad. That's the point of all this, isn't it?"

"Yes, it is."

She had the feeling that when he said the words, he was reminding them both of the reason for their marriage. He didn't want either of them to forget it.

* * *

In the barn the following morning, Brooks made sure he concentrated on the chores and not on Jazzy. That was hard, though. Her soft voice got under his skin as she talked to the horses. It was tough not to watch her jeans pull across her backside as she carried feed to the stalls. While he replaced water buckets, he remembered the meal she'd cooked last night, the way the house had smelled so good, the fresh-baked biscuits that had fallen apart when he'd broken them. He found himself easily imagining coming home to her every night.

"Are you going to play gin rummy all day today with Dad?" he asked from across the stall.

"Not *all* day. If you need me to work on anything for the office, I can do it here. Just let me know. I want to cook and freeze dinners so your dad can just pull them out when he needs them."

"There *are* frozen dinners."

"There are. But they have preservatives, and maybe not as tight a watch on calories, fat, all that. I found some good recipes online."

"You're going above and beyond the call of duty."

"If I sit with your dad and talk with him, it's hard to deflect some of his questions. He watches the two of us like a hawk. At least if I'm busy, he can't ask me about...us."

Brooks knew staying here was hard for Jazzy, too, and he shouldn't take his frustration out on her. "Tonight, instead of talking and playing gin, we'll make out the guest list. You can bet he'll have opinions on that. We should also decide on food. The women in the church's social club can provide a down-home meal with fried chicken if we'd like that. After all, your family is traveling all the way from Thunder Canyon. A hot meal would be good."

"That would be nice," she agreed. She studied him for a few moments, then commented, "You were awful quiet this morning while we were doing chores. Are you worried about the wedding?"

He wasn't worried about the wedding. He was concerned about what came after and the attraction he was beginning to feel toward Jazzy that he didn't understand and couldn't deflect.

"The wedding should pretty much plan itself. When are you going to get a dress?"

"I found one online. It should be here soon."

"Won't your mom and sisters be disappointed you chose a dress without them?"

"I don't want to spend too much time around them right now, Brooks, for the same reason I don't want to sit and talk with your dad. They'll understand I have to do this on short notice."

But he saw the look in Jazzy's eyes and knew she wasn't convinced of that. Were they making a mess of their lives? He knew this was right to do for him, but Jazzy? She was the kind of girl who still had stars in her eyes, who dreamed of bridal veils and babies. He'd bet on it.

For that reason, he thought about another errand he should run. He really should buy Jazzy a wedding present, just something small to tell her he appreciated what she was doing. He didn't know if Crawford's General Store would have anything, but they might. Nina ordered some unique gifts simply because Rust Creek Falls inhabitants didn't always want to travel to

Kalispell to find what they needed. He'd stop in there sometime today because things were only going to get more hectic before the wedding.

"Is there anything I should know about the horses? Should I come out to check on them during the day?" Jazzy asked as she stroked a gray's nose.

"No, I'll let them out into the pasture before I'm done here. Why don't you go on up and start Dad's breakfast."

"Trying to get rid of me?" she asked teasingly.

Yes, he was. But he couldn't tell her that. When he didn't answer right away, she asked, "Brooks?"

"Once Dad's up, he doesn't like to wait around for breakfast. I don't want him coming out here and thinking he can help. Maybe you can head him off at the pass."

"I'll do that."

When she swished by him, he almost reached out and pulled her into his arms. But he didn't.

At the doorway to the barn, she stopped. "Sunnyside up eggs, or scrambled?"

"Any way you want to make them."

She flashed him a smile and was gone.

Brooks groaned and picked up a pitchfork.

A wedding present for Jazzy.

Brooks strode through Crawford's, not knowing what he was looking for, just hoping that when he saw it, it would be right. He was hoping he could find that one special thing that he knew she'd like. Jewelry was always the best bet, but thinking about it, he hadn't seen Jazzy wearing much jewelry. Of course she wouldn't to work with animals or painting or helping with construction at the new elementary school.

Pearls were a traditional wedding gift. His dad had given his mom pearls. In fact, he knew they were still kept in his dad's safe. But this wasn't going to be a traditional wedding. It wasn't going to be a real marriage, so traditional didn't work.

He glanced at vases and candy and even boots. He spotted sparkly earrings and a necklace that would have hung practically to her navel. But then his gaze fell on the right thing, the perfect thing, something that was necessary yet something that could be a little fashionable, too. The Montana Silversmith's watch. His gaze targeted the rectangular-faced one with the black leather band and the scrollwork in silver and gold that made the band fancy.

When he saw who was behind the counter today, he smiled. It was Nina Crawford. She was looking as pretty and fit as usual, yet when his gaze ran down over the front of her, even in the oversize T-shirt, he could see the small bump.

"Nina, it's good to see you."

She frowned and laid her hand on her tummy. "It's good to see you, too, Brooks. I guess you noticed." She leaned close to him and whispered, "I just started showing, almost overnight."

"That's the way it happens sometimes. At least that's what I've heard." Though he did wonder who the father was.

Nina asked, "How can I help you?"

"Can I see that watch?" It was inside the case.

"That's a woman's watch."

"Yes, I know."

"Are you dating someone?" She sounded surprised and he knew why. Most everyone in town knew he'd said more than once, he'd never get married. But never say never.

"I'm not just dating someone. I'm going to marry someone."

"Why, Brooks Smith! Who's the lucky girl?"

"Jazzy Cates."

"One of those volunteers from Thunder Canyon?"

"That's right. She's been helping out here since after the flood. I thought this would be a nice wedding present."

"It's a *beautiful* wedding present. Any woman would love to have it." She stood back and eyed him again. "I just can't believe you're getting married. Did the flood change the way you look at life? It did for many folks around here."

He couldn't say it did, really, though Jazzy had maintained it had changed her outlook some. "Not so much. I guess I'm just feeling it's time to put down roots and forget about the past."

"That's not so easy to do," Nina said. "Take the mayoral election for instance. Collin Traub versus my brother. In the past, there was a family feud between the Traubs and Crawfords that no one even remembers anymore. But the bad feelings are still there. Who are you voting for?"

"Collin did a good job after the flood, bringing everyone together."

"You're kidding, right?"

"No, I'm not. I saw him in action."

Nina crossed her arms over her chest, "And my brother didn't do a good job?"

Now he'd set his foot in it. "It's going to require some thought, but I think my vote's going to be for Collin."

"I should charge you extra for the watch."

"But you won't."

She gave him a wry smile. "No, I won't. Do you want it gift wrapped?"

"You do that here?"

"Sure do. I have a pretty gold foil that should do the trick, if you have time to wait."

"I have a few minutes. Thanks, Nina. I really appreciate it."

"I don't need you here," Barrett said for about the tenth time.

Jazzy and Brooks exchanged a look across the kitchen table.

Barrett motioned to the papers Jazzy had spread across the table—pictures of wedding cakes and flowers, a list of guests and a to-do list that ran on for two pages. "You have lots to do and not much time to do it in. And you can turn off that damn monitor, too," he told Brooks. "After tonight, I'm on my own. You have better things to do than babysitting."

Brooks wasn't sure he was ready to leave just yet. But he also didn't want his dad's blood pressure going up every time he thought about them being there. "I'll make you a deal."

"Uh-oh. Sounds like I'm going to get the short end of the stick again."

Jazzy laughed and Brooks realized the sound broke the tension. She seemed to be able to do that easily.

"Jazzy and I will leave, but I come out here to help you with the chores first thing in the morning and at the end of the day. And she stops in at lunch to make sure you're eating properly."

Barrett narrowed his eyes. "I don't mind seeing her pretty face at lunch, and I'll take your help with the chores in the morning. But I'm on my own after that."

"Dad—"

"Don't give me that tone of voice, son. You want to help out with the animals, fine. You want to help out at the clinic, fine. But then I need my private time."

"Another condition, then. You get one of those new smartphones so we can talk face-to-face."

"I don't need—"

"Mr. Smith, I think you need to put Brooks's mind at rest. He won't be able to work if he's worried about you. Is a new phone such a bad thing?"

Barrett sighed. "You two aren't going to give up, are you?" After a lengthy pause, he decided, "All right, a new phone, Brooks helping out with the animals and with the practice, and you keeping me company at lunch. But don't think that's going to go on forever, either."

"We'd never think that," they said in unison, and then they both laughed.

Barrett shook his head. "You're even beginning to sound like a married couple. So did you set the date?"

"I talked with the reverend tonight," Brooks said. "Next Wednesday evening. Jazzy and I are going to the social hall tomorrow to check things out."

"I'm paying for the reception," Barrett said.

Brooks looked at him, surprised. "You don't have to do that."

"That's not a matter of *have to*. I want to. It's the least I could do for all you're doing for me. Why don't you two go take a last check of the barn, so I can watch my TV in peace."

This time, Brooks didn't argue with his father. He hadn't seen Jazzy all day, and he'd missed her. It was an odd feeling, one he couldn't remember having even with Lynnette.

"I'll grab my jacket," Jazzy said and did just that. She pushed all the papers into a pile and slipped them into a folder.

Once they were outside and walking toward the barn, she said, "I think your dad wants some peace and quiet."

"He's used to living alone. I can see why having us around is tough."

"So which cake did you like?" she asked him. "The one with the little pedestal, the layer cake with the flowers in pink and yellow around the border, or the all-white cake with a dove sitting at the edge of each layer? Melba said she can do any of them. She's a terrific baker and offered to do it when I told her we were getting married."

"It really doesn't matter to me, Jazzy. Just choose one. Any one will be all right, as long as the cake's good." He could see that wasn't what she wanted to hear. She wanted him to be enthusiastic. But he was having trouble with enthusiasm for this wedding when it was going to be fake. Certainly he didn't want more than that, did he?

She stopped him with her hand on his arm. "You really don't care?"

The night had turned cool and very damp. Suddenly snow flurries began floating around them. "It's not that I don't care, Jazzy. I want you to have what you want. Doves or pedestals don't make a difference to me. But if they do to you, pick the one that makes you happy."

She gazed up at him, and in the glow of the barn's floodlight, he could see she looked confused.

"So it's not that you don't care, you're just not particular."

"That's the gist of it. Though I do prefer chocolate cake to something...exotic."

"Like white?" she teased.

He took her by the shoulders and gave her a gentle little shake. Her hair fell over his hand, turning him on. When Jazzy was around these days, he got way too revved up. Maybe he should keep his distance from her until the wedding. That wasn't going to be so hard unless...

He had something to ask her...to invite her to do. "We're getting married next week." If he said it often enough, he might believe it.

"I know," she said softly.

At that very moment, kissing her was the top thing on his to-do list. But he had to cross it off. "When we leave Dad's, you'll be going back to Strickland's till the wedding. But when we move in together...I just want you to know you can trust me. I have two bedrooms and you'll have your privacy in yours."

"I wasn't worried about—" She stopped and looked him straight in the eyes. "I trust you."

She trusted him. That was a vote of confidence he had to live up to.

"Are we eventually going to move to Rust Creek Falls?" she asked.

He'd been giving that some thought. "That makes sense, too. Since the Kalispell practice found someone to replace me, there's no need for me to stay there.

After we're married, we'll look around and see what's available."

"It sounds like a plan."

The snow was coming down a little heavier now, and Jazzy raised her face to it. A few flakes landed on her eyelashes—pretty, long, blond eyelashes. She opened her mouth and caught a few flakes on her tongue, giving him a grin.

His stomach clenched, his body tightened and he knew his plan to keep his distance would go along just fine as long as he didn't kiss her.

Chapter Nine

Jazzy stood in the social hall of the church the following evening, still not quite believing she was planning her wedding.

Her wedding.

She'd never thought it would be like this. Her chest tightened and her eyes grew misty.

Standing beside her, Brooks must have realized her emotions were getting the best of her because he asked, "Is something wrong?"

"Not really," she said, her voice betraying her.

He lifted her chin, and his touch excited her as it always did. "What is it?" he asked gently.

She summed it all up the only way she could. "It's our wedding day. I never thought it would be like this— just something to plan and get through."

He studied her for a very long time.

Then he asked, "Do you have that CD you burned at the office today of your favorite songs?"

"Yes," she said warily, glancing toward her purse that was sitting on one of the tables.

"Hold on a minute. I'll be right back."

When he started to stride away, she clasped his arm. "Where are you going? We really should get back to your dad." They would be moving out this weekend. She'd be going back to Strickland's until they married and Brooks would be staying at his condo once more.

"If we're leaving him on his own this weekend, we have to trust him to behave. But I asked Charlie to make an unexpected visit after we left tonight. They're probably deep into a discussion about what teams are going to make it to the Super Bowl this year."

When he turned away from her again, she asked, "But where are you going?"

"Patience, Jazzy. I'll be right back."

Men said they didn't understand women. That was definitely a two-way street.

For a few minutes, Jazzy believed Brooks had deserted her. Maybe that's what she expected. In the end, wasn't this kind of marriage all about that? Leaving each other with no strings? Unfortunately for her, she was going to have strings.

She wandered about the hall, thinking about flowers for the tables. Maybe white mums...

Brooks reappeared. He ordered, "Give me the CD."

She did and he went to a little door mounted on the wall and inserted a small key. He opened it, manipulated whatever was inside, and came back to her without the CD. Moments later, her music began playing and he opened his arms to her. "Okay, let's take a spin and see how it feels."

Was he serious? She felt a little ridiculous.

"Come on, Jazzy. Let's do more than plan. Let's practice our first dance."

When she still hesitated, he offered, "Look, I can understand you don't want me to treat our wedding as if it's just an appointment on the calendar. I'm not. Let's dance."

She felt a bit foolish now. After all, their wedding *was* an appointment on the calendar. It wasn't a *real* wedding. That fact made her so deeply sad.

Gratefully, Brooks didn't see her underlying confusion because he went on, "I think we've been trying to avoid the pretense of the whole thing. You hate deceiving Dad as much as I do. We just have to keep remembering the greater good."

So that's what he thought they were both doing, pretending for the greater good. *She* wasn't pretending. As world-shaking as it was, she'd fallen in love with Brooks Smith! Who knew that could happen in these strange circumstances? All she knew was that she never felt this way with Griff or anyone else, for that matter. She was an experienced dater. Truth be told, she hadn't even gone on anything resembling a date with Brooks. But each time they were together, it felt like a date. Each time they were together, she was sinking deeper into a whirl of emotion—and she wasn't sure how she'd ever pull herself out.

Gosh, she should write a country song.

Stepping closer to Brooks, she let him take her into his arms. His clasp was loose at first as the music swirled around them. As she gazed up into his eyes, however, his hold tightened a bit and then a bit more. She liked the feel of his strong arms around her. She liked the feel of the softness of his T-shirt against her cheek. He was so...so...male and she felt as if she were drowning in that...drowning in him.

She had to distract herself before she started weaving dreams that would never come true. "Do you really believe your dad will be okay if we leave?"

"He's not giving us any choice. I found someone to help him with chores morning *and* evening. He's the son of one of Dad's neighbors. And I'm going to insist Dad keep his cell phone on him at all times. I'll be at his practice during the day if I'm not out on call, so I can check on him between patients. With Charlie checking, too, all the bases will be covered."

All the bases except home base...her heart.

"I really want to rent a place in Rust Creek Falls so we're closer to Dad," Brooks continued. "But I checked with the real-estate agent. Since the flood, a nice place is hard to find. My condo in Kalispell will have to do until something becomes available. In fact, why don't we take a drive there when we're finished here?"

Touring the condo where Brooks lived would tell her even more about him. "Sure."

Suddenly Brooks released her, but he didn't go far. He reached into the pocket of his jeans. "Before I forget." He withdrew a chain with two keys. "There's a key to my place, and a key to Dad's."

She held them in her palm and the reality of living with Brooks shook her a little. She pocketed the keys. "Thank you."

"You're welcome." Taking her in his arms again, he brought her closer.

She'd watched couples dancing on TV. She'd danced
with a few of her dates, too. But the pleasure of dancing with Brooks surpassed anything she'd watched or
anything she'd ever felt. Now that they were pressed
even closer together, she let his thighs guide hers. She
let her cheek actually rest against his shirt. She could
feel him breathing.

Although she fought against it, a happily-ever-after
dream began to take shape and there was nothing she
could do about it.

On Friday, Jazzy slipped Brooks's key into his door
lock and opened the door. Then she waved to Cecilia
who gave her a thumbs-up sign and drove away.

Everything seemed under control in Barrett's clinic,
and Brooks was going to be out on calls all day. There
hadn't been any appointments at the Buckskin Clinic.
For now, any emergencies that came in there were being
forwarded to his dad's place, anyway. So Jazzy had told
Brooks, barring any unforeseen circumstances, Cecilia
would drive her to his place and she could make them
dinner. His father seemed to crave more privacy and independence now that he was feeling better, and Brooks
had liked the idea.

She picked up the bags she'd rested on the porch
while she was opening the door and went inside. It was
one floor with two bedrooms, a spacious living room,
a small dining area, and a basic kitchen. It was obvious
he didn't spend much time here. There wasn't a loose
sneaker or a stray newspaper or magazine anywhere.
The kitchen looked pristine, as if he never cooked in it.
Most of all, she admired the floor-to-ceiling fireplace.
She could imagine being curled up on the tan cordu-

roy sofa that sat opposite, sharing a cozy evening with Brooks. Maybe more than a cozy evening.

Thoughts like those were invading her waking as well as sleeping hours now, and she wasn't pushing them away quite as forcefully. After all, love made you think about all aspects of being together. She now knew exactly what had caused those looks on Laila, Abby and Annabel's faces when they'd been falling in love.

Whenever Brooks entered her mind, she had to smile. Whenever she thought about him caring for an animal, her heart warmed. Whenever he got close, her stomach fluttered. All signs she'd never had before. Now she knew what they all added up to—love. This marriage wasn't going to be one of convenience for her. She was going to mean those vows when she said them. And Brooks…well, maybe a year would make a difference. Maybe, in their time together, he'd tumble head over heels in love with her, too.

She planned supper for around six-thirty. The time had seemed reasonable. After all, a pot roast could cook a little longer if Brooks was late. She'd wrapped baking potatoes in foil before popping them in the oven. Blueberry cobbler would stay warm for a while or could be reheated in the microwave. But at seven-thirty, she was still telling herself all that as she worried in earnest. At eight o'clock she got the call.

"Are you all right?" She tried to keep the note of panic from her voice.

"I'm fine. There was a break in fencing at one of the ranches and some calves got wound up in barbed wire. I ended up working by flashlight and I didn't have a cell signal to call sooner. Sorry about that."

"It's okay. I'll have dinner ready for you when you get home."

"It's probably ruined."

"Nope. The meat might be a little stringy, but it's salvageable. What's your ETA?"

"About fifteen minutes."

"Sounds good. See you then."

Jazzy hung up the phone, relieved that Brooks was okay. More than relieved, really.

Fifteen minutes to the dot later, she heard the garage door go up. She heard the door open into the mudroom. When Brooks appeared in the kitchen, she couldn't help but gasp. He was practically covered in mud!

"I haven't been calf-roping, but close to it," he joked.

He unbuttoned his jacket and shrugged out of it. It was wet as well as muddy, and he didn't know where to lay it.

She took it from him and plopped it in the mudroom sink. "I can get clothes from your room if you don't mind me opening your closet or drawers."

"I don't mind. I don't want to track mud in there. Second long drawer in the dresser. Just grab sweatpants and a sweatshirt."

Hurrying off to his room, she switched on the light and looked around. There was a four-poster, king-size bed, a dresser with a detached mirror, a chest of drawers by the closet and a caned-back chair next to the bed. His bedspread was imprinted with mountains and moose, and the blinds were navy like the background of the spread. This was a thoroughly masculine room, and when she thought about that bed and him in it—

Quickly she went to the dresser and pulled out pants and a shirt, then hurried back to the mudroom. He'd shut the door. She could hear the spigot from the sink running, so she knocked.

"I'm washing off," he said. "Just drop them on the other side of the door and I'll grab them."

After they were married, would she be able to open that door and just walk in? Would he want her to?

Crossing to the kitchen, she pulled the food from the oven and arranged their plates. The vegetables had practically disintegrated, but the meat was surely tender. She fixed two plates, but instead of arranging them on the table, she took them into the living room and set them on the coffee table.

When Brooks came into the living room, he looked like a different person from the mud-splattered one who'd come home.

"Soap and water make a difference," she teased.

"Soap and water might not make a difference for those clothes."

"That's why man invented washing machines. You'd be amazed."

He glanced at the meal on the coffee table. "I already am."

She patted the sofa next to her. "Come on. I bet you're cold. It's supposed to go down to freezing out there tonight. A hot meal will help you warm up again."

He smiled and sat on the sofa beside her. That butterfly feeling in her stomach wasn't because of hunger.

They ate side by side. Jazzy was aware of every bite Brooks took, each sideways glance, the lift of his smile that said he approved of her cooking. She finished before he did, and she went to the kitchen for the whipped cream and cobbler.

After Brooks laid his head back against the sofa

cushion for a moment, he eyed her soberly. "Do you know, I've never had a meal like this cooked for me before?"

"So no woman has tried to make inroads to your heart through your stomach?" she asked in mock horror.

To her surprise, instead of taking a lighter road, he admitted, "Lynnette didn't cook. We had takeout or meals at a local diner, much like Dad does." He paused and added, "And I haven't dated much since then."

And she knew exactly why. Handing him the cobbler, she said, "I'll cook when I can, for your dad, too."

"I think you're going to deserve more than a piece of land when our year is up."

Did that mean he could possibly give her his heart? But then he added, "I might have to raise your salary."

She felt her hopes wither but she wouldn't let him notice. "Try the cobbler," she encouraged brightly.

He did and she did. When she glanced over at him, she saw he was watching her with that deep intensity that darkened his eyes. A ripple of excitement skipped up her spine.

"What?" she asked.

He leaned toward her and stroked his finger above the skin over her lip. "Whipped cream."

She could imagine him using that voice in bed with her. She could imagine him using that voice in between kisses, in between—

He lifted his finger to his lips and licked off the whipped cream he'd taken off hers. Then he leaned closer to her.

Jazzy's insides were all a-twitter. Maybe he was going to kiss her. Maybe she'd actually feel his lips on hers, like she'd dreamt about for so many nights now.

But as soon as she had the thought, he must have realized what he was doing. His expression closed down, that dark, male intensity left his eyes, and he was once again essentially her business partner. Nothing more.

That was it, she thought. She'd have to deal with a year of wanting him to kiss her...a year of wanting more than that.

But she had *her* pride, too. She certainly wouldn't throw herself at him. She wasn't going to set herself up for a huge fall. She'd have to be as calm and practical about this as he was.

Calm and practical, she told herself once again. "We really should get back to your dad's."

Brooks's expression didn't change, though she could feel his body tense beside her. "Just let me get my boots."

As he hiked himself up off the couch and strode toward his bedroom, she whispered to herself once more, "Just be calm and practical, and you'll be fine."

But she didn't believe it.

The next few days sped by as Jazzy manned the phones at Brooks's clinic and tried to forget that he'd almost kissed her, tried to stop asking herself the question—why *hadn't* he kissed her? The day before the wedding, she was getting ready for work in the morning when Cecilia came to her room.

After Jazzy let her friend in, Cecilia said, "I'm kidnapping you this morning."

Jazzy ran her brush through her hair. "What do you mean *kidnapping* me?"

"I told Brooks you had something important to do for the wedding this morning. He said that was fine. There aren't any appointments on Buckskin Clinic's schedule and you could take the morning off."

"Then I really should go check on his dad—"

"Nope. You're going with me to Bea's Beauty Salon. *You* are getting a makeover."

Jazzy spun around. "A *makeover?*"

"A hair trim, some highlighting, and I brought a bunch of makeup along. We're going to get you ready for the wedding."

At first she was going to protest, but then she thought about her relationship with Brooks thus far. She thought he found her attractive, yet something was holding him back. Maybe his past romantic history. Maybe his broken engagement. Maybe he just didn't want to delve under the surface of the murky waters of their business arrangement. Maybe all of the above. But Jazzy knew she wanted more than a marriage on paper. If she was going to be married to Brooks, then she wanted to be *married* to him. She was afraid if she told him that, he'd call off the whole agreement. Possibly this whole deal had made her a little crazy. They certainly hadn't known each other very long. But she felt more sure of this marriage than she'd felt about anything in her life.

"My family's arriving today," she murmured. "Abby and Cade are driving my car up and parking it at Brooks's condo."

"All of your family is coming?"

"Everyone."

"But you don't look as happy about it as you should. What's going on, Jazzy?"

Oh, no. She couldn't confide this marriage of convenience to anyone. Not anyone. Not for her sake, not for Brooks's sake, and not for his dad's sake.

"Just jittery, I guess. Maybe a day at the salon is just what I need," she joked.

She'd never been that fashion-conscious or put much store in spending hours in front of a mirror. But Cecilia didn't wear gobs of makeup and she certainly looked pretty. Maybe she couldn't find a guy because she didn't care about all that as much as she should.

Not that she wanted just any guy anymore. She wanted Brooks Smith.

"I have something I want to show you." Jazzy went to the small closet, reached up for a hanger, and brought out her wedding dress for Cecilia to see. It was a Western-cut, three-quarter length dress with just the right amount of fringe. "I bought it online, what do you think?"

"I think it's *perfect* for you. Oh, Jazzy, you're going to look so pretty."

Jazzy reached up to the shelf above where her clothes were hanging and pulled down a Western hat with a bit of tulle around the brim and down the back. "And this goes with it."

"I'm so glad you showed that to me. We'll keep that in mind when we're getting your hair done. I have you set up for a manicure and a pedicure at the same time. A facial first."

"Cecilia, that's too much."

"Nonsense. It's part of my wedding gift to you…and Brooks," she said with a wink. "Believe me, he'll appreciate it when you're done over."

Done over.

"So what are you wearing tonight for the rehearsal dinner?" Cecilia asked.

"There isn't a rehearsal, per se. We're going to dinner

with our families and then the minister is going over the basics at the church. I'm not having bridesmaids. Jordyn will be my witness. Brooks's dad is going to be his."

"So where are you all going to dinner tonight?"

"The diner. They've reserved a big table. I just hope my family behaves. You know how they can get. Mom tried to talk me out of getting married. Dad asked a lot of questions. Laila, Abby and Annabel would have taken over the ceremony and everything about the reception if I hadn't put my foot down...hard. Brooks and I had everything planned and we knew exactly what we wanted. I wasn't going to let my family mess with that. We don't want a big shindig for Brooks's dad to have to deal with. I've explained that to everyone more than once so I hope they'll be on their best behavior."

"You don't want a fuss or argument that could cause a heart attack."

"Exactly. I'm worried about Barrett as it is, how he's going to be, how he's going to feel, what he's going to think."

"Think about you and Brooks?"

"And about my family's attitude. Barrett actually believes in love at first sight. He and his wife had it. So he's going to be right in there rooting for us. He could be at odds with my parents."

Cecilia suddenly took Jazzy's hand. "Jazzy, what do you want?"

"I want a happy, committed, long-lasting marriage with lots of babies."

"Have you and Brooks talked about babies?"

"No. But we have time." They had a year...at least. She had to be hopeful.

Cecilia ran her hand down the delicate fabric of the

wedding dress and the silky fringe at the sleeves. "This really is magnificent. That means everything that goes with it should be, too. Do you have shoes?"

"High-heeled boots. I ordered those online, too. But they're a little big. I'll stuff tissue in the toes and in the back." Pulling them out from the bottom of the closet, Jazzy showed Cecilia the calf-high boots.

"I was hoping you'd have open-toed shoes, so everyone could see your pedicure."

"It's mid-October in Montana. I don't want my feet to freeze."

Cecilia shrugged. "The boots will make you look sexy. Brooks will still be taller than you, even with those heels."

Actually, Jazzy liked the effect of Brooks towering over her. She liked the fact that when he hugged her, he surrounded her.

"What color for the toenails and fingernails? What will you be wearing *after* the wedding?"

Jazzy certainly hadn't thought about *that,* either. They'd be going back to Brooks's condo. It wasn't as if they were going anywhere special. "I guess I'll wear something I brought along."

"You are not talking flannel pajamas, are you?"

"No, I brought along a nightgown and robe."

"Yeah, I bet it's the kind you feel comfortable in. That's not what you need. Something else we're fitting in this morning. We'll be stopping at the General Store. Nina has a rack of nightgowns and robes. Maybe if there's time when we're done, I'll drive you into Kalispell to a cute little dress shop I know there. You need something special for tonight, too, Jazzy. Something that shows your family you know exactly what you're doing…something that shows this town that this wedding isn't of the shotgun variety."

"Is that what everyone's saying? That I had to get married because I was pregnant?"

"I've heard it at the beauty salon, around the General Store, around the volunteers at the elementary school."

"I hope you squelched it."

"You know each one of those gossip conversations is like a little bonfire. It takes a lot of water to douse them out. The best thing would be seeing you looking slim and confident and ready to go into this marriage as if it's just any other marriage. And it *is* like any other marriage, right?"

Oh, how Jazzy wished that were true. "It's a marriage that Brooks and I will work at to make last."

That's what she had to believe.

That evening when Jazzy took off her coat at the diner, all eyes in the place seemed to be focused on her. Especially Brooks's.

Cecilia had insisted she buy a red dress. The one she'd chosen was simple and sleek enough—even understated with its high neckline and just-above-the-knee hem. But there was a slit in the side and when she turned around, there was a keyhole in the back.

But Brooks wasn't looking at her back; he was looking at her front, and boy, was he looking at her front. Not only the dress, but her hair and her face, too. She'd used mascara, lipstick and some kind of powder that almost shimmered on her skin. With her newly highlighted blond hair tapered around her face in a fresh style, she'd never felt more confident as a woman.

Brooks was looking at her as a very stunned man.

"There she is," Barrett said with a wide smile. "I knew she wouldn't run out on you."

But Brooks didn't seem to hear his father. He couldn't seem to take his eyes off her. And she couldn't take her eyes off him. He'd worn a dressier Western shirt tonight with bolo tie and black jeans with boots. Tall and handsome and ultimately sexy, she found herself trembling just standing there.

"Don't you look beautiful," her mother said, motioning to the chair next to her. "Not that you don't always look pretty, but tonight something's…different."

"She's dressed to bowl over any guy she meets," Brody said, not looking as if he approved.

But she squelched that statement right away. "Only one guy," she assured them all. Was she acting or had she really said that? She meant it.

Brooks stepped closer to her like a fiancé would, took her hand and squeezed it.

Leaning close to her ear, he murmured, "You look gorgeous."

Was he acting, too?

He led her to the chair her mother had gestured to and pulled it out for her. She sank down onto it before her legs gave way. This was some way to start the evening with her head feeling as if it were filled with cotton and her mouth totally dry.

Brooks took his seat next to her and they faced her family. He covered her hand with his again and she knew to everyone gathered there, they looked like a loving couple.

Yet her father was frowning as he stared at them. "So tell me again why you're rushing into this marriage so fast, without giving us all breathing space, and time to get used to the idea."

Her whole family had come—Abby and Jackson, Laila and Cade, Annabel and Thomas, Jordyn Leigh, Brody and her parents. Jazzy knew Jordyn was on her side. After she'd seen the phone picture of Brooks Jazzy had sent her, she'd insisted he was too good to let go. But the rest of her family... She had to make this good.

However, before she could open her mouth, Brooks, protective as ever, stepped in. "I'm not sure you can explain the bond that forms when two people just click, sir, the way Jazzy and I did from the beginning."

That definitely didn't allay her father's concerns. "So you're just going to move up here, away from us, without discussing it with the family?"

Jazzy exchanged looks with Abby, Annabel and Laila who'd gone through the process of falling in love. Her look said *Help me out here, sisters!* Abby did. "You know how true love works, Dad. You've seen me and Laila and Annabel go through it. When it's right, it's right."

"We won't see you very much," her mother said, a little sadly.

Brooks assuaged her mom's concerns. "We'll visit you often. Jazzy's going to want to make sure you're part of our lives, and I will, too." The look he sent Jazzy said he meant that.

"You folks can stay with me the next time you're in town," Barrett told them. "Brooks still considers me an invalid and won't let me overdo anything. I'd be glad to have the company." He stared at Jazzy's dad. "I hear you're good with horses. I've got a few."

The tension around the table eased. The two men

began talking ranch life. Jordyn gave her a thumbs-up sign. Brody, however, eyed her suspiciously as if he still didn't believe what was going on. Her sisters and their husbands fell into conversation, too.

Brooks interlaced his fingers with hers on the table, leaned close and said only loud enough for her to hear, "It's going to be all right."

But as she felt the heat between them, as his breath fanned her cheek, as his gaze unsettled her the way no other could, she thought about her vows tomorrow and wondered if everything *could* be all right.

Chapter Ten

Brooks knew he must be crazy. Today he was going to marry a woman he was seriously attracted to, yet he didn't intend to sleep with her! If that wasn't crazy, he didn't know what was.

He adjusted his tux, straightened his bolo tie, wishing all to heck that Jazzy hadn't almost knocked his boots off last night when he'd seen her in that red dress. And when he pushed her chair in and saw her skin peeking through that cutout in the back, he'd practically swallowed his tongue.

There was a rap on the door. He was in the anteroom that led to the nursery area in the back of the church. He knew Jazzy was in a room across the vestibule that was used exactly for situations like this—brides and their bridesmaids preparing for a wedding.

Preparing for a wedding.

After the dinner last night, and the suspicious and wary glances of her family, he'd retreated inward. He knew that. He also knew it had bothered Jazzy. But how could he explain to her that she turned him on more than he'd ever wanted to be turned on? How could he explain to her that this marriage of convenience might not be so convenient, not when it came to them living together?

Still he was determined to go through with this. Their course was set. He wasn't going to turn back now.

After a deep breath, he opened the door. Jazzy's sister Jordyn stood there with an unsure smile. She'd been the one person to treat him like the brother-in-law he was going to be.

"Everything's all set," she said. "Once you're in place at the altar, the organist will start the processional."

Stepping into the vestibule, he saw his dad beckoning to him from the doorway that would lead up to the altar. He also saw Jazzy's dad looking more like a soldier than a father, standing by the door to the room where she'd emerge.

Mr. Cates frowned at Brooks.

Brody stood at the entrance to the church, his mother on his arm. He was ready to walk her up the aisle. But when he glanced over his shoulder and saw Brooks, his mouth tightened and Brooks saw the disapproval in his eyes.

If he were a betting man, he'd bet that someone in Jazzy's family would stand up and protest at that point in the wedding when the minister asks, "Is there anyone who sees a reason that these two shouldn't be joined in matrimony?"

"Abby, Annabel and Laila will give you a chance," Jordyn assured him as if she could read his thoughts.

"And because *they* will, their husbands will, too. Mom and Dad and Brody will come around as long as they see you make Jazzy happy. And you will, won't you?"

After the way he'd left Jazzy last night, with him all silent and brooding, he'd wanted to do something nice to reassure her. So he'd bought a bottle of champagne to celebrate when they got back to his place tonight. That's when he'd give her the watch. He wanted her to be happy, and he'd do his best to see that happen. But no one could *make* someone else happy. Everyone had choices, and those choices either led to success or failure.

So he was truthful with Jordyn. "I want Jazzy to be happy."

Jordyn gave him an odd look, as if she suspected everything might not be what it seemed. Then she confirmed it when she said, "I trust Jazzy to make the right decisions for herself. I'll be around if she needs me. Don't you hesitate to call me if she *does* need me."

"I won't," he promised, and he meant it.

Brooks crossed the vestibule and approached his father. When they were standing next to each other, Barrett pounded Brooks on the back. "I'm glad you asked me to be your best man. You could have had Gage Christensen or even Dallas Traub, for that matter."

He and Dallas had been friends for years, but since his divorce and gaining custody of his three kids, Dallas had had even less time for friendship than Brooks had.

"I wanted *you,* Dad."

"This day makes me happier and prouder than you'll ever know. Jazzy will be good for you. She'll ground you like your mother grounded me. You and me—we're going to have to have a talk one of these days, about marriage and everything that goes with it."

"I think I learned the facts of life a long time ago, Dad," Brooks said with a smile, trying to lighten the atmosphere a bit.

His father's face grew a little red. "That's not what I mean. There are things…there are just some things we need to talk about."

The minister emerged from behind the altar and Brooks nudged his father's arm. "We can talk. But right now, I think it's time for me to get married."

His father chuckled and side by side, they walked up the aisle to the front of the church.

Jazzy felt like a princess. It was silly, really. This dress wasn't all tulle and lace. It was more like a dressy, Western dress. But it was white and her boots were white with three-inch spiked heels, and Cecilia had made sure her hat was tilted just right on her head with the tulle flowing down the back of her dress. Mostly she felt like a princess because she could see Brooks waiting for her at the altar, all handsome and starched and pressed, with shiny black boots, and a look in his eyes that was lightning hot.

Last night she'd been worried because he'd turned so quiet, so expressionless, so unlike the Brooks she knew. What would he be like today after they were married?

That thrill of anticipation ran down her spine. He was going to be her husband.

Her dad stood beside her and held out the crook of his arm for her to put her hand through. She knew he wasn't on board with this wedding, but she couldn't keep living her life to please her parents. At thirty, it was well past time she flew the coop. She could see her mom sitting in the front pew, her sisters and their husbands in the pew behind that.

Jordyn Leigh, however, was going to lead the way on the road to this future. She'd worn a pretty, royal blue dress that, in Jazzy's estimation, was just right for this ceremony. She and Brooks hadn't wanted pomp and circumstance and long gowns. They'd wanted simple and quiet and just plain friendly.

The organ music began and with a spray of yellow mums clenched in her hands, Jordyn glanced over her shoulder at Jazzy and then started forward.

Jazzy held on to her bouquet of lilies and white mums even more tightly, afraid she'd drop it. She was that nervous. As the scent of the flowers wafted up to her, she used the look in Brooks's eyes as her guiding light. He couldn't look at her like that and not feel something, could he?

Whether he felt something or not, she was going to marry him and see where the future led them. Exciting couldn't even describe the ripple of emotion inside of her. Everything about today was going to be memorable.

Just as she reinforced the thought, Laila turned toward her and snapped a picture with her camera. Abby and Annabel had cameras, too, and knowing her sisters, everything about today would be recorded.

Tears pricked in her eyes. She blinked fast and smiled.

The church aisle really wasn't that long, but her walk down toward the altar seemed to take forever. But she didn't falter as the look in Brooks's eyes drew her forward.

Once Jazzy was at the front of the church, her fa-

ther solemnly kissed her and she took her place beside
Brooks.

"You look beautiful," he said in an almost awed
voice.

"You look pretty spiffy yourself."

At her words, the awkwardness they both seemed
to be feeling drifted away. He smiled, one of those
Brooks smiles that affected her in a way she didn't understand, that made her feel hot and giddy and altogether a woman.

Beside Brooks, his father beamed at Jazzy and in that
moment she felt a few doubts about what she was doing.
What would happen to Barrett's feelings about her in
a year if she and Brooks separated? But she couldn't
think about that now. Today they were joining their
lives. Somehow this would work out.

The minister welcomed their family and guests.

Jazzy handed her bouquet to Jordyn as she and
Brooks joined hands. His was warm and dry and firm,
decisive in its hold on hers. She felt fragile and beautiful and supportive beside him. The words of the ceremony became a blur as the minister talked, as she and
Brooks responded.

They each said "I do" calmly as if they knew what
they were doing.

Then Brooks's voice was low but strong as he said,
"I, Brooks Smith, take you Jazzy Cates to be my law-
fully wedded wife...to have and to hold from this
day forward...for better or for worse...for richer, for
poorer...in sickness and health...to love and to cherish
until death do us part."

She repeated those same words, looking straight into
his eyes so he'd know she meant them. Now his reac-

tion was more stoic, yet the nerve in his jaw worked. The ceremony was affecting him, too. He just didn't want anyone to see that.

As Brooks slipped the gold band onto her finger, she could hardly breathe. When she slipped the gold band onto his finger, a hush over their guests seemed to emphasize the importance of the moment. They held hands and gave their attention to the minister as he said a few words about love and marriage, bonds, promises and a union that made the world go round.

They bowed their heads as the minister bestowed a blessing, and then he said the words the whole church was waiting to hear.

"I now pronounce you husband and wife." In a low voice, he said to Brooks, "You can kiss her now."

Well, of course, they *had* to kiss. They had to show everyone they meant what they'd said...the promises they'd made.

Brooks's arms went around her and there was only a moment of hesitation before he bent his head to her. His lips found hers unerringly as if this had been a long time in coming. She certainly felt as if it had, but then maybe he was just determined to get it over with. Yet as his lips settled on hers, it certainly didn't seem as if he wanted this kiss over with quickly. This meeting of lips took on more than a perfunctory air. It went on longer than she thought it would. In fact, she didn't know how long it went on because she lost track of time and place and the fact that there were guests watching them.

Apparently, Brooks forgot, too, because his arms held her a little tighter and he didn't raise his head and break their kiss until the minister cleared his throat.

She should feel embarrassed, she really should. But

she was so awed by the desire behind what had just happened that she couldn't even think of anything else. She probably couldn't have found her way out of the church. But Jordyn handed back her bouquet. Brooks took her arm and, in the next moment, they were walking down the aisle to the smiles and applause of their family and friends.

She was married. Brooks was her husband. The full reality of that hadn't set in yet.

They walked down the aisle to the back of the church, through the vestibule to the reception hall. Once inside, Brooks took her elbow and spun her around. "I had to do that, Jazzy. I had to make it look good." There was something in his voice that was a little unsettled as if making the kiss look good had unsettled him. And here she'd thought the kiss had really *meant* something.

"You certainly made it look good. I'm not sure what my parents thought of it, but afterward your dad was grinning from ear to ear."

"They'll all be in here in a minute. We just have to be clear about how we're handling it. No honeymoon now because of taking care of Dad's practice, as well as setting up mine. We'll be moving back to Rust Creek Falls as soon as we find a good place. Not a house, though. Not yet."

"Your father's going to think we're planning to build on your grandmother's property."

"I'm not going to tell him we will. If that's what he thinks, fine."

Her hand on his arm, looking up into his eyes, she said, "Brooks, I don't like deceiving anyone, especially not him."

But Brooks didn't have a chance to respond because

their guests started pouring in and they began receiving them like a newly married couple would.

Brooks's dad pounded him on the back, congratulating him. Jazzy's sisters gathered around and gave her a group hug. She and Brooks got separated more than once as guests migrated to their tables and conversations abounded. They had almost greeted the last of their guests and Brooks had stepped aside to speak to the minister, when Dean took Jazzy's arm.

"I can't believe you went through with this so quickly."

"You're going to be doing the same soon."

"That's different and you know it. I'm still getting the feeling that something's off here. That all of this happened too fast."

"Dean, Brooks and I just got married. Why can't you simply wish us well?"

"Maybe you married Brooks to escape Thunder Canyon and your family, but is that a valid reason? Shelby and I are getting married because we can't live without each other."

"Are you judging what I feel?" Dean was an old enough and good enough friend that she could ask the honest question.

He shook his head. "I'm just hoping you're head over heels in love and this isn't something other than that."

Looking him straight in the eye, she assured him, "I'm head over heels in love." That thought still shook her up, made her feel queasy, instilled in her the knowledge that she could easily be terribly hurt.

But it was absolutely true. She loved Brooks Smith.

Dean's eyes widened a bit as he could see the truth.

He gave Jazzy a big hug. "Then congratulations. I hope the two of you have a lot of happy years together."

She was hoping for one year that would stretch into a lifetime.

Jazzy sat beside Brooks during their wedding dinner, wondering what he was thinking. He smiled, but the smile didn't light up his eyes. He spoke to their guests, but there was a surface quality about it that troubled her. Every once in a while, he'd reach over and squeeze her hand or drop his arm around her shoulders. But the gestures felt forced. She just wanted to give him a hug... nestle in his arms. That's what a wife would do when she was feeling unsure.

Jordyn, who had taken over as facilitator for the day—and Jazzy was so grateful because this sister wanted to help, not interfere—tapped Jazzy on the arm and addressed Brooks, too. "It's time to cut the cake. Are you ready?"

She and Brooks hadn't really talked about this...or prepared a script. This would be a go-with-the-flow moment.

Brooks stood without a word and held Jazzy's chair for her. Once she'd gotten to her feet, he took her arm and escorted her to the table where the multilayered cake stood.

"You can have the top layer to take along," Jordyn told them. "For a midnight snack," she teased with a wink as if she imagined what they'd be doing then.

What would they be doing at midnight? Jazzy wondered. Sleeping? Pacing their separate bedrooms, thinking about whether or not they'd done the right thing? How many doubts was her new husband having?

"I bought you a special cake-slicing knife so you'll remember this moment," Jordyn said with a smile and handed them a cake knife with their names and the date engraved on the handle.

"Oh, Jordyn," Jazzy said with tears filling her eyes. "Thank you."

As she hugged her sister, flashes from cameras went off and she realized her family was recording the moment. She heard Brooks sincerely thank Jordyn, too.

Then it was time. With friends and family looking on, Brooks's hand covered hers over the handle of their first wedding gift. There was a stack of presents on the table beside the cake. Even though this was a sudden wedding, their guests were taking the opportunity to give them something to start them on their way.

Brooks's hand was large, warm and encompassing. When he gazed down at her and gave her a half smile, Jazzy's breath hitched.

Brooks himself took care of the slice of cake, sliding it onto a paper plate. Then he offered it to her. They each broke off a piece, knowing what they were supposed to do.

Brooks lifted the bite of cake and icing to her lips, never taking his eyes from hers.

Flashes from cameras again burst around them.

She opened her mouth, and when she took the bite from his fingers, her tongue touched his thumb and icing slid along her upper lip.

The sound of a spoon tapping a glass rung in her ears. As if the sound had to be translated, a woman called, "Kiss that icing away!" More tinkling on glasses. After all, this was a wedding reception.

Brooks leaned in and kissed her. The icing became

the sweetest confection she'd ever tasted as Brooks's tongue slipped along her lips and she kissed him back.

When he broke away, she blinked, tried to find her equilibrium and realized it was *her* turn now. If he kissed her like that again... She was careful picking up his piece of cake. He was careful as he ate it from her fingers. Everyone clapped. She tried to smile along with Brooks as they both seemed to be relieved that tradition was over.

As Jordyn oversaw the slicing of the cake for guests, some of them chatted with Jazzy and Brooks. Dallas Traub, who Brooks had introduced in their receiving line, approached them. "I just want to tell both of you not to be strangers. We've all been so focused on recovering from the flood, we haven't had time for anything else. After spending so much time with my rug rats, I could use adult conversation."

Earlier, Jazzy had learned that Dallas lived on his family's ranch—the Triple T—but had his own house on the property that had seen some damage from the flood, but not the devastation others had experienced.

"I'd like to see your ranch sometime. And meet your children." After all, it was only polite to make Brooks's friend feel comfortable.

"We'll set up a time soon," Dallas assured them. Then he clapped Brooks on the back and walked away.

"He's been through a rough time," Brooks said almost to himself. "That's when family counts most."

Jazzy imagined he was thinking again about the reason for this wedding—not true love, not a lifelong commitment, but rather his dad's health.

Had they done the right thing?

* * *

A short time later, as Brooks and Jazzy were min-
gling with their guests, Brooks watched Jordyn go to
the podium and pick up the microphone. She tapped it
and smiled. "It's time for the first dance between Jazzy
and Brooks as a married couple," she announced. Turning to the CD player on the wall, she started the music.

It was one dance, Brooks thought, as he offered his
hand to Jazzy. Surely he could get through one dance.

He thought of the first time he and Jazzy had danced
when they'd looked over the social hall. And their kiss
after the ceremony, not to mention the sensual tasting
of the wedding cake—

He had to look at this logically. This day was simply
an exception to the agreement they had made. Today,
they were pretending in front of a larger audience than
his dad. Today would be over before they knew it.

His wedding day. When he'd imagined it with Lynnette, he'd had dreams. Now he just wanted his dad's
good health. He just wanted the year to pass quickly so
he and Jazzy could get on with their lives.

As Brooks forced a smile and took Jazzy in his arms,
he was glad they'd had that one practice dance. That
way this wasn't so awkward.

Just like last night when Jazzy had appeared in the
diner in her red dress, he'd been bowled over by the
way she'd looked in her wedding dress as she'd walked
down the aisle on her father's arm. It was so feminine
with its lace and high neck. Yet it had a touch of Western sass, too, with its fringes and peek-a-boo sections
that gave him a glimpse of skin. And those boots with
their heels…

Taking her in his arms and bending his head to her,

he said, "I don't know how you can dance in those things."

"These boots were made for dancing," she joked, but her smile wobbled just enough that he knew this day wasn't easy for her, either. He was glad he'd bought the roses, champagne and watch for tonight.

When he leaned toward her, he got caught in the fragrance of her perfume. It was musky-sweet and fit Jazzy perfectly. "Are you okay?" he asked seriously, in spite of everyone watching.

"As okay as you," she returned with her usual spunk. But then she added, "Though I'm glad we're not in a fishbowl all the time. It's downright unnerving."

"Now you know how celebrities feel," he bantered, hoping to make her smile again.

She didn't just smile. She laughed. And he realized how much he enjoyed the sound of it.

"Maybe I should simply think of my family as groupies!"

Flashes popped as both Laila and Abby took photos of them.

"They're going to make an album for us." Jazzy was watching him for his reaction.

"Your family is just doing what families do."

"Maybe we should have gotten married by the justice of the peace. It would have been simpler the whole way around," she murmured.

Tearing his gaze from Jazzy's, he caught sight of his father watching them. His broad smile said it all.

"Just look at my dad, Jazzy." He maneuvered them so she could see Barrett.

After the moment it took for her to absorb his message, she sighed.

Brooks didn't know what that sigh meant because everyone began clinking their spoons on their glasses so he and Jazzy would kiss.

"Here we go again," he said, tightening his arms around her, drawing her close so her body was pressed against his. She didn't resist or try to lean away.

When his lips met hers, he intended to make the kiss quick. He intended for it to simply be a brushing of lips on lips.

But with Jazzy, nothing was ever exactly as he intended it to be.

Her perfume was like a magic spell, drawing him into its aura. Jazzy was so femininely alluring, his hand came up to caress her cheek. Careful not to disturb her hat, he angled his mouth over hers and almost forgot about "pretend." His lips felt so right on hers.

In the nick of time, before he took their public kiss into the private realm, he pulled away. Jazzy almost tripped over his boot and he caught her up against him so they didn't have a mishap.

Charlie called out, "Careful those kisses don't knock you off your feet!"

Everyone laughed. Everyone except him and Jazzy. They couldn't seem to unlock their gazes.

And they didn't until Jordyn announced, "Now my dad will dance with Jazzy and Brooks will dance with my mom. Everyone else, join in and enjoy the music."

Brooks had to let Jazzy go. Tearing his gaze from hers, he realized he didn't like that idea at all.

That night on the porch at Brooks's condo, Jazzy held the top layer of foil-wrapped wedding cake, still not quite believing what had taken place. She and Brooks had said their vows, he'd kissed her so passionately her hat had almost popped off. When he'd licked that icing—

He set her suitcase down on the porch and unlocked the door, glancing at her. "You packed light when you came to Rust Creek Falls. One suitcase? Most women would have three."

"I'm not most women." She wanted to say, "I'm your wife now," but she didn't.

He gave her a very long look that made her shift the layer of cake from one hand to the other, then he opened the door.

Jazzy caught the scent of roses as soon as she walked inside. Immediately she spotted the vase on the side table and went straight to it. The blooms were huge and red, giving off a beautiful scent.

"They're wonderful!"

"I thought you might like them."

She wanted to cross to him and kiss him all over again in a way that wasn't simply for show, but she didn't have that freedom.

While he carried her suitcase to the guest bedroom, she looked around the place and noticed a fire was laid on the grate. Maybe they'd cozy up together in front of it.

Brooks returned to the living room. "I'll light a fire. I have champagne, too. We can celebrate. I've never seen my dad happier."

His dad. That was the reason they'd done this, and she couldn't forget it. "Champagne would be nice," she agreed.

When Brooks started for the kitchen, she followed with the cake. "I'll find a plate."

"Top left cupboard. You'll have to learn your way around," he said with a smile.

That smile. She sighed, found two plates and unwrapped the cake.

Five minutes later they were sitting on the sofa with a fire dancing on the grate, sharing bites of cake. Brooks had taken off his jacket and rolled up his sleeves.

"It was a nice wedding," she said as a preamble.

"Yes, it was," he agreed. "But I'm not sure your parents approve of me, or your brother, either."

Her dad had questioned Brooks about his practice and so had her brother. They hadn't smiled much and Jazzy wished, as she had in the past, that they'd just trust her judgment.

Brooks took the bottle of champagne he'd pulled from the refrigerator, unwrapped the foil around the top, and then popped the cork. It bounced across the room and they both laughed. He poured the champagne into two tumblers, only filling them about a third of the way. As he picked up her glass, as well as his, and handed it to her, the bubbles danced and popped.

"Before today, I hadn't had champagne since my sister's wedding."

"Then it's about time." He clinked his glass against hers. "We pulled it off."

Yes, they had. "My parents will be harder to convince if and when we visit them."

"It will be fine, Jazzy, really it will. Jordyn's on our side. She still lives at home, right?"

Jazzy nodded and took a couple of swallows of her champagne. "She'll be a good buffer. I wish I could confide in her, but it's difficult for sisters to keep secrets from one another. I'm afraid if I tell her, she'll tell Abby, Abby will tell Laila, Laila will tell Annabel…"

"You can talk to *me*."

Yes, she could talk to Brooks about everything but what she felt for him. She took another swallow of champagne and realized she'd drained her glass. He drank his, too, picked up the bottle, and poured more for both of them. They were sitting close together, the sleeve of her dress rubbing the sleeve of his shirt, their knees brushing every now and then.

"I spoke to Charlie tonight," she said.

"He keeps Dad on track as much as he can."

"Did he tell you your dad wants to do the chores himself?" Jazzy asked him. "He doesn't want Travis helping him."

"Travis has his orders from *me*. He's supposed to listen to me, not to Dad."

"Charlie insists your dad's stubborn."

"He doesn't know how to sit still unless his favorite program's on the TV," Brooks grumbled. "He's eating the meals you're making him, though. That's a good sign. And he walks up and down the drive, going farther each day. When bad weather sets in, I don't know what he'll do. Maybe I can get him a treadmill for Christmas."

"Do you think he'd use it?"

"I can set it up in the basement and make him a gym area. If I have to, I'll go there and work out with him."

She drank more champagne, then laid her hand on Brooks's arm. His forearm was as muscled as the rest of him, the dark brown hair there was rough under her fingertips. "You're a good son."

"We haven't been close enough in my adult years. Maybe now that will change."

"I think it will...if you both want it to."

Brooks reached to the shelf under the coffee table and brought out a wrapped package. She hadn't noticed it under there, though now the gold foil gleamed in the lamplight.

"Brooks, what's this?"

"Just a little something for you to remember today. Open it."

Jazzy's fingers fumbled as she tore the paper off the box with a Western scene. "Montana Silversmiths." Taking the lid from the box, she saw the watch inside. Lifting it out, she examined the scrollwork on the band, the pretty face.

"Oh, Brooks, it's beautiful! Thank you."

"Put it on and see if it fits."

It fit her wrist as if it had been made for her.

Brooks poured more champagne into the two glasses. Then he looked at her as he'd looked at her when she'd walked up the aisle toward him, when she'd taken his hand and faced the minister. "You've been a good sport about all of this."

"I have a dream, too," she said, knowing Brooks would think she was talking about the rescue ranch, not about their marriage.

The longer they gazed at each other, the more the fire crackled and popped, the more the electric tension in the air seemed to draw them together. She didn't want this moment of closeness to end. Maybe those champagne bubbles had gone to her head, but she thought she saw desire in his eyes.

He took a strand of her hair in his hand and then

played with it between his fingers. "So silky and soft. In that hat and your dress, you looked as if you'd just stepped off the pages of a fashion magazine."

"I'm just Jazzy," she said with a small laugh, feeling all trembly inside. "The same girl who got to know Sparky because of you. The same girl who got scratched by Mrs. Oliver's cat. The same girl who will never be a calf roper."

He laughed at that and leaned a little closer. "I have no doubt you could be a calf roper if you set your mind to it."

"I'd rather set my mind on other things."

It seemed as if he would, too, because instead of just touching her hair, his hand delved under it and slid up the back of her neck. She tilted her head up to gaze into his eyes and he leaned even closer.

Something in the air changed. Instead of conversation and banter, Brooks seemed to want something else, and so did she. The kiss after their ceremony flashed in her mind, right before his lips settled on hers. Their kiss with the taste of icing between them was still a sweet memory. But this time as he kissed her, he didn't stop with the pressing of lips on lips or a slight lick of his tongue. Now Brooks's tongue slid along her lips, and she didn't hesitate a second. She opened her mouth to him. He tasted her and she tasted him. He was champagne and icing, and she was tempted by both.

Apparently, he was, too, because his tongue explored her mouth, searching, asking, maybe even demanding. She gave in to his desire...and hers. She responded with everything she had. Her arm went around him and she became intoxicated by the scent of his cologne and the scent of him and the idea that they were husband and wife. She could feel every bit of Brooks's desire. When his fingers went to the zipper on the back of her dress, she anticipated what might happen next. But the sound of the rasp of the metal changed everything. Brooks's fingers froze as he did, too.

He broke their kiss, raised his head and looked as if he'd done something terribly wrong.

Before she could tell him that she liked what they were doing, that after all, they were married, that maybe something new could come of their partnership, he gruffly said, "I'm sorry, Jazzy. I know we have an arrangement and I never intended for this to happen. I just wanted to celebrate a little and show you how much I appreciate what you're doing. This is essentially a business deal, and neither of us should forget that."

A business deal. She'd really never thought of this as strictly business, but clearly, *he* had. The flowers and the champagne and watch were just to show his appreciation.

And the kiss? Well...

She was a woman and he was a man, and he had needs that he apparently wasn't going to satisfy.

"I guess the champagne went to our heads," she murmured.

"I guess," he said gruffly.

"Thank you for the watch. I really like it."

"Good."

So Brooks had once again turned into the monosyllabic remote man he'd been the night before their wedding. Because he felt he'd done something wrong?

So she said the one thing that she knew would make this easier for both of them. "I'd better turn in. I have to unpack and...set up my alarm. Do you want me to go to your dad's with you in the morning?"

"That's up to you."

"I'll go with you. We wouldn't want him to think something's wrong." She stood, feeling a little shaky from everything that had happened today, just wanting to make a fast exit.

He stood, too. "I'll have to make sure the fire's out, so I might be up for a little bit. Good night, Jazzy."

She murmured, "Good night," and headed for her room. As she did, she felt the air on the back of her neck where her zipper had been lowered a bit, and she wondered just what would have happened if both of them had had one more glass of champagne.

Chapter Eleven

The next morning, breakfast was awkward and quick. Jazzy cooked scrambled eggs while Brooks fried bacon. She put the toast in and waited for it to pop while he took everything to the table.

Halfway through eating, Brooks said, "You don't have to go along to check on Dad. I can drop you at the clinic."

That certainly would be easier with this tension between them but not necessarily the best thing to do. "I don't mind. Besides, wouldn't your dad think it was odd that we weren't together the day after our wedding?"

As she'd watched yesterday, Brooks had done some fast talking to both their parents about why they weren't taking a honeymoon yet—what with setting up both clinics and so much to do, they thought they'd wait. With a sigh, Jazzy realized she didn't even know where

Brooks would like to *go* on a honeymoon. She wouldn't care. Anyplace holed up alone with him overnight would be terrific.

If last night had really been their honeymoon—

Once outside in Brooks's truck, their gazes met and she could easily see Brooks was thinking about last night's kiss, too. Yet he obviously didn't want to talk about it or their marriage. He started the truck and aimed it in the right direction.

This tension between them was more than she'd bargained for. This tension between them felt as if it could explode at any moment. She just hoped when it did, they were both ready for the consequences.

When they arrived at the Bar S, Brooks pulled around back to the clinic. But when he rounded the curve in the driveway, he spotted his dad's truck and his father climbing into it.

"What the hell?" he mumbled, as if this was one more stress he didn't need.

Jazzy clasped his arm. "He might be just driving into town to get something at the General Store. His doctor said it was safe for him to drive."

"Jazzy, I know what the doctor said," Brooks snapped. "But I also know Dad always pushes the boundaries, so it's never as simple as it seems. He wouldn't have driven the truck around back unless he wanted to load up a few supplies. I know him. You don't."

That stung because she felt as if she'd come to know Barrett pretty well over the past couple of weeks. True, she didn't know all of his habits, but she did know he wanted to feel better. The two of them had talked about what he needed to do for that to happen. She was hurt Brooks would dismiss her so cavalierly.

"I might not know your dad as well as you do, but during the time we spent together, we talked, probably more than you've talked to him in the past few years."

Brooks looked startled at that observation, but he obviously didn't want to have a conversation about it now. He climbed out of the truck and jogged over to his dad.

Jazzy got out and followed him. All right, so she was going to let *him* handle it. Let's see how well he did that.

"Where are you going this early, Dad?"

With the door to his truck hanging open, Barrett looked from Brooks to Jazzy. "The better question is, what are you two doing here so early? It seems to me you'd be late on the day after your wedding." There was a twinkle of slyness in his eyes that made Jazzy feel uncomfortable.

"Off-topic, Dad. Where are you headed to?"

"It's not like I'm going to drive across the state. Stewart Young called. He has a horse that went lame and he wants me to look at him."

"I can do that," Brooks said in an even voice that told Jazzy he was keeping what he really thought under control.

"Stewart doesn't want *you,* he wants *me. I'm* the one who's handled his horses for thirty years. *I'm* the one he trusts. Besides, I've got to start getting out again. I'm not going to sit in that house like an invalid. That's no better for me than doing too much."

In a way, Jazzy knew he was right. Yet she could also see Brooks was afraid his dad would do something he shouldn't, get involved in something he shouldn't, overexert himself in a way he shouldn't.

Mediating, she suggested, "Why don't both of you go?"

They both swung their gazes toward her in a challenging way. All right, she'd take on two Smith men at once if she had to.

Focusing on Brooks's dad, she suggested, "You can consult with Stewart while Brooks does the actual physical exam. That way you can get out, but Brooks won't worry about you. I can hold down the fort here until you get back. If something comes up at Brooks's clinic, I'll call you. That's what cell phones are made for."

Barrett didn't look happy but he wasn't protesting, either. Still, he eyed them suspiciously. "So tell me again why you're here so early."

Brooks pushed up the rim of his Stetson. "We're here early so maybe we can finish early."

Barrett harrumphed. "I guess the whole evening together would suit the two of you." He noticed the watch on Jazzy's wrist. "That's pretty."

"It was a wedding gift from Brooks." She knew that would please Barrett.

"It's good to know my son *does* have a romantic bone in his body. I guess there's hope."

When Jazzy looked down at the watch, but then back at Brooks's expression, she wasn't so sure.

With troubling insight, Brooks realized whenever he was with Jazzy, he felt like a different person. Sometimes stronger. Sometimes way too unsettled. Their kiss last night weighed on his mind. His brusque attitude this morning did, too. Somehow they had to figure out this marriage.

After his visit to Stewart Young, he'd dropped her

at the Buckskin Clinic. She'd taken care of calls that had come in and referred patients to his dad's clinic where Brooks could see them. It was all a bit confusing for now, but they'd get into a routine, and slowly as his dad came back to work, he'd spend more time at his own clinic.

Eventually his father would say to him, "Let's join our practices," and then they'd get a partner that would take some of the load off them both. It was easy to see the way this should go. He just wished his dad wasn't being so stubborn about it.

After he finished at his dad's, he picked up Jazzy. On the drive home, they decided to order pizza instead of worrying about cooking. They'd been silent in the truck again, though, and Brooks wished they could get back the easy camaraderie they'd had at the beginning of their relationship. What had happened to their friendship?

It had gotten sidetracked by circumstances that had taken on a life of their own.

At his place, he decided against a fire tonight. No more cozy atmosphere. No more thinking about pleasing Jazzy with flowers or champagne. That had given off the wrong signals. He wasn't interested in romance, he told himself, just in an easy companionship between them. Jazzy got herself a glass of water, and he called the pizza establishment he favored most.

He put his hand over the phone. "What do you want on your pizza?"

"It doesn't matter," she said without her usual enthusiasm.

"Tell me *something,* Jazzy, or I'm going to load it up with what I want."

"Pepperoni," she shot at him. "And plenty of onions."

Okay, so she wasn't interested in romance, either.

After he placed the order, she said, "I'm going to give Jordyn a call in my room. Let me know when the pizza arrives."

Before he could blink, she was gone from the kitchen into her bedroom and had closed the door.

For some reason, that closed door annoyed him. Not that he wanted to listen in on her conversation, but it set up another barrier between them.

Restless, he grabbed two plates and set them on the table. Then he rummaged in the drawer for silverware and pulled napkins from the counter. Next on his list was to find an apartment in Rust Creek Falls. It would definitely be more convenient. He could call Rhonda Deatrick now and leave a message. Going to the phone again, he was about to do that, when his doorbell rang.

Couldn't be the pizza already.

When he opened the door to Gage Christensen, he smiled. He'd invited Gage to the wedding but he hadn't been there.

"I know, I didn't show up for the big shindig. I had an emergency call and had to go out. And Lissa's in New York. So I thought I'd stop by now and congratulate you both." He had a package in his hands. "Something I thought you could use other than a toaster."

"Come on in." But as soon as Brooks said it, he realized he shouldn't have. Not because he didn't want Gage there, but because Jazzy was in her own room, not his master suite. Gage had been here before. He knew the setup.

At that moment, Jazzy emerged from the guest bedroom. When she saw Gage, she stopped. Gage handed her the wedding present, but exchanged a look with Brooks.

"You two haven't known each other very long. You weren't dating when Jazzy and I had dinner."

They both kept silent.

"You fell hard overnight?"

"Didn't *you?*" Brooks shot back.

Gage's face turned ruddy. "Maybe. I suppose it does happen." After another long look at both of them, he said, "If the two of you need to talk about anything, I'm around."

Suddenly, his cell phone beeped. He gave a shrug and said, "Excuse me," and checked it. "I've got to get back to the office. Now."

Halfway to the door, he stopped. "Are you coming to the meeting tomorrow night at the town hall? Nate Crawford is supposed to have an important announcement."

They hadn't talked about it, but the meeting would give them something to think about other than this marriage of convenience. "Sure, we'll be there," Brooks responded.

After Gage was gone, Jazzy looked at Brooks. "Do you think he guessed that…this isn't a real marriage? Are we doing the best thing for everyone?" she asked.

"It's too late to have second thoughts now." Though he *was* having second thoughts. Being married to Jazzy for a year and keeping his hands off her was going to be torture.

"Why don't you open Gage's present? We really should open the rest of the stack tonight."

Jazzy sat on the sofa, the box in front of her on the

coffee table. She tore off the wrappings and on the out-side of the box they could read PRESSURE COOKER.

"Oh, it's one of those advanced foodie pressure cook-ers that're supposed to be easy. You can brown every-thing right in it then let it steam. A meal is supposed to be ready in about half the time," she explained.

"Sounds practical."

"Gage put some thought into this. It's a great new-lywed gift."

Yes, it was. When Gage had decided on it for them, he hadn't realized how appropriate it would be. A pres-sure cooker. Brooks felt as if he were inside a pressure cooker right now, just waiting for it to blow.

The community meeting was just getting underway when Brooks and Jazzy slipped inside the town hall. Jazzy kept stealing glances at Brooks to try to guess what he was thinking. Gage's visit stretched like a wire between them. Was what they were doing wrong, or simply advantageous to them both, as well as Brooks's dad? She wasn't sure anymore. But if it was right, why didn't it feel right?

The folding chairs were packed tight together to fit the most people in. Jazzy's shoulder rubbed against Brooks's but he didn't look her way, though she did look his. He'd dropped her at his clinic this morning while he went to his dad's. All of the appointments Jazzy had made for Brooks at Buckskin Clinic were set up for to-morrow. That seemed to be the easiest way to handle this for now. So they'd be working together tomorrow. Maybe some of this tension would dissipate then.

Irene Murphy saw them and waved. "Congratula-tions," she called, a few feet from where she was sitting.

A gentleman seated in back of them clapped Brooks on the shoulder and wished them all the best, too. Gage was across the room and just raised his brows. Jazzy didn't know what he was thinking.

Nate Crawford was running the meeting. He banged his gavel on the podium for some order. After thanking everyone for coming, he read a list of the community's accomplishments since the flood. Utilities had been restored, roads repaired, bridges rebuilt.

He went on, talking about the progress on the elementary school and how volunteers had come from all over to help.

The side door to the town hall opened and shut. To distract her attention from Brooks, Jazzy turned to look to see who the newcomers were. A couple walked in followed by—

Jazzy felt her whole body go a little cold. Oh, my. What was Griff Wellington doing here?

As if his eyes were drawn by a magnet, they came to rest on her. It didn't take a genius to figure out he was here to see her. He must have heard about her marriage.

Nate was still speaking and everyone was listening to him. Jazzy raised her hand to Griff, an acknowledgement that she'd seen him, but she wasn't going to disrupt the meeting to go to him. That would look odd.

Brooks nudged her shoulder. "Who's that?"

Maybe he was as aware of her as she was of him. She stayed silent, trying to figure out how to explain.

Before she could, Brooks noted, "You've gone pale."

"Don't be silly. It's just a little cold in here."

"Not with all these people, it isn't. Who is that guy?"

Some of the other meeting-goers had turned to look

at them. Jazzy whispered, "Not now. I'll explain later, okay?"

Brooks gave her a look that said he would indeed expect an explanation later. She wished now she had told him about Griff and her almost-engagement. She wished now she'd told Brooks *she'd* broken it off. But it just hadn't seemed important. Or had the real reason for not telling him been she didn't want him comparing her to the fiancée who had broken her engagement with *him*. Whatever the reason, the die was cast and she'd have to figure this out as she went.

She felt Brooks's gaze on her from the side and she felt Griff's gaze on her from the back. He must have found a seat behind them. The hairs on her neck prickled and she had the feeling she was in for a stormy night. Not at all what she'd planned. She'd hoped she and Brooks could talk and maybe get back on an easy footing. But now this.

Jazzy tried to concentrate on Nate's words once more.

"The reason we called this meeting tonight, the main one, anyway, is that I have some good news for this town. Lissa Roarke's blog and personal diary about life in Rust Creek Falls since the flood has gotten some attention back in New York City. She's going to be on a national morning talk show. I spoke with her myself this afternoon, and she believes that once she's on that show, donations and even more help are going to come rolling in, which will be an even greater help with the reconstruction efforts. So maybe we can really be the town we were before the flood, even better."

Everyone applauded. Gage looked proud enough of

Lissa to burst. But all Jazzy could think of was Griff standing in the back of the hall, waiting for her.

Jazzy grew more antsy the longer the meeting went on. Brooks glanced at her more than once, and she tried to stay calm. She realized, although she'd dated Griff, she didn't really know him very well because she didn't know why he was here and she had no idea what his reaction was going to be to seeing her, to talking with her, to hearing the news of her marriage, if he hadn't heard it yet. But she did know Brooks and the fact that she hadn't told him about Griff weighed heavily on her.

After the road construction foreman spoke, after a couple of ranchers had their say about what they still needed to get their places back to running in top shape, after Nate thanked everyone for coming, the meeting finally ended.

Jazzy tapped Brooks's arm. "I have to speak to someone. It will only be a few minutes."

After Brooks gave her a piercing look, she added, "I'll be right back." Then she slipped away before he could ask her any questions.

When Griff saw Jazzy, his expression was somber. "Can we step outside?"

This was a small town full of people who knew each other. At gatherings like this, they liked to chat. They started forming groups now, doing just that.

Jazzy nodded. Though she started to follow Griff, she glanced back over her shoulder and saw that Brooks's gaze was tracking her.

Once outside, Jazzy glanced up at the beautiful full moon that was lighting up the front of the town hall. It was a momentary distraction before she had to face Griff. However, squaring her shoulders, she did.

"How are you?" she asked.

"I'm good. How are *you?*"

"I'm great," she said brightly, but then dropped the pretense. "Why are you here, Griff?"

"I ran into Abby, or rather she ran into me at the store. She made some excuse about needing new running shoes, but I don't think she runs, does she?"

"She might have taken it up lately." Jazzy always defended her sisters and brother, no matter what.

He nodded his head in concession. "Fair enough. Anyway, she told me you got married. I couldn't believe it. I wanted to ask you myself. Is it true?"

"She wouldn't have lied to you."

Griff looked up into the thousand stars, and then back at her. "No, I suppose not. Is it that guy you were sitting next to?"

"Yes, Brooks Smith. He has a veterinary practice."

"Ah," Griff responded, as if that made sense somehow. "A love of animals. Is that what bonded you together? This is awful quick."

"A love of animals is one of the things that brought us together."

"You never looked at me the way you look at him."

"Griff, don't."

He sighed. "I should have seen our breakup coming. But I guess I was just hoping that I was as right for you as you seemed to be for me."

"Was I really *right* for you? Think about it. We became friends, but—"

"We never had grand passion? I suppose not. Maybe I just wanted to settle down and start a family so badly that I ignored what I *should* have in favor of what we *did* have."

Jazzy had shared embraces and kisses with Griff, details of their lives, the hopes for a future, so it didn't seem odd for her to take his hand now. "I never wanted to hurt you. That's why I broke off our involvement when I did. Don't you see?"

"And you didn't know this Brooks Smith before you left Thunder Canyon?"

"Oh, no! I never would have dated another man behind your back."

"I didn't think so, but I had to have that question answered, too. So you love him?"

"More each day."

Griff gazed into her eyes for a moment, squeezed her hand, then leaned in and kissed her on the cheek. "I wish you well, Jasmine Cates Smith, I really do. Once I get over some hurt pride, maybe when you come back to Thunder Canyon, we can stay friends, and I can meet your guy."

Leaning away, she responded, "I'd like that."

Griff gave her a little salute and then he walked away. She watched after him, knowing he was a good man, knowing he'd make someone a wonderful husband.

She jumped when Brooks's voice startled her. "So… who is he?"

Jazzy glanced around at the people who had started to trickle out of the town hall. Nina Crawford stopped and said to the two of them, "Congratulations on your wedding." She whispered to Brooks, "Even if you don't think you're going to vote for Nate." She'd moved away when another burly gentleman waved to Brooks.

"Can we talk about this when we get home?" Jazzy asked. "A little privacy would be good."

"We can talk in the truck. I don't think I want to wait until we get home."

He was right about that. Or maybe he just didn't want to have to look at her while they were having the talk. He'd have to keep his eyes on the road.

They had parked some ways down the street and they walked that way on what Jazzy knew could be a romantic evening, with that big, full moon and all the stars.

Brooks waited until they were in his truck, buckled up, and then out on the road toward Kalispell. "So spill it," he said in a brook-no-argument voice.

She figured the best way to tell it was just to tell it. "Griff and I dated back in Thunder Canyon."

"Dated, or were dating when you left?"

"Past tense. Laila saw him looking at engagement rings and she told me. He and I had been going out for a few months and I just didn't feel— I just knew he wasn't the one. So I broke off our relationship." She could see Brooks's mouth tighten, his hands wrap more securely around the steering wheel.

"So he thought you were serious enough to get married, and then you broke up with him."

She knew what he was comparing this to. "It's nothing like your relationship with Lynnette."

"Isn't it? And even if it isn't, you didn't tell me about it. I thought you were an honest woman, Jazzy."

That hurt. It hurt terribly. "I *am* honest. I *was* honest. Did you want me to tell you about everyone I dated in the last five years?"

"I told you about Lynnette."

Yes, he had confided in her about his fiancée, and why hadn't she told him about Griff?

"Brooks, I didn't intentionally keep it from you. It

just never came up. It didn't seem important." Not after she'd met him. Not after she'd realized the difference in being around Brooks. It had been nothing like being around Griff.

But she could see he wasn't buying it. She could see he still thought she'd been dishonest with him. There was really no way to change his mind.

When they arrived back at Brooks's place—Jazzy couldn't quite think of it as home yet—he took off his jacket and went to the kitchen. There he pulled a bottle of beer from the refrigerator.

Jazzy followed. "We can talk about this more if you want."

"There's nothing to say, Jazzy. You lied by omission. I don't know if I can forget that."

"Maybe I did it because I didn't want you comparing our friendship or relationship or whatever it is, to yours and Lynnette's."

He gave her a hard stare and unscrewed the cap of the bottle. "That's an excuse but I don't know if it's a good one."

If he understood she'd been falling in love with him, it might be, but she certainly couldn't tell him that now.

"I didn't tell you about Griff because it was over, because I had started a new life here in Rust Creek Falls. You're acting so self-righteous, telling me I'm not an honest woman. Yet you're lying to your father. *We're* lying to your father. How do you account for that? Are *you* a dishonest man?"

He looked totally taken aback as if he'd never put those things in the same category. "That's not the same at all, Jazzy, and you know it. My dad's health was at stake."

"And your relationship with him, and my relationship with my family and friends, too. Maybe my relationship with you is at stake here. Think about it, Brooks, then tell me if we're so different."

His attitude rankled. He was as stubborn as his father. But she loved him, anyway. That, most of all, was what made her turn away. That, most of all, was what made her hightail it out of the kitchen and head for the guest room.

Chapter Twelve

Jazzy stood in the exam room beside Brooks, their bodies not touching if they could help it. She was there because she was more aid to Maggie Bradshaw and her son Timmy who'd brought a rescued kitten in than she was to the vet who had only monosyllabic replies to anything she said. Well, two could play that game. There wouldn't be any conversation. There wouldn't be any closeness. There might not even be a marriage of convenience for much longer.

The little boy, who was about five, was crying. "Momma says if she's sick, we can't keep her!"

Brooks knelt down beside Timmy, making eye contact. "When you first brought her in, I took a blood sample to do testing. I'll find out in a few minutes whether she's sick or not. So how about if you wipe those tears until we find out if we have something to worry about?

I'm giving her a flea treatment, but I have a little comb here, and I'd like to show you how to use it. Do you think you could do that?"

Timmy looked at Brooks as if he'd given him the biggest job in the world. "I can do that."

Brooks nodded to Jazzy. "Can you help him with that?"

It was the first, since last night, that his voice had held a little bit of tenderness...that gentleness she knew so well.

"Sure, I can. I have a stepstool over here, Timmy. You can climb up on that and you'll be right in line with the table."

Timmy glanced over his shoulder at his mom. "I want to keep her."

His mom looked pained as if she wanted to say yes, but yet didn't know if she could take care of a sick cat. The fuzzy, yellow tabby hadn't shown any symptoms yet, but she was only about a month old, and had somehow survived the outdoors. Maybe she was sturdier than she appeared.

"We think she's been sleeping under our porch," Mrs. Bradshaw said. "Timmy came in and got me as soon as he saw her so we could feed her, and she was hungry. If we keep her, is there anything we should know about food?"

"Food in small portions with water in between. Always make sure she has plenty of water, and make sure it's kitten food," Jazzy instructed, then she checked with Brooks. "Right?"

"Right on," he admitted. "I'll go check on the test."

Jazzy showed Timmy how to lift the comb through the fine fur, looking deep at its roots for dirt and any fleas they might find. In about twelve hours, the treatment would take care of the pests, but it would be good to get the dirt out.

Jazzy explained, "In three days, you should give her a bath in no-tears baby shampoo with tepid water, a warm room, and a nice fluffy towel for drying afterward. Some cats don't mind a bath as much as you think. You might want to have a pitcher of water there to pour over her to rinse her. It would be better to start in the morning so she could dry off in a patch of sunlight."

A short while later Brooks was back and he was smiling. "She tested negative for feline leukemia and FIV."

"I told her about the bath," Jazzy said.

He glanced at her. "Right. I understand you don't have any other animals?" he asked Mrs. Bradshaw.

"No, we don't. With food costs the way they are, it just seemed better not to. But this little one found us."

"Do you have a room you can keep her in for the next couple of days? One that you'll be able to clean up fairly well, just in case a flea or two escape?"

"We have a sunroom. Would that be all right?"

"In October, that should be perfect. Keeping her there will serve two purposes. It will make sure the fleas are gone. You can also give her a small space to explore a little at a time. In a few days, she'll learn every aspect of that room, then she'll be ready to go exploring elsewhere. She's scared, dehydrated and malnourished, so she's going to need a few days to perk up and feel like her real kitten self again. You're sure there weren't any other kittens close by?"

"Not that we could find. And we did look."

Brooks plucked the kitten from the table and knelt down again in front of the boy. The kitten had curled in Brooks's arm looking up at him with little golden eyes that were trusting and innocent. "Want to hold her?" Brooks asked.

It was obvious Timmy did, but hadn't known if he should. Now, however, Brooks helped him and showed him the best way to hold the kitten so she wouldn't slip away.

"This is good when she's sleepy," he said. "If she gets squirmy, just forget holding her and let her down. She won't want anyone to hold her then and she'll be able to get away, no matter what you do. But when she's sleepy, she'll probably want to cuddle with you."

Timmy looked at his mom. "Can she sleep on my bed, Mommy? Please…please?"

"Maybe it will be a good idea if she does," Mrs. Bradshaw answered. "You won't be so lonely. Ever since his dad left, he's had bad dreams."

"I'm sorry to hear about your husband leaving Rust Creek Falls," Brooks empathized. "You're certain he's not coming back?"

"This place was just too small for him to begin with. He never stayed in one place long before I met him. We came from New Mexico."

"That's a long way," Jazzy said.

"Oh, we stayed in a few states in between, but when we got here, I settled in. I joined a quilting club and a knitting club. Jay wasn't enamored with the place *before* the flood. After the flood, he said there was simply no reason to stay. But I disagreed. Now more than ever, this is a real community. We have to stick together. But he didn't see that. He just wanted to go his own way and said it was time."

"I'm sorry," Jazzy said.

"Being a single mom isn't so bad," she said to Jazzy. "I don't have to consult anyone else about my decisions. But Timmy misses him, and maybe this kitty is the answer to a prayer."

"What are you going to name her?" Jazzy asked.

"Porch," Timmy answered quickly, as if he'd already thought about it. "That's where we found her. Wouldn't that be a good name?"

Brooks laughed. "I think that's a great name. You'll never forget how she came into your life. You've got to promise me you'll help take good care of her, that you'll help to feed her and give her water. A kitten like this has to eat even more often than you do. Do you think you can be that responsible?"

"I can feed her."

"I'm sure your mom will help and show you at first. But then we'll see how much of a big boy you can be."

It was obvious to Jazzy that Brooks would make a wonderful father. When he looked up, their gazes met, and she wondered if he guessed what she was thinking. They'd never talked about children because they never expected their marriage to be a real one. She wanted children, but she wanted to do it right.

Brooks was helping the kitty back into her box. "I'll take her out to the desk for you. Jazzy will give you an itemized bill."

"My husband would have had a fit if he had seen what this was going to cost. But I figure, I'll just use the money he would have spent on beer this month."

Jazzy typed a few things into the computer and printed out the bill. Maggie wrote a check and handed it over.

Just as Timmy and his mom were leaving, Paige Dalton came into the office, surprising Jazzy. Paige was a fifth-grade teacher who was holding classes in her home. But she couldn't be holding classes if she was out and about. Jazzy had seen her over at the school several times and had liked her, though she really didn't know too much about her.

"Paige, it's good to see you. What brings you here? Do you have a small animal in your purse?"

Paige laughed and pushed her dark brown hair away from her cheek. "No, I don't. Not this time, anyway. I have a question for Brooks."

Brooks was watching mother and son leave, and Jazzy wished she could read his mind. Was he wondering what it would be like to be a father someday? Did he want to be a dad?

At the sound of his name, he turned toward Paige. "Hi, Paige. How can I help you?"

"The children have off today to work on special projects at their own homes. We're doing holiday customs around the world. Some of them are making baked goods. Some of the guys are building structures like the Eiffel Tower. Some of them are writing reports or recipes. Anyway, I gave them the day to work on them at home. And tomorrow is their presentation to the rest of the class. It should be fun. I'm taking our curriculum as is and trying to make it suit to what's happened around here. Teaching from my home is different from being in a classroom. Actually, they seem to be learning well in a relaxed atmosphere, but they do miss the socialization with their friends."

"I imagine they would," Jazzy said.

"So what do you need?" Brooks asked.

"Would you come talk to the class about being a veterinarian? I'm sure they'd love to hear. We're trying to do a different career each week, and I want to broaden their outlooks." She took a step closer to him. "I understand how busy you are, helping out with your dad's practice as well as this one. I'd only need about an hour of your time, and I think it would mean a lot to the children."

"I can't say no to the children now, can I?" Brooks asked with a smile. "Sure, I can spare an hour. What day next week would be good for you?"

"How about next Friday? Late morning...around eleven?"

"Jazzy will pencil it in." He motioned to the exam room. "I'm going to clean up in there."

Paige and Jazzy were left alone in the reception area. As Brooks disappeared, Paige put her hand over her mouth. "Oh, my gosh, I didn't even congratulate the two of you on your wedding. Best wishes!"

Jazzy didn't know what to say, so she just said, "Thank you."

"You got married really fast. It must have been a whirlwind romance."

Jazzy wasn't a mind reader, but she could see Paige seemed a little wistful. Was it because she wanted a whirlwind romance of her own? Or because her own heart had been broken?

Jazzy just hoped this marriage of convenience wouldn't break *her* heart.

* * *

The following evening, Jazzy made supper—soup again, so she could take some to Barrett—wondering how she could break the tension between her and Brooks. Clamping the lid on the soup, she turned it down to simmer, hoping Brooks wouldn't be too late.

As soon as she thought it, the garage door opened. She realized she was nervous and anxious as he came from the garage into the kitchen and strode into the mudroom.

She called a "hello" but he must not have heard her over the water running because he didn't call back. When he appeared in the kitchen, he'd discarded his jacket. There wasn't a welcoming expression on his face. He looked so serious, she was afraid of what might come out of his mouth next.

However, all he said was, "Do I have time to take a shower before dinner?"

"Sure. The soup can keep. The longer it cooks, the better it tastes."

Usually he bantered back. But after their argument last night, he obviously wasn't bantering. Had that been their first fight? Was he going to forgive her for not telling him about Griff, or for the things she'd said about what they were doing concerning his dad?

Chopping vegetables for a salad, she heard the shower running. She imagined him standing naked under that shower. She imagined tan lines from his working outdoors, let alone the muscles that would ripple when he moved. She imagined his wet hair, brown and slick, his smile as he beckoned her into the shower with him…

Abruptly, she cut off the fantasies. From what was

going on between them right now, that kind of envisioning belonged on another planet.

She'd finished making the salad and was slicing a loaf of crusty bread that she'd picked up at the bakery when she realized the shower had gone off a long while before. Was Brooks staying in his room to avoid her? Maybe he was making phone calls.

Leaving the kitchen, she walked down the hall to his bedroom. His door was partially open, and when she peeked inside, she saw him standing at the window, sweatpants riding low on his hips as he stared out into the black night. Something was off. Something was wrong.

She simply couldn't stay away. She had to know what was going on in his head. He didn't seem to hear the door when it creaked open because he didn't turn toward her.

"Brooks?" she called softly.

He still didn't turn toward her.

Crossing to the window, she touched his arm. "Is something wrong?"

His face still had the strained expression she'd seen when he walked in. His eyes bore a look of turmoil as he finally turned to look at her. "I'm a veterinarian and I'm supposed to stay detached from the animals I treat."

She had a bad feeling and dreaded what was coming. "It's hard to stay detached."

"I'm usually good at compartmentalizing—keeping the business of being a veterinarian on one side, patient care on the other side, personal life underneath it all. But today— I lost a foal. It was stillborn. Nothing I could do."

Looking away from her again, she knew he didn't want her to see the emotion he was feeling.

"I'm sorry, Brooks." She really could think of nothing else to say. No words helped in a situation like this.

He must have heard the heartfelt understanding in her words. He must have seen the longing in her eyes…her desire for everything between them to be right again. His voice was deeply husky as he said, "Jazzy."

Impulse led her to wrap her arms around him in a hug, to lift her face to his. Impulse must have gotten to him, too…because he bent his head and kissed her.

This wasn't a light, feathery kiss. This time, Brooks's mouth on hers was decidedly masterful, absolutely possessive, totally consuming. His tongue breached her lips in a way that said he needed—wanted—this kiss as much as she did.

She didn't need to breathe. All she wanted to do was feel—feel Brooks's desire in the way his arms tightened around her, feel it in the way his tongue swept her mouth, feel it in the way his body hardened against hers. His skin was hot as her hands explored his bare back. His muscles were taut under her fingertips. He was strength and desire and gentleness…and she loved him. Oh, how she loved him.

She thought it over and over again though she didn't say it. Too much was happening at once. Had he forgiven her for not telling him about Griff? Were his feelings going deeper, too? Did he want exactly what she wanted tonight?

He certainly seemed to because as she stroked her hands down his back and around to his hips, as her thumbs fingered the drawstring on his sweatpants, he groaned and broke off the kiss. For a moment she thought he might want to part like he had the other night, but tonight he looked at her differently.

Tonight he shook his head as if he couldn't fight desire anymore. Tonight he said, "I want you, Jazzy. Do you want me, too?"

No words of love there. Yet she heard deep emotion in his voice and saw it on his face. She was going to give in to it...give in to passion and hope for love.

"I want you." She put as much feeling into those three words as she could manage.

With a deep groan, he lifted her into his arms and she wrapped her legs around him. His fervent kisses distracted her so she didn't even realize he had carried her to the bed. As she sat on the edge of the bed, she clung to him, rubbing her nose into his neck, letting everything about him encompass her. His large hands slid under the hem of her sweater.

"You're going to have to let go of me if I'm going to get this off you."

She didn't want to let go of him, not ever.

He swiveled their bodies until he was sitting beside her on the bed, too. Lifting her sweater over her head, he made quick work of her bra and stared at her as if she were a beautiful piece of artwork...or a fascinating sculpture...or a woman he cared about. Maybe even...loved.

"You can touch me," she said softly, so wanting to hear what he felt about her.

He gave her a wry smile. "So can you."

They reached for each other at the same moment.

She untied the drawstring at his waist. He unsnapped her jeans.

In no time at all, they were naked on his big bed, facing each other, touching. Every stroke and every kiss meant so much because it had been taboo for so long. Ever since that first night when they'd flirted at the Ace in the Hole, they'd experienced the sexual electricity that had brought them to this moment.

When she laced her fingers in his hair, he caressed her thigh, his hand doing enticing things she could feel down deep inside. Her fingers played in his chest hair. After a speaking glance that said he was going to get serious now, he lowered his head to her breast. The tug of his lips on her nipple inspired sensations she'd never felt before. His tongue laving it made her call his name. His smile, filled with deep male satisfaction, led her to reach for him, enfold him in her hand, and feel the pulsing of his blood. He let out a long breath that told her she affected him just as he affected her.

But apparently he'd had enough of the foreplay. Sliding his palm to the apex of her thighs, he knew she had, too.

"Don't move," he rasped, as he reached for the nightstand and pulled out the drawer.

She kept her eyes closed, her breaths coming in short, shallow pants because each kiss and touch had readied her for what came next. She heard the rustle of foil, the packet tearing. A moment later, he was back with her, kissing her lips until she clung to him like a vine.

He rolled her onto her back and rose above her, but he didn't move to enter her. Gazing at her, he said, "I was jealous of that man you dated, and I took it out on you. I shouldn't have. You're the most honest woman I know."

It was an apology, and she knew saying he was jealous was hard for Brooks. There was no reason to dwell on it, or their argument. She reached for him and when he entered her, she felt wonderfully whole. She arched up to Brooks, wrapped her legs around him, and took him deeper. His groan of satisfaction made her feel proud, made her feel driven to give him everything she was and everything she could be. Each of his thrusts took her to a new plane of sensation. The melding of their bodies created a swirl of emotion she couldn't begin to grasp.

When they'd stood at the falls a couple of weeks ago, she'd felt awe near to this. But not anything this wide and deep and high. Not something as cataclysmically earth-shattering. This was *love*. It was so totally consuming that she didn't know if she'd ever be herself again.

As she held on to Brooks, light shattered, feelings washed over her, her body trembled and then shook with a climax so overwhelming, tears came to her eyes. Brooks's release came immediately after, and as they gasped for breath together and held on to each other, she knew their lives would never be the same.

The first sign that something was wrong was the way Brooks rolled away from her, with his eyes closed, and without a smile. The second was his terse "I'll be right back," as if they had something important to settle.

Jazzy's head was still spinning from making love

with him, and she hoped she was wrong about the feeling of doom that was stirring in her heart. Moments before, it had been filled with hope.

When Brooks returned from the bathroom, he didn't slide into bed with her, but rather sat on the edge. "That was a huge mistake."

She didn't know what she had expected to hear, but that wasn't it.

She was about to tell him she didn't regret anything about making love, when he said, "I think we should split up. We'll tell my dad it didn't work out. I'll still give you my grandmother's land, though."

Stunned, she couldn't begin to make sense of his words, let alone respond to them.

He went on, laying out his case. "Even if we tried to make a real marriage of this, I can't give you the marriage you deserve. With my own practice, watching over Dad's, I won't have time to sleep, let alone nurture a relationship. My mom had to cover for my dad more times than I can count. Whenever I had a school function, or sports event, she didn't complain, but he wasn't around. He was always working. When she got sick, my grandmother was there more than he was."

"Are you saying that I'm so different from your mom?"

"Oh, you're different all right, Jazzy. You say what you think. Even if she resented the time Dad worked, she never said. You couldn't be like that."

"How do you know I'd resent it?"

"I just know."

To her dismay, she realized he was thinking of

Lynnette again. He might not be comparing her to his mother, but he was comparing her to another woman who'd let him down. And that just made her angry.

"This isn't about your mom *or* your dad working too much. It's about *your* broken engagement. It's about a woman being unfaithful to you and walking out."

His silence told her she'd hit the mark. Still, he concluded, "No matter what it's about, we'd end up hating each other. I don't want that. Do you?"

Reaching for the sheet, she pulled it up, feeling the need to cover her body where she hadn't such a short time ago. But now everything was different. Brooks had succumbed to desire in a moment of weakness. He didn't love her. He couldn't, not if he wanted to end their marriage.

To top it all off, he began dressing quickly. And then he pulled his duffel bag from the closet.

"What are you doing?"

"I'm going to give Dallas a call and go bunk with him and his kids. I'm sure he won't mind, and he won't ask any questions."

"That's all you're concerned about, questions?" Brooks was building a new wall around himself, and Jazzy knew there wasn't anything she could say to knock it down. She'd found the man of her dreams and he didn't want her. He didn't need her.

All she could think of to say was, "Your father's going to be so upset."

Brooks gave her a long, hard look. "Not any more upset than he would be at the end of the year. This was a crazy idea. We were both foolish for thinking it could work."

With his boots on now, jeans and sweatshirts in his duffel, he was ready to go.

"I'm not going to stay here, Brooks. It's *your* place, not mine."

"Stay as long as you need to. This is *my* fault, not yours, Jazzy. I'll see a lawyer and get that land transferred over. I'll keep my word."

Then as if he couldn't stand to look at her another moment longer, he left.

Chapter Thirteen

Jazzy absolutely didn't know what to do. She'd cried most of the night. This morning she was trying to look at her options. But her feelings kept getting in the way. Should she go back to Thunder Canyon? Should she leave Brooks forever? She really couldn't think about that in spite of what he'd said.

Yet she knew she couldn't stay here in his condo. She couldn't walk into his bedroom and remember what they'd done...how she'd felt...how he'd claimed her. It would be impossible to stay here without envisioning the future she'd hoped they'd be able to share.

Tears threatened again. She swiped them away, knowing this was her own fault for risking her heart. Maybe she should have married Griff who was safe. But, no. She hadn't wanted safe and she still didn't. She wanted Brooks. But if he didn't want her, what could she do?

Picking up her cell phone, she dialed the number for Strickland's Boarding House. Fortunately, Melba answered. She certainly hadn't wanted to leave a message. "Melba, it's Jazzy Cates."

"Hi, honey. How are you? Getting used to married life?"

So what could she say to that? She could hang up and think of something else. She could drive herself back to Thunder Canyon.

Not yet.

"Melba, I need to know if you still have the room I was renting."

Silence met her question.

"You want your room back?"

"Is it still available?"

"Yes, it is. Did you and your young man have a fight?"

If it had been a fight, they could make up. If it had been a fight, maybe she would have gotten out all of her feelings. If it had been a fight, there could still be hope.

"You could say that. I just need to be by myself for a while."

"Well, come on back, honey. You know that coffee is always brewing and there's hot water for tea. I baked apple bread, too. Comfort food."

"Thanks, Melba. I'll be over soon."

After Jazzy packed her suitcase, after she got into her car and switched on the ignition, she backed out of Brooks's driveway. Instead of heading for town and Strickland's, she headed for the Bar S. She didn't expect Brooks to be at his dad's clinic this early. In fact, she didn't want to see him. She couldn't see him. Not until she felt as if she had her emotions all under control. But she *did* want to see his father. She had something to say to him and she just hoped he was in a receptive mood.

Barrett had a mug in his hand when he opened the door. "It's tea," he said with a broad smile. "Herbal. I've still cut caffeine out of my diet."

"Good for you," she said with as much enthusiasm as she could muster. She knew Barrett missed his coffee as much as he missed donuts. She'd brought him soup because she and Brooks hadn't eaten any last night, and she knew his dad liked it. Besides, it was a good excuse for stopping by.

She had two containers in the bag, and she said to him, "I brought you soup, enough to eat and freeze. Do you have a few minutes?"

"Sure. That teenager Brooks hornswoggled into helping me with chores won't get here for about an hour. He's catching on, but I still have to supervise."

Jazzy went inside the house to the kitchen. She stowed a container of soup in the refrigerator and the other one in the freezer. Barrett's freezer was still fairly stacked with other dinners she had made for him. Maybe they'd be the last. Maybe she wouldn't be seeing Barrett again. That thought deeply saddened her.

"Okay, missy. Sit down and tell me what's going on. You don't have the usual spring in your step. What did my son do now?"

For some reason, Barrett's comment made Jazzy angry. "You've got to stop blaming Brooks for trying to do the right thing."

Barrett looked a little surprised at her explosion. "You *do* need to sit down. You need some of this herbal tea more than I do." He pulled out a chair for her and pointed to it.

As she sat she said, "Brooks didn't do anything wrong. He tried to do something right."

Barrett sat across from her and hiked up one brow. "And—"

"He's the most honest, value-oriented man I know. The only thing he did was try to...try to protect *you*."

After a long pause, Barrett's voice was wary as he encouraged, "Go on."

She was going to get it all out. Every bit of it. There was simply no reason why she shouldn't. Simply no reason why Barrett shouldn't know all of the truth. "If you had just trusted Brooks enough to hand down the practice to him...if you had been reasonable about your own health, then I never would have gotten caught up in a pretend marriage that turned out to be not so pretend!"

Barrett leaned back in his chair and eyed her. "Let's slow down a bit so I can make sure I understand what you're saying. You think I should have handed the practice down to Brooks?"

"Of course you should have. Or at least formed a joint venture after he graduated. It wasn't his fault Lynnette took up with another guy. She didn't have what it takes to be a veterinarian's wife. She didn't have what it takes to live in a small town. You blamed him for that."

"Is that what he said?"

"Of course that's *not* what he said. He blamed himself, too. And that was reinforced by *you* blaming him."

"I never knew why they broke up," Barrett muttered. "He didn't tell me. He just said something about long hours and her not wanting to live in a small town."

"That was only part of it. And she blamed the breakup on that. But she hurt him badly, Mr. Smith, and that's why he hasn't wanted to get involved with anyone since."

"Until you came along."

She sighed, took a deep breath and plunged in. "The night I officially met Brooks, he'd argued with you about your health. He was so frustrated and so worried. That's why he decided to set up a private practice. I happened to be on the bar stool next to him. We'd run into each other before that, but not officially introduced. That night, we talked. He asked me to come work for him."

"Must have liked you right away to do that."

"Maybe so. I don't know. But the icing on our wedding cake was because you wouldn't listen to reason when you were in the hospital. That day, Brooks asked me to marry him. We made a deal. He offered me his grandmother's land if I married him for a year. He figured in a year, he could help get your health turned around and then everything would go back to normal."

She shook her head. "There is no normal. Last night, he realized…he realized it's not going to work. He wants to split up. He doesn't want to be married."

Barrett cocked his head, studied her carefully and she suspected he could see way too much. He cleared his throat. "I can see the Smith pride has gotten us both into a peck of trouble. I *do* trust Brooks. But the truth is—I could see him going down the same road I took. I'd been a true workaholic all my life. I saw my family suffer because of it. I knew only one thing could save Brooks—if he found a woman he cared about as much as he cared about himself…as much as he cared about his furry patients. I wanted him to find that woman and build a life with her. I wanted him to marry and settle down so he'd have a reason to come home."

Jazzy's dejection must have shown on her face.

"He said the marriage isn't going to work out, huh? Do you believe that?"

When Jazzy didn't respond, Barrett leaned across the table and patted her hand with his. "Do you love him?"

She couldn't keep the tears from her voice. "I do."

"You know what? I think he loves you, too, whether he admits it or not. I've seen the way he looks at you. And you can't tell me he would have gotten himself tied up to a woman if he didn't care for her. I don't know what happened between the two of you, but give him a little time and maybe he'll come to his senses."

"What if he doesn't?"

Barrett's heavy brow hiked up. "Then he's a danged fool."

Brooks finished with his last patient of the morning at Buckskin Clinic, checked out Mr. Gibbs with his Doberman pinscher, handled the man's check and watched him leave. Then he glanced around the empty reception area, heard no sounds of Jazzy moving around in the exam rooms and realized how much he missed her. He not only missed her by his side here in the office... he missed her, period. Had she driven back to Thunder Canyon? Or was she still at his place?

His place. He had begun thinking of it as *their* place. Everything—every memory, every touch and kiss—that they'd experienced last night came back to haunt him. Thinking about it all was like a punch in the gut. He thought about staying with Dallas and his kids again tonight. The boys had been a distraction, that was for sure. But even Dallas's kids couldn't distract him from the memory of the look in Jazzy's eyes when he'd said he wanted out...when he'd said their deal was no longer a deal...when he'd said his father might as well know sooner rather than later.

His dad.

Brooks had to settle everything with him now. He didn't want his father finding out about the breakup of his marriage from somebody else.

Fifteen minutes later, Brooks was in his father's kitchen, watching his dad ladle soup from a plastic container into a bowl. "You look as if you need some lunch," Barrett said. "What's up?"

Brooks didn't know where to begin. "Jazzy and I... we—"

Barrett pushed the soup into the microwave, shut the door and set the timer. "You and Jazzy what?"

"We don't...we didn't have a real marriage. She's probably on her way back to Thunder Canyon."

With those words the rest of Brooks's sorry tale poured out—how they'd connected at the Ace in the Hole, how she'd agreed to work for him, how he'd come up with the brilliant idea of a marriage of convenience. "I made an appointment to see a lawyer this week and transfer Grandma's land to her." He expected a blowup from his father at that, but he didn't get it.

"Are you sure you want to do that?" was all his father asked.

"Jazzy deserves it for putting up with this whole situation. For—"

"*Why* does Jazzy deserve it? She went into this thing with open eyes just like you did. Fools, both of you. But consenting fools."

"Look, Dad, we just never realized what was going to happen. We thought we could keep it a business agreement and we couldn't."

"So feelings got involved?" his father asked.

"Hell, yes, feelings got involved," Brooks erupted, standing up, walking around the table. "And there's not a thing I can do about them. I'm not marriage material. Working the two practices is going to keep me swamped up to my eyeballs. Besides, there's a reason Lynnette broke our engagement. There's a reason she fell for someone else. She said it was the hours, but it was something deeper than that. I was missing something—something as a man—that would keep her there."

Had this been the real reason he hadn't dated for the past four years? Was this the real reason he kept himself guarded where women were concerned? He was clearly lacking some special ingredient he needed to be a good husband and maybe a father someday.

"Brooks," his father said sharply.

He stopped pacing and stared at his dad.

"You're missing *nothing*. Did it occur to you that your relationship with Lynnette was missing something? Maybe *she* was missing a loyalty factor that led to her infidelity."

Brooks's mouth dropped open.

"Jazzy was here earlier. She explained what the two of you did. She gave me a dressing-down because I didn't trust you enough to hand over my practice. She told me about Lynnette and added that my lack of faith in you didn't help the situation. I've got to tell you, son. I *do* have faith in you. I *am* proud of you. But I wanted you to find a woman like your mom who could ground you. I wanted you with a woman who could make a home for you. I wanted you to have a wife to be the center of your world...who could keep you from working too long and too much. I should have made your mom the center of my world and I didn't. If I had, maybe she wouldn't have died so soon. If I had, maybe I would have seen the symptoms. *I* would have, should have been taking care of her at the end, not your grandmother. I did everything all wrong, and I didn't want you doing it wrong, too."

Brooks had never known any of this. But that's because he and his dad had never really talked. Not about the kind of things that mattered. Stunned, he asked, "So you blame yourself for Mom's death?"

"I blame myself for not loving her the right way. I blame myself for being pigheaded, in denial and too focused on work that served like a shield so I didn't have to give too much of myself. Don't you make the same damn mistake."

The microwave beeped. Barrett removed the soup bowl and put it on the table. "So what happened between you and Jazzy that made this whole thing blow up?"

Oh, no. Brooks wasn't going there.

Barrett narrowed his eyes. "Fine. My guess is your marriage of convenience got a little inconvenient. You're both confused because things happened so fast."

"I'm not confused," Brooks said, realizing now he had been miserable since he'd left Jazzy in his condo.

"Do you want out of the marriage?" his father demanded to know.

Last night when he'd made love to Jazzy, he'd realized in a blinding flash of earth-shattering proportions that he *had* been making love to her. It wasn't just sex. It had been so much more that the experience had rattled and disconcerted and even panicked him. He'd given her his word their marriage would be a business deal. He'd gone back on his word, which was something he *never* did.

"Not confused, huh?" his father asked with a sly smile. "Seems to me you're *plenty* confused. So think about a few things. How would you feel if Jazzy left for Thunder Canyon and never came back? How would you feel if you didn't see her every day? Just how would you feel if Jazzy Cates Smith got involved with someone else?"

Brooks didn't know where to turn. Facing those questions made him want to ram his fist through a wall. And why was that?

The fact was that the sexual electricity between him and Jazzy had wired him since he'd met her. But even more than that, her sweetness and caring, her perky outlook, lifted him up above a place where he'd been. She'd become the sunlight in his days, the moonlight in his nights. She'd become someone he treasured, a woman he respected...and *loved.* Jazzy had become the epitome of everything he'd been running from and everything he'd hoped for.

She was everything he wanted.

"So," Barrett drawled. "If you're not confused, just what do you feel for her?"

Brooks sighed. "I love her."

"Then why are you sitting here eating lunch with me? Go get her."

"I don't know where she is. She might have driven back to Thunder Canyon."

"She didn't. Not yet. She's at Strickland's."

Brooks started for the door.

Barrett called after him, "For what it's worth, she's in love with you, too. She has to be to put up with me."

Brooks prayed his dad was right as he climbed into his truck and picked up his cell phone. He skimmed through his contacts and dialed Strickland's, hoping to get Melba. He did.

"Melba, its Brooks Smith. Is Jazzy there?"

"I just took her a cup of tea a little while ago. Do you want me to get her?"

"No. I just wanted to make sure she was there."

"She's pretty upset," Melba told him. "Are you going to upset her more?"

"I certainly hope not. Can you keep her there if she tries to go out? I should be there in about twenty minutes."

"She's not going anywhere. She doesn't want anyone to see her crying."

Brooks felt as low as he could possibly feel. The last thing he'd ever wanted to do was hurt Jazzy. So he told Melba, "I'll see what I can do about that."

Twenty minutes later to the minute, he stood in front of Jazzy's door, a bouquet of roses in his hand. Thank goodness Nina had had some fresh flowers. Maybe they'd at least get him in to talk to Jazzy. He knocked.

Jazzy called through the door, "I'm okay, Melba. Really. I don't need any more tea."

"It's not Melba," he called back.

When Jazzy opened her door, slowly, as if she was afraid to let him in, he could easily see she was miserable, too. He held out the roses to her, taking in everything about the woman he loved, trying to absorb the fact that she held his future happiness in her hands.

"I know these will never be enough to make up for all the mistakes I made. But I want you to come home with me."

Jazzy's expression changed from cautious to defiant. "I did that before and you left."

"That's because I was a fool."

She didn't take the roses, and she crossed her arms over her chest. "You're not a fool anymore? What's changed?"

He deserved that. He deserved her not making this easy. He stepped inside her room, closed the door and laid the roses on the bed. Then he faced her, knowing this couldn't be done in half measure. "I didn't ask you to marry me on a whim."

Jazzy's arms uncrossed as she dropped them to her sides…and she waited.

Taking a risk, he took her hands in his and pulled her closer. "I might not have realized it the exact moment I sat on that stool at the Ace in the Hole, but you're everything I should have been looking for, everything I missed, everything I want. I love you, Jazzy. I don't know when it happened and I don't know why. Maybe it was when you first smiled at me. Maybe it was when you painted my office. Maybe it was when we went to the Falls. I know now it was before I said 'I do.' Making love with you was absolutely incredible. But I felt overwhelmed with desires I didn't even understand. But now I do."

Since she wasn't pulling away, since she seemed to be listening, since her eyes were glistening with unshed tears, he pulled her arms up around his neck and held her in a loving embrace. "I want a real marriage with you, Jazzy. I want to build a life, a future, a home with you. Can you forgive how stupid I've been and be my wife through thick and thin, better and worse, today and forever?"

"Oh, Brooks…"

When she said his name like that all he wanted to do was love her forever—

His heated kiss exposed his longing, his desire, the love he felt and the love he hoped to feel in the future.

She broke off the kiss, cupped his face in her hands, and said, "I love you, too, Brooks. I want to stand beside you, work beside you, fall asleep in your arms every night and have your babies."

"Babies?" he asked with a quirked brow.

"Babies," she assured him.

Sweeping her into his arms, he laughed and carried her to the single bed. When he kissed her again, he didn't stop and neither did she. They'd found their future in each other's arms.

Epilogue

Jazzy and Brooks walked through the field, holding gloved hands. The weather had turned colder, but they didn't care about the chill. This was something they wanted to do. They glanced at each other often, then studied their surroundings.

When they stopped in the midst of field grass about two hundred yards from the road, Jazzy said, "I can tell Mom and Dad are accepting our marriage now. They want to know how they can help with plans for the house."

"Our visit with them over the weekend brought us closer. When your dad and I went riding, he was almost friendly!"

"They could see we're in love."

Brooks grinned at her. "Because we didn't leave our bedroom till late Saturday morning?"

"Maybe," Jazzy said with a laugh. "Or maybe it's because when we look at each other, anyone within fifty feet can tell. We give off signals like Laila and Jackson, Abby and Cade, Annabel and Thomas do."

"Give me a signal," Brooks said, teasing her and bringing her close for a kiss. Their passion caught fire until Brooks broke away and raggedly stated, "If we don't want to make love in the middle of a field in freezing weather, we'd better concentrate on why we came." He waved to the east. "I can see the house sitting on that rise. Do you want one story or two?"

"I like those plans you found for a two-story log home. And I was thinking..."

"Uh-oh. Always dangerous."

She swatted his arm.

He hugged her, amusement dancing in his eyes. "Just teasing. What were you thinking?"

"I could start taking business courses online so I know how to run the operational side of a horse-rescue ranch. What do you think?"

"I think that's a terrific idea. Self-serving on my part because I want as much time with you as we can manage. To that end, I'm interviewing two possible partners this week. One is driving all the way from Bozeman. I'm video conferencing with the other. Dad's going to sit in."

Suddenly they heard a truck rumbling down the access road. "Speak of the devil," Brooks said in an amused tone.

Barrett climbed from his truck and leisurely walked toward them. "I thought I'd give you two a little time out here then come put in my two cents before you go back to Kalispell. Which, by the way, seems like a commute you don't need."

"Nothing in Rust Creek Falls is available, Dad. I spoke with the real-estate agent again this morning."

"Actually, something *is* available," his father assured him.

"Just what do you know that we don't?" Brooks kept his arm around Jazzy's waist.

"I was thinking," his father said.

"It's going around," Jazzy joked with a glance at Brooks.

Barrett ignored her comment and went on, looking a little...nervous? "It will take at least six months for you to get a place built. Especially if we have a rough winter. In fact, you might have to wait until spring to start construction."

"That's possible," Brooks conceded.

"So why don't you come stay with me?" Barrett hurriedly continued. "You can have the whole upstairs and as much privacy as you want. You can even make a spare bedroom into your own sitting room with a TV. After work, you can go your way and I can go mine. What do you think?"

Jazzy was totally surprised by the offer and Brooks seemed to be, too.

Brooks said, "I can't give you a decision right now. Jazzy and I will have to talk about it."

"Talking is a good thing when you're married. I'll let you to it. But don't stay out here too long or you'll freeze your tails off."

As quickly as Barrett had appeared, he gunned the engine of his truck and drove away in a spit of gravel.

Brooks squeezed Jazzy nearer to combine their warmth. "We could go sit in the truck."

"You think this is going to be a long discussion?" she asked, studying his face.

"I don't know. Is it? Tell me what you honestly think. Shouldn't newlyweds have total privacy?"

"That depends. It seems to me if we want privacy, we can find it—in the barn, in the clinic at the end of the day, in an upstairs hideaway. I really think your dad means what he says. We could have our own place up there. And...we wouldn't have to worry about him."

"It would be temporary...just until we get the house built."

"Exactly. Who knows? Till then maybe we can convince him to date."

"You are *such* an optimist."

"Isn't that why you married me?"

He shook his head. "I married you because I was falling hopelessly in love with you."

"And I with you."

As snowflakes began a fluttering shower around them, they kissed again with a fire that could warm any cold winter day...a fire that could last a lifetime.

* * * * *

Kissing Paige Dalton was not the smartest thing he'd ever done.

On the other hand, he knew it had been inevitable, that they had been moving inexorably toward this moment since he'd walked her home from the town hall debate earlier in the week.

One kiss—just to prove to himself that she didn't have the same hold on him that she used to. Except that one kiss had proven him wrong. She tasted just like he remembered—right down to the cherry lip balm she'd favored when she was sixteen. Just one kiss, and he knew that he wanted her as much now as he'd always wanted her.

Maybe even more…

MONTANA MAVERICKS:
RUST CREEK COWBOYS:
Better saddle up. It's going to be a
bumpy ride!

A MAVERICK UNDER THE MISTLETOE

BY
BRENDA HARLEN

First published in Great Britain 2013
by Mills & Boon, an imprint of Harlequin (UK) Limited,
Eton House, 18-24 Paradise Road, Richmond, Surrey TW9 1SR

© Harlequin Books S.A. 2013

Special thanks and acknowledgement to Brenda Harlen for her contribution to the Montana Mavericks: Rust Creek Cowboys continuity.

ISBN: 978 0 263 90157 3

23-1113

Harlequin (UK) policy is to use papers that are natural, renewable and recyclable products and made from wood grown in sustainable forests. The logging and manufacturing processes conform to the legal environmental regulations of the country of origin.

Printed and bound in Spain
by Blackprint CPI, Barcelona

Brenda Harlen is a former family law attorney turned work-at-home mum and national bestselling author who has written more than twenty books for Mills & Boon. Her work has been validated by industry awards (including an RWA Golden Heart® Award and the *RT Book Reviews* Reviewers' Choice Award) and by the fact that her kids think it's cool that she's "a real author."

Brenda lives in southern Ontario with her husband and two sons. When she isn't at the computer working on her next book, she can probably be found at the arena, watching a hockey game. Keep up-to-date with Brenda on Facebook or send her an email at brendaharlen@yahoo.com.

To Chris R., Christyne, Leanne, Karen and Vikki—
brainstormers, researchers and community planners
extraordinaire. Thanks for making the writing of this
book not just easier but a lot more fun.

To Susan Litman—for keeping us on track while still
letting us color outside of the lines. (And yes, I know
that's a mixed metaphor :))

With thanks also to my good friend Anna Perrin,
who always has the solutions to my last-minute plot
problems (even if I can't always use them).

Chapter One

In Sutter Traub's opinion, Rust Creek Falls was as irresistible—and fickle—as a woman. Once upon a time his heart had belonged to this town and he couldn't have imagined ever living anywhere else. Then she'd turned him out and turned her back on him.

Just like the only woman he'd ever loved.

Of course, he'd come back when she'd needed him—the town, that was, not the woman. Because Paige Dalton had *never* needed him, and she wouldn't ever ask for his help if she did, and thinking about her now was only going to stir up memories and feelings he didn't want stirred up.

So he focused his attention on the reason that he was standing in the back corner of town hall now: the imminent election. When his brother Collin had recently announced his intention to run for mayor of Rust Creek Falls, Sutter had impulsively volunteered to be his campaign manager. Which had resulted in him spending a lot more time in town over the past few months than he'd ever intended when news of the floods had first brought him home, which meant that he wasn't going back to Seattle before the last ballot was counted.

But for now he just wanted this debate to be over.

It was the last public face-off between the two mayoral candidates—Collin Traub and Nathan Crawford—before the citizens of Rust Creek Falls went to the polls on Thursday, and though it had just gotten underway, Sutter wished it was already done.

He couldn't have said why, but he had an uneasy feeling about the event. It might have had something to do with Nate's smug expression when they'd been setting up. It was as if he had something up his sleeve and, knowing the Crawfords, Sutter didn't doubt it for a minute.

As the debate progressed, he gradually began to relax. Collin was comfortable in front of the crowd, answering questions easily and confidently. He had a clearly defined plan to return Rust Creek Falls to its former glory and he made sure the residents knew it. Nate focused more on the history of the town than its future, and more on why he was the better candidate to fix the problems than how he was going to do so. But both candidates were—at least to all outward appearances—respectful of one another, and the spectators seemed to be listening to each side.

But when Thelma McGee—the former mayor's mother and moderator of the event—stood up to announce that the debate was finished, a member of the audience loudly pushed back his chair and rose to his feet.

A Crawford supporter, Sutter immediately suspected, and the gleam in Nate's eyes made him think that there was nothing spontaneous about the man's actions.

He was a military man in a dress uniform with his medals proudly displayed on his chest, and Sutter's heart immediately began to pound. One sleeve of the man's uniform hung loose because he had no arm to put through it. Not just a decorated veteran but a wounded war hero.

Perspiration beaded on Sutter's brow and trickled down his spine.

Thelma, bless her, never wavered. "I'm sorry, sir—"

"Master Sergeant Dean Riddell." He barked out the name as if it was a military order.

"Yes, well, we've run out of time tonight and—"

"Time is irrelevant when our boys are fighting to protect our freedoms. And I want to remind the good people of Rust Creek Falls that they need to know if these candidates support our armed forces."

"While your concern is acknowledged and appreciated, the eventual mayor of Rust Creek Falls has no voice with respect to military activity or spending. This is strictly about local politics."

While Sutter heard and silently applauded her point, no one else did, because they'd all started talking and debating among themselves.

"Ladies and gentlemen—" Collin tried to settle the crowd while Nate just sat back with his arms folded across his chest and a smug smile on his face. "Do I need to remind you that my brother, Major Forrest Traub, is a decorated war hero, too? He fought valiantly and tirelessly for his country—for all of us—and I have never been anything but supportive of his efforts and his sacrifices."

"Can you say the same thing about your campaign manager?" the master sergeant demanded.

And Sutter knew the damage had been done. It didn't matter that everything Collin said was true; what mattered to these people was that there was mud to be slung—and it was Sutter's fault that Collin was the one wearing it.

He'd been young and impetuous and probably a little too outspoken in his efforts to convince his brother that he'd already gone above and beyond in the service of his country. He'd vehemently objected when Forrest had announced his intention to reenlist for another tour, because he'd just wanted his brother to stay home and be safe.

But Forrest had chosen to go back, and when he returned to Rust Creek Falls again after his medical discharge, Sutter had known the scars on his brother's leg were insignificant compared to the damage to his soul. Thankfully, months of physical therapy and falling in love with Angie Anderson had started healing his body and his heart—but his relationship with his brother was going to need something more.

Obviously no one in Rust Creek Falls had forgotten Sutter's objections. And while he acknowledged and accepted that he would always be haunted by the mistakes of his past, he hadn't expected that anyone else would have to pay for his outspokenness. Listening to the crowd, now thoroughly stirred up by Master Sergeant Riddell, he finally realized that his presence could hinder Collin's campaign rather than help—exactly as Nate Crawford had intended.

They were still murmuring and bickering when another spectator stood up on the other side of the room. And Sutter's heart began to pound even harder inside his chest when he recognized Paige Dalton.

He hadn't seen her enter the hall, hadn't known she was there. That in and of itself was a surprise, because Sutter had always had a sixth sense where Paige was concerned. A sixth sense that had been honed by self-preservation since his return to Rust Creek Falls a few months earlier.

Looking at her now, she took his breath away. It wasn't just that she was beautiful, but the way she stood—with her spine stiff and her chin up—she looked like a warrior ready to take on the entire population of Rust Creek Falls, or at least those who were assembled in town hall tonight. She was wearing a soft pink peasant-style blouse over a raspberry-colored skirt. Her long, dark brown hair hung straight down to the middle of her back, and her dark chocolate-colored eyes were focused and intense.

He braced himself for her attack. He didn't care what Master Sergeant Riddell or anyone else in Rust Creek Falls thought about him—except insofar as it might impact Collin's hopes of winning the election—but he'd never stopped caring about Paige and he hated knowing that she was disappointed in him.

"Can we focus on what's relevant here?" she said to the crowd. She didn't yell—in fact, she raised her voice just enough to be heard. And as she continued to speak, her volume dropped further, forcing others to stop talking in order to hear what she was saying. "First, and most important, is the fact that it is *Collin* Traub who is running for office, not Sutter.

"Second, regardless of whether any of us agree with statements that Sutter made with respect to his brother's decision to reenlist five years ago, those statements were *his opinion,* it was *five years ago,* and we need to *focus on the issues* that are relevant to Rust Creek Falls *in the present* and the *candidates who are actually running* in this election."

She paused a moment to take a breath and to give everyone a minute to think about what she'd said before she continued. "But even if it was Sutter instead of Collin who was running for mayor, he would get my vote because he's the type of man who's willing to stand up for what he believes, regardless of popular opinion or what anyone else might think. That is a man of conviction, and that is the kind of man who gets things done, and what Rust Creek Falls needs right now is someone who can get things done.

"Thankfully, that is a trait he shares with his brother Collin. And that is why *Collin* Traub is the type of man we need in charge of our town during this difficult time.

"With all due respect, Master Sergeant Riddell, the

army isn't coming here to rebuild our town. And I think you would agree that our servicemen and women have more important things to do. That leaves it up to *us,* the citizens of Rust Creek Falls, to figure out the best way to get things done—and the best person to help us do so. I think that person is Collin Traub."

Then she picked up her jacket and calmly turned to walk down the aisle between the folding chairs and out the door.

"Thank you again for your time tonight—"

Thelma McGee was speaking again, but Sutter didn't hang around to listen to what the moderator said. He needed to see Paige. He wasn't entirely sure why, he just knew that he did.

He slipped out through a side door and raced around to the front of the building. Paige couldn't have had more than a two-minute head start on him, but she seemed to have vanished into thin air. He scanned the dimly lit street and finally spotted her when she neared a lamppost at the end of the block.

"Paige—wait!"

She paused at the corner of North Main Street and as he drew nearer, he saw the reluctance on her face. She looked as if she'd rather bolt than wait, but she held her ground until he reached her side. Then she turned east up Cedar Street, obviously wanting to be out of sight of town hall when the crowd dispersed.

He didn't blame her for not wanting be seen with him. They'd both grown up in this town where almost everyone knew everyone else, and it was safe to assume that most of the residents knew at least some of Sutter and Paige's history together.

"I just wanted to thank you," he said when he fell into step beside her.

"I didn't do it for you," she told him.

"Why did you do it?"

"Because Nate's been running an underhanded campaign since Collin threw his hat into the ring, but dragging a war veteran into this debate solely to discredit your brother…" She trailed off, shaking her head. "That's a new low, even for Nate."

"Are you sure he set it up?"

"I saw him talking to the master sergeant before the debate," she confided. "I have absolutely no doubt that he planted him in the audience to stir up trouble."

"Well, I don't think the tactic was nearly as successful as he'd hoped, not after your little speech."

She shrugged. "I was there because I want to be an informed voter. My personal bias aside, I wanted to hear what the candidates had to say, how they responded to questions. Everything I saw and heard tonight confirmed my belief that Collin is the best mayoral candidate, and I wanted to make sure that people left the hall talking about him—not you."

"Well, I appreciate what you said, anyway," he told her. "I know it couldn't have been easy to speak up in my defense—even if it was for my brother—after… everything."

After…everything.

Sutter's words echoed in Paige's mind, making her wonder if that was really how he thought about the fact that he'd broken her heart and shattered her hopes and dreams. Had their relationship been so meaningless, and their breakup so inconsequential to him, that he could just categorize those events as "everything"?

She looked up at him, amazed and annoyed that even after five years a simple glance was enough to make her heart pound. Of course, he probably had that effect on a lot of women. At six feet two inches, with the solid, muscular build of a real cowboy, he turned heads no matter where he went. The thick, light brown hair, deep blue eyes and quick smile kept those heads turned in his direction. She deliberately tore her gaze away.

It infuriated her that after five years, her heart was still aching from his callous dismissal, while he seemed completely unaffected. But there was no way she was going to ask for clarification. Instead she only said, "It was a long time ago."

"Was it?" he challenged, his voice quieter now and tinged with a hint of sadness.

Or maybe she was only hearing what she wanted to hear.

"I'll admit, there are days when it seems like our relationship was in a different lifetime," he told her. "And there are other days when I would swear it was only yesterday. When I can close my eyes and see you right in front of me, reach out as if to touch the softness of your skin, breathe in and catch the scent of your perfume."

She wouldn't let the soft seduction of his words or his voice sway her. "I think you've been breathing in something that's not legal in this state without a prescription."

"Ouch—that was harsh."

"What kind of response did you expect?"

"I don't know," he admitted. "Maybe I just wanted to know that you think about me sometimes, too."

"I don't. Because it wasn't yesterday—it was five years ago, and I have too much going on in my life right now to think about what used to be or might have been."

But her words were a lie. The truth was, she didn't just think about Sutter sometimes. She thought about him far too often. It didn't seem to matter that he'd been gone for five years, because her heart had never quite healed. And even after all that time, whenever she saw him—which, thankfully, hadn't been very often before the horrible flood had brought him back to Rust Creek Falls—it felt like ripping the scab off of the wound.

And yet when a stranger who didn't even know him started attacking his character, Paige couldn't seem to help herself from flying to his defense. Because regardless of what had happened between them, she knew that deep inside Sutter was a good man. The man she'd once loved more than anything.

"So tell me what's going on in your life," he said now.

She turned to look at him. "Why?"

"Because I want to know."

"Well, I've been teaching my fifth-grade class in my living room because we don't have a school anymore—which is one of the reasons I'm so invested in the outcome of this election. We need to get the new school built because our kids deserve better than what we've been able to do for them so far."

"Fifth grade?" Sutter frowned. "I think Dallas's eldest is in fifth grade."

She nodded. "Ryder's in my class."

"He's had a rough go of it…since his mother walked out."

"It hasn't been easy on any of the boys." She felt herself softening in response to his obvious concern about his nephew, just a little, and steeled herself against it. "But when one person walks out of a relationship, it's inevitable that someone else is going to be hurt."

His gaze narrowed. "Are we still talking about Ryder?"

"Of course," she agreed, the picture of innocence. "Who else would we be talking about?"

"Us," he said bluntly. "I thought you might have

been referring to the end of our relationship—when you dumped me."

She hated that he could still see through her so easily. "I wasn't talking about us, and I didn't dump you," she denied. "I simply refused to run away with you. Because that's what you did—you ran."

"I'm back now," he told her.

And standing close to him, it was all too easy for Paige to remember the way she used to feel about him. Far too easy to want to feel that way again. Thankfully she wasn't a naive teenager anymore, and she wouldn't let it happen. Because sooner or later Sutter would leave Rust Creek Falls again. He always did.

"Yes, you're back now," she acknowledged. "But for how long?"

Sutter's gaze slid away. "Well, as Collin's campaign manager, I'll be hanging around until the election."

His response was hardly unexpected, and yet Paige couldn't deny that she felt a pang of disappointment in response to his words. "Yeah, that's what I thought."

"It's not easy being here," he reminded her. "No one has ever welcomed me back with open arms."

She would have. If he'd come home at any time during those first six months that he'd been gone, she would have welcomed him with open arms and a heart so full of love for him that it was near to bursting.

But he hadn't come home, not at all in the first year or for a very long time after. And the longer he was gone, the more she realized that the overwhelming love she felt for him wasn't reciprocated—at least not in the way she needed it to be if they were going to build a life together.

Instead, they'd each moved on without the other. By all accounts Sutter was doing very well in Seattle. Apparently he'd opened his own stables in the city and had established quite the reputation for himself. Paige had been sincerely happy to hear the news and genuinely pleased for him, because she was more than content with her own life in Rust Creek Falls.

She loved her job, she lived close enough to her family that she saw them regularly—although she sometimes wondered if maybe a little *too* frequently—she had good friends and she even went out on occasion. She didn't want or need anything more—and she certainly didn't want Sutter Traub turning her life upside down again.

"You saw that tonight," he pointed out to her. "No one has forgotten what happened, why I left, and no one will miss me when I'm gone again."

She could tell that he believed it, and her heart ached for him. "This is your home," she told him. "Whether you choose to live here or not, this is where you belong— with your family and your friends and everyone else who cares about you."

He managed a wry smile, but his tone when he responded was more wistful than skeptical. "Would you be included in that list?"

Chapter Two

"Of course," Paige agreed. "Despite everything that's happened between us, we've always been friends."

Even as the words tumbled out of her mouth, she wished she could haul them back. Because as much as she believed coming home and making peace with his family was the right thing for Sutter, she knew it wouldn't work out so well for her. Not when even this brief conversation had her churned up inside.

"Well, speaking in confidence to a friend," Sutter said, "I'm afraid Collin's fighting an uphill battle in this election."

She was surprised, and grateful, for the change of topic. "What makes you say that?"

"The fact that every time I go into town, I hear rumblings—and none of them are very subtle."

"What kind of rumblings?"

"Just the other day I was at the general store and I heard Ginny Nigh comment to Lilah Goodwin that it's a sorry state when people nowadays don't understand the importance of family values. It used to be that when a man got a woman pregnant, he did the right thing and married the mother of his child."

"You think she was talking about Clayton?"

"I know she was. Of course, she didn't mention the fact that Clay didn't even know Delia was pregnant until she showed up on his doorstep with the baby—or the fact that Delia turned around and hightailed it out of town only a few days later."

"Leaving your brother with the son he never knew he had—which, to me, proves that he *does* understand family values. He stepped right up to be a daddy to Bennett and never tried to pawn him off on anybody else."

He smiled, just a little. "I wish you'd been at the store with me."

But of course they both knew that such an occurrence would have generated gossip of a different kind.

"Anyway, you shouldn't worry about Ginny—everyone knows she's just an old busybody."

"Unfortunately, she isn't the only one who's been talking. Even the minister in church the other day was talking about wedding vows and that 'till death do us part' needs to mean till death and not until one of the spouses decides he or she has had enough."

"Pastor Alderson has never made any secret of the fact that he's opposed to divorce."

"And Dallas is divorced—but he only took the step to end his marriage after his wife walked out on him and the kids."

"I think most people around here know that the divorce was instigated by Laurel's abandonment."

"Do they?" he challenged. "Or do they see it as proof that the Traubs don't reflect the traditional family values that are a cornerstone of Rust Creek Falls?"

"Collin has to pick his battles," Paige said reasonably. "He can't expect to win every argument on every issue, so he should focus on what he's doing and not worry about rumors."

"That's what we've been trying to do," Sutter admitted. "The purpose of his national online initiative to help rebuild Rust Creek Falls was designed to give people a reason to look past the devastation and focus on the positive."

"'A vote for Collin Traub is a vote for success and prosperity for the future of Rust Creek Falls,'" she quoted.

He grinned. "You've been reading our press."

"I've been reading everything in the press," she clarified. "I like to make an informed decision."

"Are you seeing anyone?"

She stopped in the middle of the sidewalk, stunned by the abrupt change of topic. "How is that any of your business?"

"Maybe it's not," he admitted. "But I heard that you've been keeping company with a foreman at the lumber mill, and I want to know if it's true."

"It's true." She started walking again. "I've been dating Alex Monroe for a few months now."

"Is it serious?"

"Again—none of your business," she said, because she wasn't going to admit to Sutter that her relationship with the other man wasn't anywhere close to being serious.

Alex was a great guy. He was attractive and well mannered and she enjoyed spending time with him. Unfortunately there was no real spark or sizzle between them, nothing to make her think that their relationship would ever progress to the next level.

Her sisters, Lani and Lindsay, claimed that Paige wouldn't ever be able to have a serious relationship with Alex—or any other man—so long as she was still carrying a torch for Sutter. She, of course, denied that was true, because she'd given up hope that Sutter would come back to her a long time ago.

But standing beside him now, she was suddenly overwhelmed by the memories of what they'd once shared, and she realized that maybe she had been comparing other men to "the one who got away." But she didn't think that was so unusual. After all, Sutter had been her first love and her first lover, and she couldn't imagine any subsequent relationship having that same depth and intensity.

And she wasn't going to waste even another minute of her time worrying about it tonight. She started walking again, and he fell into step beside her.

A few minutes later, she paused outside a two-story saltbox-style house with steel-blue clapboard siding and wide white trim around the front door and windows.

"This is mine," she said, and felt a familiar thrill when she spoke those words. Two years earlier, when she'd put in her offer for the house, she'd been excited—and then absolutely terrified when it was accepted. Gradually the terror had subsided, beaten back by endless weeks and months of intense manual labor to scrub and shine and prep and paint until she felt as if it was well and truly her own.

He gave the house a quick once-over. "Nice," he said approvingly.

She didn't want or need his approval, but she found herself smiling anyway. Because it *was* nice. More important, it was hers.

"Are you going to invite me in for coffee?" he asked.

"No."

His brows lifted. "Just no? You're not even going to make up some kind of lame excuse as to why you can't invite me in?"

"I don't need to make up an excuse," she told him. "The fact is, tomorrow is a school day and I have lesson plans to review."

The smile that flashed across his face actually made her knees weak.

"For a minute it was almost like we were back in high school," he said.

She'd thought the same thing as soon as the words were out of her mouth. There had been a lot of times when Sutter had tried to convince her to stay out with him instead of going home to finish her homework or study for an upcoming test. And a lot of times when she'd let herself be convinced. And when he'd finally walked her home, they'd still been reluctant to part, so they'd stood in the shadows of the back porch of her parents' house and kissed good-night. He'd spent a lot of time kissing her good-night.

Obviously he was remembering the same thing, because he took a step closer and said, "Are you going to let me kiss you good-night?"

"No." Though she knew she should hold her ground, she took an instinctive step back.

Sutter smiled knowingly. "Are you busy Thursday night?"

This second abrupt change in topic made her almost as wary as his previous request. "Why?"

"It's election night," he reminded her. "And the candidates and their supporters will be gathered at town hall for the results. Since you've declared your support for Collin, I thought you might want to be there."

She did believe Collin was the best candidate and he was definitely going to get her vote, but hanging out with his family and friends at town hall meant being around Sutter, and she wasn't sure if that was something she could handle.

"I'll think about it," she finally agreed, because once he'd made the offer, she knew that she wouldn't be able to *not* think about it. But she also knew that there was no way she could go.

The only hope she had of protecting her heart was to stay as far away from Sutter Traub as possible.

Since it wasn't an outright refusal, Sutter decided not to press Paige for a firm commitment. He simply waited until she'd unlocked her door, then he wished her a good night and headed back to town hall. He hadn't realized how far they'd walked until he had to make the trek back again without the pleasure of her company.

He'd enjoyed walking and talking with her like they'd done so many times before. But that was the past. He retraced his steps as he'd lived the past five years of his life—without her. And he tried not to think about everything they'd once meant to one another, and everything they'd lost.

Paige Dalton had been his soul mate and best friend. His heart had belonged to her, wholly and completely. She was the one woman he'd imagined spending the rest of his life with. He'd even proposed marriage before he'd left town, but she'd turned him down and turned her back on him, and he'd gone to Washington alone.

The transition from Rust Creek Falls to Seattle hadn't been an easy one, and for the first several months Sutter had doubted it would be a successful one. He'd tried working at various office jobs in the city, but he never found one that seemed to fit. Or maybe he was just too restless to sit behind a desk all day. It was only when he heard about a job opening for a horse trainer at a local stable that things began to turn around for him.

He'd always been good with animals and he'd quickly established a reputation for himself with the local horse set. After a couple of years working for someone else, he had both the money and the confidence he needed to venture out on his own.

Three years earlier, he'd opened Traub Stables, and he was gratified by its success. He was also pleased that his business had created a second market for CT Saddles—Collin's custom-made saddles and leather-goods business. That was all Sutter wanted—all he needed. Or so he'd believed until he'd come back to Rust Creek Falls again.

When he'd left town five years earlier, he'd vowed that he would never return. Of course, he'd been younger and more impulsive then, and the simple fact that his family was in Rust Creek Falls guaranteed that he wouldn't be able to stay away forever. Despite the harsh words that had been thrown around in the Traub household, he could never really turn his back on his family—even if he felt they'd turned their backs on him first.

So when he'd heard the news about the flood, he had to come home to make sure everything was okay at the ranch. Of course, it had taken him some time to get everything in order with his business so that he could feel comfortable leaving for a couple of weeks. And even then, his apprehension had increased with every mile that drew him closer to the Triple T. There was still tension in his family—most notably between Sutter and Forrest—and it had occurred to him that he might not be welcome. Especially if his war-hero brother had also decided to return.

Both Forrest and Clayton were living in Thunder Canyon these days with their new wives and, in Clayton's case, children. But Sutter was certain they would also be drawn back to Rust Creek Falls, eager to do anything they could to help out not just the Traub family but the larger community.

Another reason that Sutter had questioned his impulse to return was the possibility that he might run into

Paige Dalton. A possibility that had turned into a certainty when he found out that Collin was marrying Willa Christensen—a friend and colleague of Paige's.

Of his five brothers, Collin was the only one who got Sutter and who hadn't judged him for his less-than-enthusiastic support of Forrest's decision to return to Iraq. So when Collin had asked Sutter to be his best man, he hadn't even considered refusing. He hadn't found out until later that Paige would be Willa's maid of honor.

The wedding had been simple but beautiful. And Sutter and Paige had both focused on their respective duties and pretended to be oblivious to one another. At least, Sutter was pretending. And he'd *tried* to focus on his duties, but Paige had always been a distraction.

She was the most beautiful girl he'd ever known. Now that girl was a woman and even more of a distraction. Willa had been a gorgeous bride, and Sutter had been thrilled to see his brother so obviously in love and more contented than he'd ever been, but it was the bride's maid of honor who had caught—and held—Sutter's attention.

Her long dark hair had been fashioned into some kind of loose knot on top of her head, but a few strands had escaped to frame her delicate heart-shaped face. Her dark eyes had been enhanced with makeup, her sharp cheekbones highlighted and her sweetly curved lips had been painted a glossy pink color.

Her dress was a long, strapless column of pale lilac silk that hugged her curves. She'd been more skinny than thin as a girl, but there was no doubt she was a woman now. A woman with silky-smooth skin and beautiful shoulders that had seemed rather chilly whenever she'd turned them in his direction.

Unfortunately, her obvious disinterest had done nothing to cool the blood running through his veins. But he'd managed to get through the wedding without giving in to the desire to touch her, and he'd breathed a sigh of relief when the event was over.

He'd done a pretty good job of avoiding Paige in the months that had passed since then—until tonight, when his need just to see her and talk to her had overridden his common sense and sent him chasing after her.

When he'd offered to manage Collin's campaign, he'd claimed it was simply because he believed that his brother truly was the best person for the job—especially considering that the only other candidate was Nathan Crawford. He hadn't been willing to admit, even to himself, that Paige Dalton had been a factor in his decision to stay in Rust Creek Falls a little longer. Maybe he'd been an idiot where she was concerned, but he wasn't a masochist. Once bitten, twice shy and all that.

But now, three months later, he was still in Rust Creek Falls and still hoping to catch a glimpse of her around every corner. And that, he knew, was a definite sign that it was long past time to go back to Seattle.

He'd been making occasional trips back and forth, not so much to keep an eye on his business, because he trusted his stable manager absolutely, but to ensure that he was able to give the personal touch to his major clients. But he'd never stayed in Seattle more than a few days before he'd found a reason to return to Rust Creek Falls again. He decided now that he needed to get back to his real life before he let himself start believing that he could ever come home to stay. Because the more time he spent here, the more he remembered how it had felt to be part of the close-knit community, and the more he craved that sense of belonging again.

The town had come together and had made impressive headway with respect to the repairs that were needed.

It never ceased to amaze him how people managed to overcome their differences and work together in times of crisis. In fact, Collin and Nate had worked side by side on the Recovery Committee with Sheriff Gage Christensen—Willa's brother—and Thelma McGee.

Sutter had pitched in wherever help was needed and, as a result, had occasionally crossed paths with Paige. Each time he saw her, he was reminded of what they'd once had—and what he'd lost. And almost every night since his return, he dreamed of her when he went to sleep.

That was just one more reason that he was looking forward to going back to Seattle—so he could sleep through the night without dreams of a sexy, dark-eyed brunette disturbing his slumber. Not that the distance had helped him forget about Paige completely, but it had forced him to accept that she'd chosen a life without him. And he knew the best thing for him now was to get back to that life without her. Except that he'd made his brother a promise, and that meant that Sutter was going to be in Rust Creek Falls until the last ballot was counted.

His faith in his brother had not wavered once since Collin had announced his candidacy. If anything, the more he learned about his brother's plans and ideas for the town, the more convinced he was that Collin was the right man to lead Rust Creek Falls through this crisis and toward a better, stronger future. Unfortunately, instead of promoting his own ideas, Nathan Crawford was more interested in slinging mud at the Traubs.

For some reason that Sutter couldn't even pretend to understand, the Traubs and the Crawfords had been at odds for generations. According to the widely circulated rumors around town, the feud had originated with a business partnership gone wrong. Of course, that was only one version of the story and, depending on the telling, even it had several variations and discrepancies as to which party had done the wrong.

In any event, the animosity that existed between the families since before Sutter could remember had come to a head a few years earlier when Collin and Nate had gotten into a fight over accusations that Nate's girlfriend was stepping out with his nemesis. Collin's announcement that he would run against Nate in the election had further exacerbated the tensions.

"Where did you disappear to?" Collin demanded when Sutter finally got back to town hall.

The majority of the crowd had dispersed, leaving only a handful of people in the building: volunteers stacking up chairs and sweeping the floors, Willa in conversation with a young couple who were just as likely to be talking to her about their daughter who was in her kindergarten class as an issue regarding Collin's campaign.

"I needed some air," Sutter told his brother.

"You didn't follow Paige?"

He scowled. "I'm not a stalker, but yes, I did talk to her. I wanted to thank her for the things she said."

"Her words did interject rationale and reason into an uncomfortable situation—at least for the moment."

"She promised that you have her vote," Sutter told him.

"I'm grateful for that," Collin said. "But I'm more concerned about you."

"You've got my vote, too."

His brother cuffed the side of Sutter's head. "I meant that I'm concerned about you and Paige."

"There is no me and Paige—there hasn't been for a long time." Of course, knowing that fact didn't stop him from thinking about her—or wanting her. "Besides, she's seeing Alex Monroe."

"I know that she's gone out with him a few times," Collin admitted. "I don't know that it's exclusive, though."

"It doesn't matter," Sutter insisted. "My life is in Seattle now, and she made it clear a long time ago that she has no intention of ever leaving Rust Creek Falls."

"Your business is in Seattle," his brother agreed. "But your family is here."

"Now you sound like Paige," he grumbled.

"Really?" Collin seemed intrigued by the idea. "Well, where you choose to live is your decision. I just want to be sure that you're not planning to go anywhere before the election."

"I'm not, unless you want me to."

"I don't."

"That whole scene tonight—it happened because of me."

"It happened because Nate Crawford doesn't know how to play by the rules."

Sutter couldn't deny that was true, but he still hated to think that his brother could lose the election because of him. Certainly the tide of popular opinion had turned against him in a heartbeat tonight, until Paige's timely interjection.

"Desperate times call for desperate measures," Willa said, coming over to join in their conversation. "And I think Nate is feeling more than a little desperate."

Collin slid his arm around her. "Why do you say that?"

"Because he knows he's going to lose this election, and the defeat is going to be that much harder to take for a Crawford beaten by a Traub."

"While I appreciate your confidence, you might want to hold off on the victory speech until the votes are actually counted," Collin told her.

Secretly, Sutter couldn't help but agree with his

brother. As much as he appreciated Willa's optimism about her new husband's chances in the election, he didn't share her faith. He truly believed Collin was the best candidate for the job, but Nate Crawford had run a clever campaign. Instead of focusing on his plans to return the town to its former glory—no doubt because he knew that Collin was leaps and bounds ahead of him in that regard—he'd chosen to focus on his family's place in the town's history, and on digging up dirt on his opponent.

Not that there was much dirt to be found on Collin, which was surely why Nate had expanded his smear campaign to encompass the whole of the Traub family. And in doing so, he'd had more success.

Sutter could only hope that Nate's efforts would be in vain.

Chapter Three

Sutter said goodbye to Collin and Willa and headed back to the Triple T. He bypassed the main house and went directly to Clayton's residence on the property. Since Clay had moved to Thunder Canyon, his place had become a guest house for visitors, and although Sutter wasn't technically a guest, he felt more comfortable there than in the main house.

Mostly he appreciated the privacy and the solitude, and he was grateful for both tonight. He didn't feel like making idle conversation with anyone, especially not his well-meaning but undeniably interfering mother, and especially not if she'd somehow gotten wind of the fact that Paige had been present at the town hall debate.

Ellie had always liked Paige, and despite the breakup with Sutter she hadn't yet given up hope that they might somehow find their way back to one another. So she made a point of keeping him apprised of what was going on in Paige's life—including the fact that she was dating the mill foreman.

Sutter knew that the information hadn't been intended to hurt him but to spur him into action, his mother expecting that he would charge into town and sweep Paige off her feet and into his arms again. Even if he'd thought such a grand gesture might be successful, Sutter knew that he had no right to interfere in her life now. Five years earlier, they'd made their own choices and gone their separate ways.

And now she was dating Alex Monroe.

That fact was more difficult to accept than he wanted to acknowledge. He didn't know Alex well, but he knew who he was and he had nothing against the guy. He just didn't like the idea of Paige with anyone else.

Which was admittedly hypocritical considering that he'd hardly lived like a monk in the five years since he'd left Rust Creek Falls. But the truth was, he hadn't been with anyone since Paige who had made him forget about her.

He'd fallen in love with her when he was barely seventeen, and with the innocence and conviction of youth, he'd been absolutely certain that he would love her forever. They'd talked about their future together, when they would get married, where they would live, how many children they wanted. And he'd believed that she loved him, too—right up until the moment she'd told him she couldn't marry him.

Even five years later, the memory of that impulsive and rejected proposal stung. Because even now he knew he wasn't completely over his feelings for Paige, while she seemed to have moved on without so much as a backward glance in his direction.

The fact that she'd bought a house proved to him that she still wanted most of the same things they'd talked about. That she hadn't let him get past the front door proved that he wasn't a factor in any of her plans.

Which, of course, made him wonder if Alex Monroe was. Had she invited him in for coffee? Had he been given a tour of Paige's house? Had he seen her bedroom? Spent the night in her bed?

Sutter scowled, acknowledging that those were questions he probably didn't want to know the answers to—even the speculation was making him crazy.

He deliberately turned his thoughts to why she'd moved out of her parents' house. Maybe she'd wanted to be closer to her job, although a couple of blocks hardly made a difference. In a town like Rust Creek Falls, commuting times were never a concern.

More likely she'd wanted her own space, more independence. Paige had always been close to her family, but she'd often chafed at their rules and restrictions. It was a common complaint of many teenagers, but she was a grown woman now, an incredibly beautiful woman living alone in a house that was probably just waiting for the children she'd always wanted.

He poured himself a glass of whiskey and swallowed it in a single gulp. The liquor burned a path down his throat and into his belly, but it didn't touch the aching emptiness in his heart. So he poured himself a second drink and was considering a third when he realized what he was doing. He pushed the bottle aside and headed to bed.

It had been a lot of years since he'd drunk himself into a stupor over a woman, and even that hadn't helped him forget either the pain or the loneliness. Of course, it had been Paige then, too, and he wasn't going to go down that path again.

It was a decision he found himself questioning later. If he'd consumed enough alcohol to pass out drunk, maybe he wouldn't have been able to dream. Because when he finally did fall asleep, his dreams were filled with images of Paige, past and present. Memories mingled with fantasy in an enticing montage that teased and tormented him through the night.

When he finally woke the next morning with his heart pounding and the sheets twisted around his body, he actually ached for her.

Teaching wasn't an easy job at the best of times, and these were definitely not the best of times. There was so much going on in the town, so many families who had been displaced and so many demands on Paige's time and attention that she sometimes didn't know which direction to turn. As if all of that wasn't enough, Sutter Traub had planted himself in the middle of everything by getting involved with his brother's mayoral campaign and churning up a lot of feelings she'd thought were long dead—or at least deeply buried.

She walked around the long table that had been set up in her living-room-turned-classroom to check on the mock campaign posters her students were creating. Early on in her teaching career, she'd realized that kids learned more easily and maintained information more readily when they could relate the lessons to real life, so she'd talked about the recent flood during a unit on environmental studies and had worked the upcoming election into their discussion about governments.

The latter had certainly given her some insights into the political leanings of many local families, and though the class seemed fairly evenly divided between "Team Crawford" and "Team Traub," she was optimistic that Collin would emerge victorious. But right now she tried to focus her thoughts not on the upcoming election but on the current lesson.

She really did love her job and looked forward to the start of every day, approaching each subject with equal enthusiasm. She had her own personal favorites, of course, but she tried not to let that bias show. She wanted her students to experience and enjoy everything. She loved being able to open their minds, to encourage their curiosity and nurture their creativity, and gloried in each and every one of their successes. And because she was so completely engaged with her students, she hurt when they were hurting.

And she knew that Ryder Traub was hurting. Sutter had been right about the fact that Dallas's eldest son was having a hard time adjusting to his mother's abandonment. He wasn't acting out, as was often the case with children going through difficult transitions. Instead, it was as if he'd drawn into himself, disengaging from the other students and the activities in the classroom. He wasn't uncooperative—he always did the work that was required of him—but Paige could tell that he was just going through the motions.

She tried to draw him out, but that wasn't an easy task when she had sixteen other students to attend to. Not that they all came to class every day, which was another reason teaching in her home was a challenge. It was as if the parents figured it wasn't an actual school, therefore, she couldn't actually be teaching. And that only made it harder to impress the importance of every lesson upon her students.

When the day was over and the last student had gone, she realized she needed more markers and stickers to replenish her cupboard. Sometimes she would go to the specialty classroom resource store in Kalispell, but for everyday supplies she could usually find what she needed at Crawford's General Store.

Unfortunately, she sometimes found more than she wanted, as was the situation when she realized it was Nate Crawford behind the counter instead of his sister.

She forced a smile as she emptied her basket. "Where's

Nina?" She wasn't just making conversation but was genuinely concerned about the woman, who was nearing the
end of her pregnancy.

"She had an appointment—" he automatically began
to scan Paige's purchases "—so I said I would cover the
store. It gives me a chance to connect with the people of
our town on a more personal basis."

Which Paige interpreted to mean that any poor soul
who wandered in for essential grocery items was likely
getting a healthy dose of Nate's campaign propaganda
along with every loaf of bread and quart of milk. "It
always helps the voters to know their candidates," she
agreed.

He totaled her order and she gave him her money.

He made change, but didn't immediately pass it across
the counter. "I feel as if I should warn you about something."

"I'm sure that's not necessary."

"I know you have…a history…with Sutter Traub," he
continued anyway. "But your public declaration of allegiance could make you unpopular in this town."

"I don't need to be popular—I'm not running for office." She picked up her bag and held out her hand for
her change.

"No," he agreed, finally giving her the money. "But
maybe your new boyfriend needs to know that you're
running around with your ex."

Paige knew that she'd done nothing wrong, that there
was absolutely no reason for her to feel as if she had, but
that knowledge didn't succeed in alleviating her guilt.
Because the truth was, the whole time she'd been with
Sutter the night before, she hadn't once thought about

Alex—not until Sutter had specifically asked her about the other man.

She didn't know if that said something about her relationship with the mill foreman or if it was simply a side effect of being near Sutter. She'd been dating Alex for a couple of months now and, after fifteen minutes in Sutter's company, she'd barely remembered his name. It was embarrassing to admit, even if only to herself, and Alex certainly deserved better than to be an afterthought.

So when she got home, she surveyed the contents of her refrigerator to ensure that she had the groceries she needed to put together a decent meal—because she was *not* going back to Crawford's for another dose of Nate's self-righteousness—then called Alex to invite him to come over for dinner. Though he seemed surprised by the impromptu invitation, he immediately accepted.

She set the table, even putting out candles and a bottle of wine, then set about preparing the meal. She was going to spend some time with Alex tonight and forget about Sutter Traub once and for all.

Sutter figured he must be a glutton for punishment. Why else would he have decided to drive down Cedar Street before he headed home the following night? It wasn't as if it was on his way. It wasn't really *out* of his way, but the most direct route would have been to continue along Main to Sawmill, since he had to cross the river at the Sawmill Street Bridge. Instead, he turned onto Cedar, then North Pine, so that he passed by Paige's house.

And in passing by Paige's house, he couldn't possibly miss the battered truck parked outside of it. He knew that the Cruze parked in front of it belonged to Paige, and he suspected that the truck belonged to Alex Monroe, because he'd seen the same vehicle in the parking lot at the mill every day. His mother had warned him that Paige was dating the foreman, and Paige herself had confirmed it, but he still hadn't wanted to believe it. But the truth was hard to deny when it was right in front of him.

She hadn't invited Sutter in for a cup of coffee the night before because it was a school night. Well, it was a school night tonight, too, and she didn't seem to have any qualms about having company. Or maybe she didn't consider Alex company. Maybe—

Don't go there.

He sharply reined in his wandering thoughts and continued on his way.

He'd honestly thought he'd let her go. When he'd driven away from Rust Creek Falls five years earlier and Paige had decided to stay, he'd known that was the end for them. And yet every time he was near her he felt the chemistry that had always sizzled between them. That sizzle warned Sutter that they weren't as over as he wanted to believe.

Except the fact that she was at home tonight with her new boyfriend suggested that he might be the only one who felt they weren't over. And that really sucked.

His mother had said that she was making pot roast for dinner, one of his favorites, but he'd declined her invitation to join the family—as he'd declined most of her invitations since returning to Rust Creek Falls. Too much had been said and done for Sutter to pretend otherwise, so aside from working with his father and brothers on the ranch, he usually kept to himself and prepared his own meals at Clay's house. Tonight, he pulled into the parking lot of the Ace in the Hole instead.

He climbed the rough-hewn wooden steps and opened the screen door beneath the oversize playing card—an ace of hearts—that blinked in red neon. The bar was dimly lit and buzzing with conversations that mostly drowned out the Johnny Cash song emanating from the ancient Wurlitzer jukebox that still played three songs for a quarter. A long wooden bar ran the length of one wall and the dozen bar stools that faced the mirrored wall reflecting rows of glass bottles were already occupied, with several other patrons crowded in between the stools and leaned against the bar.

The booths that lined the outer walls were also filled, as were most of the wooden tables that surrounded the small dance floor in the middle of the room. Discarded peanut shells crunched under his boots as he made his way to one of those tables near the mostly unused stage in the far back corner. He pulled out the ladder-back chair and settled onto the creaky seat. The round wooden table was battered and scarred but appeared to be clean.

"What are you doing here?"

Sutter looked up, startled to see Paige's sister Lani standing at his table. She was wearing a pair of jeans and a plaid shirt, so it was only when he saw the apron around her waist and the order pad in her hand that he realized she was his waitress.

And not a very happy one, judging by her tone, so he kept his deliberately light and said, "I was hoping to look at a menu."

She tossed a single laminated page on the table. "That's the menu—look all you want."

"You probably don't get very many tips with an attitude like that," he mused.

"I'll give you a tip—stay away from my sister."

He looked around. "Is Lindsay here, too?"

Lani's eyes narrowed. "You know very well that I'm talking about Paige."

Ellie's roast beef with a side of gentle prying suddenly seemed infinitely more palatable than substandard pub fare with prickly attitude, but no way was he going to let Paige's little sister run him off.

"And I've barely seen her in the three months that I've been back in Rust Creek Falls," he pointed out to her.

"You saw her last night," Lani noted.

"Yeah, and here's a news flash for you—it was a public meeting at town hall."

"You walked her home."

He didn't bother to ask how she knew. This was Rust Creek Falls, where anyone might have seen them and no one could ever keep a secret for very long. "Actually, she would probably say that she was walking alone and I just happened to be beside her."

"Good."

"How about a beer while I try to decide between the cheeseburger and the bacon burger?"

"We're out of bacon."

"In that case, I'll have the cheeseburger and a draft beer."

She nodded and took the menu back, but she didn't move away from his table. "Alex Monroe is a good guy—and he's good to Paige."

"Have I said anything to the contrary?"

"The fact that you're still in Rust Creek Falls says plenty."

"I'm here because I'm helping Collin with his campaign."

"Then you're going back to Seattle after the election?"

"Not that it's any of your business," he felt compelled to point out. "But yes, I'm going back to Seattle after the election."

"And that's why she's better off with Alex," she said triumphantly. "Because he won't leave her."

"But does he love her? And does she love him?"

"She's with him," Lani said firmly. "That's all that should matter to you."

He didn't want to admit she was right, so he only shrugged, as if he was bored by the whole conversation. "Are you going to get my drink now?"

"Maybe." She turned away and went to another table, where a young couple had just sat down. She took their order, immediately returned with their drinks, then went back to the bar again and finally brought Sutter his beer.

The election was in two more days, and then his job here would be over. He should probably hang around a little while longer to tie up any loose ends, but he figured it was safe to assume that he'd be back in Seattle within a week. Back to the freedom and contentment of being anonymous, back to the big city where there weren't memories of Paige Dalton in every direction he turned.

He should forget the burger and get back to the ranch to start packing so he didn't have to spend any more time in Rust Creek Falls than was absolutely necessary. Except that leaving this town meant leaving Paige again, a prospect that was just as unappealing now as it had been five years earlier.

She's better off with Alex.

Sutter suspected that Lani was right, but he wasn't going to believe it was what Paige wanted until he'd heard it directly from her lips.

Paige really liked Alex, but she wasn't in love with him. And while she'd hoped that her feelings for him might grow and deepen with time, as she dished up the peach cobbler she'd made for dessert—using canned fruit in the recipe because there were no fresh peaches to be found in Montana at this time of year—she realized that wasn't likely to happen. At least not so long as Sutter was in Rust Creek Falls.

Not going to think about him, she reminded herself sternly.

The admonishment snapped her attention back to the present but failed to banish all thoughts of the other man from her mind. Which probably wasn't so surprising, considering her extensive history with Sutter. But that was what it was—history. He was her past, and Alex was her future.

Except that she was starting to question whether that was really true. She might want to think she and Alex could have a future, but the more time they spent together, the more difficult it was to imagine they would ever be anything more than friends.

He was an attractive man—objectively she knew this was true—but she wasn't attracted *to* him. Her heart didn't start to pound as soon as she saw him, her blood didn't hum when he was close and her knees didn't go weak when he kissed her. She guessed that Alex probably felt the same way, because he'd never tried to push her for more than the few kisses that they'd shared.

So why had she invited him to dinner tonight? Had she been hoping that he would say or do something to somehow change her mind about their relationship? That he would take her in his arms and kiss her until she was breathless and panting and wanted nothing more than to haul him upstairs to her bed?

As she poked at her dessert, she acknowledged that was what she'd been hoping. And when he'd walked through the door, Alex *had* kissed her. The kiss had been warm and pleasant...and over almost before it began.

"That was a fabulous meal," Alex said, pushing his empty plate aside.

She forced a smile. "I'm glad you were able to make it on such short notice."

"It wasn't a hard decision, considering all that I had waiting at home was a frozen dinner."

"So it was the home cooking and not my company that compelled you to accept my invitation?"

He reached across the table and linked their fingers together. "I always enjoy spending time with you, Paige."

"Why do I feel as if there's a *but* coming?"

His lips curved, but the smile didn't reach his eyes. "But lately I've found myself wondering if there's any hope for a future between us so long as you're still hung up on Sutter Traub."

"I'm not hung up on Sutter," she immediately denied. "In fact, I've barely even seen him since he came back to Rust Creek Falls."

"Because you've been avoiding him," Alex guessed.

She pulled her hand away and stood up to clear the dishes from the table. "Because I don't want to see him."

He followed her into the kitchen. "Why would it matter if you didn't still have feelings for him?"

She hated that he could so easily see a truth that she'd only recently acknowledged to herself. "Our relationship didn't end amicably," she admitted. "So there are probably some unresolved issues."

"Then you need to resolve them," Alex said gently.

"I need to move on with my life."

"You're an incredible woman, Paige. And I've enjoyed the time I've spent with you, but you're never going to move on with your life until you put your history with Sutter behind you."

"It's five years behind me," she protested.

"I stopped by town hall on my way home from work to catch the last part of the debate last night," he told her. "And when you stood up to defend Sutter Traub, there was more passion in your words than in any of the kisses we've ever shared."

She didn't know how to respond to that except to say, "I'm sorry."

"Don't be," he said. "And don't ever settle for less than everything you want."

"You're dumping me, aren't you?"

He shook his head. "I'm letting you go so that you can figure out what you want. If you decide that's me, you know where to find me."

He tucked a strand of hair behind her ear, then lowered his head and touched his lips to hers. It was a nice kiss. Light and friendly, and completely uninspiring. She wanted to feel heat or tingles—*anything*—in response to his touch, but there was nothing.

As she watched Alex drive away, she silently cursed Sutter Traub and the possibility that his kisses had ruined her for any other man.

Chapter Four

Sutter was one of the first voters lined up when the polling station opened on Thursday morning, right behind Collin and Willa, who followed Nathan Crawford. Sutter wouldn't have been surprised to learn that Nate had camped outside of town hall to ensure that he was able to cast the first ballot.

There was a steady stream of voters throughout the day. Some of them wore their allegiance proudly on their lapels in the form of buttons that proclaimed Crawford or Traub, and by Sutter's estimation, they were fairly equal in number—and far outnumbered by the voters who came in grim faced and solemn with no indication as to how they were voting or why.

Nate had several factors in his favor. Aside from his campaign being widely supported and well funded—although no one in town really seemed to know where his money was coming from—he'd lived and worked in Rust Creek Falls his entire life. He was friendly and generally well liked, and he always knew what was going on with everyone in town. Of course, that probably had something to do with the fact that Crawford's General Store was the shopping mecca of Rust Creek Falls and people tended to chat while they browsed, making it the central point of information dissemination, too.

Collin, on the other hand, tended to keep to himself and mind his own business. He lived on Falls Mountain and operated independently out of a renovated work-shop on the property. He'd inherited CT Saddles from their great-uncle, Casper Traub, but it was Collin's artistic craftsmanship that had really put the business on the map. He made custom saddles and tack and pretty much anything of leather, and he'd used the same focus and attention to detail that had made the company a success to develop a solid plan to rebuild the town and revitalize the economy.

The polling station closed at 6:00 p.m., at which time Thelma McGee taped up the tops of the boxes and took them into the back room to be counted by the independent vote counters. The first step was to divide the ballots into separate piles: Crawford, Traub and spoiled ballots. Then each pile was counted once, then counted again to double-check the results.

The candidates were entitled to be present during the counting of the ballots, along with an authorized representative. Nate Crawford was there with his campaign manager, Bill Fergus. His parents, his sister, Nina, several close friends and a handful of campaign workers were waiting outside for the results.

Of course, everyone was there in anticipation of a celebration, but only one candidate could win. And Sutter couldn't help but think that if his brother lost, it would be his fault, that he'd tainted Collin's campaign by being part of it. Because he was afraid his family would share that belief, he decided it was somehow less stressful to hide out with Thelma and watch the votes being counted than to wait with his family for the results. So Sutter stayed in the room while Collin opted to remain outside with Willa and the rest of the family, claiming he was too nervous to watch.

It was nearly nine o'clock before the final results

were tallied, and although the numbers were close, when Thelma McGee emerged from the back room it was to announce that Collin Traub was the victor. Of course, Nate Crawford was furious, and although Sutter heard him grumbling and predicting dire consequences for the town, he couldn't dispute the results. For the benefit of the local reporter who was hanging around, he offered Collin a terse congratulations and a brief handshake, then walked out of town hall with his family and supporters trailing after him.

While Collin and Willa and the rest of "Team Traub" were laughing and hugging, Sutter found himself looking around the small gathering of supporters for Paige, but she wasn't there. He knew he had no right to be disappointed. She hadn't made him any promises, but he'd hoped that she would show up anyway. He'd wanted her to share in the victory he was sure wouldn't have happened if not for her words at the town hall meeting earlier in the week.

Her absence was proof to Sutter that she wanted to maintain a certain distance between them, that the brief conversation they'd shared after that meeting hadn't bridged the gap of five years. And maybe that was for the best.

He forgot about Paige—at least for a minute—when he got back to the ranch and discovered that the rest of the family had already gathered there. Bob and Ellie, of course, along with Braden and Dallas and Dallas's three boys—Ryder, Jake and Robbie. Clayton and Antonia had made the trip from Thunder Canyon with their two children, Bennett and Lucy, in tow, as had Forrest and his new wife, Angie.

Ellie had the champagne in the fridge—and sparkling grape juice for the kids and the nursing mother—so that as soon as everyone was gathered, the drinks were ready to be poured. As hugs and kisses were exchanged all around, Bob popped the corks and started the bubbles flowing. It was a joyous celebration—thankfully with enough people around that Sutter could avoid having any direct communication with Forrest.

When the glasses had been distributed, Sutter raised his and called for attention to toast Mayor Collin Traub. Everyone joined in, clinking crystal and adding congratulations and advice, and Forrest leaned over to tap his glass to Sutter's.

It wasn't a big deal—or it shouldn't have been. But to Sutter it was huge. Because in that moment, Forrest had looked him directly in the eye. Not a word had passed between the two of them, but somehow Sutter felt as if the vise that had been squeezing his chest eased, just a little. For the first time in a long time, he actually felt as if he was part of the family, as if he was home.

This is probably a bad idea.

As Paige turned her vehicle into the long drive that led toward the Triple T Ranch, she was seriously questioning the wisdom of her impetuous decision to come here, and yet she couldn't stay away. She'd been pleased to hear about Collin's victory, but her thoughts weren't focused so much on the new mayor as his campaign manager. Which was why she knew this was a bad idea.

And yet she didn't turn her car around; she didn't drive away. Instead, she parked at the end of the long line of vehicles and tried to ignore the pounding of her heart.

She could hear talking and laughing from inside even as she made her way to the door, and she wondered if anyone would be able to hear the ring of the bell over the cacophony of sounds. But her finger had barely lifted from the buzzer when the door was opened and she was face-to-face with Sutter.

"You didn't come to town hall."

She was taken aback by his greeting. Not the accusation of the words so much as the hurt beneath them. She hadn't intended to hurt him. Truthfully, she wouldn't have thought that she could. They were supposed to be beyond that.

But somehow, only two days after vowing to put him out of her mind, she was at his door. And no matter how many times she told herself that she hadn't come to see him, she knew it was a lie.

"I figured I'd already made enough of a public statement at town hall on Monday night."

"Well, you're here now, so you can join the party," he said. Then he pulled her into his embrace and swung her around.

Unable to do anything else, Paige held on as the world spun around her. Even when he released her and her feet were back on solid ground, her head continued to spin. And Paige knew it wasn't a consequence of the physical motion as much as the euphoria of being in Sutter's arms again.

This was definitely a bad idea.

"I'm glad you came."

His smile was so real, his joy so evident, she couldn't help but want to share in the emotion of the moment with him. But that was a dangerous wish, so she said, "I can't stay—I just wanted to congratulate Collin."

The brightness of his smile faded just a little. "Of course," he agreed, and led her to the living room. "Look who decided to join the party."

In response to Sutter's announcement, everyone turned. And Paige realized that every member of the

Traub family was there, including the two brothers who now lived in Thunder Canyon, more than three hundred miles away.

"I apologize for crashing the party," she said, suddenly self-conscious.

"It's not crashing when you were invited," Sutter pointed out to her.

Ellie pressed a glass of champagne into her hand. "It's wonderful to see you, Paige."

The greeting was so warm and sincere that Paige actually felt her throat start to tighten, but she somehow managed to smile. "It's wonderful to see you, too."

Everyone greeted her warmly, if not quite as enthusiastically as Sutter had done. Of course, she'd always gotten on well with his parents and all of his brothers. And when she and Sutter had broken up, she'd missed his family almost as much as she'd missed him.

"Congratulations, Mayor Traub," she said when she'd finally managed to make her way through the crowd to Collin and Willa.

"Thank you," Collin said to her. "And thank you for speaking up at the town hall meeting—you really were the voice of reason in the midst of a lot of emotional chaos."

"I'm not sure that my opinion carried any weight, but I wanted people to focus on the relevant issues."

"It carried a lot of weight," Willa told her. "And swayed a lot of on-the-fence voters."

"Well, now that those votes have been counted, your life is going to get even busier," Paige pointed out.

"We're looking forward to it," Collin said, drawing his new wife closer to his side. "We've got a lot of plans for this town."

"And we're going to need a lot of help to implement

those plans," Willa said, her gaze shifting from Paige to the man standing behind her. "Which is why we're hoping to convince Sutter to stay."

Paige looked up at him, surprised by Willa's admission and wary about his response.

"Plans are for tomorrow," he said lightly. "Tonight is for celebrating."

His response suggested to Paige that his plans hadn't changed. He'd told her that he would be going back to Seattle after the election, and she was counting on that promise. Because contrary to Alex Monroe's parting advice, she didn't want to resolve anything with Sutter—she just wanted him to be gone before he could do any more damage to her fragile heart.

But as she visited with his family, she realized how much she'd missed all of them. She'd always enjoyed spending time with them, and she'd loved his parents as if they were her own. And if anyone was surprised that she'd shown up to take part in the celebration, no one said anything to her. They welcomed her into the fold as easily as they'd always done, almost making her feel as if the past five years had never happened. As if Sutter hadn't broken her heart into a million jagged little pieces.

He reached for her hand, linking their fingers as easily as he'd done a thousand times before. Those thousand times before had been more than five years earlier, but still her pulse skipped and her heart pounded. She wanted to tug her hand away, but she worried that doing so would draw too much attention to the fact that he was holding it.

"I could use some air," he said to her. "Will you take a walk with me?"

She could use some air, too, but going outside with Sutter meant being alone with Sutter, and she wasn't sure that was a good idea. In fact, she was sure it was another bad idea in a day that had already been full of them.

He didn't wait for her response but immediately started tugging her back toward the kitchen. She went with him because it seemed less awkward than refusing. But she was all too conscious of his mother's eyes following as they left the room, and she knew that Ellie was probably speculating as to what it meant.

But it didn't mean anything. Paige wouldn't let it mean anything.

The night was chilly, and she was grateful for the sheepskin-lined denim jacket that she'd worn.

As they walked, Sutter talked excitedly about his brother's plans for the town. She could hear the pride in his voice, and she knew that he was sincerely pleased by Collin's victory.

"It's not going to be an easy job, but I don't doubt he's up to it—especially with Willa by his side."

"They're obviously both committed to the rebuilding of Rust Creek Falls," she agreed.

"And to each other," Sutter noted. "It makes a world of difference to know that someone has your back, no matter what problems might arise."

"She loves him," Paige said simply.

"You used to have my back—I don't think I really appreciated that at the time. I don't think I ever realized how much I needed your support until you weren't there anymore."

"I was still there," she felt compelled to point out. "You were the one who left."

"You're right," he admitted. "But that didn't stop me from missing you."

"I agreed to take a walk, not a stroll down memory lane."

"If the past is really the past, why are you so afraid to talk about it?"

She was afraid because she knew how dangerous it could be to talk about the past, to remember how things used to be, how good she and Sutter had been together.

"I just prefer to look forward rather than back," she told him.

"That's too bad, because I have some really fond memories of the time I spent with you."

"It's starting to snow."

"What?" He looked up, and seemed startled by the thick white flakes that were falling down around them.

She'd been surprised by the change in the weather, too, focused so intently on Sutter that she hadn't been aware of anything else. In fact, she hadn't even noticed the snow until she saw the white flakes against his dark jacket and in his thick hair.

"We should get back," she said now and turned toward the house.

Sutter caught her hand again. "You used to like walking in the snow, and I'm not ready to let go of you just yet."

He'd had no such qualms five years ago—not just letting her go, but moving more than five hundred miles away. But she didn't say any of that aloud. She didn't want him to know how much his decision had hurt, how much it still hurt.

"Do you remember the first night I kissed you?"

Of course she remembered. She remembered every little detail of that night despite the eleven years that had passed since then.

"It was a snowy night much like tonight," he continued when she failed to respond to his question. "After the high school Christmas concert.

"You were in the choir and I was in the audience, and when I looked up at you on stage—you took my breath away. I don't know if it was the song you were singing or the white robe you were wearing, but you looked just like an angel.

"And when you stepped forward to sing your solo in 'Silent Night'… I've never heard anything more beautiful. Before or after. And when the concert was finally over and everyone was starting to file out of the auditorium, I asked if I could walk you home."

He'd stuttered a little over the words, as if he was nervous. She'd been just as nervous—maybe even more so. And though her parents had been in the audience and were waiting to give her a ride home, she'd opted to walk with Sutter. She'd been just sixteen years old, and totally infatuated with him.

"I held your hand," he reminded her, then smiled. "And I remember thinking it was a good thing we were both wearing gloves, because my palms were clammy. I think I fell a little bit in love with you that night, and I was as terrified as I was excited that you'd agreed to walk with me.

"It was cold enough that we could see our breath in the air, and the snow crunched beneath our feet as we walked, but I didn't feel cold. Because with every step of the five blocks from the high school to your parents' house, all I could think about was how much I wanted to kiss you, and whether or not you would let me."

He stopped now and tipped her face up, forcing her to meet his gaze. "Do you remember any of that?"

"I remember that it was cold," she told him. "And that my fingers and toes were numb even before we got to the church."

His brows drew together. "*That's* what you remember?"

She heard the disappointment in his tone and her heart softened. "And when we got to my house, we stood behind the stand of lodgepole pines," she continued, "out of sight of anyone peering through the windows, and you kissed me."

He'd slipped his arms around her, drawing her close. Her heart had pounded; her knees had gone weak. His eyes had held hers as his head lowered slowly, until his lips brushed against hers.

Her heart was pounding and the nerves in her belly were jangling as he drew her into his arms now. She couldn't claim she didn't know what he was planning to do any more than she could claim she didn't want his kiss. When his mouth touched hers, the line between the past and present blurred. As the snowflakes swirled around them, Paige could almost believe she was sixteen again. Certainly her heart was pounding as hard and fast as it had then.

His tongue stroked the seam of her lips, a silent entreaty that she couldn't refuse. Her lips parted on a sigh, welcoming him. As the kiss deepened, she knew that this wasn't a memory. Because Sutter's kiss was that of a man, not a boy. And the innocent curiosity she'd felt as a teenage girl had been replaced by a woman's yearning.

His arms tightened around her so that they were pressed together from shoulder to thigh. Despite the thick coats they both wore, she could feel the heat emanating from his body and the answering fire that pumped through her veins. He was hot and hard—yeah, there was no mistaking the evidence of his arousal when he was pressed against her—and she wanted him just as much as he wanted her.

Do we need to make an itemized list of all the reasons that this was a bad idea?

The taunting voice of her subconscious made her pull away. But she kept her hands on his arms, holding on to him, because she wasn't entirely sure that her legs would support her. She drew in a deep breath and willed her heart to settle back inside of her chest.

She was undeniably shaken by the intensity of their kiss. Whatever she'd anticipated when she'd agreed to walk with Sutter, it wasn't this. She couldn't do this—she wouldn't get wrapped up in Sutter Traub again, especially when she knew his return to Rust Creek Falls was only temporary.

When she was sure that her legs would support her, she took a careful step back. "It's late, and I need to get home."

As she turned, Sutter said, "Who's running away now?"

She didn't respond. Because she couldn't deny that she *was* running, but she had a valid reason: he'd already broken her heart once and she wasn't going to let him do it again.

Chapter Five

Sutter held his ground as he watched her retreat, because he knew that if he chased after her, he might very well beg. And he'd never been the type to beg. So he watched her go as his own wants and needs continued to churn inside of him.

Kissing Paige Dalton was not the smartest thing he'd ever done. On the other hand, he knew it had been inevitable, that they had been moving inexorably toward this moment since he'd walked her home from the town hall debate earlier in the week.

He'd wanted one kiss—just to prove to himself that she didn't have the same hold on him that she used to. Except that one kiss had proved him wrong. She tasted just like he remembered—right down to the cherry lip balm she'd favored when she was sixteen. Just one kiss and he knew that he wanted her as much now as he had then. Maybe even more, because he knew how good they were together.

Except that Paige was with someone else now—a fact that he'd conveniently forgotten when he'd had her in his arms. He figured it was a safe bet that she'd forgotten about the mill foreman, too. There was no way she'd been thinking about another man while she'd been kissing him.

But one kiss didn't change the fact that she had a life without him. Or that her life was here in Rust Creek Falls and his was in Seattle.

And he liked his life in Washington. He was proud of the business he'd built and the success it had become. He'd made new friends and he never lacked for female companionship if he wanted it. But he'd missed his family and his friends in Montana. And he'd missed Paige.

He'd dated a lot of women in the past five years, trying to forget about her. Because he'd been certain that he would eventually meet someone who would make him forget the first woman he'd ever loved. The only woman he'd ever loved. Now, five years later, he was starting to wonder if she might be the only woman for him.

When he'd left town, he'd been full of hurt and anger, determined to prove to himself and everyone else that he didn't need anything or anyone he'd left behind. With time and distance, his indignation had eventually faded. He'd accepted that his own actions might have been a bit impulsive and not completely rational. But he still hadn't been willing to admit he'd made a mistake, and he hadn't been ready to go home. He'd left Rust Creek Falls with the intention of proving that he could make it on his own, and it had taken a while, but he'd done so. He'd built a successful business for himself in Seattle. He had a nice home and a comfortable life.

And truthfully, for the first year after he'd opened the doors of his stables, he hadn't had time for anything else. But lately he'd begun to feel that something was missing. When he went home to an empty house at the end of the day, he considered that it might be nice to have some company—and for more than just a few hours. In fact, it might be nice to share his life with someone.

Except that he hadn't met anyone in Seattle who inspired him to think of long-term plans. He'd met a lot of attractive, intelligent and fascinating women, but he couldn't imagine spending the rest of his life with any one of them. Because when he'd been barely twenty years old and head over heels in love with Paige Dalton, they'd made plans for their future together. Obviously things hadn't turned out the way they'd planned, but he couldn't forget the dreams they'd shared—and he couldn't imagine any other woman occupying the space she still held in his heart.

When Paige's taillights disappeared at the end of the long drive, he finally headed back toward the house and the party still going on inside.

"Everything okay?" Collin asked when he returned.

"Everything's fine."

"Good, because I wanted to talk to you about some of the ideas Lissa Roarke had to generate national interest in the rebuild of Rust Creek Falls."

"I was your campaign manager. The campaign is over," Sutter pointed out to him. "You don't need my advice or opinion on anything anymore."

"I need your help."

He shook his head. "I'm sure Lissa has everything under control, and I have to get back to Seattle."

"You're really going to leave?"

"That was always the plan," Sutter reminded him.

"I know," his brother admitted. "But I thought—I hoped—things had changed."

His mind drifted back to the kiss he'd shared with Paige. That all-too-brief moment had proved to Sutter that his feelings for her were as strong and steadfast as ever.

"No," he said. "Nothing has changed."

Ellie Traub couldn't sleep. And when she couldn't sleep, she ended up tossing and turning, disturbing Bob's sleep. The alternative was to slip out of bed and pace. When the boys were younger, Bob used to tease that she was going to wear out the floor by the window. She'd put an area rug on the floor—not really to protect the wood but to muffle her steps so that he wouldn't hear her.

She'd paced for each and every one of her boys on numerous occasions, some more than others. She'd done a lot of pacing when Forrest was in Iraq. It was the hardest thing in the world for a mother to know that her child was in danger and not be able to do anything to help. When he came home wounded, she only cared that he was home. Yes, he had scars—physical and emotional—but he was alive and the healing could begin.

She'd hoped that Sutter might come home then, too. She hadn't realized how deeply he'd been wounded by the falling-out with Forrest and, consequently, the rest of the family. But he'd come home when he'd heard about the floods because he'd known the family needed him, and that gave her hope that he might someday come home to stay for good. Seeing him with Paige Dalton tonight further bolstered that hope.

Ellie had always liked the young schoolteacher. Even when Paige and Sutter were in high school together, she'd thought that they were well suited. Paige had spent a lot of time at the Triple T back then—so much that Ellie had begun to think of her as part of the family. In fact, she'd been certain that Paige would be her daughter-in-law someday. And then Sutter had left town and broken Paige's heart.

She'd come to the ranch tonight—ostensibly to congratulate Collin, but Ellie hadn't missed the looks that had passed between Paige and Sutter, or the crackle in the air whenever they stood close to one another. Whatever had been between them clearly wasn't over—but was it enough to keep her son in Rust Creek Falls?

"I thought that once the election was over you'd stop pacing the bedroom floor at midnight," Bob said.

Ellie froze. "I'm sorry if I woke you."

"Why don't you tell me what's on your mind?"

Because it was obvious that something was, she replied without hesitation, "Sutter."

"You're worried that he's going to go back to Seattle now," he guessed, shifting so that he was sitting up in bed, leaning back against the headboard.

She nodded.

"He's a grown man—he has to make his own choices."

"I understand why he left—and I know we bear some responsibility for that, for letting him think that our decision to support Forrest meant we didn't support him. But I didn't think he'd stay away for so long."

"He's built a life and a career for himself in Seattle."

She lowered herself onto the edge of the mattress. "I want him to come home."

"He came home when we needed him," Bob pointed out.

"I want him to stay," she insisted stubbornly.

He lifted a hand and gently brushed her hair away from her face. "I want that, too, but it's what Sutter wants that matters."

"I think he'd stay this time, if Paige asked him to."

Bob sighed. "Ellie."

"I know she's been dating the mill foreman, but even a blind person could see that there are still sparks between her and Sutter."

"I know you like Paige and that you'd like nothing better for them to get back together, but you have to let them live their own lives."

"Did you see them together tonight?"

"Yes, I saw them. But they're not together anymore," he reminded her.

"He still loves her."

"Did he tell you that?"

"As if he would."

"Then let it be," he suggested.

She folded her arms over her chest.

He smiled and leaned forward to brush his lips against hers. "I love you, Ellie."

Even now, after forty years of marriage, his kiss warmed her inside. And when he eased her back onto the mattress, she didn't protest.

"I love you, too," she told him. "And I love the life we have together, so why is it wrong to want the same happiness for my children?"

He settled her head onto his shoulder and held her close. "It's not wrong to want it—it's only wrong if you try to manipulate it."

She sighed softly. "I'm not trying to manipulate, just to…nurture the possibility."

"Right now, you should try to go to sleep," he suggested.

She closed her eyes and followed his advice.

The flowers confused her.

Paige scowled at the gorgeous bouquet of yellow and orange gerbera daisies on her dining room table and tried to figure out what they were supposed to mean. Not their symbolic meaning, but why Sutter had sent them. The brief message on the card—"Thanks for always having my back, S."—was an echo of what he'd said to her the night before, so the flowers were redundant. Beautiful but redundant.

So why had he sent them? Was it because of the kiss? It

had been one kiss—a simple and inconsequential meeting of their lips. Okay, the fact that she'd tossed and turned through most of the night suggested that it might not have been quite as inconsequential as she wanted to believe. Still, it was only one kiss.

But it was a kiss that made her want more.

She turned her back on the flowers and returned to the lesson she'd been teaching before the ring of the bell had interrupted. Of course, she should have realized that the delivery would not go unnoticed. And she should have expected that her class of fifth graders would be more interested in the flowers than the chapter of the book she'd instructed them to read and summarize.

As soon as she returned to the living room and asked if there were any questions, Allyson's hand shot into the air.

"Who are the flowers from?"

"A friend," she said, because it seemed the simplest if not necessarily the most accurate response.

"Your boyfriend?" Emma asked, not bothering to put her hand in the air.

"No, just a friend."

"A boy friend or a girl friend?" Becky wanted to know.

Paige drew in a breath and mentally counted to ten. "Let's forget about the flowers and concentrate on chapter three for the next twenty minutes," she suggested. "Now, who can tell me what it was about mules that made them ideal for working in the coal mines?"

David, one of the more focused students in her class, raised his hand. "Because they were sure-footed and strong."

"That's right," she agreed. "Anything else?"

His attention dropped back to the book, and his classmates followed suit, looking for the answers to her questions in the passage they'd read.

Paige exhaled slowly, confident that her students were back on track.

The rest of the day went fairly smoothly—until her sisters stopped by after dinner.

Paige was just washing up the dishes when she heard the cursory knock at the back door before Lani and Lindsay walked in.

"Mom sent leftover meat loaf," Lindsay said.

"Thanks." Paige took the container from her sister and put it in the fridge. There was no point in reminding her mother that she'd been living on her own for almost two years now—it wouldn't stop Mary from sending food, just like her repeated assertion that she didn't like meat loaf hadn't stopped her mother from trying to get her to eat it.

"Is that the only reason you stopped by—to perform your assigned meals-on-wheels duty?"

"No. We're actually heading out for movie night and thought you might want to come with us," Lani told her.

There wasn't an actual movie theater in Rust Creek Falls, but every Friday night was movie night in the high school auditorium. Of course, they were never new releases. Sometimes they were recent movies, but more often they were classic films or family favorites.

"What's playing?"

Lani named the film, and although it was one of Paige's favorites, she shook her head. "I've seen it at least a dozen times."

Lindsay shrugged. "So have we, but it happens to be what's playing tonight."

"I'd rather stay home and mark spelling tests." She folded her towel and draped it over the handle of the oven.

When she moved away, Lani spotted the flowers.

"Well, well... Does this mean you've finally taken

your relationship with Alex to the next level?" she teased her sister.

"Only you would equate a simple bunch of flowers with sex."

"Actually, I'd hope for something a little fancier than daisies after sex."

Lindsay frowned at the bouquet. "Didn't Sutter always give you gerberas?"

He had, because he knew that they were Paige's favorites. Not as elegant as lilies or as fancy as roses, but simple and beautiful.

Before she could say anything, Lani reached forward to snag the card that she'd tucked in with the blooms, and Paige silently cursed herself for not tearing it into pieces and tossing it into the trash.

"These are from Sutter," she said accusingly, then turned to Paige, her hands fisted on her hips. "Why is Sutter Traub sending you flowers?"

"I don't know," Paige insisted, though the guilty flush that swept her cheeks certainly suggested otherwise. "Maybe because I told him that I would vote for Collin and Collin won the election."

"I voted for Collin, too," Lindsay said. "I didn't get any flowers."

"So did I," Lani noted. "And I don't believe for a minute that the new mayor's brother sent flowers to thank you for marking an X on a ballot, so spill."

"There's nothing to spill," Paige said.

"We're your sisters." Lindsay's tone was more persuasive than demanding. "You can tell us anything."

"If there was anything to tell, I would," Paige assured her. "But there is nothing to tell."

"How about the fact that you were at the Triple T last night?" Lani challenged.

She frowned. "How do you know that?"

"I saw Ellie at the library this afternoon, and she commented about how pleased she was that you went by to congratulate Collin last night."

"Yes, I went to the Triple T to congratulate Collin last night."

"And of course Sutter, as Collin's campaign manager, would have been there, too," Lani noted.

"Yes," she said again. "Sutter was there."

"And?" Lindsay prompted.

"And we talked a little—mostly about Collin's plans for Rust Creek Falls."

"Mostly," Lani said, zeroing in on that single word. "Which means that you talked about other things, too."

Paige sighed. "The weather, because it was cold and starting to snow."

"Just like the first night Sutter kissed you, when you were in high school," Lindsay remembered.

She rolled her eyes. "And you wonder why I don't tell you anything?"

"So there is something you aren't telling us," Lani decided.

"You don't have to tell us," Lindsay said. "But it's obvious that Sutter has somehow managed to get under your skin again."

"He hasn't," she denied, though not very convincingly.

Lindsay touched her hand. "You were in love with him once," she reminded her gently.

Paige just nodded.

"And he stomped all over your heart," Lani said, her tone not at all gentle.

"Thanks for the reminder," Paige said drily. "I'd almost forgotten that part."

"Sorry," Lani said, not sounding sorry at all. "I just

want to make sure you don't forget—and that you don't give him a chance to do it again."

"No worries there," Paige assured her. "Now that the election's over, I don't think he'll be hanging around Rust Creek Falls too much longer."

Lindsay cast another worried glance at the vase filled with flowers. "I wouldn't be so sure."

"Why do you say that?" Lani demanded.

"Because I can and do hate Sutter for what he did to Paige, but he was never the type of guy to play fast and loose with a girl's heart. These flowers—*Paige's favorite flowers*—make me think that he's not over our big sister."

"I don't care if he is or isn't, as long as he goes back to Seattle," Lani said.

"I appreciate your concern," Paige said to her sisters. "But there's really no need for it. My heart is completely Sutter proofed now."

Even if Sutter had heard Paige's proclamation, he wouldn't have been dissuaded. And he wouldn't have believed it, anyway. Because when they'd kissed the night before, he'd felt the connection, as strong and undeniable as it had been five years earlier.

And that was why he was at her door at eight o'clock on Friday night. He'd tried calling first—in fact, he'd called several times during the day. He knew that she was home because she was teaching, and he could understand why she wouldn't want to interrupt a lesson to answer the phone. Still, he didn't understand why she hadn't found five minutes in the several hours that had passed since her students went home to return his call.

He knew it was possible—even probable—that she might be out with Alex Monroe. Or that he might be at her house again. It was a chance he was willing to take.

He wasn't willing to let Paige pretend he didn't exist any longer. But he was relieved when he saw that only her car was in the driveway.

She opened the door in response to his knock, but she didn't look happy to see him.

"What are you doing here, Sutter?"

He held up the plastic-wrapped plate. "I brought celebration cake."

She eyed the plate warily. "Why?"

"Because my mom's cheesecake used to be your favorite."

The wariness was replaced by interest. "That's your mom's mile-high cherry cheesecake?"

"As if I would show up here with any kind of imitation."

"Are you going to hand it over or do I have to invite you inside?"

"An invitation would be nice," he told her.

She stepped away from the door.

"And a cup of coffee would be even nicer."

"Would you like a cup of coffee?"

"How could I possibly say no to such a gracious offer?"

Her lips curved just a little as she led the way to the kitchen.

He glanced around the room, noted the glossy white cabinets, deep blue backsplash, granite countertops and stainless-steel appliances. Instead of a kitchen table there was an island, with four stools set up in counter-style seating. He spotted the bouquet of daisies tucked in the back corner of the counter by the refrigerator.

"I see you got the flowers."

"They're beautiful," she acknowledged with more than a hint of reluctance in her tone. "But they really weren't necessary."

"I know they weren't necessary, but I wanted to give you flowers."

"Why?" She measured out coffee grounds, dumped them into the paper filter.

"Do I need a reason?"

She poured water into the reservoir. "You need to understand that what happened last night shouldn't have happened, and that it won't happen again."

He smiled. "'What happened last night' makes it sound like it was a much bigger thing than it was."

"It wasn't a big thing at all—it was just a kiss."

"So why are you so bent out of shape over a bunch of daisies?"

"I'm not," she immediately denied, then huffed out a breath. "Okay, maybe I am."

"Then maybe you need to figure out why."

"Because our relationship was over five years ago. Because the flowers were delivered while I was in the middle of a lesson with my class. Because my sisters were here earlier and demanded to know why you were sending me flowers." She ticked the reasons off on her fingers as she enumerated them, then she looked at him. "I think any of those reasons would suffice, so pick one."

Sutter winced. "I didn't think about the fact that your students would be here." He looked around. "Where do you put them?"

"Not in here," she admitted. "I have sixteen if they all show up."

"If?" he prompted.

"Attendance has been a bit of a problem since the flood," she told him. "Some parents don't seem to understand that I'm following the curriculum—teaching essential subjects to their kids so they're not behind when we do get back into a real classroom. They seem to think that because this isn't actually a school, attendance is optional."

"So where is the classroom?"

She opened a pair of French doors and led him into the living room, where her furniture—a butter-yellow sofa, two matching armchairs with ottomans and a set of glass-and-metal occasional tables—had all been pushed back against the walls to make room for the long folding tables and chairs that occupied the middle of the room.

"And you spend the whole day in here with sixteen kids?"

She laughed softly. "You're feeling claustrophobic just thinking about it, aren't you?"

"A little," he admitted, not surprised that she'd read his thoughts so easily. No one had ever understood him like Paige. In fact, when he'd first told her about his job interview at a management company in Seattle, she'd warned that he wouldn't last behind a desk, that he'd go crazy stuck in an office.

"Actually, I try not to keep them cooped up in here all day. If the weather's nice, I walk them down the street to the Country Kids Day Care so they can run around outside—that's our physical education component. And if there's research to be done, we go over to the library to use the computers there."

The coffeepot hissed, signaling that it was finished brewing. Paige turned back to the kitchen and poured two mugs of coffee. He took the one she handed to him, shook his head when she offered cream and sugar. He'd always taken his coffee black, and he saw that she still did, too.

He settled onto one of the stools at the island while Paige cut the slice of cheesecake down the middle, then transferred one half to a second plate. She carried the plates and forks to the island, but instead of sitting beside him, she remained standing on the opposite side.

She cut off a piece of cake, then slid the fork between her lips. Her eyelids closed and a sound of pleasure hummed in her throat. "Mmm. This is even more incredible than I remembered."

The expression on her face was pure bliss—a both tempting and painful reminder that she was a sensual woman who enjoyed indulging in all kinds of pleasures.

"Ellie Traub's secret recipe," he said lightly. "She doesn't let anyone step foot in the kitchen while she's making it."

"She let me help her with it once."

"She did not."

"She did," Paige insisted. "She was making it for the baby shower, when Laurel was pregnant with Robbie."

"Mom always did like you best," he said, managing to coax another smile from her.

She polished off the last of her cake, then picked up her mug of coffee and sipped.

"Do you want me to apologize for the flowers?" he asked.

She glanced at the colorful blossoms and sighed softly. "No. I don't want you to apologize."

"What do you want?"

"I want you to go back to Seattle." She looked at him now, her gaze steady and sure. "I *need* you to go back to Seattle."

Chapter Six

Paige saw the disappointment and hurt on his face, but she didn't—couldn't—let herself be swayed by emotion. He'd asked what she wanted, and she wasn't going to feel guilty about giving him an honest answer.

Except that deep in her heart, she knew that it wasn't an honest answer. She didn't want Sutter to go back to Seattle—she wanted him to stay in Rust Creek Falls forever. But she knew that wasn't an option, so the next best thing was for him to leave as soon as possible before she started wishing for things she knew she couldn't have.

"Because you're afraid of what might happen between us if I stay," he guessed.

Paige didn't know what irritated her more—the cockiness of his tone or the fact that he was right. Of course, she had no intention of admitting as much.

"Nothing's going to happen between us," she told him in her firmest teacher voice.

"Something already happened," he reminded her.

"You kissed me," she acknowledged in a deliberately casual tone. "It wasn't a big deal."

"I might have started it, but you kissed back pretty good," he pointed out. "In fact, I'd say a lot better than pretty good. And it was a big deal."

She felt her cheeks flush. "I did kiss you back, and I shouldn't have."

"Because you feel guilty about Alex?"

It was an easy excuse, and preferable to the truth—which was that one kiss from Sutter had made her want a lot more kisses, a lot more touching, a lot more everything. And that was a dangerous way of thinking.

"No," she admitted. "Alex and I aren't seeing one another anymore. But that doesn't change the fact that I have no intention of starting something with you again."

"I'd say it's already started," he told her.

She shook her head.

"Are you really trying to deny the chemistry between us?"

"We didn't break up because of a lack of chemistry," she reminded him.

"You're right," he admitted. "But the more time I spend with you, the more difficult it is to remember why we did break up."

"Because you were determined to get out of Rust Creek Falls and I didn't want to leave. And that hasn't changed."

"Maybe it has," he said. "Why won't you at least give us a chance?"

She shook her head again.

"I'm not the same man I was five years ago," he told her. "And I'm not going to walk away from what I want this time."

"Whether you stay or go is your choice—but don't make the mistake of thinking it has anything to do with me."

"If I stay, will you go out with me?"

"No."

"I'm not asking you to make any life-altering decisions, I'm just asking you to spend some time with me."

She picked up the empty plates and carried them to the sink. She refused to let herself even think about his invitation. No good would come from spending time with Sutter—and despite her assurance to her sisters, she knew that her heart wasn't nearly as Sutter proof as she wanted to believe. In fact, it was already softening as her resolve was weakening.

"Just one date," he cajoled. "And if you don't have a good time with me, I'll back off."

"Really?"

"Really," he assured her.

"Just one date?" she asked, still skeptical.

"One date. Whatever you want to do."

Paige considered for another minute, her common sense warring with her curiosity. And in the back of her mind, it occurred to her that if he was offering to do anything she wanted, she really could use his help with something. She finally nodded. "Okay."

"How does tomorrow night sound?"

She shook her head. "Tomorrow morning. Early."

"How early?"

"You can pick me up at eight."

Sutter suspected that his Saturday-morning date with Paige was going to be unlike any other date he'd ever experienced. His first clue was the hour—obviously she wasn't planning a candlelit dinner and romantic movie, but he didn't care. All that mattered was that he would get to spend time with Paige. But as he made his way into town Saturday morning, it occurred to him that the only time he'd been at a woman's house at eight in the morning was when he'd spent the night before in her bed.

Unfortunately, he hadn't spent Friday night in Paige's bed. But he did pick up breakfast for both of them—if donuts and coffee from Daisy's Donuts could be considered breakfast. Since she hadn't told him what their plan was for the day, he'd dressed casually in a pair of jeans and a flannel shirt with his favorite leather jacket. He'd nicked his jaw when he was shaving, so he double-checked his face in the rearview mirror to make sure he didn't have any tissue stuck to the cut before he exited the vehicle.

She met him at the door, obviously eager to get going—wherever it was they were going. She was dressed just as casually in jeans, a zip-up hoodie and jean jacket. But he couldn't help but notice how the softly faded jeans molded to the sweet curve of her buttocks, or how the layers she wore on top emphasized the slenderness of her frame. She had running shoes on her feet and her long dark hair was pulled back into a ponytail.

Aside from the simple silver hoops that hung from her ears and the pink gloss on her lips, she wore no decorations or makeup. Of course, Paige had the kind of natural beauty that didn't require any artificial enhancement. She looked young and fresh and as beautiful as always. And when she smiled at him, his heart actually ached.

"You made it." Her eyes lit on the paper cup holder in his hand and her smile widened. "And you brought coffee?"

"And donuts," he told her.

"What kind?"

"Powdered sugar with lemon filling."

She reached for the bag. "It's not fair that you know all my weaknesses."

"And some much more interesting ones than cheesecake and powdered-sugar donuts."

"One date," she reminded him, pulling a donut out of the bag. "And then you're going to back off."

She sounded so optimistic he might have been insulted if he didn't believe that her desperation to get him out of her life was a reflection of the depth of her feelings for him. "I will back off," he agreed. "If you don't have a good time."

She bit into the donut. "The fact that I'm going to enjoy this doesn't count."

"Okay, the good-time register doesn't start until the coffee and donuts are done and we're at… Where are we going?"

"To the elementary school."

"Isn't it still under repair?"

"Yep." Her lips curved, just a little. "You know how to swing a hammer, cowboy?"

"I think I can figure it out."

The repair of the school was coming along slowly but surely. The first part—tearing out everything that had been damaged by the flood—had been completed fairly quickly thanks to the large number of residents who had volunteered to help out. The second part—rebuilding what had been destroyed—was a bigger task, and a more costly one. Numerous delays had held up the work, mostly resulting from a lack of funding.

The school board's insurance company was dragging its feet, insisting that more information was needed before it could settle the claim. Of course, without money there wasn't a lot that could be done. Some supplies had been donated, and a small fund had been collected from residents to help with the rebuild.

But the reality was that almost every family in Rust Creek Falls had been affected by the flood, and while everyone wanted to help, most were in the same predicament, with their time and resources stretched too thin to be able to stretch any further. Even the generous donation that Lissa Roarke, a transplanted Manhattanite now engaged to Gage Christensen, had procured from a New York–based nonprofit organization called Bootstraps hadn't been enough to finance the project.

So Paige was more than a little surprised when they arrived and found twice the usual number of volunteers and every one of them busy at work. The site was buzzing, not just with activity but with information. Apparently Lissa had recently appeared on a national morning show to discuss the plight of Rust Creek Falls, and the result had been an unexpected influx of both monetary donations and building supplies. Having funds and materials made a huge difference, and of course the townspeople had done the rest, volunteering their time and labor. Those who couldn't provide physical labor brought other things to the table—literally.

A handful of picnic tables had been set up on the property and from noon until about two o'clock, there were platters of sandwiches and a steady supply of Crock-Pots filled with hot soups and stews to fuel the workers. There were also plates of cookies, bowls of fruit and vats of coffee.

Paige and Sutter focused their efforts on her fifth-grade classroom. They worked with Dean and Nick Pritchett, who expertly measured, cut and installed the last of the drywall, following behind to tape and mud the seams and nails. Of course, Dean and Nick were finished long before Paige and Sutter, leaving the two of them working alone together for most of the afternoon.

"Is this how you spend every Saturday?"

"For the past few weeks," she admitted. "For a long time there wasn't anything to do because we were stuck waiting for permits and funding. Considering that, it's amazing how much progress has been made in such a short time."

"Are all of the teachers here?"

"Not just teachers, but support and admin staff, parents and a lot of citizens who have no direct interest in the school and their own work to do. It's the way that towns like Rust Creek Falls work."

"I haven't been gone that long," he noted drily.

"I know," she admitted. But at times it had felt like forever. "And I know life in the big city hasn't changed you too much."

"How do you know that?"

"Because you came all the way from Seattle when you heard about the flood."

"It isn't all that far."

But she knew that it was. More than five hundred miles, and there were times she felt as if it might as well have been five thousand because of the distance the move put between her and Sutter.

"Well, I know it meant a lot to your family, that you came home." She leaned over and touched her lips to his cheek. "And it meant a lot to me that you were willing to help out here today."

When she started to draw back, he slipped his arm around her waist and held her close. "I was willing to do anything, so long as it meant spending some time with you."

"Why?"

"Because I miss you. I didn't even realize how much until I came home and saw you again."

She'd missed him, too, which was exactly why she didn't want to go down the same path again. "Spending time together is only going to make it harder when you leave again."

"But you had a good time today, didn't you?"

"I feel good about what we accomplished here," she allowed.

"C'mon, Paige. Just admit you had a good time."

"I had a good time."

"Me, too," he said, and smiled as he lowered his head toward her.

She lifted her hands to his chest. "What are you doing?"

"You kissed me," he said. "Now it's my turn to kiss you."

"It was just to thank you for helping out today."

His mouth hovered just a fraction of an inch above hers. "Then you can consider this a thank-you for letting me help out," he said, and captured her lips.

Paige knew she should pull away, because letting Sutter kiss her again was a tried-and-true recipe for heartbreak. But as soon as his mouth touched hers, all thoughts of resistance were forgotten. In that first moment of contact, she couldn't seem to focus on any of the dozens of reasons that this was a bad idea. She could only think that this was exactly what she wanted.

Her eyes drifted shut; her body swayed toward him. His hands slid up her back, drawing her closer. He tilted her head back, deepened the kiss. The hands she'd lifted to hold him at a distance slid over his shoulders to toy with the soft, silky strands of hair that touched his collar.

He touched the tip of his tongue to her lips, delved inside when they parted for him. Her arms had wrapped around him and her breasts were crushed against his chest, her hips aligned with his. Despite the layers of clothes between them, she could feel the heat of his body, the imprint of his hands, the press of his erection. Heat rushed through her veins, pooled low in her belly.

There was definitely chemistry between them.

Very potent chemistry.

But as she'd reminded him the night of the election,

the attraction between them had never been the issue. Right now, in the comfort of his arms, she had trouble remembering what the issue had been. What had come between them? And why had she ever let him go?

When he finally eased his lips from hers, they were both breathless. After a moment, he said, "Now that makes it official."

She realized that she was still in his arms, her cheek resting against the warm flannel of his shirt so that she could feel the steady beat of his heart. She forced herself to take a step back. "Makes what official?"

"It's not really a date unless it ends with a kiss," he told her.

It was the perfect excuse to say goodbye and find her own way home. They'd spent the day together working at the school—not a traditional date by any stretch of the imagination, but he had allowed her to choose the venue—and now it was over.

And yet she heard herself say, "If our date is ended, does that mean you're not going to buy me dinner?"

He seemed just as surprised as she was by the words that came out of her mouth, but he recovered quickly. "I'll buy you dinner," he agreed readily. "But I think I'm going to need a shower first."

She glanced down at her mud-spattered clothes. "Me, too."

"You know, it would conserve water if we took that shower together," he suggested.

She shook her head. "Your environmental consciousness is impressive, but I don't see that happening."

He just grinned. "Can't blame a guy for trying."

Paige had just stripped out of her clothes when there was a knock on the door. Thinking that Sutter had forgotten something—or was pretending that he'd forgotten something in the hope of catching her half-dressed—she hastily tugged on her robe and went to the door.

"Yes, I believe in conserving…" The words faded away when she realized it wasn't Sutter on her porch but her middle brother. "Oh, Travis. Hi."

His brows drew together as his gaze skimmed over the robe. "You were expecting someone else?"

She sighed and stepped away from the door. "I wasn't expecting anyone. Sutter just left and—"

"So that *was* him—the guy you were with at the school?"

"Yes, we were both at the school." She went to the fridge and pulled out a bottle of the beer that she kept on hand for whenever one of her brothers visited—which they rarely did.

Anderson, Travis and Caleb were all busy with their own lives, but she knew that they were never far away. And though she didn't often call on them for help, it was comforting to know that they were close if she needed anything.

Her brother's scowl deepened as he twisted the cap off the bottle. "Why was he there?"

"Because we need all the help we can get if we have any hope of getting the kids back into that building for the beginning of the new year," she reminded him. "Why are *you* here?"

He straddled one of the stools at the island. "I ran into Nate as I was fueling up at the gas station."

"And that was so noteworthy you had to stop by to tell me about it?" Since it seemed as if her brother was settling in, she considered pulling another beer out of the fridge for herself. Except that she was going to be seeing Sutter again in a while, and the last thing she needed was to have her ability to think clearly compromised by alcohol, especially when just being near Sutter tended to cloud her mind.

"I stopped by because he happened to mention that he'd seen you with Sutter Traub."

She doubted he had just happened to mention it—knowing Nate Crawford, it was more likely he'd deliberately tattled to her big brother. "So?"

He frowned at her response. "You're not denying it?"

She leaned back against the counter and folded her arms across her chest. "Rust Creek Falls is hardly a booming metropolis. As long as Sutter's in town our paths are going to cross, and I don't have to explain my actions to anyone—not to you and certainly not to Nate Crawford."

"What about to Alex Monroe?"

"My relationship with Alex isn't any of your business, either," she told him. "But if it was, I would tell you that we aren't seeing each other anymore."

"Because of Sutter?"

"Because our relationship wasn't going anywhere."

"I always liked Sutter, but I don't want you to get hurt again," Travis said sincerely.

"I don't want that either, but I'm not going to cut Sutter out of my life just because we have a history."

"It's not the history that worries me but the present," he said.

"You don't need to worry at all," she assured him.

"Just...be careful."

"I always am. That's why I've got half a dozen condoms in my purse."

His jaw dropped open; she laughed.

"Relax, Trav. I'm kidding."

He closed his mouth, cleared his throat. "Actually, I

hope you're not kidding. Not that I want to know about your sex life—or even if you have one—but if you do, you should take precautions."

He was adorably flustered and earnestly sincere, and she lifted herself up on tiptoes to kiss his cheek. "Thanks for the sex ed lesson, big brother. I'll keep that in mind."

Sutter didn't pay too much attention to the speed limit on the way to the ranch, and when he got back to Clayton's house, he took a quick shower. He'd made some progress with Paige today, as evidenced by the fact that she'd been the one to suggest they extend their date to include dinner, and he was determined to build on it.

But he knew that if he left her alone for too long, if he gave her too much time to think, she might change her mind about going out for dinner with him. And he didn't want to risk that happening.

Less than an hour after he'd dropped her off, he was back at her house, freshly showered and cleanly shaven, but there was no response to his knock on the door. Her car was in the driveway and there were lights on inside, so he knocked louder.

Finally the door was flung open. "Sorry," Paige said. "I'm running a little behind schedule."

A fact that was verified by the thick terry robe she was wearing and her dripping-wet hair. He stepped into the foyer.

"My brother stopped by," she explained. "Not for any particular reason as far as I could tell, but…"

He was only half-listening to her words, far more intrigued by the droplet of water that was slowly tracking its way down her throat, then over her collarbone before finally disappearing into the hollow between her breasts.

He didn't have to be a rocket scientist to figure that

she'd heard the knock at the door and thrown on her robe without even toweling herself dry. Which meant that she was naked beneath the robe, and that one tug of the belt knotted at her waist would—

He forced himself to sever the thought and curled his fingers into his palms to resist the urge to reach for her.

"Sutter?"

He yanked his gaze from her chest. "Yeah?"

She huffed out a breath and drew the lapels closer together. Despite her apparent indignation, the flush in her cheeks and the darkening of those chocolate-colored eyes proved that she was feeling the same awareness that was heating his blood.

"I said there's beer and soda in the fridge, if you want a drink while you're waiting."

"Sorry, I wasn't paying attention," he admitted. "I was thinking about how incredibly hot you look right now."

She pushed her sodden bangs away from her face. "I'm a complete mess."

"Do you remember when we cut through the woods on the way home from that party at Brooks Smith's house and you slipped on the log bridge?"

She shuddered at the memory. "It wouldn't have been a big deal if I'd fallen into water, but the recent drought had reduced the stream to a trickle, and I ended up covered in muck and leaves."

And when they'd got back to the ranch, they'd stripped out of their muddy clothes and washed one another under the warm spray of the shower. Of course, the scrubbing away of dirt had soon turned into something else, and they'd made love until the water turned cold.

"Even then—covered in mud from head to toe—you were beautiful."

"You only said that because you wanted to get me naked."

"Just because I wanted to get you naked doesn't mean it wasn't true. And speaking of naked..."

"I should put some clothes on," Paige realized.

"Don't go to any trouble on my account."

She lifted her brows.

He smiled. "Actually, I didn't mean that as a come-on."

"Really?"

He gently brushed the pad of his thumb beneath her eye. "You look tired."

"I thought I was beautiful."

He smiled. "Incredibly beautiful, but tired. And if you don't feel up to going out, I can go to Buffalo Bart's to get some takeout."

He could tell that she was tempted. But she was also wary. No doubt she was thinking about the fact that takeout would mean coming back here, to her house, where they would be alone together. She shook her head.

"I appreciate the offer," she said, already heading for the stairs. "But I think it would be better if we went out."

"Even if I promise not to jump your bones?"

She paused on the bottom step and sent him a sassy smile. "Maybe you should be worried that I might jump yours."

Chapter Seven

When Sutter pulled into the parking lot of the Ace in the Hole, it was mostly full. Of course, dining options in Rust Creek Falls were extremely limited. Aside from this loosely termed bar and grill (which was much more bar than grill and definitely rough around the edges), there was Buffalo Bart's for wings and a few other fast foods, and Daisy's Donut Shop for coffee, pastries and light lunch fare.

Paige recognized several vehicles in the lot, and belatedly accepted that walking through the door beside Sutter could very well escalate what was supposed to be a casual dinner to an event. Most of the longtime residents knew that Paige and Sutter had been an item in high school and beyond, and not one of them would have been surprised to hear the ring of wedding bells for the two of them. But that wasn't how things had played out. Instead, Sutter had spoken out against his brother's decision to reenlist and had left Rust Creek Falls, and Paige had been left nursing her broken heart.

Sutter pulled open the door and gestured for her to enter. As they made their way to a vacant booth, several people lifted their hands in greeting or spoke a few words, and Paige didn't doubt that they were the subjects of some murmured conversations. There had been speculation, of course, after she'd spoken up in Sutter's defense at the mayoral debate, but most of that had died down within a few days because they hadn't been seen out and about together. Being here tonight changed that.

"I should have asked if your sister was working before we came in here," he said, sliding into the seat across from her.

"My sister?"

"Lani," he clarified. "I came in last week for a burger and she was my waitress."

"She doesn't actually work here," Paige told him. "She just fills in for a friend sometimes. Courtney works at a couple of different places and Rosey can't always schedule her hours around the other job, so whenever there's a conflict, she asks Lani to cover her shift."

"That's good, because if Lani was relying on tips to pay her bills, she should learn something about customer service."

Paige grinned ruefully. "I'm sorry if she gave you a hard time."

"You don't have to apologize for your sister," he told her. "And I can't blame her for being mad at me. Because I can see that from her perspective I didn't just leave Rust Creek Falls—I left you."

Paige shrugged, forced herself to respond casually. "From my perspective, too, but I survived."

"I never doubted that you would. And at the time, I didn't see that I had any other choice but to go," he confided. "Although I realize now that leaving town so soon after Forrest reenlisted only cemented everyone's impression that I didn't support him or his military career."

The waitress—and it was Courtney who was working in their section tonight—came to take their drink order. Sutter asked for a draft beer and Paige nodded to indicate that she would have the same. Usually she preferred wine, but the selection at the Ace in the Hole was limited to red or white house wine, which was whatever happened to be the cheapest bottle available from Crawford's that week.

She waited until Courtney had gone to get their drinks before she responded to his comment. "It doesn't matter what other people thought—or even what they think now."

"That sounds good in theory," he agreed. "But the first time I came back to Rust Creek Falls, Clovis Hart wouldn't let me fill up my tank at the gas station."

"You're kidding."

He shook his head. "I knew that speaking out against Forrest's decision wouldn't go over well with a lot of people—but I didn't expect it would make me persona non grata to the whole town.

"By the time I got to the Triple T, I was on empty. I had to ask Braden to come into town with jerry cans so that I would have enough fuel to drive out of town again."

"I'm surprised you ever wanted to come back again after that," she admitted softly.

"Despite the falling out with my family, they're still my family," he told her. "And despite the fact that our relationship was over, I still looked for you every time I was home. I didn't expect a smile or even a wave, I just hoped to catch a glimpse of you in a crowd somewhere."

"I tried to lie low whenever I heard that you were in town," she admitted. "Because it hurt too much to see you."

"It hurt me, too. You were such a huge part of my life, and then…" His words trailed off as Courtney returned with their beverages.

She set the glasses down. "Did you want anything to eat or just the drinks?"

"We definitely want food," Sutter said, looking to Paige for direction.

"We'll share the nachos grande," she decided.

"For an appetizer maybe," Sutter said.

"Bring the nachos," Paige said to Courtney. "We can order something else after that if we're still hungry."

"Nachos," he said, shaking his head after Courtney had gone.

"They've upsized the order since you left. The nachos are more than enough for both of us," Paige assured him.

"I guess we'll find out," he said. "But next time, I'm taking you to Kalispell to a real restaurant."

She sipped her beer. "What makes you think there's going to be a next time?"

"You had a good time today," he reminded her.

"I did," she agreed. "But I'm already having second thoughts about being here with you."

"So I'm not the only one who feels like an animal trapped in an enclosure at the zoo with spectators pressed against the fence staring at us?"

"No, you're not."

"I don't care if people talk about me—I'm used to it," he said sincerely. "But I don't want to make things difficult for you."

She lifted her glass to her lips. "I guess it just bothers me that everyone who sees us together automatically assumes I'm going to fall for you again—and have my heart broken all over again."

"Everyone?"

"My sisters, my brothers, my friends—even Irene Murphy in the feed department at Crawford's warned be to be careful."

"I would never intentionally hurt you," Sutter told her.

"I know," she said, and she did know. But his lack of

intent hadn't prevented it from happening. When he'd left Rust Creek Falls—and left her—she'd felt as if her heart had been ripped out of her chest.

Yes, he'd asked her to go with him, but he had to have known there was no way she could do so when she was in the middle of her required yearlong in-class supervised teaching experience. And he hadn't been willing to wait five months for her to finish. In fact, he'd been so eager to get out of town she doubted he would have been willing to wait five days.

Thankfully, she'd had her teaching to keep her busy. The work—her own and that of her students—occupied most of her waking hours throughout the day. But for the longest time, dreams of Sutter continued to haunt her nights, and she'd wake up in the morning missing him.

He'd been gone about a year, and she was almost halfway through her first year as a "real" teacher when she decided that she'd been missing him long enough. When she'd crossed paths with Jeremy Wellwood, a local high school teacher, at a conference and he'd asked her to go out, she'd accepted the invitation, determined to forget about Sutter once and for all.

They'd gone into Kalispell to the North Bay Grille for dinner. The meal had been delicious and Paige had really enjoyed chatting with Jeremy and getting to know him a little bit better. They'd talked some more on the drive back to Rust Creek Falls, and when he'd walked her to her door and Paige had thanked him for a wonderful evening, she had been sincerely grateful because she'd had an excellent meal and fascinating company and she hadn't thought of Sutter at all.... Okay, maybe she'd thought of him once or twice, but he hadn't preoccupied her every thought, and that was definite progress as far as she was concerned.

Jeremy was an attractive man, and if her heart didn't beat a little bit faster when he smiled at her, that didn't mean she wasn't attracted to him. She'd figured that only proved that she wasn't a schoolgirl anymore. She was simply past the stage where she was going to get all starry-eyed and weak-kneed over anyone.

And then Jeremy had kissed her. His lips were a little too soft, a little too moist and his technique a little too practiced. Or maybe it was just that his lips weren't Sutter's lips. And when he'd touched her, she'd wanted to pull away rather than lean into him. Because his hands weren't Sutter's hands.

Alone in her bed that night, she'd realized that she'd been subconsciously comparing every man she met to Sutter—and had found them all lacking in some way. The realization frustrated her, because she wanted to share her life with someone, to marry and have a family. For years she'd believed she would have that family with Sutter. But he'd made it clear that he had no intention of coming back to Rust Creek Falls for anything more than the occasional visit, so she had to stop wanting what she couldn't have and think realistically about her future.

When Jeremy called her again, she'd ignored her reservations and agreed to another date. Over the next few months, there were several more dates until she finally decided she was ready to take the final step. The next time he'd invited her back to his place, she'd accepted. She had sex with him, and after she went home, she'd cried herself to sleep.

He called her the day after, but she admitted that she was still not completely over her ex. It didn't seem to matter that Sutter had been gone for almost two years. He was still firmly entrenched in her heart.

She felt horrible about what had happened with Jeremy. She'd liked him and enjoyed spending time with him, but she hadn't cared about him as much as she'd cared about proving that her relationship with Sutter was firmly in the past. She'd thought that sleeping with someone else would make her forget the only man she'd ever loved. Instead, it had proved to her that physical intimacy without real emotion was cheap and meaningless.

After that, she'd vowed that she wouldn't fall into bed with another man until she was sure that she genuinely cared about him and could imagine a future for them together. Alex Monroe was supposed to have been that man, and she'd honestly thought they were heading in that direction—until Sutter came back to town.

She was twenty-seven years old and she'd had only two lovers. She wasn't sure if that was admirable or pathetic. Was her limited experience a reflection of discriminatory taste or simple disinterest? And what did it mean that her formerly dormant libido was humming whenever she was around Sutter?

Thankfully, Courtney returned to their table, saving Paige from further introspection.

The nachos were heaped on a platter and layered with spicy ground beef, melted cheeses, diced tomatoes, sliced black olives and jalapeños, with bowls of sour cream and salsa on the side. Sutter's eyes widened when the waitress slid the platter into the middle of the table.

"Still think you're going to need more than this?" Paige teased him.

He shrugged. "I guess that depends on how much you're going to eat."

She lifted a chip heavy with meat and cheese from the top of the platter. "As much as I can."

He grinned and gestured for Courtney to bring them a couple more drinks.

They both dug into the chips, eating more than talking until they'd devoured half of them. The nachos were salty and spicy, and Paige downed her second draft fairly quickly. She'd never been a heavy drinker, but she was thirsty and the beer went down easily, so when Courtney asked if she wanted another, she nodded. Sutter shook his head in response to the same question but ordered a soda, no doubt conscious of the fact that he was driving.

"I almost forgot how much you liked Mexican," he noted.

Paige wasn't eating with as much enthusiasm now, but she continued to pick at the chips. "My second favorite kind of food."

"What's the first?"

"Anything sweet," she admitted.

"I'd love to take you to Seattle sometime," he said. "There's a little restaurant tucked at the end of a residential street that serves seriously authentic Mexican. The menu is written in Spanish, the tamales are homemade and the margaritas are icy and tart."

Her brows lifted. "You don't strike me as the margarita type."

"I'm not," he admitted. "But Jenni guzzles them down like water."

She didn't want to ask. His life in Seattle was none of her business, but he'd dropped the name so easily, her curiosity was undeniably piqued. "Who's Jenni?"

"Jenni Locke—the head trainer at my stable."

"I thought most trainers were men."

"I'd say the majority probably are," he agreed. "But there are increasing numbers of women in the field and I have to say Jenni is one of the best I've ever known."

She traced the ring of condensation on the table with her fingertip. "How long has she been with you?"

"Since the beginning."

"You must know her pretty well, then."

"You work closely with someone for three years, you get to know them pretty well," he agreed.

"Are you...involved?"

He paused with a nacho halfway to his mouth. "What?"

She shook her head. She hadn't meant to ask the question and wasn't sure she wanted to know the answer. "Forget it."

Of course he didn't forget it. Instead, he said, "Do you mean *romantically* involved?"

"I shouldn't have asked. It's none of my business."

He dropped the nacho onto his plate. "I would have thought you knew me better than to think I'd be kissing you if I was involved with someone else."

"Five years is a long time," she reminded him. "I'm not sure I know you at all anymore."

"I haven't changed, not that much. And to answer your question—no. Jenni and I are not, and never have been, romantically involved.

"She is, however, one of my best friends in Seattle. In fact, she and Reese, my stable manager, are probably my two best friends. Although that might be simply because we spend so much time together," he admitted wryly. "But we also have a lot in common, including a vested interest in the success of Traub Stables."

She hesitated on the verge of asking another question to which she might not like the answer, but decided that she had to know. "Do you miss being there?"

"I miss the routines," he admitted. "I miss looking around and knowing that everything I see is mine." He held her gaze across the table. "But right now, I don't want to be anywhere but exactly where I am."

And right now, that was enough for Paige.

* * *

Paige nibbled on a few more chips, then pushed the platter closer to Sutter. "I'm done."

He was close to being done himself but unwilling to admit defeat. He picked up a nacho and dunked it in salsa. "How about you?" he asked her. "Do you love teaching as much as you thought you would?"

"Even more," she said, then stifled a yawn.

"Tired?"

She nodded. "It's been a long day."

"And a busy one," he agreed.

"But it's starting to look like we might actually make our target of having the school ready for the new year."

"Which means you'll get your living room back."

She smiled. "I don't mind so much. It beats the alternative of not being able to hold classes at all—I can't imagine the kind of mischief some of my students would get into if there wasn't any structure to their days."

"That would be their parents' problem, not yours," he pointed out.

"Says the man from the big city."

"What's that supposed to mean?"

"Just that maybe you have forgotten how things work in towns like this—any problem is everyone's problem, whether it's a natural disaster or a kid who goes around causing trouble because he's got too much time on his hands."

"What about a kid who swipes a red licorice rope in a misguided attempt to impress a pretty girl?"

"Usually a parent's reprimand is sufficient to ensure that kind of delinquent behavior doesn't become a habit."

"I was reprimanded by my father's hand on my butt," he reminded her.

"And I kissed your cheek to apologize for getting you into trouble."

"Not the one that hurt."

She smiled. "I'd almost forgotten about that."

"I didn't," he told her. "I was ten years old, and it was my first kiss."

"And I still have a weakness for red rope licorice," she admitted.

"I'll keep that in mind." He leaned back in his seat and picked up his soda. Looking around, he noticed the empty stage at the back of the room. "Do they ever have live music here anymore?"

"Maybe two or three times a year. Rosey figures the jukebox is all she needs to provide in the way of musical entertainment—and it's already paid for."

"Then she hasn't changed at all in the past five years," he mused.

"The only thing that's changed is the menu," Paige told him. "Although wings and burgers are probably still the most popular items, she did upgrade the nachos and added wraps and even salads."

"Salads?"

"Not standard cowboy fare," she acknowledged. "But it has brought more women here at lunchtime."

The jukebox Paige mentioned had been eating up quarters all night with a standard assortment of country-and-western tunes playing consistently in the background, so he was pleasantly surprised to hear one of Shania Twain's biggest hits start up.

"Do you remember this song?" Sutter asked.

Paige nodded but kept her gaze firmly fixed on the glass she held between her hands. "It was a huge hit when we were in high school."

"*And* the first song we danced to at your junior prom," he reminded her.

She just nodded again.

He glanced toward the center of the room, where a few couples had ventured onto the dance floor. He tipped his head in that direction. "What do you think—want to hit the dance floor for old times' sake?"

This time, she shook her head. "No, thanks."

"Why not?"

"People started talking as soon as we walked through the front door—imagine how the goship would spread if we stepped onto the dance floor together."

"I'm not afraid of a little gossip."

"'Cuz you don't live here."

"Was it really that bad when I left?"

"No," she said. "It was worse. And not jus' 'cuz people talked about our breakup, but 'cuz they all felt sorry for me. 'Poor Paige—dumped and abandoned by her boyfriend.'"

He winced. "You should have told them the truth—that *you* dumped *me*."

"I didn't *dump* you. I wanted you to stay." She picked up her glass again and frowned when she discovered that it was empty.

"Did you want anything else? Soda? Coffee?" He didn't suggest another beer because he'd noticed, even if she hadn't, that she was starting to slur her words just a little.

"No," she decided, shaking her head. "I'm ready to go."

He paid the bill, then stood up. She slid out of the booth, ignoring the hand he offered to her. He figured it was like the dance floor—she didn't want to give the locals anything to talk about.

The rusty hinges of the screen door protested when she pushed it open. She paused on the porch to draw in a deep breath of the cold night air.

Sutter stopped beside her. "Are you okay?"

"I'm not sure," she admitted. "My ears are buzzing, and my head's floating—" she held a hand about six inches over her head "—somewhere around here."

"You never were much of a drinker," he remembered.

"I'm still not." She drew in another breath. "I prob'ly shouldn't have had the shecond beer."

"I think it's more likely the third that you're feeling."

She turned her head to look at him, her brow furrowed. "I didn't have three."

"Yeah, you did."

"Well, that would 'splain the buzzing in my ears."

He led her to his truck, helped her into the cab and made sure she was buckled in before he went around to the driver's side.

She didn't say much on the short drive back to her house. When he pulled into her driveway, he realized it was because she'd fallen asleep. He opened her door and nudged her awake.

"Come on, sleeping beauty. You're home."

He walked her to the door to make sure she got inside safely. He didn't intend to go any farther, except that she squinted at the key she pulled out of her pocket and couldn't quite slide it into the lock. He covered her hand with his own to help guide her movements. The deadbolt released, and he turned the knob.

"Do you have any acetaminophen?"

"D'you have a headache?"

He smiled. "Not for me—for you."

"I don't have a headache," she told him.

"You might in the morning," he warned.

She went to the kitchen, poured herself a glass of water and shook a couple of tablets out of the bottle she located in the cupboard.

"You want me to take you up to your bed now?"

She looked up at him, her solemn gaze considering him. "Yeah," she admitted on a sigh. "But I don' think thatsa good idea."

Chapter Eight

Sutter had to smile, not just at her erroneous interpretation of the question but her unexpected reply to it.

"I was only asking if you wanted me to help you upstairs and get you settled," he clarified, though his own thoughts had now shifted in a very different direction.

"You can't help me get shettled—you make me *un*shettled."

"Not nearly as unsettled as you make me, I'll bet."

"D'you ever lie awake at night thinkin' 'bout me and wishin' I was there?"

"Every night," he admitted.

"D'you dream 'bout me?"

"Every night," he said again.

"Good," she decided. "'Cuz I dream 'bout you, too."

"What do you dream about?" he asked, because he was curious and she seemed to be in the mood to talk.

Her lips curved as her eyes drifted shut. "I dream 'bout you kissing me, touching me. And it's so real.... I can almost feel your hands on my body." She took his hands now and moved them to her breasts. "I *want* to feel your hands on my body."

Oh, damn—he had *not* anticipated this, and his own body's response was immediate and undeniable. As all the blood in his head migrated south, he knew he should pull his hands away, but hers held his immobile, and he felt her nipples bead beneath his palms.

"Touch me," she said.

He couldn't seem to help himself. His fingers gently kneaded the tender flesh; his thumbs brushed over the tight buds. She moaned low in her throat, a sensual sound of appreciation that made his whole body ache with want.

"Kiss me."

There was no way he could refuse. Not that she gave him much choice in the matter. Even before the words were out of her mouth, her hands were linked behind his head, urging his mouth down to hers.

She might be feeling some effects from the alcohol, but it hadn't affected her coordination at all. She fastened her mouth on his in a kiss that was soft and warm and incredibly sweet. Then her tongue slid between his lips to dance with his, and the flavor changed to something hotter, spicier and infinitely more dangerous.

In some distant part of his brain, it occurred to Sutter that one of them should think about this rationally—and he didn't think it was going to be Paige. With sincere reluctance, he eased his mouth from hers.

"It's late," he said.

Her only response was to take his hand and start up the stairs.

Since Sutter was pretty sure she was heading toward her bedroom, he tried to hold back. "I really have to be going."

But his resistance made her stumble on the next step. With a muttered oath, he scooped her into his arms and carried her up.

"First room on the right," she told him.

He stepped just inside the door and set her back on her feet. She slipped her hands beneath the hem of his T-shirt, slid her palms over his chest. She pushed the fabric up and pressed her lips to his chest, where his heart was beating a frantic and desperate rhythm.

He tugged her hands away. "Honey, you're just a little bit—" *Topless,* he realized, his jaw on the floor. Before he'd managed to get a complete sentence out of his mouth, she'd tossed her shirt aside and her bra had immediately followed.

She'd asked him to touch her, to kiss her, and he wanted to do that and a whole lot more. But he was a grown man with at least a tiny bit of self-control, and he managed to restrain himself. At least until she took his hands and brought them to her breasts again. His eyes closed, but he didn't know if he should swear or pray for forgiveness, because when she drew him back to the bed, he let her. Then he lowered his head.

He laved her nipple with his tongue, tasting, teasing, then drew the turgid peak into his mouth and suckled. She gasped and arched against him, her fingers threaded through his hair, cupping the back of his head, silently urging him on. He complied, using his lips and tongue and teeth until she was panting and squirming.

He wanted to make love with her more than he wanted to take another breath, but it wasn't going to happen tonight. Not when he knew that Paige didn't really know what she was doing. He might curse his conscience, but he couldn't ignore it.

He pulled away and tried to catch his breath and cool his blood. Her pajamas were neatly folded on top of her pillow. He picked up the top and tugged it over her head.

She blinked at him, apparently confused as to why he was suddenly dressing her instead of *un*dressing her. As he tugged the long-sleeved shirt into place, he kissed her again, because he was afraid that if he gave her a chance to say anything else, he might forget all the reasons that making love with her tonight was a bad idea.

Her hand slid between their bodies to rub over the front of his jeans, where his erection was straining painfully. "You do want me," she realized.

"Wanting isn't the problem."

"Wha's the problem?"

"Three beers," he muttered, and moved off of the bed.

She blinked. "Huh?"

"When we make love, I want to be sure you'll remember it in the morning."

"I'll remember," she told him. "I've never been able to forget."

He picked up her pajama bottoms, holding them out at arm's length to her.

"No one else has ever made me forget," she said as she snatched them out of his hand.

"Forget what?"

She stood up abruptly—and swayed just a little when she got to her feet. He started to reach out to steady her, then dropped his hand again, deciding that any physical contact at this point could be more dangerous than Paige falling over.

She unsnapped the button at the front of her jeans and began wiggling out of the snug-fitting denim. He knew he should look away—if not for the sake of her modesty then for his own peace of mind. But the slow, sensual movement of her hips held him spellbound.

"How it felt to make love with you," she finally answered his question.

When the denim pooled at her feet, she was clad in a pair of pale pink bikini panties with delicate lace trim. He swallowed hard and took a deliberate step back, away from her.

"You're not the only man I've ever been with." She finally covered up those delectable little panties with her pajama bottoms. Also pink but decorated with fat white cartoon sheep.

"I didn't expect that I was," he said. He hoped she wouldn't name names, because he was wound up tight enough right now to want to hunt down all of her other lovers and beat them mercilessly for daring to touch the only woman he'd ever loved.

She pulled back the covers on her bed. "I thought if I slept with shomeone else, I'd fin'ly get over you."

He'd fallen into the same trap too many times before he'd accepted the truth: he would never get over Paige. He could build a new life and even have other relationships, but she would always own his heart.

He moved forward now, but only to pull the comforter up over her. "If it's all the same to you, I'd really rather not hear about your other lovers right now."

"Lover," she said, rubbing her cheek against her pillow.

He stilled. "What?"

"Singular, not plural." She yawned. "There was only one after you."

He stood there for a minute, trying to make sense of what she was saying. The words were simple enough, but the implications were enormous. And his heart seemed to swell inside his chest, buoyed by the possibility that she might still love him, too.

"I bet you've been with lotsa women," she murmured.

Now that she was snuggled under the blankets, he figured it was safe enough to sit on the edge of the mattress. He gently brushed her hair off of her cheek. "No one who ever made me forget about you," he told her honestly.

"You shouldn'ta come back."

"Do you really wish I'd stayed away?"

"No," she admitted. "I wish you'd never gone."

"Since I'm here now, will you spend the day with me tomorrow?"

Her eyes were starting to close. "Thas not a good idea."

"Let's try a different answer," he suggested, and brushed his lips gently over hers. "Say, 'Yes, I'll spend the day with you, Sutter.'"

"Yes, I'll spend the day…" The words trailed off as she drifted into sleep.

Paige awoke in the morning with her throat dry and her head pounding. She eased herself carefully up in bed and pressed her hands to her throbbing temples. A quick glance at the clock revealed that it was almost ten o'clock. Beside the clock was a glass of water, a bottle of acetaminophen and a note: "Take two, drink all the water and call me when you're up." Sutter hadn't signed it, but he had left his cell phone number.

She took the two pills, drank the water and headed to the shower.

There were some fuzzy patches in her memory of the previous evening. Not of the time they were at the Ace in the Hole, but afterward. She thought she'd dozed off on the drive home, then she remembered Sutter walking her to the door.

Had he kissed her good-night?

Her mind suddenly flashed with an image of his hard, strong body pressed against hers. Of those strong, talented hands stroking her skin. Of his hot, hungry mouth devouring hers. Was it a memory or just a fantasy? Either way, the mental picture had her blood racing and her heart pounding, so maybe it was better that she didn't remember.

And it would be really good if she could clear all thoughts of Sutter from her mind before she walked into church.

Her family was already seated in their usual row when she arrived, but she hovered at the back for a few minutes, waiting until the service was about to begin before taking her place beside Lindsay. She figured her tardiness would save her from any interrogation. In truth, it only delayed it.

When the service was over and everyone filed out again, her parents went downstairs for their usual coffee and chitchat with friends and neighbors. Sometimes Paige and her sisters would join them, but she declined the invitation today and Lani and Lindsay opted to leave with her.

"I didn't see Alex in church," Lani noted.

"That's not unusual," Paige said.

"I know," her sister admitted. "But Mom was hoping to invite him to dinner tonight."

"That would be a little awkward," Paige warned.

"Why?"

"Because we broke up."

"When?" Lani demanded.

"A few days ago."

"Are you seeing Sutter now?" Lindsay asked.

"No," she replied, immediately and firmly.

"But you were at the school with him yesterday," Lani noted.

"Yes, because Sutter was bugging me to go out with him, and I suggested that we go to the school as an alternative."

"And after you finished at the school?" Lindsay prompted.

Paige sighed. "Obviously you know someone who saw us at the bar last night."

"Half the town saw you at the Ace in the Hole last night," Lani informed her.

"We were at the school late, and we were both hungry when we finished, so we went to grab a bite to eat."

"Did he kiss you good-night?" Lindsay asked.

"I'm not getting involved with Sutter," Paige said firmly.

Her sisters exchanged glances.

"He kissed her good-night," Lani decided, not sounding the least bit happy about it.

She sighed. "Yes, he kissed me. But that's no reason to make it into something bigger than it is."

"I still can't believe you dumped Alex," Lani grumbled. "He's a great guy."

"He is a great guy," Paige agreed. "And I didn't dump him."

Her sister rolled her eyes. "I doubt he dumped you."

"It was a mutual decision," Paige told them.

"So he wasn't heartbroken?" Lani challenged.

"He definitely wasn't heartbroken," she confirmed.

"Did you want him to be?"

"Of course not," Paige denied. "But considering that we've been dating for a few months, I didn't expect him to be so...unaffected."

"Which, I guess, tells you everything you needed to know about that relationship," Lindsay noted.

"I did really like Alex."

"But he's not Sutter."

"Will you stop trying to make this about Sutter?"

Lani shook her head. "Will you stop trying to pretend this is about anything but Sutter? If he hadn't come back to Rust Creek Falls, if he hadn't kissed you and made you remember what the two of you used to have together, you'd still be with Alex."

"We're just worried about you, Paige," Lindsay said gently.

Paige understood that her sisters were thinking about what was best for her—and no doubt remembering how completely heartbroken she'd been when Sutter had left Rust Creek Falls five years earlier. "I appreciate that," she told them. "But I assure you, there's no reason to worry. I'm not going to get hung up on Sutter again.

"Yes, I've kissed the guy a couple of times. And yes, he is a fabulous kisser. But I have no illusions that a few kisses are going to lead to anything else, because I know that Sutter isn't going to stay in Rust Creek Falls."

"And if he asks you to go to Seattle with him again?"

She just shook her head. "He's never even hinted in that direction, and he knows that my life is here."

"I know that's what you said five years ago," Lindsay agreed. "Because you were trying to convince Sutter to stay, and because you didn't want to be too far away when Gram was so sick. But even when he packed up and left town, you waited for him to come back. You didn't believe he would stay in Seattle for five months—never mind five years."

She was right. Paige hadn't expected that Sutter's move would be permanent. She hadn't believed he would stay away from his family. She hadn't wanted to believe that he would stay away from her. But when she'd refused to go with him, he'd taken that to mean that their relationship was over. She'd tried to explain all the reasons that the timing wasn't good, but he was determined to go—with or without her.

And still she'd thought he would return. But the days had turned into weeks, the weeks into months and the heart that had felt so battered and bruised by his decision to leave Rust Creek Falls had shattered into a billion pieces.

She'd thought about going after him—more times than she wanted to admit. She'd thought about packing up and following him to wherever he was. Because her life felt so empty without him, because she felt incomplete without him.

But even after her grandmother had finally lost her battle with multiple sclerosis and passed away, Paige had had her pride. It hadn't kept her warm at night, but it had refused to let her chase after him. Besides, she'd believed that what she'd told him was true. He had to make peace with his family, and he was never going to do that from five hundred miles away.

And truthfully, she'd been more than a little insecure about their relationship at that point, and terrified by the thought of leaving everything familiar to start a new life in unfamiliar surroundings. It was a testament to how much she'd loved Sutter that she'd even considered it, but his willingness to leave his family in the face of conflict made her wonder if some kind of disagreement might cause him to leave her, too. In the end, that was exactly what happened—they'd had differing opinions as to how he should handle the clash with his family, and he'd left.

The fact that he'd come home now, that he'd heard about the flood and had come back to help his family, gave her hope that he hadn't turned his back on Rust Creek Falls completely. But if he thought his return meant that he could just pick back up where he'd left off with

Paige, he was sorely mistaken. She wasn't going to give him another chance to break her heart.

The problem was, she enjoyed spending time with Sutter. She felt comfortable with him—maybe too comfortable. Because she inevitably let her guard down around him, which meant that she would have to make a concerted effort to avoid him. A more difficult task than she'd imagined when she turned onto her street and saw his vehicle parked in front of her house.

The shiny new truck with the Washington State plates stood out from the more weathered pickups that most of the locals drove and was a tangible reminder of how far he'd gone since he'd left Rust Creek Falls—and proof that he'd chosen to make his life somewhere else and without her.

With that thought in mind, she steeled her resolve and met him on the porch. "What are you doing here, Sutter?"

"I'm here to pick you up."

"Why?"

"Because you got to choose what we did yesterday, so today it's my turn."

"Except that I never agreed to do anything with you today."

"Actually you did," he told her.

She frowned. "When?"

"Last night. When I brought you home after dinner."

Since her memories of last night were still a little fuzzy, she couldn't say for certain that she hadn't. "You had to know that I had a little too much to drink last night."

"How is the head today?"

"Fine." *Now.* "But I'm a little bit…hazy on what was said after we left the restaurant, which means I can't be held responsible for any agreements I might have made. And if you were an honorable man—"

"If I *wasn't* an honorable man, we would have had this conversation several hours ago—in your bed."

That snagged her attention. "What are you talking about?"

"You invited me to spend the night with you."

Her cheeks flamed as the fantasy/memory of their bodies pressed close together shimmered in her mind again.

"I did not," she said, but her denial lacked both strength and conviction.

"You did, too," he told her. "Lucky for you, I realized that you weren't thinking clearly and I didn't take you up on the offer. But I was more than a little tempted."

"I wouldn't have let anything go that far—I don't sleep around."

"I know."

The simple, matter-of-fact statement made her wonder. "Did I tell you that last night, too?"

"Yep," he agreed.

Three beers and she apparently lost not only her inhibitions but control of her mouth. "Did I admit that I've only slept with half a dozen other guys since you left?"

"Actually you said it was only one."

His words made her humiliation complete. Not only had she been intoxicated enough to throw herself at him, but her lack of a sex life since he'd been gone was tantamount to an admission that she'd never gotten over him.

A change of topic was definitely in order. "My parents are expecting me at their house by five o'clock for dinner."

"I'll make sure you're back before five," he promised. "So what did you want to do today?"

* * *

He took her to the Triple T.

Paige should have suspected they would be going to the ranch when Sutter suggested that she change her clothes. She swapped the long skirt she'd worn to church for a pair of jeans and tugged a thick sweater on over her blouse, then tucked her feet into a pair of cowboy boots.

When she realized where they were headed, the nerves inside her belly started to twist into knots. She had more than a few reservations about their destination, mostly because there were so many memories for her at his family's ranch and she didn't want those memories dredged up. Or maybe she was more worried about the feelings evoked by those memories.

He drove past the family homestead and parked his truck by the barn. There were a couple of horses saddled and tethered in the closest paddock. "Obviously Rusty got my message," he said, guiding her toward the waiting animals.

Just the sight of the gorgeous palomino with the golden coat and luxurious blond mane and tail made Paige's throat tighten. Buttercup was the mount that she'd always used when she'd gone riding with Sutter at the Triple T, and she'd sincerely missed the horse when she'd stopped going out to the ranch after he'd gone.

"Do you remember Buttercup?"

"Of course," she admitted, stroking the animal's muzzle with easy affection. "But I don't recognize her companion. Where's Maverick?"

"I took him to Seattle with me."

"Oh. Of course." She should have realized that. Maverick had been Sutter's pride and joy. He'd raised him and trained him, and it made perfect sense that he would have taken the horse with him when he left.

"I wanted to take Buttercup, too," he told her now. "Because the two of them were accustomed to spending a lot of time together, but I couldn't do it. It seemed like I'd be taking her away from you."

"So who's this?" she asked, nodding her head toward the bay gelding with the white blaze on his forehead.

"Toby," he said, and the horse whinnied in acknowledgment.

"Smart," she noted.

The horse nodded his big head; Paige chuckled.

"I packed a picnic lunch for us," Sutter said, checking the saddlebags to ensure it was there. "I figured we'd both be hungry after being out in the fresh air for a while."

"How long is a while?"

"I promised to have you home before five o'clock, and I will," Sutter assured.

"I wasn't thinking about the time so much as I was thinking about my butt," she admitted. "I haven't been on the back of a horse in a long time."

The statement seemed to surprise him. "You used to love riding."

"I loved riding with you." And when he was gone, it wasn't the same. Besides, it wasn't as if she could just take a drive out to the Triple T and saddle up one of the horses to navigate a familiar trail. Her brothers had horses, but again, it had never been the riding she'd enjoyed as much as the company when she'd been with Sutter.

"Do you want to do this?"

"Right now I do," she said. "But I'm well aware that some long-neglected muscles might regret that decision tomorrow."

"I'm more than willing to give you a full-body massage to help loosen up anything that feels tight when we're done."

"That's an interesting offer—" and more tempting than she was willing to admit, especially when being close to him had her feeling tight and achy all over "—but I think I'll pass."

"Well, if you change your mind…"

"I'll let you know," she promised him.

Chapter Nine

It might have been a while since Paige had been on the back of a horse, but she obviously hadn't forgotten anything. She looked good in the saddle, with the wind blowing her long dark hair away from her face, her cheeks pink with cold and her eyes sparkling with happiness.

They rode for almost an hour before they reached the top of the bluff where they'd spent a lot of time during those long-ago summers. There was a trio of silver maples clustered together on one side of a man-made swimming hole and, low on the trunk of the fattest tree, Sutter had carved a crude heart with "ST + PD" inside it. Paige had added the inscription "4EVR."

"Do you want to walk for a bit, to make sure you can still feel your legs?"

"Sure," Paige agreed.

Sutter dismounted, then took Buttercup's reins to hold her steady so Paige could do the same. She slid to the ground, keeping a hand on the horse's flank to maintain her balance.

"You okay?"

She nodded. "But I think having my feet on the ground for a little bit is a good idea."

They walked in companionable silence for a few minutes, enjoying the quiet of the day and the spectacular scenery of the ranch. He'd grown up on this ranch and had taken it for granted for a lot of years. It was only when he'd moved to Washington that he'd realized how much the Montana landscape was part of his heart and soul. There were a lot of things to love about Seattle, and he did, but it wasn't in his blood the way Rust Creek Falls had always been.

The distinctive "kee-eee-arr" of a red-tailed hawk sounded, and Paige stopped to watch the raptor slowly turning in circles as it surveyed the open field for any sign of prey. "They're such graceful creatures."

"Graceful…and vicious," Sutter noted as the hawk swooped down to snag some unsuspecting critter in its claws.

She winced. "Yeah, that, too."

"I guess that means it must be lunchtime."

"Suddenly I'm not very hungry."

Hungry or not, he saw that she was shivering. "You're cold," he said, and silently cursed himself for not realizing it sooner.

"A little," she admitted. "I didn't realize how chilly it was today."

"You're more sheltered from the wind in town," he noted. "Out here, there are no barriers against Mother Nature or her whims."

"I wouldn't want any," Paige said honestly. "Although I wouldn't have minded a heavier jacket."

"I'd planned for us to have a picnic, but now I'm thinking that's not such a great idea."

"Outdoor picnics are better suited for the summer," she suggested.

"We had a lot of them." He stepped up behind her, partly to block the wind but mostly because it gave him an excuse to be close to her, and wrapped his arms around her. She leaned into his embrace, her head tipped back against his shoulder. "We'd spread a blanket in the sun by the swimming hole, eat whatever we'd managed to steal from my mom's kitchen for lunch, take a dip in the water to cool off if it was hot and sometimes you'd let me kiss you."

He wondered if she ever thought about those long-ago summer days, when they'd spent so much time out here, swimming and kissing and sometimes a whole lot more.

Not that there was any chance of anything like that happening today. It was too cold to even unzip a coat, never mind get naked and busy. Although just thinking about the busy part had him feeling all kinds of hot and bothered on the inside. He banished the enticing thoughts from his mind. "Can you ride a little bit farther?"

"Farther into the middle of nowhere?" she asked warily.

He grinned. "We're not as far away from civilization as you think."

He helped her up into the saddle and then he mounted Toby and started away. Ten minutes later, they'd arrived at their destination.

"This is Clayton's place, isn't it?" Paige asked.

"And my temporary home away from home." Sutter tied up the horses and proceeded to fill the trough so they could drink.

While he was doing that, she unpacked the saddlebags. "You're not staying at the main house?"

"I haven't spent a night under that roof since I left," he admitted.

"Oh, Sutter." Her eyes filled with tears.

"Don't feel sorry for me, Paige. I know why things are the way they are."

"Then maybe you can explain it to me."

"I didn't toe the family line."

"You stated a differing opinion—and you had valid reasons for it."

"Valid doesn't mean forgivable," he told her.

"You have to know your mother didn't mean it when she said that if you couldn't support your brother, you weren't welcome in her home."

"My mother doesn't usually say things she doesn't mean."

She frowned. "Are you telling me that, in the past five years, you've never once talked to her about this?"

He opened the door, gestured for her to enter. "What's to talk about?"

She shook her head. "You need to talk to her," she insisted. "Otherwise you're never going to let go of the hurt you're carrying inside."

He led her through the foyer, past the den on one side and the living room on the other and into the eat-in kitchen at the back. "Coffee?"

"Yes, please."

He measured out the grounds, poured water in the reservoir.

"I was mad at her for a long time, too," Paige commented.

"I'm not mad at her."

"You should be," she said. "You had a disagreement with Forrest and she supported your brother, not just taking the side of one son over the other but doing so publicly."

"Okay, maybe I'm a little mad." He took a couple plates out of the cupboard and unwrapped the sandwiches.

"And hurt."

He opened a bag of potato chips and dumped some onto each of the plates. "Let's eat."

She huffed out an exaggerated breath. "You're such a man."

"Thanks for noticing."

"It won't kill you to talk about your feelings," she told him, carrying the plates to the table.

He poured the coffee into two mugs and took a seat across from her. "And what if you're wrong about that?"

"Okay. I'll tell you about mine," Paige decided.

He picked up half of his sandwich, bit into it.

"I was mad at your mother for a long time, too, because I blamed her for your decision to leave Rust Creek Falls," she confided.

"It wasn't her fault."

"That doesn't matter—feelings don't need to be rational, they just need to be." She looked at the sandwich on her plate: thickly sliced ham between slices of fresh bread slathered with mustard, just the way she liked it. But she picked up her mug, sipped her coffee instead. "And it was easier to blame her than to accept that it might have been my fault."

"It wasn't your fault, either," he said in the same deliberately casual tone.

She nibbled on a chip. "I felt as if I'd let you down—but you let me down, too."

"What did I do?"

"You left."

"I'm pretty sure we talked about that," he said drily.

"But I didn't believe you would actually go," she admitted. "I knew you were angry and upset, but I still didn't think you would leave. And when you did, I was sure you wouldn't be gone for very long." She gave him a wry smile. "Obviously I forgot how stubborn you can be."

"Said the pot to the kettle," he noted wryly.

She opened her mouth to protest, then shut it again. "Okay—I could have called and tried to keep in touch."

He didn't ask why she hadn't, for which she was grateful, because she wasn't entirely sure how she would have answered that question. Because the truth—that it hurt too much to know that he was so far away—was too revealing.

"Speaking of keeping in touch—how are things in Seattle?" she asked in a somewhat desperate attempt to redirect her thoughts. Thinking about her history with Sutter was only going to lead to heartbreak; she needed to remember that his present was far away from Rust Creek Falls—and her.

"Everything seems to be under control."

"Seems to be?"

"I have complete faith in Jenni and Reese."

Jenni, she remembered, was his trainer—the one who drank margaritas. And Reese—she tried to remember what he'd told her about him. "Reese is your stable manager?"

He nodded. "And all-around go-to guy."

"Still, you must be itching to get back and check on things for yourself." She kept her voice light, determined not to let him know how much the knowledge that he would be leaving again tore her up inside. Because he'd made her no promises, and he'd certainly never pretended that he was back in Rust Creek Falls to stay.

"There doesn't seem to be any urgent need, and right now I'm more concerned about what's happening here."

"Everything is on track here—thanks to Lissa Roarke. It's amazing how much attention she's drawn to Rust Creek Falls and the devastation done by the floods."

"I wasn't talking about the status of the town, but the status of us."

"I want us to be friends, Sutter. But anything more than that—" she shook her head "—just isn't going to happen."

Sutter seemed to consider her statement for a long minute before he responded. "I can accept being friends," he finally agreed. Then he flashed the smile that never failed to make her knees weak. "For a start."

As the weather continued to grow colder and the occasional dustings of snow started to accumulate, Paige began to appreciate not having to leave her house to go to work. Although holding classes in her home provided a whole other set of challenges, especially when the kids started bouncing off the walls in anticipation of the upcoming holidays. Right after Halloween, their thoughts had fast-forwarded to Christmas, and every one of her students was excited. Everyone except Ryder.

Paige couldn't help but notice that the more the other kids talked about the upcoming holiday, the more withdrawn Sutter's eldest nephew became. She wished there was some way to reach him—to bring him out of himself and get him involved in something.

A recent staff meeting at the principal's house had included a discussion about the elementary school's annual Christmas production. Some of the teachers wanted to cancel it this year, suggesting that their time and attention were better spent on other things. Paige was relieved when the principal insisted that was exactly why the kids needed it more than ever.

Of course, Ryder had no interest in auditioning for the play. In fact, when she suggested it to him, he shook his head. "I don't wanna be in any stupid play." Then, as if aware that his comment might have sounded disrespectful, he quickly added, "ma'am."

Paige didn't press the issue. She understood that some kids lived for the opportunity to get up on stage and others preferred to stay in the background. So she waited a couple of days, and then she casually mentioned that there was a lot of work to be done on the scenery for the play. Though he had a tendency to downplay his talent, Ryder was quite artistic. She didn't expect him to jump up and volunteer, and he didn't, but when she told him that she would appreciate any help he could give her on the project, he silently nodded his agreement.

While her days were busy with her students, Paige knew that Sutter was keeping busy, too. He was usually at the ranch, helping his father and his brothers with whatever needed to be done at the Triple T, but when he had time to spare, he made his way into town and invariably found somewhere else to lend a hand.

And whenever he was in town, he stopped by to see Paige before he headed home again. And the more time she spent with him, the more difficult it was to remember that they were only friends.

If she didn't see him every day, he called or texted. Sometimes more than once. She knew that she was playing a dangerous game, but every time she tried to put on the brakes or pull back, Sutter was there. And it would only take one stroke of a fingertip over the back of her hand or a casual brush of his lips against hers and she would forget all the reasons why getting involved again was a bad idea.

With each day that passed, Paige couldn't help but notice that everything seemed better when she was with Sutter. She'd thought she was perfectly content with her life, but with Sutter she was truly happy, and at the same time frustratingly discontented. Because every time he kissed her or touched her, he made her want *more*.

And as one day turned into the next, it got harder and harder for Paige to keep him at a distance. It didn't seem to matter that she knew it would be a mistake to get involved with Sutter again, that it was only a matter of time before he left Rust Creek Falls and headed back to Seattle.

Because the longer he stayed, the more she found herself hoping that he'd stay forever. She knew that wasn't a fair or reasonable hope when he had a business in Seattle, but still it blossomed inside her heart.

And if he asks you to go to Seattle with him again? Lindsay's words echoed in her mind, giving her pause. If he wouldn't stay—would she be willing to go? Her head cautioned against it, but her heart was quietly pounding, "Yes. Yes. Yes." But it was a moot question, because he hadn't asked her.

On Wednesday, Sutter spent the afternoon helping rebuild fences in town, so she invited him to come over for dinner when he was finished. Although he didn't show up at her place until almost seven o'clock, she was just pulling the chicken out of the oven.

"I was going to apologize for being late, but apparently I'm not."

"You are," she told him. "But I'm running behind schedule, too."

"Had to keep some unruly students after class?" he teased.

She just shook her head. "And I have to renege on our plans for tomorrow night."

"Why's that?"

"I have four pounds of ground beef that need to be made into meat loaves."

"You don't even like meat loaf."

She wondered how, after five years, he remembered that when her own mother never did. "It's for my mom," she admitted. "She was carrying a basket of laundry up the stairs and fell and broke her collarbone."

"Ouch," he said, reminding her that he'd suffered the same injury when he'd been thrown from a horse when he was thirteen. "That's not fun."

"No," she agreed. "That's why dinner's late—my dad was in court today so she called me, and I spent three hours at the clinic with her this afternoon."

"Is there anything I can do to help?"

She was touched that he would ask. Especially considering that neither of her parents had been warm or welcoming since his return. But Sutter had always been willing to lend a hand wherever it was needed, as evidenced by his return to Rust Creek Falls despite the tension that remained between him and his parents.

"Thanks, but my sisters have made a schedule of household chores and meal preparation. I'm on dinner prep Tuesdays and kitchen cleanup Thursdays. They've even got Caleb scheduled to do laundry, which makes me doubly grateful that I have my own washer and dryer."

"Are you scheduled for anything on Saturday?"

"Not officially," she told him. "But I'll probably be at the school for a few hours in the morning, and then I need to get started on my holiday baking."

"It's only the middle of November."

"It's not *only* but *already* the middle of November," she clarified. "And with my mom being laid up, I offered to do her baking, too."

"Do you want a few extra pairs of hands?"

She eyed him warily. "I'd say it depends on who those extra hands belong to."

"Me and my nephews."

"I can't quite picture you decorating sugar cookies."

"Well, if it was up to me, I'd show you a more creative

use of icing and sprinkles, but since I promised to take Dallas's boys for the day, that will have to wait."

The heat in his gaze practically singed her from the tips of her toes to the top of her head. And the slow, sexy smile that curved his lips made all of her female parts ache and throb. It was too easy to imagine what he was thinking, and now she was thinking it, too, and wishing that he wouldn't have the boys with him on Saturday.

"You should check with your nephews first," she told him.

"Why?"

"Because I get the impression that Ryder isn't too excited about the holidays."

"Probably because it was the day after Christmas last year that Laurel walked out," Sutter told her.

She hadn't been sure of the exact date, but she'd remembered that it had been sometime around Christmas because it had been a hot topic of conversation in town after the holidays—the fact that Dallas's wife had packed up and walked out, not just on her husband but her children.

Paige still didn't understand how Laurel could have done such a thing. Maybe she'd fallen out of love with her husband—and considering the man's grumpy attitude of late, Paige could understand how that might happen. But she didn't understand how any woman could abandon her children, and Paige's heart broke for the three beautiful boys who had been left behind.

"That would certainly explain his less than jolly attitude," she acknowledged.

"You didn't know?"

She shook her head. "Not any of the details."

"She didn't even talk to him about it," Sutter told her

now. "He just woke up on the morning of December 26 and found a note on her pillow."

"I heard it mentioned that one of the Triple T's ranch hands disappeared around the same time as Laurel."

"I heard the same thing, and if she fell in love with someone else, that might be some explanation for wanting out of her marriage. But whether it's true or not, I don't know. Dallas certainly never confided in me."

"At least she didn't try to take the boys."

"I'd like to think she knew she'd get one heck of a fight from the whole family if she tried, but the truth is, I don't think she wanted them."

"You don't think she's just waiting to get settled somewhere else before she comes back to get them?"

He shook his head. "My understanding is that the divorce papers gave full custody of the boys to Dallas."

"I don't get that—a woman walking away from her children."

And she knew that it wasn't an isolated case. In fact, Sutter's brother Clayton had experienced a similar situation. Although he hadn't been married to the mother of his child—in fact, he hadn't even known his girlfriend had been pregnant until Delia had showed up with the baby in her arms. And when Clayton had let her in the door, she'd dumped the baby in his lap and taken off, concerned about nothing so much as her own ambitions.

Clayton had lucked out, though, when he'd gone to Thunder Canyon and met Antonia Wright. Although she'd been pregnant with another man's baby when they met, the two had fallen in love and married, giving his son, Bennett, and her daughter, Lucy, a more traditional family.

She hoped, for his sake and that of his children, that Dallas would also find someone else to love. But she didn't hold out a lot of hope of that ever happening unless his surly attitude changed. In the meantime, she was pleased to know that the now-single dad was accepting the help that was offered by his family, because raising three active boys alone couldn't be easy.

"If you think the boys want to make cookies," she finally said to Sutter, "you can bring them over after lunch."

Sutter had just picked up the boys from Dallas's house when his cell phone rang. He recognized the number and immediately connected the call.

"I'm hands-free with kids in the car." He issued the warning because his friend's language was sometimes creative and colorful, and Sutter didn't want to have to explain to his brother the how or why if his kids went home with new words in their vocabulary.

"Kids? Heck, Sutter. You've been gone even longer than I realized."

"Funny, Reese. What's up?"

"Doug Barclay's been making noise—he's got Dancer's Destiny entered in the All American Stakes at Golden Gate Fields and he wants to discuss some concerns with you before then."

"I'll give him a call," Sutter promised.

"I got the impression that he wants to see you."

"Are there any problems with Dancer's Destiny?"

"Not that I'm aware of."

"Then I'll give him a call." He crossed over the Sawmill Street Bridge. "Was there anything else?"

"Yeah, we've got four more orders for custom-made saddles. I've sent the details to Collin."

"That's great," Sutter said. But he also knew it wasn't the type of news that warranted a phone call, especially if Reese had already been in contact with the new CT of CT Saddles.

"And I was wondering if you had any idea how much longer you were going to be in Rust Creek," Reese asked now.

"Not offhand."

"But the election's over, right?"

"The election's over," he confirmed. "And Collin's starting to settle in as the new mayor, but…some other issues have come up."

"All right," Reese finally said. "I'll tell Doug that you'll be in touch."

"Thanks. Hey, is Jenni there?"

"No." His friend responded to the question almost before Sutter had finished speaking. "She's, uh, she's in the arena, working with one of the yearlings."

"Okay. Tell her I'll catch up with her later."

"Sure."

Sutter had barely disconnected the call when Ryder said, "Who's Jenni?"

There was more than a bit of an edge to his voice that had all kinds of questions churning in Sutter's mind, but he only said, "She works at my stables in Seattle."

"Is she your girlfriend?"

"Ew—girls are gross," Robbie chimed in.

Sutter stifled a smile. "No," he said in response to Ryder's question. "Jenni isn't my girlfriend."

"Because Miss Dalton's your girlfriend, right?"

Suddenly he understood the edge to his eldest nephew's tone. Although Dallas had tried to keep the details of their mother's abandonment from the kids, Ryder had likely heard rumors about his mother having a boyfriend. And as much as he hated to label his relationship with Paige, especially in any way that put boundaries around it, he decided that, under the circumstances, it wasn't just wise but necessary.

"Miss Dalton and I have been friends for a long time," he informed his nephews.

"You sent her flowers," Ryder said, accusation in his tone.

"Did you kiss her?" Jake wanted to know.

"Ew," Robbie said again. "Kissing's gross."

"How do you know?" his brother challenged. "How many girls have you kissed?"

"None."

"Kissing is not gross," Sutter said. "Not when it's an expression of caring between two people who really like one another."

"Jake likes Mikayla," Robbie said.

"Do not," his brother denied hotly.

"Do, too."

"Do not."

"Boys!"

They immediately fell silent.

He pulled into Paige's driveway and shifted into Park, then he turned to face the three of them in the backseat.

"Girls are not gross and kissing is not gross, although when I was six, I probably thought so, too," he admitted to Robbie.

He shifted his gaze to Ryder. "Miss Dalton is not my girlfriend, although she used to be and I'm hoping that she might one day be again.

"But for today—" he looked from one to the other, including all of them now "—I would appreciate it if you put any other comments or questions on this topic on hold until the drive home."

And maybe by then he'd be one step closer to having Miss Dalton as his girlfriend again.

Chapter Ten

Paige had borrowed some aprons from the supply that Willa kept for her kindergarten class, and she made sure the boys were washed up and their clothes covered before she let them loose in the kitchen. She'd actually started baking the night before, making a couple dozen gingerbread cookies for Sutter's nephews to decorate. Those were in a plastic container in the cupboard, in reserve for when the boys got bored or tired of helping.

Robbie was, of course, totally enthused. He was on his knees on a stool at the island, digging a measuring cup into the bag of flour before Paige even had a chance to ask them what they wanted to make first. Jake headed straight for the bowl of minimarshmallows and immediately set about trying to figure out how many of them he could cram into his mouth. When he finally stopped gagging, he was thirsty from all the sugar, so Paige got him a glass of milk. Robbie decided that he needed a drink, too, but he wanted juice.

Ryder declined her offer of milk or juice with a polite, "No, thank you," then stood in the background, quietly waiting for instructions. She could tell that helping to bake cookies wouldn't make his top-ten list of favorite things to do—heck, it probably wouldn't make a list of the top one hundred—but he didn't protest.

She decided to put Ryder in charge of measuring the liquid ingredients because he was patient and meticulous and less likely to spill anything. Jake was assigned the task of measuring the dry ingredients, and Robbie got to wield the spoon and mix everything together.

"I thought you were going to help with this," Paige said to Sutter, who seemed content to stand back and watch the sloppily choreographed chaos in the kitchen.

"Absolutely," he agreed. "But my job doesn't start until the first batch comes out of the oven."

"What's your job?" Jake asked.

"Quality control."

"What's that?" Robbie wanted to know.

"It's a fancy term for someone who eats the cookies under the pretense of testing to see if they taste good," Paige informed him.

"I wanna be quality control," Robbie decided.

"Me, too," Jake agreed.

"Everyone will get to sample the cookies," she promised. "But we need to make them first."

They made a lot of cookies. And when they'd done as much as they could do, Paige got out the gingerbread cookies and various colored icings and decorations. The boys were each given half a dozen gingerbread cookies to decorate however they wanted. Ryder went heavy on the black icing, claiming that he was making ninja gingerbread men. Jake was more interested in eating than decorating. Robbie liked the colored sugars and holiday sprinkles and his philosophy was the more the merrier.

True to his word, Sutter worked quality control, sampling at least one of everything. But Paige didn't mind, because he didn't hesitate to lend a hand wherever it was required. He stood at the stove and melted marshmallows for the crisp-rice squares, dutifully chopped pecans for the thumbprint cookies and unwrapped dozens of caramels for the caramel nut bars.

When the boys were finished decorating, Paige gave them each a plate with a couple of cookies and a glass of milk. She didn't have a video-game system to occupy them, so they settled for watching a movie on television. Actually, Ryder played some game on his father's old cell phone in front of the television while his younger brothers watched the movie and Paige continued to work.

She still had peanut-butter bars and shortbread and lemon-snowdrop cookies to make, but she was happy with the progress she'd made today. She hadn't been sure if the extra hands Sutter had offered would be a help or a hindrance, and she suspected they'd been a little of both. But in the end, it didn't really matter because she'd sincerely enjoyed spending the afternoon with all of them.

Unfortunately, being with Sutter and his nephews made her think about the children she'd thought they would someday have together. She still wanted to get married and have a family, but she'd resigned herself to the fact that it wouldn't be with Sutter. Until spending time with him had that dream stirring again, and she knew that could be very dangerous. Because five years after Sutter had gone, she knew she still wasn't over him. She wondered if his coming back now and becoming friends would make it easier or harder for her when he went away again.

She rolled her head, trying to relieve the stiffness in her neck. Sutter settled his hands on her shoulders and began to knead the tight muscles. She moaned in sincere appreciation.

"Feel good?"

"Incredible," she admitted.

He dipped his head to whisper in her ear. "I could make you feel even better."

The husky promise in his voice had all her female parts standing at attention, but because she knew there was little chance of him following through, she managed to tease, "Right here and now?"

"Maybe not," he admitted, and sighed. "Are you ready to take a break?"

"I shouldn't," she said. "I still have so much to do."

"Ten minutes," he cajoled. "Come and sit down on the couch and watch the movie."

"Because nothing puts me in the holiday spirit like rampaging dinosaurs," she said drily.

She walked in at the scene where the brother and sister were hiding in the kitchen. She didn't particularly like scary movies, and although she agreed that the velociraptors were pretty low on the evil scale in comparison to knife-wielding psychopaths in goalie masks, she gasped out loud when one of the dinosaurs charged at the girl and crashed into a metal cabinet.

Ryder didn't look up from his screen. Jake glanced back at her and snickered, but Robbie climbed up on the couch beside her and snuggled close. Whether to offer her comfort or be comforted didn't matter to Paige. Within minutes, he was half-asleep with his head in her lap. She brushed a lock of hair off of his forehead. It was soft and silky, his cheeks were still round, his blue eyes—when they were open—still filled with innocence and wonder. Since the Traub genes weren't just evident but dominant in each of Dallas's sons, it was easy enough to imagine that Sutter's little boy might look very much like the one cuddled up against her. Robbie was fighting sleep, and perilously close to losing the battle until a roar from the screen had his eyes popping wide again. He shifted so that he was sitting up again, and stifled a yawn.

"Do you want me to see if I've got any books you might like better than this movie?"

He nodded.

Unfortunately she didn't really have anything age appropriate for a six-year-old, but she found some paper and crayons and sat him at the island to color while she cut and boxed up her goodies.

He'd drawn a couple of pictures—a boy on a horse, a house with a dad and three boys. But then he seemed to run out of ideas or interest.

"Do you want to do something else?" Paige asked him.

Robbie nodded. "Can you help me write a letter to Santa?"

"Absolutely." She closed up the box she'd finished packing, then sat down on the stool beside him.

"Dear Santa," he began, and she dutifully put the pen to fresh sheet of paper.

"I hope you had a good year and have lots of snow at the North Pole. Thanks for the presents you brung last year. I liked the dragon-lair building set best, but the pajamas were okay, too."

She fought back a smile as she carefully transcribed his words. But her smile faded at what came next, and an uncomfortable premonition filled her heart.

"This year for Christmas, I don't want any toys. Please bring my mommy home instead." He looked up when Paige stopped writing, his little brow furrowed. "You hafta write that."

Instead, she put the pen down and turned to face him. "I don't think Santa can bring her back, Robbie," she said gently.

"Even if I don't ask for nothin' else?"

"Unfortunately, only your mommy can decide if she wants to come back. I know you miss her, but—"

"I don't really miss her," he interjected, his tone matter-of-fact. "I just thought if she came home, Daddy wouldn't be sad anymore."

"How do you know your daddy's sad?"

"'Cuz he doesn't laugh anymore." He scraped at a drop of dried icing with his fingernail. "If Santa can't bring my mommy home, can he bring me a new mommy?"

"I think Santa's more accustomed to filling his sleigh with toys," she told him. "And the elves count on little boys and girls wanting toys, because it's their job to make them."

Robbie sighed. "Then I guess I wouldn't mind a deluxe neon alien-invasion spaceship."

After the movie was finished, Sutter packed up the boys—and the cookies that Paige insisted on sending home with them—and drove back to the Triple T. He considered returning to town, but he didn't want to push for too much too soon. He was confident that they would get to where he wanted to go. He just needed to be patient.

On the bright side, Sutter figured he was conserving electricity taking so many cold showers. In fact, he was just out of the shower, lounging on the couch with his feet up and a cold beer in his hand, when Dallas came in.

He gestured to the bottle his brother was holding. "Got another one of those?" he asked.

"Got several," Sutter told him. "Help yourself."

Dallas did, and settled into an oversize chair, his feet stretched out in front of him.

"The boys settled in for the night?"

"Just," Dallas told him. "They were so pumped up on sugar, I didn't think they were ever going to fall asleep."

Sutter lifted his bottle to his lips, drank deeply. "I suppose that's my fault?"

His brother just shrugged.

"They had a good time today, and if they were a little hyper when they got home, well, they're boys."

"That's what Mom said," Dallas admitted.

"You called in the cavalry?"

"She invited us up to the house for dinner."

As he knew she did every night. Ellie loved to cook for her sons and grandsons, and Sutter didn't blame his brother for taking her up on the offer. After working on the ranch all day, Sutter had enough trouble figuring out what he wanted to eat, never mind trying to feed three hungry—and picky—boys.

"What was for dinner?"

"Pork chops, scalloped potatoes, corn and mac and cheese."

Sutter's stomach growled.

"You could have come for dinner, too," Dallas told him. "I know Mom invited you."

And Sutter had declined, as he did almost every day. The one exception was Sunday lunch, when he knew there would be enough family members around the table to defuse the awkwardness. "She did. I already had other plans."

"With Paige?"

"With one of those handy microwavable trays that provides a complete meal, including dessert, in only a few minutes."

His brother wasn't sidetracked by his response. "It seems like you've picked back up with Paige Dalton again."

"Why does it sound as if you disapprove?"

Dallas shrugged. "It's not my place to approve or

disapprove—I'm just concerned that you don't realize you're wasting your time with her."

Sutter was more intrigued than annoyed by the statement. "How do you figure?"

"Because you keep telling everyone your life is in Seattle, and Paige is no more likely to leave Rust Creek Falls now than she was five years ago."

"A lot can change in five years," he told his brother.

Dallas was silent for a long minute before he finally said, "A lot can change in one year—and not always for the better."

"Paige isn't Laurel," Sutter pointed out.

"You're right—Laurel actually said yes when I asked her to marry me, and look how well that turned out."

Sutter frowned, not just at the bitterness in his brother's tone but at the blunt reminder that he'd proposed to Paige before he'd left town—and she'd turned him down. And yeah, that rejection had torn him apart at the time, but with some space and distance, he understood why she'd said no—and why it had probably been the right answer at that time.

Now, five years later, he hoped they would get to the point where he could ask the question again—and get a different answer this time. Because the more time he spent with Paige, the more time he wanted to spend with her. He wanted a life with her, a future, a family.

Watching her with his nephews today, he'd been more convinced than ever that she would be a fabulous mother. She hadn't been fazed by Robbie's exuberance, she hadn't flinched when Jake dropped a carton of eggs on the floor and she'd actually managed to tease a couple of smiles out of Ryder.

She'd been patient and attentive, and when she looked at him over a tray of unbaked and slightly mangled sugar cookies and smiled, he realized that he'd never fallen in love with another woman because he was still in love with Paige. And he didn't think it was too much of a stretch that she might still be in love with him, too.

Of course, she'd claimed to be in love with him five years ago, and—as Dallas had so kindly reminded him— she'd still turned down his proposal. She'd loved him then, but not enough to go to Seattle with him. And if she did still love him now, did she love him enough to give him a second chance? Did she love him enough to want a life with him, even if that life was outside of Rust Creek Falls?

"It's nothing against Paige personally," Dallas said now. "I just don't want you going through what I went through, and I can see you're heading in that direction."

"How do you figure?" Sutter challenged.

"You were high school sweethearts—just like me and Laurel. Everyone assumed you would get married some-day—just like me and Laurel. And when you proposed, you found out that you wanted to get married and she didn't."

"She never said she didn't want to marry me, she just didn't want to get married at that time and under those circumstances."

"The result was the same."

Sutter tried not to let his brother's comment rankle. He knew that Dallas was still smarting over his recent divorce and struggling to balance his responsibilities at the ranch with the demands of three young sons.

"Well, she didn't marry anyone else while I was gone," Sutter noted.

"Are you thinking she's changed her mind and will want to marry you now?" Dallas asked skeptically.

"I'm trying not to think too much and just enjoy the time we're spending together."

His brother shrugged and pushed himself to his feet. "Your time to waste," he decided, and dropped his empty beer bottle on the end table. "Since I can't find enough hours in a day, I better go. Thanks for taking the kids. And for the cookies."

"You should thank Paige for the cookies," Sutter pointed out.

"Yeah," his brother agreed, but they both knew he probably wouldn't go out of his way to do so.

The door closed behind Dallas, leaving Sutter alone with his thoughts again. He wondered about his brother's warnings, but he wasn't going to let Dallas's sour attitude dissuade him. Instead, he found himself thinking about Reese's unexpected phone call from earlier that day.

Sutter was in regular contact with his stable manager. In fact, he would guess that they probably exchanged no less than half a dozen text messages or emails on a daily basis. Which was why he'd been surprised to hear Reese's voice on the phone. The personal communication suggested to Sutter that there was more on his stable manager's mind than Doug Barclay's horse or Collin's saddles.

He felt a little guilty that he wasn't in Seattle to help with whatever Reese needed—but not guilty enough to be willing to leave Rust Creek Falls right now when he was finally making some progress with Paige. Not as much progress as he'd like, of course, considering his extremely high level of sexual frustration, but he was confident about the direction in which things were moving. And the kisses they'd shared reassured him that what he was feeling wasn't entirely one-sided.

But as much as he wanted Paige in his bed, he wanted more than just sex. He wanted a life with her. A future. A family. Unfortunately, there were still a lot of barriers to getting what he wanted. Even if Paige still loved him as much as he loved her, would that love be enough? It certainly didn't solve the problem of geography, and the more than five hundred miles that separated Rust Creek Falls from Seattle would definitely put the "long distance" in the relationship.

What he wanted—what he'd always wanted—was for Paige to choose to go to Seattle with him. But was it fair to expect her to leave her family, her friends and a job she obviously loved in order to start all over again in another city just to be with him? Maybe not, but he figured if she really loved him, she would be willing to do it.

With his brother's words echoing in the back of his mind, he accepted that even if she'd loved him five years ago, she hadn't loved him enough to make that choice. Was it foolish to hope that this time she might decide differently? That she might love him enough to give up her home and her job to build a new life with him?

And if he loved her enough, wouldn't he be willing to do the same?

He scowled at the idea of walking away from everything he'd built in Seattle. But the prospect of walking away from Paige was even more unthinkable.

Which meant that he had to figure out another option.

He picked up the phone and called Reese.

Chapter Eleven

Paige did some more baking after Sutter and the boys left, and when she finally fell into bed later that night, she was exhausted. And still she couldn't sleep. Despite the weariness of her body, her mind refused to stop churning. Because at some point between the crisp-rice squares and the caramel bars, she'd realized that she was still in love with Sutter.

She'd promised herself that she wouldn't fall in love with him again, that she wouldn't make the same mistake twice. And she hadn't. Because the truth was, she'd never stopped loving him.

Unfortunately, she knew that loving Sutter didn't miraculously make everything okay. There were still a lot of obstacles to overcome if they had any hope of maintaining a relationship and building a future together. The geographical distance was only one of those obstacles and, Paige feared, not even the most significant one.

A fact that was confirmed when she went to her parents' house after school on Monday to take her mother grocery shopping.

She didn't mind making the trip to Kalispell, but she was a little frustrated that her mother had been relying exclusively on her daughters for help since the accident that broke her collarbone. The traditional division of labor in her parents' home had never bothered her before, probably because her mother had willingly—and happily—performed all of the domestic chores.

But now that Mary's arm was in a sling, those duties had fallen to Lani, Lindsay and herself while Anderson, Travis and Caleb expected to show up for meals that would be ready and on the table with no effort on their parts. And God forbid any of them should actually pick up a dusting cloth or push the vacuum cleaner around, although Lani's schedule suggested that she hadn't given up hope.

Caleb had seemed willing to tackle the chore assigned to him, but he'd screwed up so badly with the washing machine he'd been permanently banned from the laundry room. He didn't seem overly disappointed about the banishment, making Paige suspect that his screwup had been deliberate.

"Heads up," Lindsay warned under her breath when she opened the door. "Mom heard that you broke up with Alex."

"Because of Sutter," Lani interjected.

Her tone made Paige suspect that her mother had probably heard the news from her sister, but she knew that didn't really matter. If she hadn't heard from Lani, she would have heard it somewhere else eventually, because nothing stayed a secret for very long in Rust Creek Falls. And she'd rather her mother know the truth than think that she was running around with Sutter behind Alex's back.

"It wasn't because of Sutter, and it was hardly a national secret," she informed both of her sisters.

But she was uneasy. Her mother didn't have strong opinions about a lot of things, but she'd clearly expressed her disapproval when Sutter spoke out against his brother's return to Iraq. And when Paige had started dating

Alex Monroe, Mary had been pleased by this "proof" that her eldest daughter was finally over her "silly infatuation" with "that Traub boy" and building a relationship with "a good man." Which meant that, regardless of the reason for the breakup of that relationship, Mary Dalton wasn't likely to be happy about it.

Throughout the drive to Kalispell, Paige kept waiting for her mother to say something about Alex or Sutter, but she seemed content to talk about other matters.

At the meat counter, they saw Carrie Reynolds—a friend of Paige's from high school who now lived and worked in Kalispell. Carrie fluttered her fingers in front of Paige to show off the diamond solitaire on her finger. After Paige had admired the ring and offered congratulations, Carrie said, "We're planning a June wedding. I really hope you can come. And Sutter, too, of course."

"I can only speak for myself," Paige said. "And I will be there."

"But you and Sutter are back together, aren't you?"

She shook her head.

Her friend frowned. "Really? Because I heard from Megan who heard from Rena that you're the reason he's back in Rust Creek Falls."

"Then somebody misheard something." Paige kept her voice neutral and deliberately did not look at her mother. "He came back because of the flood."

"But you've been spending a lot of time with him, haven't you?"

"I teach full-time and I've been helping with the reconstruction of the elementary school—I don't have a lot of time to spend anywhere else. In fact, I have tests I have to mark when I get home, so we should be going."

"Oh. Okay."

"But it was really good to see you," Paige told her. "And congratulations again."

"Thanks. And you should think about bringing Sutter to the wedding anyway. It's always more fun with a plus one."

Mary waited until they were back home and almost finished putting away the groceries before she said to Paige, "I didn't realize that Sutter was still in town."

"He is," she confirmed.

"Have you been out to the Triple T to see him?"

"Yes, I've been to the ranch, and he's been to my house."

Her mother didn't respond, but the thinning of her mouth was a sure sign of her disapproval, which Paige honestly didn't understand.

"You used to like Sutter," she reminded her.

"I did," Mary admitted begrudgingly. "Until he showed his true colors, and they weren't red, white and blue."

Paige sighed. "He didn't want his brother to go into a war zone and risk getting blown up. That doesn't make him unpatriotic, it just makes him human."

Her mother pursed her lips again. "The rest of the Traub family supported Forrest's decision, everyone except Sutter. And then he ran out on his family—and on you."

Paige could hardly claim that he hadn't run out on her when she'd accused Sutter of exactly the same thing. But she also realized that the situation hadn't been quite as black-and-white as she'd wanted to believe, and that she hadn't been an innocent victim. She'd made her choices as freely as he'd made his, and they were both responsible for the consequences.

"It was his choice to leave," she acknowledged now. "But only after he felt that everyone had turned their backs on him."

"He turned his back on his brother first, when all Forrest wanted to do was fight for his country."

"He was scared for his brother. Why can't you understand that?"

"If his brother wasn't afraid to go to war, then he should have been brave enough to support him."

"Because going back to Iraq turned out so well for Forrest," Paige said drily.

"He's a hero," Mary said firmly.

"I don't disagree," she said. "But his time overseas changed Forrest, and Sutter knew that if he went back, it would make things worse, not better."

"You think he somehow knew his brother's Humvee was going to get blown up?"

"I think he knew that Forrest would come home with scars."

"Last time I saw Forrest, he was getting along just fine. You can barely even notice the limp anymore."

"I'm not talking about the injury to his leg," Paige said. "I'm talking about the scars none of us can see—the ones that mark his heart and his soul."

"He seems happy enough with his new bride."

Clearly there was no way she was going to win this argument with her mother, though that didn't stop her from trying. "But it took him a long time to get there."

"And from what I've heard, with no help from his brother," Mary said. "What has Sutter done to mend their relationship?"

"I don't know," she admitted. "But I know he's changed. He's not the same man he was five years ago."

"And hopefully you're not the same woman," Mary said bluntly. "Because when he left, you cried for weeks."

"Yes, I cried," she admitted. "Because he wasn't just

my boyfriend, he was my best friend, and I didn't want him to go."

"I couldn't stand it if he hurt you like that again."

She sighed. "I know you only want what's best for me, but I'm twenty-seven years old—don't you think I know what's best for me?"

"Not if you think it's Sutter Traub," Mary said implacably.

Paige knew her mother meant well—honestly, she did—but that knowledge did nothing to stifle the urge to scream at her for being so completely unreasonable. Instead of screaming, she carefully folded the empty grocery bags and tucked them into the drawer reserved for that purpose.

"I really have to get home. I've still got those tests to mark for tomorrow."

"You're not going to stay for dinner?"

She shook her head. "I've got leftover meat loaf at home," she reminded her mother, then kissed her cheek.

"Call when you get home," Mary said, as she always did when her daughter headed out the door.

"I will," Paige confirmed, because it was easier to acquiesce than to remind her mother—for the thousandth time—that she lived less than a five-minute drive away.

Tonight that five-minute drive wasn't nearly long enough to diffuse her frustration, although Paige didn't know if she was more frustrated with her family or herself.

She was twenty-seven years old—she didn't need their approval. But they were her family, and she didn't like to be at odds with them over anything. The Dalton and Traub families had known one another forever and had always gotten along well. That hadn't changed when Sutter had left Rust Creek Falls. The only thing that had changed was that he had suddenly become an outcast, not just to her family but to the whole town, including his own.

Paige had never really understood how that had happened. She might not have agreed with Sutter's position regarding his brother's reenlistment, but she understood. If one of her brothers had decided to pick up and join the army during a war, she would be incredibly proud of him—and absolutely terrified *for* him. She would have felt all the same things that Sutter had felt, and she didn't like that he'd been made a scapegoat for daring to speak aloud what many others had been thinking and feeling.

She'd had words with Ellie Traub not long after Sutter had left town, when she'd crossed paths with Sutter's mother at the library. Those words played back in her mind now.

"Have you talked to Sutter?" Ellie's tone was hopeful, almost desperate.

Paige shook her head.

Disappointment had the other woman's eyes filling with tears. "I wish you'd gone with him. I hate knowing that he's so far away—and all alone."

It wasn't in Paige's nature to be disrespectful, and she loved Ellie like a second mother, but the unfairness of the statement demanded a response. "Well, I wish he hadn't left Rust Creek Falls at all," she said coolly. "But what choice did he have when his own mother told him he wasn't welcome in her home?"

"I didn't mean it like that," Ellie protested, and started to cry. "I never wanted him to go. I only wanted him to support his brother."

Of course, her tears had only made Paige feel worse. They'd ended up crying together—bound by their love for Sutter and their grief that he was gone—and they'd made their peace with one another. Unfortunately, Paige didn't know how to get her parents to make peace with Sutter's choices.

Part of it was her own fault. She knew her family was protective of her because Sutter had broken her heart. What should she have done—act as if it didn't matter that he'd left Rust Creek Falls? She'd never been very good at hiding her feelings, and there had been no way she could have pretended that he hadn't broken her heart wide-open.

Sutter was sitting on the top step of Paige's front porch when she got home. Her heart gave a little jolt when she saw him. She'd experienced a lot of those jolts lately, actual surges of emotion through her system that churned up everything inside. She'd seen him fairly regularly over the past couple of weeks, and she knew her reaction wasn't just the effect of his presence on her recently reawakened hormones, but a stronger and deeper yearning in her heart.

He smiled when he saw her, and his obvious pleasure made her feel all warm and tingly inside.

"What brings you into town tonight?"

"I needed some space."

"More space than you'd have tucked away in Clayton's house on an enormous ranch all by yourself?"

"Okay—maybe I wanted to see you more than I wanted space," he admitted. "Why do you look as if you're ready to spit nails?"

"Grocery shopping with my mother."

"I didn't realize you disliked shopping so much."

"I dislike being interrogated."

"About me," he guessed.

She nodded.

"I'm sorry."

"It's not your fault."

"I've been getting some grief from my family, too," he told her.

"About me?"

"Yeah. Since you came out to the ranch the night of the election, my mom's been wanting me to invite you to the Triple T for Sunday dinner."

"What did you tell her?"

"That meeting the parents is a big step, and I didn't want to rush into anything."

She smiled at that. "It is a big step—and it could send the wrong message."

"Ryder already asked if you were my girlfriend," he confided. "On the way to your place Saturday."

"What did you tell him?"

"That girls are yucky— Oh, wait. That's what Robbie said."

She smiled again. "Give him a few years. He'll change his mind. He's your nephew after all."

"Without a doubt," Sutter agreed.

"And he'll use those big blue eyes and trademark Traub smile to get exactly what he wants."

His lips curved, slowly, deliberately. "Does it work for me?"

"What do you want?" she asked warily.

"A cup of coffee?"

"I think that can be arranged."

The phone was ringing even as Paige slipped her key into the lock. She muttered under her breath as she pushed open the door and reached for the portable handset on the table in the hall.

"You said you would call when you got home," Mary said without preamble.

"I literally just walked through the door, Mom."

"Oh. Okay. Well, I just wanted to let you know that Lani is covering a shift for Courtney tonight, so on her way into work she's bringing over a piece of the pie that Lindsay made."

"I don't need any pie."

"You love pecan pie," Mary said, as if she needed reminding of the fact.

"Then you better send a big piece so I can share it."

"Are you expecting company?"

"As a matter of fact, Sutter's here."

She could almost see her mother's brow furrow. "He's there now?"

"Yes."

"You said you had tests to mark."

"I do, and I will get to that after I have a cup of coffee with a friend."

Mary was silent for a moment, and when she finally spoke she only said, "I hope it's decaf. You'll never get to sleep if you drink regular coffee this late in the day."

Paige closed her eyes and let her head fall back against the wall. "I'll talk to you tomorrow, okay?"

"Okay. I love you, Paige."

"I love you, too, Mom," she said, because she did.

Even if her mother frustrated her beyond belief at times.

Paige disconnected the call, then proceeded to the kitchen to make the promised coffee. Though she was acting as if the phone call hadn't bothered her, Sutter knew her too well to be fooled by the casual act. He also knew that Paige and her mother had always been close, and he didn't like knowing that he was the cause of any tension between them.

"Why did you tell your mother I was here?"

She finished measuring the grounds, then pressed the button to start the machine. "Was it supposed to be a secret?"

"No, I just didn't think you'd volunteer that information."

"We're not doing anything wrong—there's no reason to sneak around or for me to shove you into a closet when my sister comes to the door."

"Especially not with my truck parked out front," he noted wryly.

She shrugged. "We're friends, Sutter. I'm not ashamed of that fact."

"You're still on that friends kick, huh?"

"Because we are still friends," she said in a firm and decisive tone.

"Do you kiss all of your friends the way you kiss me?" he asked curiously.

Her cheeks flushed with color before she turned away to retrieve a couple of mugs from the cupboard. "Okay, so we're friends with some chemistry."

"Some *potent* chemistry, I'd say."

Before she could respond to that, the door opened and her sister walked in.

Lani dropped a plate on the counter and turned to Sutter. "Don't you live in Seattle now?"

"It's nice to see you, too, Lani," he said pleasantly.

Her gaze narrowed. "When are you going back?"

"I haven't quite decided yet."

Paige brought the two mugs to the island, passed one to him.

"Decide," Lani advised. "Soon."

"Lani," Paige said, a note of warning in her voice.

"If I didn't know better, I'd think you were trying to get rid of me," Sutter said to Lani.

"I am," she agreed unapologetically.

"You know what?" Paige interjected, her focus on her sister. "Sutter is a guest in my home. If you can't be nice to him, you can leave."

"I'm going," Lani said. "But only because I'll be late if I don't."

Paige sighed as the door closed again. "I'm sorry."

"No, *I'm* sorry," he told her. "I didn't realize how much your family would object to our…friendship."

She managed a smile.

"Maybe I should go back to Seattle," he said, almost to himself.

She lifted her cup to her lips, sipped. "If that's what you want."

Her tone was casual, but her refusal to look at him made him suspect that she wasn't as unconcerned about his decision as she wanted to appear.

"I don't want to cause any problems for you," he said.

"Don't make this about me."

"But it is about you," he insisted. "Or maybe it's about us."

"There is no us."

He didn't argue with her claim. In fact, he didn't say anything at all. Instead, he breached the short distance between them and covered her mouth with his own.

There was nothing tentative in his kiss this time. It was hot and demanding, and Paige was more than willing to meet his demands and counter with a few of her own. He'd always been a fabulous kisser. She'd kissed other men in the past five years, but no one had ever made her feel the way Sutter made her feel. No one else had created flutters in her belly, weakness in her knees or yearning in her heart.

She lifted her arms to link them behind his neck and

pressed her body close to his. His was so hard and strong, and every hormone in her body was jumping and dancing, begging for his attention. It had been a very long time since she'd felt this kind of desire, so sharp and fierce it was almost painful. And when he touched her, when his hands skimmed up her torso, barely brushing the sides of her breasts, she actually whimpered.

Desire pulsed in her veins, making her feel hot and weak, so hot she practically melted against him, so weak she needed his support to remain standing. His tongue delved between her lips, mated with hers in a slow, sensual seduction. His thumbs brushed over her nipples, making them pebble and ache, then circled around them, teasing and tempting. She arched against him, silently encouraging his exploration, urging him to touch, to take.

She wanted him. There was no point in denying it. But wanting and having were two very different things, and she knew it could be dangerous to indulge certain desires. Like on the rare occasions that she and her sisters went into Kalispell for brunch on a Saturday morning and she was tempted to order the mile-high chocolate cake instead of her usual spinach-and-cheese omelet. But of course, she never did. Because as much as she might want the decadent dessert, she knew it wasn't a suitable choice for breakfast. Sutter Traub was a lot more tempting than that luscious chocolate cake—and potentially much more dangerous to her heart. Not a suitable choice at all.

But still the only man she wanted.

He eased his mouth from hers. "There is, very definitely, an us," he told her.

Chapter Twelve

Paige wanted to believe that Sutter's feelings were as strong and deep as her own. But as she'd pointed out to him when he'd kissed her the night of the election, it didn't matter if he loved her or if she loved him—not so long as he wanted to be in Seattle and she wanted to stay in Rust Creek Falls.

She knew he couldn't run his business from Rust Creek Falls for the long-term, and he'd already been in town for more than four months with only brief and infrequent trips to Washington during that time. She was hopeful that his work at the Triple T with his dad and brothers would rekindle his interest in ranching and persuade him to sell his business in Seattle and move home for good. But was that a realistic possibility?

Whenever he talked about Traub Stables, she heard the pride in his voice, and she knew he was happy there. Maybe he could be happy ranching, too, but was it what he wanted? Or was it only what she wanted for him?

And even if he did stay, she knew it wouldn't work so long as there was tension within his family. Which meant that Paige had to talk to Ellie.

Monday night, after she'd done so, she called Sutter.

"Do you have any plans for dinner tomorrow?"

"Nothing specific, aside from eating," he said. "What were you thinking?"

"I was thinking you might enjoy a homemade meal at your place." She kept her tone light, deliberately casual.

"Am I cooking?"

She managed a laugh, because it seemed like an appropriate response and she didn't want him to suspect that her stomach was tied in knots. "No, you just have to show up."

"Then it sounds good to me. No, it sounds great to me."

Paige ignored the guilt that churned inside her. She didn't like misleading him, but she'd run out of other options. If Sutter and Ellie were ever going to bridge the gap between them, they needed a little shove toward the chasm. "Will you be at the ranch all day?"

"Actually, no. I'm going to be at Alistair Warren's place. He needs a hand to go through the boxes in his basement, to see if there's anything that can be salvaged."

"That sounds like an all-day job."

"He said there were only about a dozen boxes."

"And he'll have a story for every item and an anecdote about every scrap of paper," she warned him.

"Just tell me what time you want me to be home and I'll be there," he promised.

"Does six-thirty work?"

"Perfectly."

Paige had been right.

Alistair Warren had a story to go with every piece of junk in his basement, but Sutter didn't mind. The retired schoolteacher had never married, which meant that he had no children or grandchildren with whom to share the countless stories he'd amassed over seventy-four years. It also meant that what should have been a half-day job had taken the better part of a day, and still they weren't close to being finished.

Alistair held a bundle of water-stained letters in his gnarled hand. "Did you know I was engaged once?"

Sutter shook his head.

"Lizzie Carmichael was her name." The old man smiled a little at the memory. "We'd even set a wedding date. Then we got into an argument about something— honestly, I don't even remember what—and neither of us was willing to give in to the other."

He shook his head sadly. "She gave me back my ring, and I let her go. And I don't even remember why." Alistair tossed the damaged letters into the trash, then looked at Sutter. "Do you have a woman?"

"I'm working on it," he said, suddenly conscious of the late hour. "In fact, she's cooking dinner for me tonight."

"A local girl, then," Alistair noted. "Does that mean you plan on moving back to Rust Creek Falls?"

"I haven't made any firm plans."

"Women like a man to have a plan," the old bachelor told him. "So you'd better make one, otherwise you'll end up old and alone like me."

"Right now, my plan is not to be late," Sutter told him.

"What time is she expecting you?"

"Six-thirty."

"Then you'd better be on your way," Alistair advised.

Sutter nodded. "Do you want me to come back tomorrow to help finish this up?"

The old man seemed surprised by his offer. "If you don't have anything better to do, that would be appreciated."

"I'll see you tomorrow," he promised.

Twenty minutes later, he pulled into the driveway of Clayton's house. He felt a quick pang of disappointment when he didn't see Paige's car, but when he walked in the back door, he immediately recognized the scent of his favorite buttermilk-fried chicken.

He smiled at the thought that Paige had cajoled the recipe from his mother for the occasion. The smile faded when he realized that it wasn't Paige standing by the stove—but his mother.

"She set me up."

He hadn't intended to speak the words aloud—and didn't realize he had until he saw Ellie's tentative smile wobble.

"It was my idea," she said quickly.

"I doubt that." If Ellie had wanted to ambush him, she would have done so weeks earlier. The fact that she'd done so only now, after Paige had insisted he needed to talk to his mother and work things out, proved that her meddling fingerprints were all over this plan. And he wasn't entirely sure how he felt about that.

The flush that colored his mother's cheeks further confirmed his suspicions. "I just wanted a chance to talk to you, to say…"

"What did you want to say?"

His mother's eyes filled with tears. "That I'm sorry."

And that quickly, he felt the shell around his heart begin to crack, just a little.

"While I was waiting for you, I was trying to figure out what I would say," she admitted. "How to tell you everything I've been thinking and feeling, how much the regrets have weighed heavy in my heart for the past five years. I had a speech prepared, but I can't remember any of it now. All I can tell you is that I'm so sorry." Despite the tears that spilled onto her cheeks, her gaze didn't waver. "I know I was responsible for your decision to leave, but I never wanted you to go."

Leaving hadn't been his choice so much as a necessity at the time, and he'd been an outcast from his family for five years because harsh words had been spoken and difficult decisions had been made. But over the years, he'd realized that he bore as much responsibility as anyone else for those words and decisions, and if his mother was brave enough to take the first step toward bridging the gap between them, then he could at least meet her halfway.

He took three steps toward her and opened his arms. Though her eyes were still swimming with tears, he saw the quick flare of hope and then she was in his arms, holding on to him and sobbing against his shirt.

"I'm sorry, too," he said, when her sobs had finally subsided.

She pulled herself from his embrace and tried to wipe the tears from her cheeks, but they wouldn't stop falling. "Why are you sorry?"

"Because I was too proud and stubborn to come home when I wanted to."

She cupped his face in her hands. "Those are traits you come by honestly enough. Just like loyalty, which brought you home when we needed you."

"When I heard about the flood—I was so worried about the ranch, about all of you."

"I can't tell you what it meant to me to see your truck in the driveway that first day you came back—to know that you'd finally come home."

He remembered the smile that had spread across her face—and how quickly it had disappeared when he'd pointedly reminded her that his home was in Seattle now, and that he would stay at Clayton's house while he was in town to help out, so long as they needed help.

"I understand why you chose to stay here," she told

him now. "I didn't like it, but I understood. And knowing that you were just a few minutes up the road was so much better than you being in a different state.

"But if you want to move your things back to the main house, you're welcome to do so. Your room is just the way you left it— Well, I picked up some things you left lying around, and I've cleaned and vacuumed a few times since you've been gone, but it's mostly the same."

He smiled at that. "Thanks, but I'm not sure how I'd feel about living with Mom and Dad again—even temporarily—after being on my own for five years."

She nodded. "I guess I can understand why you'd want the privacy here, especially now that you and Paige are back together."

Was she only repeating what she'd heard around town, or had Paige given some indication that they were heading in that direction? "What makes you say that?" he asked cautiously.

"I guess I just assumed... You've been seeing a lot of her, and..."

"And she set this up," he said again.

"She thought it was important for us to talk," Ellie said.

"She was right."

"She obviously still cares about you."

He didn't know if it was obvious, but he hoped it was true. And as grateful as he was that Paige had helped him bridge the gap with his mother, that didn't mean he was going to confess his deepest feelings to her. Instead, he gestured to the oven. "Is that fried chicken in there?"

She nodded. "And roasted potatoes, buttered carrots and corn bread."

All of his favorites.

"Are you hungry?" Ellie asked hopefully.

"Famished," he told her.

She smiled. "Let's eat."

While Sutter was having dinner with his mother, Paige was pacing her kitchen, unable to choke down a single mouthful of the grilled tilapia and rice that she'd prepared for her own dinner. It was seven o'clock, so she knew that he would have arrived home by now—and found Ellie preparing his meal.

Paige knew that Sutter's mother had some reservations about what she considered to be an ambush, but she would be there. She loved her son too much not to do whatever was necessary to bring him fully back into the fold of her family.

Paige was confident that Ellie could handle it because she knew what was coming. Sutter, on the other hand, had no clue, and she didn't know how he would respond. It was entirely possible that he would be furious with both her and his mother.

She picked at her now-cold fish, managed a couple of forkfuls of rice before she dumped the rest of it in the garbage. She tidied up the kitchen, then she dusted and vacuumed her living room/classroom, and when a knock sounded on the front door, she nearly jumped out of her skin.

She peeked through the front window and recognized Sutter's truck. Her knees were trembling as she made her way to the door, and her heart was lodged in her throat so that she wasn't sure she'd be able to speak past it. But it didn't matter, because Sutter didn't wait for an invitation, walking right into the house when she opened the door for him.

Because her living room was still a classroom, he took a seat at the kitchen island.

Paige leaned back against the counter, facing him.

"Are you mad?"

"About what?"

Neither his tone nor his words gave away anything of what he was thinking or feeling. "About dinner tonight," she prompted.

"Why would I be mad?" he said easily. "No one makes fried chicken like my mother."

"You're deliberately misunderstanding me."

"So this isn't one of those times when you want me to misunderstand you?"

She felt her cheeks flush. "Okay—I should learn to mind my own business."

"That was my first thought when I walked into the house and found my mother in the kitchen instead of you," he admitted.

"Do you want me to apologize?"

"No." He pushed off the stool and rounded the island to stand in front of her. "I want to know why."

She wasn't ready to admit that she'd hoped if he worked things out with his family, he might think about moving back to Rust Creek Falls. "Because I don't know when to mind my own business?" she suggested instead.

"Maybe," he acknowledged. "And I guess the reason doesn't matter as much as the result."

She exhaled slowly, "Does that mean you talked?"

"Yes, we talked, we hugged, she cried. It was just like a made-for-TV movie."

The curve of her lips was probably just a little smug.

"You're dying to say 'I told you so,' aren't you?" Sutter noted.

"No," she denied. "Actually I'm just marveling over the fact that you're talking about your feelings—and still breathing."

He lowered his head toward her. "If I stop breathing, will you give me mouth-to-mouth?"

"I don't think you need to worry."

"Maybe we should take some preemptive measures—" he brushed his lips against hers "—just in case."

"Well, it's better to be safe than sorry, isn't it?"

"Absolutely." His fingers combed through the ends of her hair, tugging gently to tip her head back so that he could capture her mouth more completely.

His tongue delved between her lips, tangled with hers. Desire, hot and heavy, flooded her system, pulsed between her thighs. Her body quivered like a racehorse at the starting gate, eager to finally end three seemingly endless years of celibacy.

Except her mind wasn't nearly as ready as her body to forgive and forget and get naked. So when his hands skimmed down her back and over her buttocks and she was very close to melting into a puddle at his feet, she forced herself to pull away instead.

"What are we doing here, Sutter?"

"Well, I don't know about you, but I was hoping to get to second base," he teased.

She managed a smile. "Okay, but beyond the obvious. Why? Why are we going back down a road that's only going to lead to a dead end?"

"How do you know that it will?"

"Because nothing has really changed. Aside from your relationship with your mother, which is great, but somehow I don't think you've suddenly changed your mind about going back to Seattle."

"Can't we just enjoy the journey without worrying about the destination?"

"Maybe you can," she said. "But I can't. Because one trip to Heartbreak Falls was enough for me."

"You weren't the only one who was hurt," he reminded her.

"I know. So why would we want to go through that again?"

"Because we're not the same people we were five years ago, and I think—*I know*—things can be different this time."

She wanted to believe him, because she didn't want anything else as much as she wanted to be with him, but she wasn't quite ready to take that risk.

"Maybe they can," she finally allowed. "But one thing that hasn't changed is that Tuesday is still a school night."

"And you have a field trip planned with your class tomorrow," he remembered.

She nodded. "We're going to town hall to sort and organize the boxes and cans that have been collected so far for the community food drive."

"Maybe I'll stop by to help."

"We could use it," she told him. "Nina's done a great job promoting the food and clothing drives, and donations have been pretty steady."

The shopkeeper also planned to put up a "Tree of Hope" in the store after Thanksgiving and decorate it with tags for disadvantaged children. Her hope was that customers would choose tags, buy gifts for the children represented then return to the store with the gifts, which would be distributed to the children for Christmas. This community spirit that inspired even those who had lost so much to dig deep and find something to give to others less fortunate was yet another facet of the town that Paige loved.

"Then I'll see you tomorrow," he said, and brushed one last kiss on her lips before heading for the door.

* * *

Sutter had always known that family was important to Paige. If he'd had any doubts, the lengths to which she'd gone to ensure his reconciliation with his mother obliterated them. But he still hadn't fixed things with his brother, and he knew that was the necessary next step, because his breakup with Paige went back to his falling out with Forrest.

He'd wanted Paige to stand by him, to support him, but she'd sided with his brother instead. Or so it had seemed when he'd been twenty-three years old and had desperately needed someone to be on his side. In retrospect, he could accept that there had been no right or wrong, and that nothing that had been said or done then could have fixed what had gone wrong between him and his brother. Only he could do that.

And he needed to do it. Because fixing what was broken between him and Forrest was the only hope he had of fixing things with Paige for good. And he wanted to fix things with Paige, because she was the only woman he'd ever loved—and the woman he still loved.

He knew that she still had strong feelings for him, too, but she was wary. He understood why. The frequent references she made to his life in Seattle were proof that she expected him to leave again—because he'd told her that he would. But that conversation had taken place before the election, and a lot had changed in the weeks that had passed since then.

This wasn't his first trip back to Rust Creek Falls since he'd left town five years earlier, but he could count the number of trips on one hand, and every one of his previous trips had been of short duration. In fact, prior to this most recent visit, he didn't think he'd ever managed to stay longer than a weekend. Even when he'd planned to spend a week or two, old hurts and insecurities had reared up and driven him back to Seattle again.

He was determined to finally put those old hurts and insecurities to rest so that he could look to the future instead of the past. He knew that Forrest and Angie were in Rust Creek Falls for Thanksgiving, and he knew he couldn't delay any longer. Before Forrest had enlisted, when he'd thought he would stay in Rust Creek Falls and work on the Triple T with his father and his brothers, he'd built a small house on the property. Since Sutter didn't want to cause a scene in front of the whole family, he decided to track his brother down there.

Despite the chill in the air, Sutter felt perspiration bead on his brow as he approached the front door. Now that he was actually at the door of his brother's house, his heart was pounding in his chest and his mind was assailed by doubts and fears, the foremost one being: What if Forrest turned him away?

And he realized it was the fear of screwing up again that had held him back from making any overture prior to now. So long as he hadn't reached out and been slapped back, there was always the possibility of fixing his relationship with Forrest. But if he tried and failed— No, he didn't even want to consider the possibility.

He was relieved when the door opened and he saw that it wasn't Forrest standing on the other side but his beautiful young wife, Angie.

"Sutter?"

He couldn't blame her for being uncertain—they'd only met once before, when she and Forrest had come to Rust Creek Falls the night of the election to support Collin in his bid for mayor.

"Yeah," he said. "I apologize for dropping by uninvited—"

"You're family," she interjected, and a smile of genuine pleasure and welcome spread across her face. "Family doesn't need an invitation. Please come in."

Sutter stepped inside, and removed his hat from his head.

"Can I get you anything? A cup of coffee?" She glanced pointedly at the hands that clutched the brim of his hat. "A glass of whiskey?"

So much for thinking he didn't look as nervous as he felt. He cleared his throat. "Actually, coffee would be great, if it's not too much trouble."

"It's already on," she said, leading him back to the kitchen.

She gestured for him to sit, so he did, and she poured a fresh mug of coffee for him.

"Is, uh, Forrest around?"

"He just went out for a walk—part of his morning ritual. The exercise helps ease the stiffness in his leg and the fresh air helps clear his head. He still has nightmares sometimes," she confided, "but not as often as he used to."

"Forrest and I— We've never really talked about what he went through in Iraq," he admitted.

"Probably because you've barely spoken at all since he got back."

"He told you that?"

"He did," she confirmed, and the look she sent him was almost apologetic. "And so has everyone else in town."

"I should have figured."

Angie reached across the table and touched his hand. "But you're here now, and that's what matters."

"I guess we'll have to see if your husband shares that opinion."

As if on cue, the back door opened and Forrest came in.

"Sutter." Forrest looked from his brother to Angie, as if she might have the answers to the questions that were undoubtedly spinning through his mind.

"I hope it's okay that I stopped by."

"Sure. I'm just…surprised." He looked at his wife again, silently—almost desperately—pleading.

Angie poured another mug of coffee and pressed it into Forrest's hands. "I'm going to head up to the main house, to see if your mom needs anything from town," she said.

Then she kissed her husband, and gently squeezed Sutter's shoulder as she passed.

Forrest didn't move until the door closed behind her, then he took a couple of hesitant steps toward the table and finally lowered himself into a chair across from his brother.

"It looks like the move to Thunder Canyon was a good one for you," Sutter noted.

The hint of a smile played around the corners of his brother's mouth. "Better than good."

"Marriage definitely agrees with you."

"I didn't think it was what I wanted," Forrest told him. "After Iraq, I was so messed up. I felt guilty for living when so many others had died. And I didn't want to be happy. I didn't think I deserved to be happy. Then I met Angie."

"And put a ring on her finger before she could change her mind?" he teased.

"Angie was the one who was in a hurry. I just wanted to make her happy." He took his time sipping his coffee, as if he was trying to figure out what else to say. "You could've come to the wedding."

"I did," Sutter admitted.

Forrest frowned. "You were there?"

Sutter nodded. "But I didn't want anyone to know I was there, so I snuck in the back of the church just as the bride was starting to walk down the aisle. By the way, interesting choice of ring bearer."

His brother inclined his head. "Apparently you *were* there."

"I'm guessing there's a story behind the dog?"

Forrest nodded. "Smiley's a therapy dog—and the reason I met Angie."

"You looked happy," Sutter said.

"I've never been happier," his brother said. "Angie wasn't just what I wanted, but what I needed. She turned my life around."

"I'm glad." He finished his coffee and decided he'd procrastinated long enough. "But I didn't come here to talk about your wedding."

"I didn't think you did."

"I wanted to talk to you… Well, I guess I just really needed to say that…I'm sorry."

"What exactly are you apologizing for?"

"For not supporting you when you chose to go back to Iraq."

"You were expressing your opinion." His gaze dropped to his leg. "And it turned out you were right to have some concerns."

"I didn't want to be right," Sutter told him. "I just wanted you to be safe. I was terrified that something would happen and I'd lose you forever." He dropped his gaze to the now-empty mug he held cradled between his palms so that he could pretend his eyes weren't blurred with tears.

"And thank God you came home and we didn't lose you forever," he continued, when he was sure he could do so without blubbering. "But the past five years have felt like forever. And I hope you can forgive me, because I'd really like my brother back."

Forrest cleared his throat. "I'd like mine back, too."

"Really?" Sutter couldn't believe his brother was letting him off the hook so easily. Except that if he considered that he'd been estranged from most of his family and Forrest had nearly been killed, none of it had been easy for either of them.

"Really," Forrest confirmed.

"Now I wish I'd had the courage to initiate this conversation when you'd first returned from Iraq."

His brother shook his head. "I wasn't ready then, and not for a long time after. Probably not until Angie pushed her way into my life."

"I'm looking forward to getting to know her and hearing her version of the story," Sutter said.

"She taught me not to live in the past," Forrest confided. "And she gave me hope for the kind of future I long ago gave up thinking I could ever have."

"I guess when you have a woman like that, you'd be crazy to let her go."

"You're thinking about Paige," his brother guessed.

Sutter nodded. "I made a lot of mistakes five years ago."

"Is she still making you pay for them?"

"No. Yes." He shook his head. "I don't even know. She doesn't seem to be holding a grudge, but she is holding back."

"You want more than she's giving you?"

"I want it all," Sutter admitted.

Forrest's brows lifted in silent question.

"Marriage, kids, forever," he clarified.

"Have you told her that?"

"Not yet."

"What are you waiting for?"

He wasn't sure. Or maybe he was worried that Paige wasn't sure. And he wasn't ready to put his heart on the line without being certain that hers was involved, too.

"If I learned nothing else in Iraq, I learned that there are no guaranteed tomorrows. If you want to be with Paige, don't wait to tell her."

Chapter Thirteen

Sutter invited Paige to Thanksgiving dinner at his parents' house, but she had to decline the invitation because her family was having their meal at the same time. When they'd dated in the past, they'd managed to get two meals out of the day because his family always had theirs at lunch and her family preferred to eat at dinnertime. But for some inexplicable reason that seemed to surprise Paige as much as it surprised him, Mary Dalton decided to have an early meal this year. Sutter half suspected that she'd deliberately scheduled her lunch to conflict with his family's plans and ensure that Paige wouldn't be able to spend the holiday with him.

His mother was bustling around the kitchen, completely in her element as she choreographed the preparations. Willa was mixing the coleslaw; Angie was mashing potatoes. Even Dallas's boys had been put to work: Ryder was putting pickles into trays, Jake was dumping dinner rolls into baskets and Robbie was helping his grandfather set the table.

When everything was ready and bowls and platters covered almost every inch of the table, they all sat down and Bob said grace. As the food was passed around, Ellie decided that—in honor of Thanksgiving—everyone should share something for which he or she was thankful. There were some subtle groans and protests, but his mother wasn't easily dissuaded.

"I'll start," she said as she added a spoonful of candied yams to her plate. "I'm thankful to Hank Pritchard for making the extension for this dining room table, but I'm especially grateful that so many of our children and grandchildren are here to sit around it with us today."

The only one of Sutter's siblings who hadn't come home for the holiday was Clayton. Sutter knew that his brother would have liked to have been there, but now he and Antonia were married and living on her family's ranch, where she managed the Wright Way boarding house with her widowed father and three brothers. And while Ellie was undoubtedly disappointed, she understood that Antonia had a family of her own and other responsibilities. That fact—along with Antonia's promise that they would come to Rust Creek Falls for Christmas—lessened her disappointment, at least a little.

Ellie looked at Robbie, who was seated to her left. "What are you thankful for?" she asked her grandson.

"That Uncle Collin married my teacher, 'cuz she smells really good."

Willa's cheeks flushed in response to the boy's exuberant comment while the other adults chuckled.

"I'm glad it's a long weekend, so there's no school until Monday," Jake declared.

"Braden?" Ellie prompted.

"This one's easy," he said. "I'm thankful that Sutter's home to help me muck out stalls."

Bob was up next, and he smiled at his wife at the opposite end of the long table. "I'm grateful that, forty years ago, I had the good sense to marry my Ellie."

Ellie's eyes sparkled with moisture as her own lips curved.

Angie was beside her father-in-law. "I'm thankful for my new husband and his wonderful family."

"I'm thankful for the support of my whole family—" Forrest looked at Sutter, then shifted his attention to his wife "—and especially for my beautiful wife."

The only one who faltered was Dallas, and Sutter could understand why he might not be feeling particularly thankful after the events of the past year. But when he finally spoke, he said, "I'm thankful for my sons—Ryder, Jake and Robbie—who are the very best part of my life."

Ellie's eyes filled with tears again. They all knew it had been a rough year for Dallas, and Sutter was glad his brother was able to appreciate how fortunate he was to have the three boys who looked at him as if he was the center of their world—and he was.

When it was finally Sutter's turn, he looked around the table, at the family he'd stayed away from for far too long, his gaze pausing on Forrest beside his new wife. "I'm thankful for the second chances that I've been given since returning to Rust Creek Falls."

Of course, thinking of second chances made him think of Paige, and the advice that his brother had given to him the day before. *There are no guaranteed tomorrows. If you want to be with Paige, don't wait to tell her.*

He'd barely touched the plate he'd heaped with the food his mother had spent hours preparing, but he pushed his chair away from the table and stood up.

Ellie looked at him, obviously startled—and not at all pleased—by his abrupt action. "What are you doing?"

"I have to see Paige."

She frowned. *"Now?"*

"Right now," Sutter confirmed. "Because she gave me a second chance, too, and I'm not going to blow it."

"I hardly think staying to finish your meal would blow anything," she chided.

Sutter looked at Forrest again. "I'm not willing to wait another minute to tell her how I feel about her."

Paige had always loved Thanksgiving, but as she sat at the dining room table with her family, she couldn't help feeling as if something—or some*one*—was missing. She wished Sutter was there, or that she was at the Triple T with his family. But with each of their families deciding to have the meal at similar times, there was no way for them to be together without choosing one over the other.

But maybe it was better this way. Maybe they needed to spend the holiday apart so that she would remember they had separate lives now. Lately she'd started to fall into the trap of thinking they were a couple again, because they'd been acting like a couple. Spending almost all of their free time together, talking every day when they couldn't see each other.

Every time her phone buzzed to indicate a text message, her heart started to beat just a little bit faster because it *might* be a message from Sutter. And if it was, she'd inevitably feel a smile steal across her face. She was acting like a lovesick teenager, further proof that she'd fallen for him all over again.

Paige and her sisters had just started clearing away the empty plates when there was a knock at the door. Visitors on Thanksgiving were unusual, as most everyone in town was celebrating the occasion with their own families. Since Paige was closest to the door, she responded to the knock—and her heart knocked hard against her ribs when she found Sutter on the porch.

He smiled. "Happy Thanksgiving."

"It is now," she said.

"Am I interrupting?"

"We just finished eating. Did you want to come in for dessert?"

He shook his head. "I just wanted to talk to you."

"Sounds ominous," she teased.

"It's not," he promised. "At least, I don't think it is."

"Then it can wait until after we have pie," she said, and took his hand to drag him into the dining room.

"We've got one more for dessert," she said brightly, dragging Sutter into the dining room.

There had been several conversations taking place around the table, and they all faded away.

"Happy Thanksgiving," Sutter said.

The chorus of halfhearted and mumbled responses immediately put Paige's back up. She understood that her family disapproved of certain things Sutter had said and done five years earlier, but if she'd gotten over them, she expected they should be able to do the same.

"I hope I'm not intruding," he said.

If he'd been anyone else—or if the same scene had played out more than five years earlier—her mother would have assured him that he wasn't and her father would have jumped up to find him a chair. Today, her mother only said, "I'm surprised to see you, Sutter. Doesn't Ellie usually host a big lunchtime meal on Thanksgiving?"

"Yes, she does. And she is," he told her. "But I slipped out early to see Paige."

"I imagine it was probably a little awkward around the table," Mary said, with false sympathy, "since your brother's home from Thunder Canyon for the holiday."

"Forrest and Angie are home, but Clay and Antonia stayed in Thunder Canyon," he clarified. "And no, it wasn't awkward at all."

"This, on the other hand, is starting to feel more than

a little uncomfortable," Paige noted. "Can't you be gracious and welcoming to a guest I've invited to join us?"

"There really isn't room for another chair at the table," her mother said primly.

Paige was stunned, as much by the dismissive tone as the blatant lie. "We've never had trouble squeezing in one more in the past."

"I didn't put the extra leaf in the table this year," Ben spoke up in support of his wife.

Her brothers, who had always been friendly with the Traub boys, said nothing. Paige wasn't sure if their silence was a deliberate decision to remain neutral or a result of the fact that they were too focused on their dessert to care about the conversation. Her sisters—especially Lani—*always* had something to say, but even they were quiet. And while Paige would have appreciated *some* support for Sutter from their corner, at least they hadn't joined the fray against him.

Paige had to take a deep breath before she could speak again. "Then I'm sure you'll all appreciate the extra elbow room since I'm not staying for dessert."

"Don't," Sutter said, touching her arm. "I didn't come over here to cause a scene."

"And *you* didn't," Paige assured him. Then, to her family, she said, "Happy Thanksgiving."

Ben scowled. "You can't just leave."

"Actually, I can. And right now, I think it's better that I do." Then she turned and walked out the door before she said something she knew she would regret.

"I'm sorry," Sutter said, when he led her to his vehicle.

"Why are you sorry?"

He opened the passenger door for her, helped her up. "Because I put you in an awkward position by showing up the way I did."

She shook her head. "I'm glad you came by."

"You're glad I caused dissension between you and your family?"

"You didn't cause it," she denied. "They did."

He went around to his side and climbed in. "They're your family, Paige. And I know, probably better than anyone, how hard it is to be at odds with family."

She nodded. "You're right. But aside from the fact that they're being completely unfair, they have to stop trying to control my life and my choices."

"Are you choosing to be with me?"

"It seems that, at least for today, I am."

"What about tomorrow?"

"I don't know," she admitted. "Right now I'm afraid to look too far ahead, because when I do, I see you back in Seattle."

"My business is in Seattle," he agreed. "Not my life."

She felt hope swell inside of her chest. "When did you come to this realization?"

"Sometime between the night of the election, when I kissed you as the snow fell around us, and yesterday, when I was talking to my brother."

She didn't need to ask—she could tell by the tone of his voice that he meant Forrest. "How did that go?"

"Much better than I expected."

She reached for his hand, squeezed it. "I'm so glad."

"Me, too. And one of the things I decided after talking to Forrest was that I wasn't going to waste any time going after what I wanted."

"And you wanted...me?"

"I've always wanted you," Sutter told her. "Even when I was five hundred miles away, I wanted you. Even after five years, I never stopped."

Wow—that was a declaration she hadn't expected.

And she didn't quite know how to respond. She could tell him that she felt the same way, because it was true. But she was wary about opening her heart so completely when she wasn't sure that there was a future for them, and if there wasn't, he would break her heart all over again.

On the other hand, he'd taken the first step in coming to her tonight—he'd stood firm despite the disapproval of her family and he'd put his feelings on the line. He hadn't professed undying love or promised her forever, but she wouldn't have trusted either of those claims if he had. She'd been in love with Sutter before and she knew there were no guarantees. What he was offering her now was honest and real, and she wasn't going to turn him away.

He pulled into her driveway, put the vehicle into Park. She waited for him to turn off the ignition, but he didn't. She looked at him, silently questioning.

"I'm waiting to see if you're going to invite me to come inside," he told her.

It seemed like a simple response, but she somehow sensed that there would be no going back if they went forward from here. She could go into the house alone and he would drive away. Or—

She drew in a deep breath. "Would you like to come inside?"

He turned off the ignition.

Paige led him into the house. Now that they were inside, alone, she suddenly felt nervous. It wasn't the first time she'd invited him into her home, but it was different this time because they both knew he wouldn't be leaving tonight.

"Can I get you anything? Beer? Soda? Water?"

Sutter shook his head. "No, thanks."

She took a glass from the cupboard and filled it with water, more because she needed something to do than because she was thirsty. She took a few sips and tried to put her scattered thoughts into some semblance of order.

He pried the glass from her fingers and set it on the counter, then he put his arms around her and drew her close. "I can almost hear you thinking, but I don't have a clue what's going through your mind."

"I'm not sure I do, either," she admitted. "I guess I'm just wondering, when you said you wanted me, did you just mean for tonight? Or are you planning to stay in Rust Creek Falls?"

"I haven't made any firm plans yet, but I'm hoping to stay here—with you." He brushed his lips against hers. "If you want me to stay."

"I want you to stay," she said, and kissed him again.

She was sure there were more questions she should ask, but right now she couldn't think of any of them. She couldn't think of anything while he was holding her and kissing her, except how much she wanted to be with him.

"Is your mother going to wonder if you made it home safely?"

Paige sighed. "She might."

"Why don't you give her a call to preempt any interruptions?"

She did so, and was grateful that Travis answered so she could leave the simple message and hang up. Then she turned back to Sutter.

"No more interruptions," she promised and, taking his hand, led him upstairs to her bedroom.

"This is the second time you've brought me up here— I hope you know what you're doing this time."

"I know exactly what I'm doing...and who I'm doing it with," she said, and brought his mouth down to hers.

She might have initiated the kiss, but he was an avid and equal participant. He kissed her again, deeply, hungrily. She pressed closer so that her breasts were crushed against his chest and the rock-hard evidence of his arousal was against her belly. Desire pounded through her veins, pulsed deep inside her.

His hands slipped under her sweater, and she quivered as those rough, warm palms scraped over her bare skin. He zeroed in on the clasp at the front of her bra and released it. Then his hands were on her breasts, and her nipples immediately pebbled in response to his touch. His thumbs circled the rigid peaks, moving slowly and teasingly closer to the aching nubs. She sucked in a breath when his thumbs finally brushed over the hypersensitive tips, and her knees actually trembled.

Because she wasn't entirely sure her legs would continue to support her, she drew him toward the bed and pulled him down onto the mattress with her. His brows winged up, but that was his only response before he captured her mouth again, nibbling on her lower lip as he continued to play with her breasts, driving her ever closer to the edge.

Her fingers were trembling as she worked at the buttons of his shirt, but finally she parted the fabric and touched him. Her hands slid over the ridges of abdominal muscles to his chest, admiring the smooth skin stretched taut over hard muscle. He was a man of so many contrasts. He had the strength to effortlessly control a thousand-pound stallion, the gentleness to bottle-feed an orphaned kitten—and the heart to do so. And when he focused his attention on a woman, he had an uncanny ability to make her feel safe and cherished even as he systematically obliterated any doubts or resistance.

Not that Paige was resisting—or ever had. Because

she'd given her heart to Sutter long before she'd ever offered her body, and he was still in complete command of both. But she knew his body as well as he knew hers, and she stroked her hands over him again, moving down his torso. She unfastened his pants and slid one hand beneath the waistband of his boxers. Here was another contrast: steel encased in velvet. She wrapped her hand around him and was rewarded with a throaty groan.

He pulled back, tugged her sweater over her head and tossed it aside. His shirt followed, then her bra, so that they were both naked from the waist up. She shivered, not from the cold but from the heat in his gaze. And everything inside of her quivered, not with fear but anticipation.

He unfastened her skirt, then shifted back on the mattress so that he could tug it over her hips and down her legs. His eyes followed the progress of the garment, and his lips curved when her silky lace panties and thigh-high stockings were revealed. He traced the lacy edge of the stockings, then his fingertips skimmed over bare flesh to trace the edge of her panties. It was a feather-light caress that arrowed straight to her core.

His eyes lifted to her face, watching her as he traced the same path again. This time his thumb brushed over the thin barrier of lace between her thighs, and she had to bite down on her lip to keep from crying out. He touched her again, and she did gasp now. His lips curved in a slow, satisfied smile. "You're ready already."

She could hardly deny it—and didn't see any reason to. Everything inside her was throbbing, aching, wanting. "It's been a while for me."

"For me, too," he told her.

"More than three years?" she challenged.

"No," he admitted. "But it's been more than five years since I've been with someone who mattered."

And her heart, already precariously perched, toppled over.

"Be with me now," she said, reaching for his pants.

But he caught her hands and gently lowered them back to the bed. "We've waited too long to rush it now."

He tugged her panties down her legs and added them to the growing pile of clothing on the floor. He shifted farther down the mattress, stroking his hands along the outside of her legs, then circling her ankles and sliding her feet back so that her knees were bent and wide. Then he lowered his head between her thighs and zeroed in on her feminine center. It only took one touch—one slow stroke of his tongue—and she shattered.

She cried out, shocked by the immediacy and intensity of the sensations evoked by his touch. The pleasure was so incredible. So overwhelming. It was simply…too much. The release was as much emotional as physical, and as her body was still shuddering with the aftereffects, she felt a tear squeeze from her eye.

But Sutter wasn't nearly finished yet, and he was already driving her toward the next peak. With his lips and his tongue, he nibbled and stroked, deliberately drawing out her pleasure. He'd always known how to take his time, how to extend the enjoyment of lovemaking for both of them. But right now she wanted him so badly that the pleasure was almost painful.

"Sutter…please."

This time she flew. One minute she was lying on her bed, the next she was miles above it, high up in the sky, soaring on the razor's edge of exquisite sensation.

As she floated slowly back toward the ground, his mouth moved up her body. He trailed kisses over her belly, between her breasts. His lips skimmed over a nipple, his tongue swirled around it. And new pleasure started to build all over again.

She reached between their bodies, wrapped her fingers around the hard length of him and stroked him slowly, enticingly. His mouth found hers again, and his tongue slid deep into her mouth then withdrew. A teasing advance and retreat. She arched her back, tilted her hips, wordlessly begging for the completion they both wanted, needed.

"Tell me you want me," he demanded.

"I want you, Sutter. Now."

Always.

But of course she didn't say that aloud. She was going to enjoy what they had together here and now without worrying about tomorrow. There was no past and no future—there was only the present.

He stripped away the last of his clothes and quickly sheathed himself with a condom. Then he rejoined her on the bed, parting her thighs and entering her in one hard thrust. Sex with Sutter had always been good, and she knew that was incredibly rare. He'd been her first love and her first lover, and they'd learned a lot together. While their initial couplings might have been a little hesitant and awkward, they had never been disappointing. Sutter had always been thoughtful and patient, more concerned with her pleasure than his own.

Obviously that hadn't changed. He gave her a moment to catch her breath, then he began to move inside of her. Slow, steady strokes that started the tension building all over again. Long, deep strokes that seemed to touch her very core. Then harder and faster, until their hearts were pounding in tandem and they were racing together toward the ultimate pinnacle of pleasure.

* * *

Somewhere in the midst of the sensual haze that had descended on his brain, Sutter heard something chime. For a moment the sound was completely foreign to him. It sounded again, followed this time by an elbow in his ribs.

"Your phone," Paige mumbled sleepily.

With sincere reluctance, he shifted so that he was sitting up in her bed and reached down to the floor for his pants and the phone that was tucked in one of the pockets.

When he pulled it free, the illuminated screen informed him that he had three new messages. *Three?* He scowled at the phone, but immediately scrolled to his inbox to check the messages.

His annoyance shifted to concern when he realized that they were all from Jenni.

Please call as soon as you get this message.

Need to talk to you ASAP.

Dammit, Sutter, this is important!

He touched his lips to Paige's forehead before he eased away. "I have to make a phone call."

"'Kay," she said, but she didn't move from her face-down position on the bed.

Her hair was spread out over the pillow like an inky spill over pale blue cotton. Her skin was paler—the color of fresh cream, the texture of finest silk. He drew the covers back a little farther than was necessary so that he could admire more of that pale skin, the line of her shoulders, the slope of her spine, the twin dimples low on her back, just above the sweet curve of her buttocks.

She'd always been beautiful, but the skinny girl he'd

first fallen in love with had grown into a very shapely woman. A very passionate woman. And though he sincerely wished the flood had never happened, it was hard to be sorry when it was the event that had brought him home—and back to Paige—again.

"Cold," she murmured.

He tugged the sheet up over her again; she sighed contentedly.

He moved toward the door to have his conversation in the hallway so he wouldn't disturb Paige. He punched the familiar number and the call was answered on the first ring.

"What's going on, Jenni?"

Chapter Fourteen

Jenni?

Though she was admittedly half-asleep and Sutter's voice sounded as if it was coming from far away, Paige had no doubt that she heard him speak another woman's name.

She strained to listen to what he was saying, but he'd closed the door so she could hear the murmur of his voice but wasn't able to decipher any specific words. But she knew that he was on the phone with Jenni—the woman who worked as a trainer at his stables and who drank margaritas. Which proved that their relationship wasn't strictly that of employer and employee.

Not that he'd denied it. In fact, he'd admitted that they were friends, but that description was both vague and open-ended. Especially considering that she'd told her family that she and Sutter were friends—and now she was naked in her bed after tangling up the sheets with him.

She rolled over onto her back and let out an exasperated sigh. She was being ridiculous and she knew it—Sutter wasn't the type of man to take her to bed if he was romantically involved with anyone else. And she'd never been the jealous type. Of course, she'd never had reason to doubt Sutter before. He'd always been the one person she knew she could count on, the one person who would always be there for her. And then he wasn't.

But he was here now, and she wasn't going to spoil what had been a wonderful evening with irrational questions or unfounded accusations. She couldn't deny her curiosity, though, and when he returned to the bedroom, she kept her tone light and asked, "What was that about?"

"I'm not entirely sure," he admitted, snuggling up behind her and wrapping his arms around her. "Jenni was kind of vague on details, aside from the fact that I'd better fix things or start looking for a new trainer."

"What are you going to do?"

"I guess I'm going back to Seattle to fix things—whatever those things are."

"She just calls and you go running?"

"It's my business, Paige. My responsibility."

He didn't even talk to her about it, or ask for her opinion or input. He just made the statement matter-of-factly, as if it should be of no consequence to her. She swallowed. "So when are you going?"

"Tomorrow."

She didn't want to ask, but she had to know if he'd meant what he'd said when he'd promised to stay in Rust Creek Falls. "How long will you be gone?"

"That I don't know," he admitted. "Until I get back and assess the situation, I wouldn't even want to guess."

"Try anyway," she suggested. "Days? Weeks? Months?"

He sighed. "I don't know, but I don't expect it would be too long."

So Paige let it go. Because she couldn't force him to give her an answer, and she couldn't force him to stay. And she was an idiot, because she'd fallen for his smooth lines and sexy smile—hook, line and sinker. And he was leaving her again.

She wanted to bang her head against the wall, but right now her head was cushioned against a nice fluffy pillow and Sutter's arm was wrapped around her middle. She should tell him to go. If he was planning to leave, he might as well go now. Her throat tightened and her eyes burned as she wondered if she was ever going to learn.

Oblivious to her inner turmoil, he snuggled closer and his breathing soon evened out, confirmation that he was sleeping. She stayed in the warm comfort of his arms and tried to convince herself that everything was going to be okay, that this time they would make it. But she couldn't stop the tears that slipped from her eyes.

Sutter woke up alone.

Paige's pillow was still indented from where she'd slept and he could smell her perfume on the sheets, so he figured she hadn't been up for very long. Still, he was disappointed that she'd managed to slip out of bed without waking him. He would have enjoyed easing into the day with her—or easing into her, he thought with a grin.

He sat up in bed, scrubbed his hands over his cheeks. He needed to shower and shave, then he wanted to make love with Paige again. They'd come together several times through the night, and still his body wasn't close to being sated. No matter how many times he had her, it was never enough. He never stopped wanting her.

He considered the possibility that she might be in the shower, but he couldn't hear the water running—which eliminated another one of his fantasies. So he showered alone and shaved with a disposable pink razor he found in the cupboard under the sink, and then he made his way downstairs. "Paige?"

There was no response.

In fact, he suddenly realized there was no sound at all. There was no scent of coffee brewing or breakfast cooking, no footsteps in the kitchen or anywhere else. Then he saw the note propped up on the counter, in front of the empty coffeepot.

It didn't take him long to scan the brief message, and as quickly as he did, his euphoric mood plummeted.

Sutter—
I'm really glad that we've found our way back to being friends again. But as wonderful as last night was, it would be a mistake to let it happen again. What we had was in the past, and I can't let myself think that we have a future together. Have a safe trip back to Seattle and I hope when you come home again that what happened last night doesn't make things awkward between us.
Sincerely,
Paige

Sincerely? For real? He was head over heels in love with her and she'd signed a kiss-off note with an impersonal *sincerely?*

He skimmed the message again as if doing so might enable him to decipher some hidden meaning, because the words on the page didn't make any sense to him.

"...as wonderful as last night was..." Okay, at least she got that part right. Making love with her had been not just wonderful but phenomenal. Even after five years, he'd remembered every little detail of how and where she liked to be touched. And he'd taken great pleasure in pleasuring her, cherishing every soft, sexy sound she made, glorying in the instinctive and sensual movements of her body, loving the way she said his name when he was buried deep inside of her.

"...it would be a mistake to let it happen again." He shook his head over that. It would be a mistake to let it *not* happen again. And he was honestly baffled to think that she could make love with him as openly and passionately as she had the night before and not believe that they were meant to be together.

He refused to accept it. He grabbed his phone and called her cell. After the fourth ring, the call went to her voice mail. He waited five minutes and tried again, but there was still no answer. He tried sending a text message, asking where she was. She ignored it.

He considered tracking her down, and Rust Creek Falls wasn't so big that he couldn't do it. He wanted an explanation—something more than a scribbled note that didn't make any sense to him. If it was really over, he wanted her to look him in the eye and tell him.

He didn't care that he was expected back at Traub Stables. Nothing was more important to him than Paige. But when she failed to answer his third phone call and another text message, he decided that it might be smarter to give her some time. If she was feeling half as churned up inside as he was right now, it might be better for both of them to talk when her emotions had settled.

Since he'd promised to return to Seattle, he would do so, even though he suspected that promise had set Paige off—that she'd assumed his decision to go back to Washington was an indication that he intended to return to his life there. But after last night, how could she not know that his life was with her, wherever she was?

Or maybe her disappearing act this morning had nothing to do with his trip. Maybe she'd simply decided, as she'd stated in her note, that their relationship was in the past and she was ready to move on—without him.

But that explanation didn't sit right with him, either. If she'd made the same claim twenty-four hours earlier, he might have believed it. But the connection between them when they'd made love had been more than the join-ing of bodies—it had been the merging of hearts. Yeah, he knew it sounded corny, but it was true. And that was why her decision to end things when they were just get-ting started again completely baffled him.

As much as he puzzled over it, he couldn't come up with an explanation for Paige's abrupt change of heart. What he did know was that the next time he saw Paige, they were going to figure things out once and for all. And by "figure things out" he meant that he was going to tell her he loved her, and when she finally admitted that she loved him, too, he wasn't ever again going to let her go.

But before he could start on the long journey to Se-attle, he had one stop to make.

She was a coward.

At the very least, she was weak—especially where Sutter was concerned. And that was why Paige had slipped out of her own bed and escaped from her own house in the early hours of the morning while the man she loved was still sleeping. Because she couldn't handle another goodbye. And because she knew that if he took her in his arms and promised to come back, she would wait for him, counting the hours, the days, the weeks. She couldn't—wouldn't—do that again.

There weren't a lot of places that she could go with-out running into someone she knew, and there were even fewer places within walking distance. She hadn't consid-ered that his truck was parked behind her car until she stole out of the house with her keys in hand and realized she wouldn't be able to get out of the driveway. At that point, any rational person would reconsider the plan and perhaps acknowledge that it was both impulsive and desperate. But she wasn't feeling very rational; she *was* feeling impulsive and desperate. And so she started to walk.

She didn't have a clear destination in mind, and it was probably by habit more than design that she turned in the direction of the elementary school. But once she thought about it, the school seemed like a logical choice. Because it was a holiday, she knew there wouldn't be many people—if any—at the site today, and she was right.

She made her way down the barren hall to her classroom and looked around at the open space. It wouldn't be too much longer before the desks and cabinets were brought in and displays were tacked up on the pristine walls. But right now it was as empty as Paige felt inside, and she sank down against the wall and let the tears flow.

A long time ago she'd been certain that she'd shed all the tears she was ever going to cry for Sutter Traub— obviously she'd been wrong. She'd had other relationships in the five years that Sutter was gone, but not one of those relationships had ever ended in tears. Because she'd never cared enough about any other man to mourn the end of their relationship.

Apparently she was destined to always love the one man who wouldn't stay with her.

He'd said that he was looking forward to a future with her, but all it took was one phone call from Seattle and he was gone. He hadn't even asked her to go with him this time. Of course, she couldn't have gone if he had asked. She had students who needed her and a lot of preparations still to make before the holidays.

As she wiped at the tears, she accepted that he was already on his way back to Seattle. He'd tried to call, several times in fact, but she hadn't answered any of his calls. In the end he'd sent her a text message, telling her that he was on his way to Seattle and he'd call when he got there. She hadn't responded to that message, either. But she'd taken it as a sign that she could return home without worrying about their paths crossing.

Sure enough, his truck was gone from her driveway when she turned onto North Pine, but she wasn't ready to go into the house yet. Not while the memories of last night were still so fresh in her mind and deeply entrenched in her heart. Groceries, she decided. She needed to stock up on supplies, which meant that she'd have to make a trip into Kalispell.

She'd just turned onto the highway when she realized she was behind a shiny black pickup truck just like Sutter's. Of course, black pickup trucks were hardly an anomaly in Rust Creek Falls, and she chided herself for the instinctive blip in her pulse. But as the vehicle slowed to turn into a driveway, she drew close enough to see the Washington State plate on the bumper.

Washington State plates, on the other hand, *were* anomalies. As she watched his vehicle bump along the long gravel driveway, she felt as if her heart was being squeezed inside her chest.

Apparently Sutter had decided to take a little detour on his way back to Seattle—to Shayla Allen's ranch.

Ten hours later, Sutter finally turned into the drive by the sign that welcomed him to Traub Stables. It was after eight o'clock, so he was surprised to see Jenni's truck still in the lot. Considering that she was invariably at the stables by six every morning, she was working extra late today.

He found her with Midnight Dancer, grooming the horse she'd helped birth two years earlier. She didn't seem particularly worried or stressed about anything, but she didn't seem her usual bubbly self, either.

"So are you going to tell me what's going on?"

"You'll have my letter of resignation tomorrow—consider this my two weeks' notice."

"Why?"

"Because I can't stay here, not if it means I have to work directly with Reese."

"I don't know if my brain's a little slow because I drove five hundred miles today or if this conversation just isn't making any sense to me," he admitted. "There've never been any issues between you before, so why—after three years—do you suddenly have a problem with Reese?"

She met his gaze head-on. "I slept with him."

These were his friends as well as his employees and Sutter liked and respected both of them, but he couldn't deny the protective instinct that rose up in him. "Did he take advantage of you?"

She laughed, though the sound was without humor. "No. Actually I probably took advantage of him."

"Should I be worried about a sexual-harassment suit?"

"I don't think so."

"Okay, you need to give me more information here. Not details," he hastened to clarify. "Please—no details. Just explain to me how you went from sleeping with Reese to wanting to give up a job I know you love."

"Because I love him, too."

"Still not seeing the problem."

She looked away, but not before he saw the shimmer of tears in her eyes. "Reese said it was a mistake—that he never should have let it happen."

Sutter winced.

"See? Even you know that's the wrong thing to say to a woman you were naked with," Jenni noted. "But instead of saying 'wow, that was incredible,' because it was incredible—"

"Details," Sutter reminded her.

"He's more concerned with the fact that our actions would be seen as unprofessional."

"By whom?"

"You."

"You're both adults—what you do on your own time is your business and absolutely none of mine. In fact, I'm quite happy to pretend we never had this conversation."

"I told Reese that's what you would say, but he was adamant. Which means that I'm either in love with a man who values his job more than he values me, or who's looking for an excuse not to get into a relationship. Either way, I can't stay here."

"Please don't make any hasty decisions."

"I'm sorry, Sutter. I know this puts you in a difficult position, but I need to move on."

"Instead of giving me your notice, why don't you take a vacation?" he suggested.

Her brows lifted. "That's your solution?"

"You've been working hard for the past few years—and even harder over the past several months. You deserve some time off, a break from the routines."

"A break from Reese, you mean?"

He shrugged. "Maybe what he needs is some time to think about what his life would be like without you in it."

"And maybe he'll decide he likes it better that way."

"If he does, then he doesn't deserve you."

She sighed. "Do you really think it will work?"

"I don't know," he admitted. "I'm probably the last person who should be giving relationship advice."

"Why do you say that?"

"Because it seems that I keep screwing up with the

only woman I've ever loved—and I actually thought things were back on track."

"This would be the girl you left behind when you first moved out to Seattle?" Jenni asked.

Sutter nodded. "But only after I asked her to come with me, and she said no."

"And when you started to get things back on track—and by that, I assume you mean you got her back into bed," she said drily, "you left her again."

"Because you called and said I was needed here."

Now it was her turn to wince. "You slept with her and then left because of a call from another woman?"

"It wasn't like that," he protested.

"It sounds exactly like that to me," she told him. "And I'm sure that's how it sounded to her."

Sutter scowled. "Then she wasn't listening to what I was saying, because I told her I would be back."

"Did you tell her when?"

"I could hardly give her a firm return date when I didn't know how long it would take to work things out here."

"You also didn't say, 'I'll be gone for a few days—a week at most—but I'm coming back to you.'"

"You think that would have made a difference?"

She huffed out an exasperated breath. "You're as much an idiot as Reese."

"At least I know what I want," he said. "Which is why I'm thinking about making a permanent move back to Rust Creek Falls." His thoughts shifted to his meeting with Shayla Allen—had it really only been earlier that morning? So much had happened since he'd awakened alone in Paige's bed that he felt as if days had passed.

He frowned now, realizing that although it hadn't been days, a lot of hours had passed and he still hadn't heard from Paige. She hadn't returned any of his calls or responded to any of his text messages, which wasn't really surprising. Based on the letter she'd left for him, she was trying to cut all ties between them. He had no intention of letting that happen.

"What would you do in Rust Creek Falls?"

He gestured to encompass the stables. "Something like this."

"Then you'll need a trainer there," she noted hopefully.

"Probably. But I *know* I need a trainer here."

She shook her head. "I'm going to check online for an all-inclusive in Maui."

Though it wasn't what he wanted to hear, he figured it was a compromise he had to accept—at least for now. He couldn't imagine Traub Stables without her, but if she insisted on leaving... "Would you really be willing to move to Montana?"

"I'd prefer Florida," she said. "But Montana would suffice."

"Why Florida?"

"Because it's as far away from Seattle as you can get while still staying in the country."

"Okay, then. I'll figure out what's going on in Montana and let you know."

"She must be one special lady," Jenni noted.

Sutter had no doubt that she was, even when she was driving him completely crazy. "I've never known anyone like her," he admitted.

"So who's going to handle things around here if I suddenly decide to take a trip to Maui?"

"I will."

"I thought you were anxious to get back to Montana?"

"I was," he agreed. "But I've decided that someone else needs some time to think."

* * *

Paige's cards had been sent, her cookies were baked and her house was decorated—aside from the tree, which she would get two weeks before Christmas. Though she spent the day with her family, she still liked to put up her own tree. Christmas was her absolute favorite time of the year—she loved everything about the holiday, especially the fact that she had all kinds of things to keep her busy and absolutely no time to waste thinking about Sutter Traub. But that didn't stop her from thinking about him anyway.

She went shopping in Kalispell with Lindsay. She'd invited both of her sisters to make the trip with her, but Lani had already committed to babysitting for a friend who needed to shop without her kids in tow.

"When's Sutter coming back?" Lindsay waited until they were resting their feet after a marathon trek through the toy store and savoring gingerbread lattes before she asked the question that Paige had been anticipating all day.

"I don't know that he is."

Her sister frowned. "Haven't you talked to him?"

"Not since the day after Thanksgiving." More specifically, not since the morning after they'd made love, but she wasn't going to share that information with Lindsay.

"He hasn't called?"

"He's called," she admitted. "Every day."

"You're not taking his calls," Lindsay guessed.

"I don't know what to say to him."

"How about 'I love you. Please come home'?"

"Except that Seattle is his home now," she reminded her sister—and herself.

"You wouldn't know it from the amount of time he's spent in Rust Creek Falls over the past four months."

"Yeah, it fooled me, too," Paige admitted.

"You fell in love with him again, didn't you?" Lindsay said, her tone just a little wistful.

She sighed. "I don't think I ever stopped."

"And yet you're still here when he's in Washington?"

"I have a job here, responsibilities I can't just abandon."

"Then why are you mad at Sutter for not abandoning his?"

"I'm not mad at Sutter."

"You're not taking his calls," Lindsay reminded her.

"I'm...confused," she admitted.

"Probably not half as confused as he is."

"Why would he be confused?"

"Because less than a week ago he was in your bed and now you're giving him the silent treatment."

Paige's jaw dropped. "He wasn't— I'm not—" She blew out a breath. "How did you know?"

"Are you kidding? When you left with him on Thanksgiving, the heat between the two of you was practically melting your clothes away before you were out the door."

"Okay, yes, he spent the night with me."

"So what really happened to cause this one-eighty?"

"He got a phone call from his trainer and practically leaped out of bed to race back to her." If it had been a genuine crisis at the stable—a sick horse, a disgruntled client, an employee embezzling funds—she would have understood the urgency of the situation. Instead, it was his trainer. His beautiful, blond, female trainer.

Not that he'd described Jenni to her in that way. In fact, he hadn't given her any details about the woman he claimed was a friend as well as a valued employee. So Paige had looked her up and discovered that Traub Stables had its own website, including bios and photos of the employees—and that Jenni Locke was undeniably gorgeous.

Paige had never had any reason not to trust Sutter. In high school there had been a lot of girls who'd liked him. All of the Traub brothers had been popular and had drawn attention wherever they went. But while she and Sutter were together, Paige had never doubted his commitment to her.

Everything was different now, though. The fact that they'd slept together didn't mean there was a commitment between them, especially when he'd left the state the very next morning.

"I'd be upset, too, if that's what really happened," Lindsay said. "But I've seen the way Sutter looks at you—the man's as head over heels as you are—and if he raced back to Seattle, it was because his *trainer* needed him to be there and not because a woman crooked her finger.

"But if that's what you really believe," she continued, "why not just cut your losses and move on? Why are you so miserable without him?"

"I know I should move on. My head is telling me to forget about him, that this emergency that called him back to Seattle was a timely reminder of the fact that we have separate lives, in separate cities. But my heart—" She sighed again. "My heart refuses to let go."

"Then maybe it's time you started listening to your heart," her sister said gently. "Go to Seattle, tell Sutter how you feel and figure out a way to make this work."

Paige wished it was that easy. But when he'd decided to go back to Seattle without even talking to her, she'd realized that she wasn't as important to him as his business. Even if he did love her, he didn't love her enough to put her first, so she shook her head.

Lindsay shook her head. "You were happy with him, and you're obviously miserable without him. If I was in your situation, you can bet I'd do whatever was necessary to be with the man I loved."

"There's one other thing I didn't tell you," Paige admitted now.

"What's that?"

"He didn't race straight back to Seattle. He made a detour first."

"What kind of detour?" her sister asked curiously.

"To Shayla Allen's ranch."

"Well, that *is* interesting."

"Interesting?" Paige said skeptically.

Shayla Allen was a young widow who didn't know the first thing about ranching, and most people in Rust Creek Falls had assumed she would sell off the property her husband had left to her when he died. So far she'd avoided doing so, and there seemed to be a regular parade of handsome cowboys stopping by the ranch to help her with one thing or another.

"Really, Paige, green is not your color," Lindsay chided.

"Because there's got to be a reasonable explanation for Sutter's visit to her ranch?" she challenged.

"There could be," her sister said. "It's not common knowledge yet, but Shayla has decided to sell the ranch and move back East. So it's possible that Sutter wasn't there to check out her assets but her real estate."

Chapter Fifteen

After she dropped Lindsay off with her assortment of packages, Paige's stomach was rumbling. Because she didn't feel like cooking, she decided to stop by the Ace in the Hole to grab a quick bite. She didn't usually venture into the bar on her own, but she hadn't been in the mood for any more company tonight—especially not the company of either of her sisters. Since Sutter had left town, Lani's smug "I told you so" attitude had been more than a little obnoxious. Lindsay was more empathetic, but her quiet understanding and sincere sympathy made Paige want to cry—and she'd done enough of that already.

She walked into the Ace in the Hole and realized there wasn't an unoccupied table in the whole place. There were a couple of empty stools at the bar, but she wouldn't feel comfortable sitting there with a bunch of men she didn't know.

And then she saw Alex.

He, too, seemed to be alone, but he'd managed to find a table. She took two steps in his direction before she changed her mind. She didn't want to put him in the awkward position of having to offer her a seat if he preferred solitude. Except that he looked up then and caught her eye, and immediately beckoned her over. The complete lack of hesitation in his response assured her that there wouldn't be any awkwardness between them, and she made her way over.

"Busy place tonight," Paige commented.

He nodded. "I managed to snag this table as a group of people was leaving. There's plenty of room if you want to join me."

"Thanks." She slid into the seat across from him. "Have you ordered already?"

He shook his head. "I was thinking about the nachos grande, but the platter's too big for one person."

"Nachos grande sounds good to me."

Alex ordered a beer; Paige stuck with soda. They chatted as they ate—about business at the mill, the progress at the school and various other local issues. It was casual and easy and Paige wondered how she'd ever thought they might have a future together when her feelings for him had always been so equable.

It wasn't until they were almost finished with the nachos that Paige noticed Dallas Traub was at the bar, deep in discussion with another man she recognized from the Triple T. A few minutes later he stood up, shook the man's hand, then turned and looked directly at her.

Paige lifted her hand to wave; his only response was a scathing glance before he headed to the door.

"Excuse me for a minute," Paige said to Alex, grabbing her jacket and hurrying after Sutter's brother.

She pushed open the screen door and stepped out. "Dallas, wait!"

He halted, then reluctantly turned back to face her. "If you want me to lie to my brother about what I saw tonight—forget it."

She was taken aback by the vehemence of his tone as much as the implication of his words, but she hadn't chased after him to have an argument in the parking lot. "While I have to admit to some curiosity about what you think you saw, I just wanted to give you something that I picked up in Kalispell today."

She shoved her arms into the sleeves of her coat as she started toward her car, and though Dallas still looked skeptical, he followed. Paige rifled through the assortment of bags in her trunk until she found the biggest one—from the toy store. She pulled out the box she wanted and handed it to Dallas.

"What is this?"

She huffed out a breath. "Did you even look at the letter Robbie wrote to Santa?"

"Of course," he said automatically.

And maybe he had looked at it, but he obviously hadn't made note of his son's request.

"Then you should know that this is a deluxe neon alien-invasion spaceship, which happens to be one of the hottest new toys this year. The girl who was unpacking the box in the store said they haven't been able to keep them in stock."

And because of that, she'd bought two—one for Robbie and one for the unnamed eight-year-old boy whose tag she had taken off of the Tree of Hope at Crawford's.

"I'm sorry if I overstepped," she said, perhaps a little stiffly. "But I didn't want to take a chance that you might not be able to find one, and it was really the only thing Robbie wanted. Well, aside from a new mommy."

He kept his gaze focused on the toy, and when he spoke again, his voice had lost most of the edge it usually carried when he was talking to her. "In that case, I guess I should say thank you. And ask how much—"

"It's a gift," she said, cutting off his question. "For Robbie from Santa."

He nodded. "Then thank you again."

"You're welcome." She closed the trunk of her car again and turned to go back into the bar.

Sutter hadn't planned to be in Seattle for more than a couple of days. His conversation with Jenni convinced him to stay longer, not just because he'd promised to cover for her so that she could take a vacation but because he needed some time to figure out his plans for his future. A future he wanted to spend with Paige.

Except that she continued to dodge his calls and ignore his text messages. He figured the advice he'd given to Jenni about Reese could apply to his relationship with Paige, as well. So he was giving her some time to think about everything that had happened between them and figure out where he fit into her life and her future. Because the contents of her letter notwithstanding, he didn't believe for a minute that her feelings for him were in the past.

But he missed her. With every day that passed, he missed her more. He tried to focus on business, catching up on everything that had happened while he was away, communicating with clients and making sure that Jenni's assistants were handling their numerous duties and responsibilities. He was pleased to note that they seemed to adjust to her absence just fine. Reese, on the other hand, was as grumpy as a bear rudely awakened from deep hibernation.

Sutter reminded himself that it was none of his business. Either they would figure things out for themselves or they wouldn't—it had nothing to do with him. Nothing aside from the fact that he could lose the best trainer he'd ever known.

Or he could take her to Montana with him. Because the more he thought about it, the more convinced he was that he could do what he was doing in Seattle back home in Rust Creek Falls. On Wednesday he got a fax from Shayla Allen's real estate agent with her acceptance of his offer on the property. He'd been expecting a counteroffer, some haggling back and forth that would draw out the process for a week or more. He hadn't expected it would be that easy, but apparently the owner was serious about selling and moving on, and now Sutter had a ranch—and a hefty mortgage—in Rust Creek Falls and no firm plans for either it or his business in Seattle.

He wanted to talk to Paige, to discuss his plans with her. It occurred to him, albeit belatedly, that they should have had a conversation *before* he put the offer in on the Allen ranch. Because Paige had been the primary factor in his decision to move back to Rust Creek Falls, and he hoped she would be pleased to learn about his plan.

But first she had to get over being mad at him—and according to Jenni, she had reason to be. Apparently he should have reassured her that he would be back, told her he would miss her unbearably and promised to love her forever.

Maybe he was an idiot—and according to Jenni, he was—but he'd thought all of that was implied. With every touch of his hands and his lips and his body when they'd made love, he'd told her that he loved her. And though neither of them had spoken the words, he'd been certain she was saying the same thing back.

But—according to Jenni again—he'd negated all of that by leaving town, hence her completely justified determination to push him out of her life forever. But this time, Sutter wasn't going to be pushed anywhere.

And he wasn't going to let her continue to ignore him, either. He decided that flowers would get her attention again, but in honor of the holiday season he ordered poinsettias this time—one for each Christmas that they'd spent apart. And he arranged for them to be delivered one at a time.

She might not be pleased by the interruptions to her schedule, but at least he'd have her attention.

The first delivery didn't come with a card. Neither did the second or the third. When the doorbell interrupted her teaching for a fourth time Friday afternoon, Paige demanded that the deliveryman tell her who had sent the flowers. He just shrugged and said, "I don't take the orders. I just deliver them."

When the bell rang again at two o'clock and she found the same deliveryman with yet another poinsettia, she was ready to scream. But he spoke before she could say— or scream—anything.

"There's a card with this one," he told her.

She forced a smile. "In that case, thank you."

As her class was finishing up a geography test, she took a moment to pry the card from the envelope. "One poinsettia for every Christmas that we were apart—and the last one I'll ever send."

It wasn't signed, but she knew it was from Sutter. She'd suspected, of course, even after the first one, because she couldn't remember the last time anyone else had sent her flowers. The cryptic reference to the five years they were apart confirmed it.

But what, exactly, did the message mean? Was he saying that they wouldn't ever have to spend another Christmas apart? And did that mean he was coming back to Rust Creek Falls?

Hope flared in her heart like a match first struck, but it burned out just as quickly. Because even if he was coming home again— For how long this time? How long would he stay before something else called him away again? She didn't want to live her life in a state of uncertainty.

But she didn't want to live her life without him, either. Because there was one thing she knew for sure: she was still, and always would be, in love with Sutter Traub.

And after dinner with her parents tonight, she was going to tell them about her decision to book a flight to Washington.

Sutter left Seattle before Jenni got back from Maui, because when Reese had asked for her flight information so that he could pick her up from the airport, he'd figured his stable manager had everything under control. And now it was time for him to take control of his life and his future. As he drove back to Montana, he tried to plan out his every action and word—he didn't anticipate arriving back in Rust Creek Falls to find Paige's driveway empty and her house in darkness.

It was just around dinnertime on a Friday night, which led him to the obvious conclusion that she'd gone somewhere to eat. Probably not the Ace in the Hole, since Dallas had told him that she'd been there earlier in the week with Alex Monroe. His brother's tone had implied that it was a date, but Sutter didn't believe it. Paige wasn't the type of woman to string someone along, so he knew she wouldn't be on a date with the other man only a few weeks after ending their relationship—and so soon after taking Sutter to her bed.

He figured her parents' house was the most likely place to find her—and the absolute last place he wanted to go considering his reception there on Thanksgiving. But he would follow Paige to the ends of the earth if he had to. Of course, the ends of the earth—wherever that might be—was, in many ways, preferable to the Dalton home, but he turned his truck in that direction anyway.

He wasn't looking for another confrontation, but as he knocked on the door, he braced himself for the possibility.

"What are you doing here?" Ben Dalton asked.

Sutter refused to be dissuaded by either the chilly tone or dismissive glance. He held the older man's gaze and said, "I need to see Paige."

"Why?"

"I have some things I need to say to her."

"I can pass on a message."

"Oh, for goodness' sake, Dad. Let him come in."

Sutter sent a quick, grateful smile to Lindsay. Ben scowled but stepped away from the door. Lani stood on the other side of her father, her arms folded across her chest. Mary stood behind her daughter, a worried frown on her face.

Great—it seemed that he had an audience, including every female member of the Dalton family except the one he most wanted to see.

"Since you're all here—I have something to say to you, too," Sutter told them. "I made some mistakes in the past, and it took me a while to acknowledge those mistakes and move on, but I hope you can do the same, because I'm not the same guy I was when I left town five years ago."

"Haven't seen much evidence of anything different," Ben said.

"You will," he promised Paige's father. "But there is one thing that hasn't changed in all of the years that I was gone—and that's how I feel about your daughter."

"How *do* you feel about her?" Lani demanded.

"Jeez, Lani, could you butt out of my life for five minutes?" Paige demanded, stepping into the room.

She was wearing one of those long skirts she seemed to favor, this one in a swirling pattern of cream and chocolate, with a cream-colored tunic-style sweater. Her cheeks were a little paler than usual and there were dark smudges beneath her eyes, and he wondered if they might be proof that she'd suffered as many sleepless nights as he had. But she was still the most beautiful woman he'd ever known, and looking at her now, his heart actually ached with wanting.

He shifted his gaze to her sister. "I don't have a problem answering your question," he told Lani. "Because I love Paige."

She looked unconvinced, but Lindsay sighed and pressed a hand to her heart. Mary worried her lip and Ben's scowl deepened.

But Sutter didn't care about any of their responses. He turned to Paige again. "It's true," he told her. "I love you."

Her eyes filled with tears, but she said nothing and made no move toward him.

So he stepped forward and took her hand. Her fingers were ice-cold and trembling. He squeezed gently. "I love you, Paige, with my whole heart. I always have and I always will."

A single tear trembled on the edge of her lashes, then tracked slowly down her cheek. His heart turned over in his chest. Whatever reaction he'd expected, it wasn't that his declaration would make her cry.

"I mean it, Paige." He was speaking only to her now, oblivious to the fact that her parents and sisters were still in the room. He dropped to one knee beside her. "I've never stopped loving you, and I never want to leave you again. I want to build a life with you, here in Rust Creek Falls. I'm hoping that's what you want, too, and that this time you'll say yes, because I'm asking you to marry me."

* * *

Paige hadn't expected to see Sutter tonight. And she certainly hadn't expected such a heartfelt declaration—or a proposal. Yes, she loved him, and yes, she'd been willing to go to Seattle to meet him on his turf to talk about the possibility of a future for them together—because that was what she wanted more than anything. But now that he was here, offering her everything she'd always wanted, she was almost too afraid to reach out and take it.

"Okay, I can understand why you'd have some reservations," Sutter said when she failed to respond. "Because I was still carrying a lot of baggage from what happened five years ago—not just with you, but with my family. And I know I wasted a lot of years feeling hurt and angry and guilty, but I'm not going to waste any more. I know I can't do anything to give us back those five years, but I'm ready to move forward now, and I really want to do that with you by my side."

It was the sincerity in his gaze as much as the earnestness in his voice that finally propelled her to action. She lifted a trembling hand to his lips, halting the flow of words so that she could speak.

"Yes," she said softly.

His lips curved, just a little. "Yes?"

She nodded. "I love you, Sutter, I always have. And I want to move forward with you, too."

"Does that mean I can get off my knee?"

"Don't I get the ring first?"

He dipped a hand into his pocket. "How did you know I had a ring?"

"You got down on one knee."

He was smiling as he retrieved the ring and slid it onto the third finger of her left hand. The exquisite emerald-cut diamond at the center was flanked by slightly smaller but equally stunning tapered baguettes. "I wanted something with three stones," he said. "To represent our past, our present and our future."

"It's perfect," she said. "But all I want—all I *need*—is you."

Finally he rose to his feet and kissed her. And in that touch of his mouth against hers, all the questions and doubts and loneliness of the past week faded away.

It was only when she heard both Lani and Lindsay sigh that she remembered they weren't alone. Reluctantly, she eased her lips from his and turned to face her parents.

"It looks like we're going to need that extra leaf in the table for Christmas," Mary said to her husband.

Ben nodded. "And for every holiday thereafter."

Their comments weren't exactly an overwhelming endorsement of Paige and Sutter's engagement, but they did represent a significant shift in her parents' attitudes from Thanksgiving, and that was a good start. Then her father took a step forward.

"You make my daughter happy and those mistakes of the past will be forgotten," he said.

And when he offered Sutter his hand, Paige saw her mother's eyes fill with tears.

"I will," Sutter said, and shook to seal his promise.

"Isn't that what you're supposed to say at the wedding?" Lindsay teased.

Sutter grinned at her. "I'm practicing."

"About the wedding," Mary began.

"*Later,* Mom," Paige said firmly. "Let me get used to being engaged first."

"All right," her mother relented. "But planning a wedding takes time—there are so many details to take care of."

But the only detail Paige was thinking about right

now was how to discreetly make a quick exit so that she and Sutter could celebrate their engagement in private.

Her fiancé, obviously on the same wavelength, said, "Before we start talking about wedding dates, I think my parents would like to know about this turn of events."

"Oh, right. Of course," Mary agreed.

So they said goodbye to her family and headed out to share the good news with his. But on the way, they decided to stop at Paige's house.

They did eventually get around to telling Sutter's family about their engagement—but not until much later the following morning.

Epilogue

Three weeks later, with the now-familiar weight of her engagement ring on her finger, Paige escaped with Sutter to Seattle for the weekend. Since the publicity from Lissa's writing had sent a mass of volunteers to Rust Creek Falls to help with the town's restoration and the new school was almost complete, they were finally able to take some time for themselves without feeling guilty.

Paige was excited to see Seattle, but mostly she was eager to get a glimpse of the life Sutter had built for himself in the city. Traub Stables was quite an impressive facility, including a thirty-stall barn, a breeding shed, an indoor riding arena, neatly fenced paddocks and even a spa to help rehabilitate injured horses. And all of the buildings were decked out for the holiday season with miles of pine garlands, enormous evergreen wreaths and countless twinkling white lights.

Not only were the buildings and grounds well maintained, but the horses she saw were all in prime condition, a testament to the quality of care they received. On the tour she also got to meet Jenni and Reese, and found out that they weren't just friends of Sutter's and employees at the stables but also recently engaged.

"You've done an incredible job here," she told Sutter.

"I didn't have to do a lot," he said. "The buildings

were in pretty good shape when I bought the property, so they needed more hands-on attention than major construction. And I got lucky that I made so many contacts when I was working at Rolling Meadows."

"You're being modest," she chided. "This place is really impressive."

"I'm proud of it," he admitted.

"It makes me wonder how you could want to leave here—to give up something that you obviously poured so much of your heart and soul into."

He put his arms around her. "Don't you know that my heart and soul are yours? Spending my life with you means that I'm not giving anything up—I'm getting everything I ever wanted."

"But if I hadn't been so insistent on staying in Rust Creek Falls, would you have chosen to live here?"

"I want to be with you, Paige."

"Reese seems like he's more than qualified to handle the day-to-day operations of the business."

"And has been since the summer," Sutter agreed. "If he wanted it, I'd sell the place to him."

"He doesn't want it?"

"He claims he's not ready for the responsibility of ownership—or the risks. He's happy to do what he does and isn't ready to take on the kind of mortgage he would need to take it off my hands."

"What if you were partners?" she suggested. "You could maintain an interest in the business but he'd continue to be responsible for the day-to-day operations."

It was an interesting suggestion and, in some ways, an obvious solution. But he was curious. "Why are you suddenly reluctant for me to sell?"

She shrugged. "I just thought it might be nice to have a place where we could get away, and it would give our children the opportunity to experience both country life and city living."

Something in her deliberately casual tone triggered his radar, making him suspect that her comment wasn't as offhand as she wanted him to think. "Children?"

"We used to talk about having kids," she reminded him. "Is that still what you want?"

"Yeah, that's still what I want." He tipped her chin up. "Are you...pregnant?"

"I don't know, but I think...I might be."

Sutter whooped with joy and wrapped his arms around her.

She laughed as he spun her around. "And to think I had some concerns about how you'd react to the news."

He set her back on her feet and tipped her chin up to brush his lips over hers. "Now can we set a date for the wedding?"

She chuckled. "I guess we'd better."

"When?"

"March," she suggested. "Then we can go on our honeymoon during spring break."

"How about we have the wedding in January and the honeymoon in March?"

"Afraid if we wait too long I might change my mind?"

He shook his head. "Nope. I don't have any doubts about anything anymore. I just want to start our life together as soon as possible."

She lifted her arms to link them behind his head, drawing his mouth down to hers. "Then I guess we're getting married in January."

As Sutter kissed his bride to be under the mistletoe, he couldn't help but marvel at all the things he had to be thankful for—because of the woman in his arms.

* * * * *

A sneaky peek at next month…

Cherish™

ROMANCE TO MELT THE HEART EVERY TIME

My wish list for next month's titles…

In stores from 15th November 2013:

☐ Snowflakes and Silver Linings – Cara Colter

& Snowed in with the Billionaire – Caroline Anderson

☐ A Cold Creek Noel & A Cold Creek Christmas
Surprise – RaeAnne Thayne

In stores from 6th December 2013:

☐ Second Chance with Her Soldier – Barbara Hannay

& The Maverick's Christmas Baby – Victoria Pade

☐ Christmas at the Castle – Marion Lennox

& Holiday Royale – Christine Rimmer

Available at WHSmith, Tesco, Asda, Eason, Amazon and Apple

Just can't wait?

Visit us Online

You can buy our books online a month before
they hit the shops! **www.millsandboon.co.uk**

1113/23

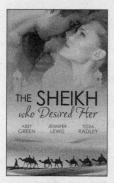

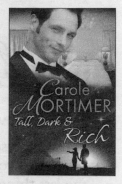

Wrap up warm this winter with Sarah Morgan…

Sleigh Bells in the Snow

Kayla Green loves business and hates Christmas.

So when Jackson O'Neil invites her to Snow Crystal Resort to discuss their business proposal… the last thing she's expecting is to stay for Christmas dinner. As the snowflakes continue to fall, will the woman who doesn't believe in the magic of Christmas finally fall under its spell…?

4th October

www.millsandboon.co.uk/sarahmorgan

1013/MB435

Come home this Christmas to Fiona Harper

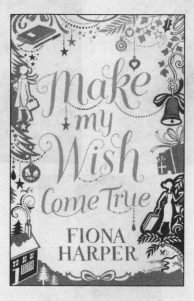

From the author of *Kiss Me Under the Mistletoe* comes a Christmas tale of family and fun. Two sisters are ready to swap their Christmases—the busy super-mum, Juliet, getting the chance to escape it all on an exotic Christmas getaway, whilst her glamorous work-obsessed sister, Gemma, is plunged headfirst into the family Christmas she always thought she'd hate.

www.millsandboon.co.uk

She's loved and lost — will she ever learn to open her heart again?

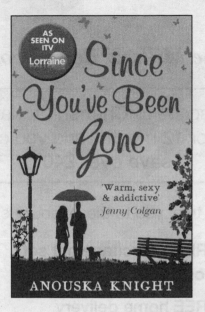

From the winner of ITV Lorraine's Racy Reads, Anouska Knight, comes a heart-warming tale of love, loss and confectionery.

'The perfect summer read — warm, sexy and addictive!'
—Jenny Colgan

For exclusive content visit:
www.millsandboon.co.uk/anouskaknight

MILLS & BOON
Book Club

Join the Mills & Boon Book Club

Subscribe to **Cherish**™ today for
3, 6 or 12 months and you could
save over £40!

We'll also treat you to these fabulous extras:

- **FREE L'Occitane gift set
  worth £10**

- **FREE home delivery**

- **Rewards scheme, exclusive
  offers…and much more!**

Subscribe now and save over £40
www.millsandboon.co.uk/subscribeme